BACHELOR DAD
ON HER DOORSTEP

BY
MICHELLE DOUGLAS

D1324108

At the age of eight **Michelle Douglas** was asked what she wanted to be when she grew up. She answered, 'A writer.' Years later she read an article about romance-writing and thought, *Ooh, that'll be fun*. She was right. When she's not writing she can usually be found with her nose buried in a book. She is currently enrolled in an English Masters programme, for the sole purpose of indulging her reading and writing habits further. She lives in a leafy suburb of Newcastle, on Australia's east coast, with her own romantic hero—husband Greg, who is the inspiration behind all her happy endings. Michelle would love you to visit her at her website: www.michelledouglas.com.

To Varuna, The Writers' House, with thanks.

PROLOGUE

Jaz hadn't meant her first return to Clara Falls in eight years to occur under the cover of darkness, but she hadn't been able to get away from work as early as she'd hoped and then the traffic between Sydney and the Blue Mountains had been horrendous.

She was late.

At least a fortnight too late.

A horrible laugh clawed out of her throat, a sound she'd never heard herself utter before. She tried to drag it back before it swallowed her whole.

Not the time. Not the place.

Definitely not the place.

She didn't drive up Clara Falls' main street. She turned into the lane that led to the residential parking behind the shops. Given the darkness—and the length of time she'd stayed away—would she even recognise the back of the bookshop?

She did. Immediately.

And a weight slammed down so heavily on her chest she sagged. She had to close her eyes and go through the relaxation technique Mac had taught her. The weight didn't lift, but somehow she found a way to breathe through it.

When she could, she opened her eyes and parked her hatchback beside a sleek Honda and stared up at the light burning in the window.

Oh, Mum!

Sorry would not be good enough. It would never be good enough.

Don't think about it.

Not the time. Not the place.

She glanced at the Honda. Was it Richard's car?

Richard—her mother's solicitor.

Richard—Connor Reed's best friend.

The thought came out of nowhere, shooting tension into every muscle, twisting both of her calves into excruciating cramps.

Ha! Not out of nowhere. Whenever she thought of Clara Falls, she thought of Connor Reed. End of story.

She rested her forehead on the steering wheel and welcomed the bite of pain in her legs, but it didn't wipe out the memories from her mind. Connor Reed was the reason she'd left Clara Falls. Connor Reed was the reason she'd never returned.

The cramps didn't ease.

She lifted her gaze back to the bookshop, then higher still to stare at the flat above, where her mother had spent the last two years of her life.

I'm sorry, Mum.

The pain in her chest and legs intensified. Points of light darted at the outer corners of her eyes. She closed them and forced herself to focus on Mac's relaxation technique again— deliberately tensing, then relaxing every muscle in her body, one by one. The pain eased.

She would not see Connor Reed tonight. And, once she'd signed the papers to sell the bookshop to its prospective buyer, she'd never have to set foot in Clara Falls again.

She pushed open the car door and made her way up the back steps. Richard opened the door before she could knock.

'Jaz!' He folded her in a hug. 'It's great to see you.'

He meant it, she could tell. 'I… It's great to see you too.' Strangely enough, she meant it too. A tiny bit of warmth burrowed under her skin.

His smile slipped. 'I just wish it was under different circumstances.'

The warmth shot back out of her. Richard, as her mother's solicitor, had been the one to contact her, to tell her that Frieda had taken an overdose of sleeping pills. To tell her that her mother had died. He hadn't told Jaz that it was all her fault. He hadn't had to.

Don't think about it. Not the time. Not the place.

'Me too,' she managed. She meant *that* with all her heart.

He ushered her inside—into a kitchenette. Jaz knew that this room led through to the stockroom and then into the bookshop proper. Or, at least, it used to.

'Why don't we have a cup of coffee? Gordon should be along any moment and then we can get down to signing all the paperwork.'

'Sure.' She wondered why Richard had asked her to meet him here rather than at his offices. She wondered who this Mr Gordon was who wanted to buy her mother's bookshop.

Asking questions required energy—energy Jaz didn't have.

Richard motioned to the door of the stockroom. 'You want to go take a wander through?'

'No, thank you.'

The last thing she needed was a trip down memory lane. She might've found refuge in this bookshop from the first moment she'd entered it as a ten-year-old. Once upon a time she might've loved it. But she didn't need a refuge now. She was an adult. She'd learned to stand on her own two feet. She'd had to.

'No, thank you,' she repeated.

Her mother had bought the bookshop two years ago in the hope it would lure Jaz back to Clara Falls. She had no desire to see it now, to confront all she'd lost due to her stupid pride and her fear.

Regret crawled across her scalp and down the nape of her neck to settle over her shoulders. She wanted to sell the bookshop. She wanted to leave. *That* was why she was here now.

Richard opened his mouth but, before he could say anything, a knock sounded on the back door. He turned to answer it, ushered a second person into the kitchenette. 'You remember Gordon Sears, don't you, Jaz?'

'Sure I do.'

'It's Mr Sears who wants to buy the bookshop.'

A ball formed in Jaz's stomach. Mr Sears owned the 'baked-fresh-daily' country bakery directly across the road. He hadn't approved of Jaz when she was a child. And he certainly hadn't approved of Frieda.

Mr Sears's eyes widened when they rested on Jaz now, though. It almost made her smile. She sympathised whole-heartedly with his surprise. The last time he'd seen her she'd been a rebellious eighteen-year-old Goth—dressed in top-to-toe black with stark white make-up, spiked hair and a nose ring. Her chocolate-brown woolen trousers and cream knit top would make quite a contrast now.

'How do you do, Mr Sears?' She took a step forward and held out her hand. 'It's nice to see you again.'

He stared at her hand and then his lip curled. 'This is business. It's not a social call.'

He didn't shake her hand.

Memories crashed down on Jaz then. The ball in her stomach hardened, solidified. Mr Sears had never actually refused to serve Jaz and her mother in his 'baked-fresh-daily' country bakery, but he'd let them know by his icy politeness, his curled lip, the placing of change on the counter instead of directly into their hands, what he'd thought of them.

Despite Jaz's pleas, her mother had insisted on shopping there. 'Best bread in town,' she'd say cheerfully.

It had always tasted like sawdust to Jaz.

Frieda Harper's voice sounded through Jaz's mind now. *It doesn't matter what people think. Don't let it bother you.*

Jaz had done her best to follow that advice, but…

Do unto others…

She'd fallen down on that one too.

Frieda Harper, Jaz's wild and wonderful mother. If Frieda had wanted a drink, she'd have a drink. If Frieda had wanted to dance, she'd get up and dance. If Frieda had wanted a man, she'd take a man. It had made the more conservative members of the town tighten their lips in disapproval.

People like Mr Sears. People like Connor Reed's mum and dad.

Jaz wheeled away, blindly groped her way through the all-too-familiar doorways. Light suddenly flooded the darkness, making her blink. She stood in the bookshop...and all her thought processes slammed to a halt.

She turned a slow circle, her eyes wide to take in the enormity of it all. Nothing had changed. Everything was exactly the same as she remembered it.

Nothing had changed.

Oh, Mum...

'I'm sorry, Mr Sears.' It took a moment before she realised it was her voice that broke the silence. 'But it seems I can't sell the bookshop after all.'

'What?'

'Good.'

She heard distinct satisfaction in Richard's voice, but she didn't understand it. She was only aware of the weight lifting from her chest, letting her breathe more freely than she had once during the last two weeks.

CHAPTER ONE

JAZ made the move back to Clara Falls in bright, clear sunlight two weeks later. And this time she had to drive down Clara Falls' main street because an enormous skip blocked the lane leading to the residential parking behind the bookshop.

She slammed on the brakes and stared at it. Unless she turned her car around to flee back to Sydney, she'd have to drive down the main street and find a place to park.

Her mouth went dry.

Turn the car around…?

The temptation stretched through her. Her hands clenched on the steering wheel. She'd sworn never to return. She didn't want to live here. She didn't want to deal with the memories that would pound at her day after day.

And she sure as hell didn't want to see Connor Reed again.

Not that she expected to run into him too often. He'd avoid her the way the righteous spurned the wicked, the way a reformed alcoholic shunned whisky…the way mice baulked at cats.

Good.

Turn the car around…?

She relaxed her hands and pushed her shoulders back. No. Returning to Clara Falls, saving her mother's bookshop—it was the right thing to do. She'd honour her mother's memory; she'd haul the bookshop back from the brink of bankruptcy. She'd do Frieda Harper proud.

Pity you didn't do that a month ago, a year ago, two years ago, when it might have made a difference.

Guilt crawled across her skin. Regret swelled in her stomach until she could taste bile on her tongue. Regret that she hadn't returned when her mother was still alive. Regret that she'd never said all the things she should've said.

Regret that her mother was dead.

Did she honestly think that saving a bookshop and praying for forgiveness would make any difference at all?

Don't think about it! Wrong time. Wrong place.

She backed the car out of the lane and turned in the direction of the main street.

She had to pause at the pedestrian crossing and, as she stared up the length of the main street, her breath caught. Oh, good Lord. She'd forgotten just how pretty this place was.

Clara Falls was one of the main tourist hubs in Australia's breathtaking Blue Mountains. Jaz hadn't forgotten the majesty of Echo Point and The Three Sisters. She hadn't forgotten the grandeur of the Jamison Valley, but Clara Falls…

The artist in her paid silent homage. Maybe she'd taken it for granted all those years ago.

She eased the car up the street and the first stirrings of excitement started replacing her dread. The butcher's shop and mini-mart had both received a facelift. Teddy bears now picnicked in a shop window once crowded with tarot cards and crystals. The wide traffic island down the centre of the road—once grey cement—now sported close-cropped grass, flower-beds and park benches. But the numerous cafés and restaurants still did a bustling trade. This was still the same wide street. Clara Falls was still the same tourist hotspot.

The town had made an art form out of catering to out-of-towners. It had a reputation for quirky arts-and-craft shops, bohemian-style cafés and cosmopolitan restaurants, and… and…darn it, but it was pretty!

A smile tugged at the corners of her mouth. She cruised the

length of the street—she couldn't park directly out the front of the bookshop as a tradesman's van had parked in such a way that it took up two spaces. So, when she reached the end of the street, she turned the car around and cruised back down the other side, gobbling up every familiar landmark along the way.

Finally, she parked the car and sagged back in her seat. She'd spent so long trying to forget Connor Reed that she'd forgotten…stuff she shouldn't have.

Yeah, like how to be a halfway decent human being.

The sunlight abruptly went out of her day. The taste of bile stretched through her mouth again. Her mother had always told Jaz that she needed to return and face her demons, only then could she lay them to rest. Perhaps Frieda had been right—what had happened here in Clara Falls had overshadowed Jaz's entire adult life.

She wanted peace.

Eight years away hadn't given her that.

Not that she deserved it now.

She pushed out of the car. She waited for a break in the traffic, then crossed the road to the island. An elderly man in front of her stumbled up the first step and she grabbed his arm to steady him. She'd crossed at this particular spot more times than she could remember as a child and teenager, almost always heading for the sanctuary of the bookshop. Three steps up, five paces across, and three steps back down the other side. The man muttered his thanks without even looking at her and hurried off.

'Spoilsport,' someone hissed at Jaz. Then to the man, 'And one of these days you'll actually sit down and pass the time of day with me, Boyd Longbottom!'

The elderly woman turned back to Jaz. 'The only entertainment I get these days is watching old Boyd trip up that same step day in, day out.' Dark eyes twinkled. 'Though now you're back in town, Jazmin Harper, I have great hopes that things will liven up around here again.'

'Mrs Lavender!' Jaz grinned. She couldn't help it. Mrs

Lavender had once owned the bookshop. Mrs Lavender had been a friend. 'In as fine form as ever, I see. It's nice to see you.'

Mrs Lavender patted the seat beside her and Jaz sat. She'd expected to feel out of place. She didn't. She nodded towards the bookshop although she couldn't quite bring herself to look at it yet. She had a feeling that its familiarity might break her heart afresh. 'Do you miss it?'

'Every single day. But I'm afraid the old bones aren't what they used to be. Doctor's orders and whatnot. I'm glad you've come back, Jaz.'

This all uttered in a rush. It made Jaz's smile widen. 'Thank you.'

A short pause, then, 'I was sorry about what happened to your mother.'

Jaz's smile evaporated. 'Thank you.'

'I heard you held a memorial service in Sydney.'

'I did.'

'I was sick in hospital at the time or I would have been there.'

Jaz shook her head. 'It doesn't matter.'

'Of course it does! Frieda and I were friends.'

Jaz found she could smile again, after a fashion. According to the more uptight members of the town, Frieda might've lacked a certain respectability, but she certainly hadn't lacked friends. The memorial had been well attended.

'This place was never the same after you left.'

Mrs Lavender's voice hauled Jaz back. She gave a short laugh. 'I can believe that.'

Those dark eyes, shrewd with age, surveyed her closely. 'You did the right thing, you know. Leaving.'

No, she hadn't. What she'd done had led directly to her mother's death. She'd left and she'd sworn to never come back. It had broken her mother's heart. She'd hold herself responsible for that till the day she died. And she'd hold Connor responsible too. If he'd believed in Jaz, like he'd always sworn he would, Jaz would never have had to leave.

She would never have had to stay away.

Stop it!

She shook herself. She hadn't returned to Clara Falls for vengeance. Do unto others...that had been Frieda's creed. She would do Frieda Harper proud. She'd save the bookshop, then she'd sell it to someone other than Gordon Sears, then she'd leave, and this time she would never come back.

'You always were a good girl, Jaz. And smart.'

It hadn't been smart to believe Connor's promises.

She shook off the thought and pulled her mind back, to find Mrs Lavender smiling at her broadly. 'How long are you staying?'

'Twelve months.' She'd had to give herself a time limit—it was the only thing that would keep her sane. She figured it'd take a full twelve months to see the bookshop safe again.

'Well, I think it's time you took yourself off and got to work, dear.' Mrs Lavender pointed across the road. 'I think you'll find there's a lot to do.'

Jaz followed the direction of Mrs Lavender's hand, and that was when she saw and understood the reason behind the tradesman's van parked out the front of the bookshop. The muscles in her shoulders, her back, her stomach, all tightened. The minor repairs on the building were supposed to have been finished last week. The receptionist for the building firm Richard had hired had promised faithfully.

A pulse pounded behind her eyes. 'Frieda's Fiction Fair'—the sign on the bookshop's awning—was being replaced. With...

'Jaz's Joint'!

She shot to her feet. Her lip curled. Her nose curled. Inside her boots, even her toes curled. She'd requested that the sign be freshened up. Not... Not... She fought the instinct to bolt across the road and topple the sign-writer and his ladder to the ground.

'I'll be seeing you then, shall I, Jazmin?'

With an effort, she unclenched her teeth. 'Absolutely, Mrs Lavender.'

She forced herself to take three deep breaths, and only then did she step off the kerb of the island. She would sort this out like the adult she was, not the teenager she had been.

She made her way across the road and tried not to notice how firm her offending tradesman's butt looked in form-fitting jeans or how the power of those long, long legs were barely disguised by soft worn denim. In fact, in some places the denim was so worn…

The teenager she'd once been wouldn't have noticed. That girl had only had eyes for Connor. But the woman she was now…

Stop ogling!

She stopped by the ladder and glanced up. Then took an involuntary step backwards at the sudden clench of familiarity. The sign-writer's blond-tipped hair…

It fell in the exact same waves as—

Her heart lodged in her throat, leaving an abyss in her chest. *Get a grip. Don't lose it now.* The familiarity had to be a trick of the light.

Ha! More like a trick of the mind. Planted there by memories she'd done her best to bury.

She swallowed and her heart settled—sort of—in her chest again. 'Excuse me,' she managed to force out of an uncooperative throat, 'but I'd like to know who gave you the authority to change that sign.'

The sign-writer stilled, laid his brush down on the top of the ladder and wiped his hands across that denim-encased butt with agonising slowness. Jaz couldn't help wondering how it would feel to follow that action with her own hands. Gooseflesh broke out on her arms.

Slowly, oh-so-slowly, the sign-writer turned around…and Jaz froze.

'Hello, Jaz.'

The familiarity, the sudden sense of rightness at seeing him here like this, reached right inside her chest to twist her heart until she couldn't breathe.

No!

He took one step down the ladder. 'You're looking…well.'

He didn't smile. His gaze travelled over her face, down the long line of her body and back again and, although half of his face was in shadow, she could see that she left him unmoved.

Connor Reed!

She sucked in a breath, took another involuntary step back. It took every ounce of strength she could marshal to not turn around and run.

Do something. Say something, she ordered.

Her heart pounded in her throat. Sharp breaths stung her lungs. Connor Reed. She'd known they'd run into each other eventually, but not here. Not at the bookshop.

Not on her first day.

Stop staring. Don't you dare run!

'I…um…' She had to clear her throat. She didn't run. 'I'd appreciate it if you'd stop working on that.' She pointed to the sign and, by some freak or miracle or because some deity was smiling down on her, her hand didn't shake. It gave her the confidence to lift her chin and throw her shoulders back again.

He glanced at the sign, then back at her, a frown in his eyes. 'You don't like it?'

'I loathe it. But I'd prefer not to discuss it on the street.'

Oh, dear Lord. She had to set some ground rules. Fast. Ground rule number one was that Connor Reed stay as far away from her as humanly possible.

Ground rule number two—don't look him directly in the eye.

She swung away, meaning to find refuge in the one place in this town she could safely call home…and found the bookshop closed.

The sign on the door read 'Closed' in big black letters. The darkened interior mocked her. She reached out and tested the door. It didn't budge.

Somebody nearby sniggered. 'That's taken the wind out of your sails, nicely. Good!'

Jaz glanced around to find a middle-aged woman glaring at her. She kept her voice cool. 'Excuse me, but do I know you?'

The woman ignored Jaz's words and pushed her face in close. 'We don't need your kind in a nice place like this.'

A disturbance in the air, some super-sense on her personal radar, told her Connor had descended the ladder to stand directly behind her. He still smelt like the mountains in autumn.

She pulled a packet of gum from her pocket and shoved a long spearmint-flavoured stick into her mouth. It immediately overpowered all other scents in her near vicinity.

'My kind?' she enquired as pleasantly as she could.

If these people couldn't get past the memory of her as a teenage Goth with attitude, if they couldn't see that she'd grown up, then…then they needed to open their eyes wider.

Something told her it was their minds that needed opening up and not their eyes.

'A tattoo artist!' the woman spat. 'What do we want with one of those? You're probably a member of a bike gang and… and do drugs!'

Jaz almost laughed at the absurdity. Almost. She lifted her arms, looked down at herself, then back at the other woman. For a moment the other woman looked discomfited.

'That's enough, Dianne.'

That was from Connor. Jaz almost turned around but common sense kicked in—*don't look him directly in the eye*.

'Don't you go letting her get her hooks into you again, Connor. She did what she could to lead you astray when you were teenagers and don't you forget it!'

Jaz snorted. She couldn't help herself. The woman— Dianne—swung back to her. 'You probably think this is going to be a nice little money spinner.' She nodded to the bookshop.

Not at the moment. Not after reviewing the sales figures Richard had sent her.

'You didn't come near your mother for years and now, when

her body is barely cold in the ground, you descend on her shop like a vulture. Like a greedy, grasping—'

'That's enough, Dianne!'

Connor again. Jaz didn't want him fighting her battles—she wanted him to stay as far from her as possible. He wasn't getting a second chance to break her heart. Not in this lifetime! But she could barely breathe, let alone talk.

Didn't come near your mother for years...barely cold in the ground...

The weight pressed down so hard on Jaz's chest that she wanted nothing more than to lie down on the ground and let it crush her.

'You have the gall to say that after the number of weekends Frieda spent in Sydney with Jaz, living the high life? Jaz didn't need to come home and you bloody well know it!'

Home.

Jaz started. She couldn't lie down on the ground. Not out the front of her mother's bookshop.

'Now clear off, Dianne Keith. You're nothing but a trouble-making busybody with a streak of spite in you a mile wide.'

With the loudest intake of breath Jaz had ever heard anyone huff, Dianne stormed off.

Didn't come near your mother for years...barely cold in the ground...

A touch on her arm brought her back. The touch of work-roughened fingers on the bare flesh of her arm.

'Are you okay?'

His voice was low, a cooling autumn breeze. Jaz inched away, out of reach of those work-roughened fingers, away from the heat of his body.

'Yes, I'm fine.'

But, as the spearmint of her gum faded, all she could smell was the mountains in autumn. She remembered how it had once been her favourite smell in the world. When she'd been a girl...and gullible.

She *would* be fine. In just a moment. If she could stop breathing so deeply, his scent would fade.

She cleared her throat. 'It's not that I expected a fatted calf, but I didn't expect that.' She nodded to where Dianne had stood.

She hadn't expected a welcome, but she hadn't expected outright hostility either. Except, perhaps, from Connor Reed.

She'd have welcomed it from him.

'Dianne Keith has been not-so-secretly in love with Gordon Sears for years now.'

She blinked. He was telling her this because… 'Oh! I didn't sell him the bookshop, so his nose is out of joint…making her nose out of joint too?'

'You better believe it.'

She couldn't believe she was standing in Clara Falls' main street talking to Connor Reed like…like nothing had ever happened between them. As if this were a normal, everyday event.

She made the mistake then of glancing full into his face, of meeting his amazing brown eyes head-on.

They sparkled gold. And every exquisite moment she'd ever spent with him came crashing back.

If she could've stepped away she would've, but the bookshop window already pressed hard against her shoulder blades.

If she could've glanced away she would've, but her foolish eyes refused to obey the dictates of her brain. They feasted on his golden beauty as if starved for the sight of him. It made something inside her lift.

The sparks in his eyes flashed and burned. As if he couldn't help it, his gaze lowered and travelled down the length of her body with excruciating slowness. When his gaze returned to hers, his eyes had darkened to a smoky, molten lava that she remembered too well.

Her pulse gave a funny little leap. Blood pounded in her ears. She had to grip her hands together. After all these years and everything that had passed between them, how could there be anything but bitterness?

Her heart burned acid. No way! She had no intention of travelling down that particular path to hell ever again.

Eight years ago she'd believed in him—in them—completely, but Connor had accused her of cheating on him. His lack of faith in her had broken her heart…destroyed her.

She hadn't broken his heart, though, because nine months after Jaz had fled town he'd had a child with Faye. A daughter. A little girl.

She folded her arms. Belatedly, she realised, it made even more of her…assets. She couldn't unfold them again without revealing to him that his continued assessment bothered her. She kept said arms stoically folded, but her heart twisted and turned and ached.

'I don't need you to fight my battles for me, Connor.' She needed him to stay away.

'*I*—' he stressed the word '—always do what I consider is right. You needn't think your coming back to town is going to change that.'

'Do what's right?' She snorted. 'Like jumping to conclusions? Do you still do that, Connor?'

The words shot out of her—a challenge—and she couldn't believe she'd uttered them. The air suddenly grew so thick with their history she wondered how on earth either one of them could breathe through it.

She'd always known things between them could never be normal. Not after the intensity of what they'd shared. It was why she'd stayed away. It was why she needed him to stay away from her now.

'Do what's right?' She snorted a second time. She'd keep up this front if it killed her. 'Like that sign?' She pointed to the shop awning. 'What is that…your idea of a sick joke?'

That frown returned to his eyes again. 'Look, Jaz, I—'

Richard chose that moment to come bustling up between them, his breathing loud and laboured. 'Sorry, Jaz. I saw you cruising up the street, but I couldn't get away immediately. I had a client with me.'

Connor clapped him on the back. 'You need to exercise more, my man, if a sprint up the street makes you breathe this hard.'

Richard grinned. 'It is uphill.'

His grin faded. He hitched his head in the direction of the bookshop. 'Sorry, Jaz. It's a bit of a farce, isn't it?'

'It's not what I was expecting,' she allowed.

Connor and Richard said nothing. She cleared her throat. 'Where are my staff?'

Richard glanced at Connor as if for help. Connor shoved his hands in his pockets and glowered at the pavement.

'Richard?'

'That's just the thing, you see, Jaz. The last of your staff resigned yesterday.'

Resigned? Her staff? So… 'I have no staff?' She stared at Richard. For some reason she turned to stare at Connor too.

Both men nodded.

'But…' She would not lie down on the ground and admit defeat. She wouldn't. 'Why?'

'How about we go inside?' Connor suggested with a glance over his shoulder.

That was when Jaz became aware of the faces pressed against the inside of the plate glass of Mr Sears's 'baked-fresh-daily' country bakery, watching her avidly. In an act of pure bravado, she lifted her hand and sent the shop across the road a cheery wave. Then she turned and stalked through the door Richard had just unlocked.

Connor caught the door before it closed but he didn't step inside. 'I'll get back to work.'

On that sign? 'No, you won't,' she snapped out tartly. 'I want to talk to you.'

Richard stared at her as if…as if…

She reached up to smooth her hair. 'What?'

'Gee, Jaz. You used to dress mean but you always talked sweet.'

'Yeah, well…' She shrugged. 'I found out that I achieved a whole lot more if I did things the other way around.'

Nobody said anything for a moment. Richard rubbed the back of his neck. Connor stared morosely at some point in the middle distance.

'Okay, tell me what happened to my staff.'

'You could probably tell from the sales figures I sent you that the bookshop isn't doing particularly well.'

He could say that again.

'So, over the last few months, your mother let most of the staff go.'

'Most,' she pointed out, 'not all.'

'There was only Anita and Dianne left. Mr Sears poached Anita for the bakery…'

'Which left Dianne.' She swung back to Connor. 'Not the same Dianne who…?'

'The one and the same.'

Oh, that was just great. 'She made her feelings…clear,' she said to Richard.

Richard gave his watch an agonised glance.

'You don't have time for this at the moment, do you?' she said.

'I'm sorry, but I have appointments booked for the next couple of hours and—'

'Then go before you're late.' She shooed him to the door. 'I'll be fine.' She would be.

'I'll be back later,' he promised.

Then he left. Which left her and Connor alone in the dim space of the bookshop.

'So…' Connor said, breaking the silence that had wrapped around them. His voice wasn't so much a cooling autumn breeze as a winter chill. 'You're still not interested in selling the bookshop to Mr Sears?'

Sell? Not in this lifetime.

'I'm not selling the bookshop. At least not yet.'

Connor rested his hands on his hips and continued to survey her. She couldn't read his face or his body language, but she wished he didn't look so darn…male!

'So you're staying here in Clara Falls, then?'

'No.' She poured as much incredulity and disdain into her voice as she could. 'Not long-term. I have a life in the city. This is just a…'

'Just a…' he prompted when she faltered.

'A momentary glitch,' she snapped. 'I'll get the bookshop back on its feet and running at a profit—which I figure will take twelve months tops—and then I mean to return to my real life.'

'I see.'

Perhaps he did. But she doubted it.

CHAPTER TWO

CONNOR met the steeliness in Jaz's eyes and wished he could just turn around and walk away. His overriding instinct was to reach out and offer her comfort. Despite that veneer of toughness she'd cultivated, he knew this return couldn't be easy for her.

Her mother had committed suicide only four weeks ago!

That had to be eating her up alive.

She didn't look as if she'd welcome his comfort. She kept eyeing him as if he were something slimy and wet that had just oozed from the drain.

The muscles in his neck, his jaw, bunched. What was her problem? She'd been the one to lay waste to all his plans, all his dreams, eight years ago. Not the other way around. She could at least have the grace to…

To what? an inner voice mocked. Spare you a smile? Get over yourself, Reed. You don't want her smiles.

But, as he gazed down into her face, noted the fragile luminosity of her skin, the long dark lashes framing her eyes and the sweet peach lipstick staining her lips, something primitive fired his blood. He wanted to haul her into his arms, slant his mouth over hers and taste her, brand himself on her senses.

Every cell in his body tightened and burned at the thought. The intensity of it took him off guard. Had his heart thudding against his ribcage. After eight years…

After eight years he hadn't expected to feel anything. He sure as hell hadn't expected this.

He rolled his shoulders and tried to banish the images from his mind. Every stupid mistake he'd made with his life had happened in the weeks after Jaz had left town. He couldn't blame her for the way he'd reacted to her betrayal—that would be childish—but he would never give her that kind of power over him again.

Never.

She stuck out her chin, hands on hips—combative, aggressive and so unlike the Jaz of old it took him off guard. 'Why did you change the sign? Who gave you permission?'

She moved behind the sales counter, stowed her handbag beneath it, then turned back and raised an eyebrow. 'Well?' She tapped her foot.

Her boot—a pretty little feminine number in brown suede and as unlike her old black Doc Martens as anything could be—echoed smartly against the bare floorboards. Or maybe that was due to the silence that had descended around them again. He hooked his thumbs through the belt loops of his jeans and told himself to stay on task. It was just…that lipstick.

He'd once thought that nothing could look as good as the mulberry dark matt lipstick she'd once worn. He stared at the peach shine on her lips now. He'd been wrong.

'Connor!'

He snapped to and bit back something succinct and rude. *The sign, idiot!*

'I'm simply following the instructions you left with my receptionist.'

She stared at him for a long moment. Then, 'Can you seriously imagine that I'd want to call this place Jaz's Joint?' Her lip curled. 'That sounds like a den of iniquity, not a bookshop.'

She looked vivid fired up like that—alive. It suddenly occurred to him that he hadn't felt alive in a very long time.

He shifted his weight, allowed his gaze to travel over her

again, noticed the way she turned away and bit her lip. *That* was familiar. She wasn't feeling anywhere near as sure of herself as she'd have him believe.

'I'm not paid to imagine.' At the time, though, her request had sent his eyebrows shooting up towards his hairline. 'Eight years is a long time. People change.'

'You better believe it!'

He ignored her vehemence. 'You told my receptionist you wanted "Jaz's Joint" painted on the awning. I was just following your instructions.' But as he said the words his stomach dipped. Her eyes had widened. He remembered how they could look blue or green, depending on the light. They glittered blue now in the hushed light of the bookshop.

'Those weren't my instructions.'

His stomach dropped a notch lower. Not her directions… Then…

'I just requested that the sign be freshened up.'

He swore. Once. Hard.

Jaz blinked. 'I beg your pardon?'

Her tone almost made him grin. As a teenager she'd done all she could to look hard as nails, but she'd rarely used bad language and she hadn't tolerated it in others.

He sobered. 'Obviously, somewhere along the line a wire's got crossed.' If his receptionist had played any part in the *Jaz's Joint* prank he'd fire her on the spot.

Jaz followed his gaze across the road to Mr Sears's bakery. 'Ahh…' Her lips twisted. 'I see.'

Did she? For reasons Connor couldn't fathom, Gordon Sears wanted the bookshop, and he wanted it bad.

She sprang out from behind the counter as if the life force coursing through her body would no longer allow her to coop it up in such a small space. She stalked down the aisles, with their rows upon rows of bookcases. Connor followed.

The Clara Falls bookshop had been designed with one purpose in mind—to charm. And it achieved its aim with remarkable ease. The gleaming oak bookcases contrasted neatly with wood-panelled walls painted a pale clean green. Alcoves and nooks invited browsers to explore. Gingerbread fretwork lent an air of fairy-tale enchantment. Jaz had always loved the bookshop, and Frieda hadn't changed a thing.

Therein lay most of its problems.

'I'll change the sign back. It'll be finished by the close of business today.'

She glanced back at him, a frown in her eyes. 'Why you?'

She turned around fully, folded her arms and leant against the nearest bookcase. To the right of her left hip a book in vivid blues and greens faced outwards—*Natural Wonders of the World*—it seemed apt. He dragged his gaze from her hips and the long, lean length of her legs. Way too apt.

But…

He'd never seen her wear such pretty, soft-looking trousers before. Mel would love those trousers. The thought flitted into his head unbidden and his heart clenched at the thought of his daughter. He gritted his teeth and pushed the thought back out again. He would not think of Mel and Jaz in the same sentence.

But…

Eight years ago he'd grown used to seeing Jaz in long black skirts…or naked.

And then she'd removed herself from his world and he hadn't seen her at all.

'Is that what you're doing these days—sign-writing?'

Her words hauled him back and he steeled himself not to flinch at her incredulity. 'Among other things.' He shoved his hands in his pockets. 'After graduation I took up a carpentry apprenticeship.' He'd relinquished his dream of art school. 'I run a building contractor's business now here in Clara Falls.'

Her jaw dropped. 'What about your art?'

Just for a moment, bitterness seeped out from beneath the lid he normally kept tightly sealed around it. 'I gave it up.'

Her head snapped back. 'You what?'

The madness had started the night he'd discovered Jaz in Sam Hancock's arms. When he'd found out the next day that Jaz had left town—left him—for good, Connor had gone off the rails. He'd drunk too much…he'd slept with Faye. Faye, who'd revealed Jaz's infidelity, her lies. Faye, who'd done all she could to console him when Jaz had gone. Faye whose heart he'd broken. When Faye had told him she was pregnant, he'd had no choice—he'd traded in his dream of art school to become a husband and father…and an apprentice carpenter.

He hadn't picked up a stick of charcoal since.

'Is that somehow supposed to be my fault?'

Jaz's snapped-out words hauled him back. 'Did I say that?'

He and Faye had lasted two years before they'd finally divorced—Jaz always a silent shadow between them. They'd been two of the longest years of his life.

It was childish to blame Jaz for any of that. He had Melanie. He could never regret his daughter.

Jaz's eyes turned so frosty they could freeze a man's soul. Connor's lips twisted. They couldn't touch him. His soul had frozen eight years ago.

And yet she was here. From all accounts a world-class tattoo artist, if Frieda's boasts could be believed.

Dianne was right. Clara Falls had no need for tattoo artists—world-class or otherwise.

And neither did he.

Silence descended around them. Finally, Jaz cleared her throat. 'I take it then that you're the builder Richard hired to do the work on this place?' She lifted a hand to indicate the interior of the shop, and then pointed to the ceiling to indicate the flat upstairs.

'That's right.'

She pushed away from the bookcase, glanced around. 'Considering the amount of work Richard told me needed doing, the place looks exactly as I remember it.'

Her eyes narrowed. He watched her gaze travel over every

fixture and furnishing within her line of sight. '*Exactly* the same.' She turned accusing eyes on him.

'That's because I've barely started work in here yet.'

Her jaw dropped. 'But…but your receptionist assured me all the work would be finished by Thursday last week.'

The muscles in his jaw bunched. 'You're sure about that?'

'Positive.'

He didn't blame her for her gritted teeth response. 'I'm sorry, Jaz, but you were given the wrong information.' And he'd be getting himself a new receptionist—this afternoon, if he could arrange it.

She pressed her lips so tightly together it made his jaw ache in sympathy. Then she stiffened. 'What about the OH and S stuff? Hell, if that hasn't been sorted, then—'

'That's the part I've taken care of.'

Several weeks ago, someone had filed an Occupation Health and Safety complaint. It had resulted in an OH and S officer coming out to inspect the premises…and to close the shop down when it had been discovered that two floor to ceiling bookcases, which should've been screwed fast to battens on the wall behind, had started to come away, threatening to topple and crush anyone who might happen to be below. Connor had put all his other jobs on hold to take care of that. The bookshop had only been closed for a day and a half.

'Why?'

'Why?' What the hell… 'Because it was dangerous, that's why.'

'Not that.' She waved an imperious hand in the air. 'Why is it your company that is doing the work?'

Because Richard had asked him to.

Because he'd wanted to prove that the past had no hold over him any more.

She folded her arms. 'I should imagine the last thing you wanted was to clap eyes on me again.'

She was right about that.

She stuck out a defiant hip. 'In fact, I'd guess that the last thing you want is me living in Clara Falls again.'

It took a moment for the import of her words to hit him. When they did, he clenched a fist so tight it started to shake. She glanced at his fist, then back into his face. She cocked an eyebrow. She didn't unsay her words.

'Are you insinuating that I'd use my position as a builder to sabotage your shop?' He tried to remember the last time he'd wanted to throttle someone.

'Would you? Have you? I mean… There's that travesty of a sign, for a start. Now the delay. What would you think? You and Gordon Sears could be like that—' she waved two crossed fingers under his nose '—for all I know.'

'God, Jaz! I know it's been eight years, but can you seriously think I would stoop to that?'

She raked him from the top of his head to his boot laces with her hot gaze—blue on the way down, green when she met his eyes again on the way up—and it felt as if she actually placed her hands on his body and stroked him. His heart started to thump. She moistened her lips. It wasn't a nervous gesture, more…an assessing one. But it left a shine on her lips that had him clenching back a groan.

'Business is business,' he ground out. 'I don't have to like who I'm working for.'

Was it his imagination or did she pale at his words?

Her chin didn't drop. 'So you're saying this is just another job to you?'

He hesitated a moment too long.

Jaz snorted and pushed past him, charged back down to the sales counter and stood squarely behind it, as if she wanted to place herself out of his reach. 'Thank you for the work you've done so far, Connor, but your services are no longer required.'

He stalked down to the counter, reached across and gripped her chin in his fingers, forced her gaze to his. 'Fine! You want the truth? This isn't just another job. What happened to your mother…

It made me sick to my stomach. We…someone in town…we should've paid more attention, we should've sensed that—'

He released her and swung away. She smelt like a wattle tree in full bloom—sweet and elusive. It was too much.

When he glanced back at her, her eyes had filled with tears. She touched her fingers to her jaw where he'd held her. Bile rose up through him. 'I'm sorry. I shouldn't have—' He gestured futilely with his hand. 'Did I hurt you?'

'No.'

She shook her head, her voice low, and he watched her push the tears down with the sheer force of her will…way down deep inside her like she used to do. Suddenly he felt older than his twenty-six years. He felt a hundred.

'I'm sorry I doubted your integrity.'

She issued her apology with characteristic sincerity and speed. He dragged a hand down his face. The Jaz of old might've been incapable of fidelity, but she'd been equally incapable of malice.

If she'd asked him to forgive her eight years ago, he would have. In an instant.

He shoved his hands in his pockets. 'Am I rehired?'

She straightened, moistened her lips and nodded. He didn't know how he could tell, but this time the gesture was nervous.

'You won't find it hard coping with my presence around the place for the next fortnight?' Some devil prompted him to ask.

'Of course not!'

He could tell that she was lying.

'We're both adults, aren't we? What's in the past is in the past.'

He wanted to agree. He opened his mouth to do precisely that, but the words refused to come.

Jaz glanced at him, moistened her lips again. 'It's going to take a fortnight? So long?'

'Give or take a couple of days. And that's working as fast as I can.'

'I see.'

He shoved his hands deeper into his pockets. 'I'll get back to work on that sign then, shall I?'

The door clanged shut behind Connor with a finality that made Jaz want to burst into tears.

Crazy. Ridiculous.

Her knees shook so badly she thought she might fall. Very carefully, she lowered herself to the stool behind the counter. Being found slumped on the floor was not the look she was aiming for, not on her first day.

Not on any day.

She closed her eyes, dragged in a deep breath and tried to slow her pulse, quieten the blood pounding in her ears. She could do this. She *could* do this. She'd known her first meeting with Connor would be hard. She hadn't expected to deal with him on her first day though.

Hard? Ha! Try gruelling. Exhausting. Fraught.

She hadn't known she would still feel his pain as if it were her own. She hadn't known her body would remember…everything. Or that it would sing and thrum just because he was near.

She hadn't known she'd yearn for it all again—their love, the rightness of being with him.

Connor had shown her the magic of love, but he'd shown her the other side of love too—the blackness, the ugliness…the despair. It had turned her into another kind of person—an angry, destructive person. It had taken her a long time to conquer that darkness. She would never allow herself to become that person again. Never. And the only way she could guarantee that was by keeping Connor at arm's length. Further, if possible.

But it didn't stop her watching him through the shop window as he worked on her sign.

She opened the shop, she served customers, but that didn't stop her noticing how efficiently he worked either, the complete lack of fuss that accompanied his every movement. It reminded her of how he used to draw, of the times they'd take their charcoals and sketch pads to one of the lookouts.

She'd sit on a rock hunched over her pad, intent on capturing every single detail of the view spread out before her, concentrating fiercely on all she saw. Connor would lean back against a tree, his sketch pad propped against one knee, charcoal lightly clasped, eyes half-closed, and his fingers would play across the page with seemingly no effort at all.

Their high school art teacher had given them identical marks, but Jaz had known from the very first that Connor had more talent in his little finger than she possessed in her whole body. She merely drew what was there, copied what was in front of her eyes. Connor's drawings had captured something deeper, something truer. They'd captured an essence, the hidden potential of the thing. Connor had drawn the optimistic future.

His hair glittered gold in the sun as he stepped down the ladder to retrieve something from his van.

And what was he doing now? Painting shop signs? His work should hang in galleries!

He turned and his gaze met hers. Just like that. With no fuss. No hesitation. She didn't step back into the shadows of the shop or drop her gaze and pretend she hadn't been watching. He would know. He pointed to the sign, then sent her a thumbs up.

All that potential wasted.

Jaz couldn't lift her arm in an answering wave. She couldn't even twitch the corners of her mouth upwards in acknowledgement of his silent communication. She had to turn away.

When she'd challenged him—thrown out there in the silences that throbbed between them that she must be the last person he'd ever want to see, he hadn't denied it.

Her stomach burned acid. Coming back to Clara Falls, she'd expected to experience loss and grief. But for her mother. Not Connor. She'd spent the last eight years doing all she could to get over him. These feelings should not be resurfacing now.

If you'd got over him you'd have come home like your mother begged you to.

The accusation rang through her mind. Her hands shook. She hugged herself tightly. She'd refused to come home, still too full of pride and anger and bitterness. It had distorted everything. It had closed her mind to her mother's despair.

If she'd come home…but she hadn't.

For the second time that day, she ground back the tears. She didn't deserve the relief they would bring. She would make a success of the bookshop. She would make this final dream of her mother's a reality. She would leave a lasting memorial of Frieda Harper in Clara Falls. Once she'd done that, perhaps she might find a little peace… Perhaps she'd have earned it.

She glanced back out of the window. Connor hadn't left yet. He stood in a shaft of sunlight, haloed in gold, leaning against his van, talking to Richard. For one glorious moment the years fell away. How many times had she seen Connor and Richard talking like that—at school, on the cricket field, while they'd waited for her outside this very bookshop? Things should've been different. Things should've been very different.

He'd given up his art. It was too high a price to pay. Grief for the boy he'd once been welled up inside her.

It would take her a long, long time to find peace.

She hadn't cheated on him with Sam Hancock. She hadn't cheated on him with anyone, but Connor no longer deserved her bitterness. He had a little daughter now, responsibilities. He'd paid for his mistakes, just like she'd paid for hers. If what her mother had told her was true, Faye had left Connor literally holding the baby six years ago. Jaz would not make his life more difficult.

Something inside her lifted. It eased the tightness in her chest and allowed her to breathe more freely for a moment.

Connor turned and his eyes met hers through the plate glass of the shop window. The weight crashed back down on her with renewed force. She gripped the edges of the stool to keep herself upright. Connor might not deserve her bitterness, but she still had to find a way of making him keep his distance, because something in him still sang to something in her—a siren song that had the power to destroy her all over again if she let it.

Richard turned then too, saw her and waved. She lifted a numb arm in response. He said something to Connor and both men frowned. As one, they pushed away from Connor's van and headed for the bookshop door.

A shiver rippled through her. She shot to her feet. She had to deal with more Connor on her first day? Heaven, give her strength.

The moment he walked through the door all strength seeped from her limbs, leaving them boneless, useless, and plonking her back down on the stool.

'Hello, again,' Richard said.

'Hi.' From somewhere she found a smile.

She glanced sideways at Connor. He pursed his lips and frowned at the ornate pressed-tin work on the ceiling. She found her gaze drawn upwards, searching for signs of damp and peeling paint, searching for what made him frown. She didn't find anything. It all looked fine to her.

Richard cleared his throat and she turned her attention back to him with an apologetic shrug.

'These are the keys for the shop.' He placed a set of keys onto the counter in front of her. 'And this is the key to the flat upstairs.' He held it up for her to see, but he didn't place it on the counter with the other keys.

Connor reached over and plucked the key from Richard's fingers. 'What did my receptionist tell you about the upstairs flat?'

Her stomach started to churn. 'That you'd given it a final coat of paint last week and that it was ready to move into.'

Connor and Richard exchanged glances.

'Um…but then you're a builder, not a painter, right?'

He'd painted the sign for the shop, so maybe…

She shook her head. 'Painting the flat isn't your department, is it?'

'No, but I can organise that for you, if you want.'

'You didn't think to check with me?' Richard asked.

The thought hadn't occurred to her. Though, in hindsight... 'She said she was contacting me on your behalf. I didn't think to question that. When she asked me if there was anything else I needed done, I mentioned the sign.' She'd wanted it bright and sparkling. She wanted her mother's name loud and proud above the shop.

'I'm sorry, Jaz,' Connor started heavily, 'but—'

'But I've been given the wrong information,' she finished for him. Again. From the expression on his face, though, she wouldn't want to be his receptionist when he finally made it back to the office. Shame pierced her. She should've known better than to lump Connor with the meaner elements in the town.

She swallowed. 'That's okay, I can take care of the painting myself.' She wanted to drop her head onto her folded arms and rest for a moment. 'What kind of state is the flat in?'

'We only started tearing out the kitchen cupboards and the rotting floorboards yesterday. It's a mess.'

Once upon a time he'd have couched that more tactfully, but she appreciated his candour now. 'Habitable?'

He grimaced.

'Okay then...' She thought hard for a moment. 'All my stuff is arriving tomorrow.'

'What stuff?' Connor asked.

'Everything. Necessary white goods, for a start—refrigerator, washing machine, microwave. Then there's the furniture—dining table, bed, bookcase. Not to mention the—'

'You brought a bookcase?' Connor glanced around the shop. 'When you have all these?'

For a brief moment his eyes sparkled. Her breathing went all silly. 'I'll need a bookcase in the flat too.'

'Why?'

The teasing glint in his eyes chased her weariness away. 'For the books that happen to be arriving tomorrow too.'

Connor and Richard groaned in unison. 'Has your book addiction lessened as the years have gone by?' Richard demanded.

They used to tease her about this eight years ago. It made her feel younger for a moment, freer. 'Oh, no.' She rubbed her hands together with relish. 'If anything, it's grown.'

The two men groaned again and she laughed. She'd actually laughed on her first day back in Clara Falls? Perhaps miracles could happen.

She glanced at Connor and pulled herself up. Not *those* kinds of miracles.

'Relax, guys. I've rented out my apartment in Sydney. Some of my stuff is to come here, but a lot has gone into storage, including most of my books. Is there room up there to store my things?' She pointed at the ceiling. 'Could you and your men work around it?'

'We'll work quicker if it's stored elsewhere.'

It took her all of two seconds to make the decision. 'Where's the nearest storage facility around here? Katoomba?' She'd organise for her things to go there until the flat was ready.

Connor planted his feet. 'We'll store it at my place.'

She blinked. 'I beg your pardon?'

He stuck his jaw out and folded his arms. 'It's my fault you thought the flat was ready. So it's my responsibility to take care of storing your things.'

'Garbage!' She folded her arms too. 'You had no idea what I was told.' He was as much a victim in this as her. 'I should've had the smarts to double-check it all with Richard anyway.'

'You shouldn't have had to double-check anything and—'

'Guys, guys.' Richard made a time out sign.

Jaz and Connor broke off to glare at each other.

'He does have the room, Jaz. He has a huge workshop with a four car garage for a start.'

She transferred her glare to Richard.

Connor shifted his weight to the balls of his feet. 'This is the last thing you should've had to come back to. You shouldn't be out of pocket because of someone's idea of a…prank.'

It was more than that. They all knew it.

'I'd like to make amends,' he said softly.

She found it hard to hold his gaze and she didn't know why. 'Okay.' She said the word slowly. 'I'll accept your very kind offer—' and it was a kind offer '—on one condition.'

Wariness crept into his eyes. Tiredness invaded every atom of her being. Once upon a time he'd looked at her with absolute trust.

And then he hadn't.

'What's the condition?'

'That you go easy on your receptionist.'

'What?' He leant across the counter as if he hadn't heard her right.

She held his gaze then and she didn't find it hard—not in the slightest. 'She sounded young.'

'She's nineteen. Old enough to know better.'

'Give her a chance to explain.'

He reared back from her then and the tan leached from his face, leaving him pale. Her words had shaken him, she could see that, but she hadn't meant for them to hurt him. From somewhere she dredged up a smile. 'We all make mistakes when we're young. I did. You did.'

'I did,' Richard piped in too.

'Find out why she did it before you storm in and fire her. That's all I'm asking. My arrival has already generated enough hostility as it is.'

Inch by inch, the colour returned to Connor's face. 'If I don't like her explanation, she's still history.'

'But you'll give her an opportunity to explain herself first?'

He glared at her. 'Yes.'

'Thank you.' She couldn't ask for any fairer than that.

They continued to stare at each other. Connor opened his mouth, a strange light in his eyes that she couldn't decipher, and every molecule of her being strained towards him. No words emerged from the firm, lean lips, but for a fraction of a second time stood still.

Richard broke the spell. 'Where were you planning on staying till your stuff arrives, Jaz?'

She dragged her gaze from Connor, tried to still the sudden pounding of her heart. 'I've booked a couple of nights at the Cascade's Rest.'

Richard let the air whistle out between his teeth. 'Nice! Treating yourself?'

'I have a thing for deep spa-baths.' She had a bigger thing for the anonymity that five-star luxury could bring. She couldn't justify staying there for more than a couple of nights, though. 'How long before the flat will be ready?'

'A week to ten days,' Connor said flatly.

She turned back to Richard. 'Is there a bed and breakfast you'd recommend?'

'Gwen Harwood's on Candlebark Street,' he said without hesitation.

Unbidden, a smile broke out from her. 'Gwen?' They'd been friends at school. The five of them—Connor, Richard, Gwen, Faye and herself. They'd all hung out together.

'Look, Jaz.' Connor raked a hand back through the sandy thickness of his hair. 'I can't help feeling responsible for this, and...'

And what? Did he mean to offer her a room too?

Not in this lifetime!

She strove for casual. 'And you have plenty of room, right?' Given all that had passed between them, given all that he thought of her, would he really offer her a room, a bed, a place to stay? The idea disturbed her and anger started to burn low down in the pit of her stomach. If only he hadn't jumped to conclusions eight years ago. If only he'd given her a chance to explain. If only he'd been this nice then!

It's eight years. Let it go.

She wanted to let it go. With all her heart she wished she

could stop feeling like this, but the anger, the pain, had curved their claws into her so fiercely she didn't know how to tear them free without doing more damage.

She needed him to stay away. 'I don't think so!'

The pulse at the base of Connor's jaw worked. 'I wasn't going to offer you a room,' he ground out. 'You'll be happier at Gwen's, believe me. But I will deduct the cost of your accommodation from my final bill.'

Heat invaded her face, her cheeks. She wished she could climb under the counter and stay there. Of course he hadn't meant to offer her a place to stay. Why would he offer her of all people—*her*—a place to stay? Idiot!

'You'll do no such thing!' Pride made her voice tart. 'I had every intention of arriving in Clara Falls today and staying, whether the flat was ready or not.' She'd just have given different instructions to the removal company and found a different place to stay.

No staff. Now no flat. Plummeting profits. What a mess! Where on earth was she supposed to start?

'Jaz?'

She suddenly realised the two men were staring at her in concern. She planted her mask of indifference, of detachment, back to her face in double-quick time. Before either one of them could say anything, she rounded on Connor. 'I want your word of honour that you will bill me as usual, without a discount for my accommodation. Without a discount for anything.'

'But—'

'If you don't I will hire someone else to do the work. Which, obviously, with the delays that would involve, will cost me even more.'

He glared at her. 'Were you this stubborn eight years ago?'

No, she'd been as malleable as a marshmallow.

'Do we have an understanding?'

'Yes,' he ground out, his glare not abating in the slightest.

'Excellent.' She pasted on a smile and made a show of

studying her watch. 'Goodness, is that the time? If you'll excuse me, gentlemen, it's time to close the shop. There's a spa-bath with my name on it waiting for me at the Cascade's Rest.'

As she led them to the door, she refused to glance into Connor's autumn-tinted eyes for even a microsecond.

When Jaz finally made it to the shelter of her room at the Cascade's Rest, she didn't head for the bathroom with its Italian marble, fragrant bath oils and jet-powered spa-bath. She didn't turn on a single light. She shed her clothes, leaving them where they fell, to slide between the cold cotton sheets of the queen-sized bed. She started to shake. 'Mum,' she whispered, 'I miss you.' She rolled to her side, pulled her knees to her chest and wrapped her arms around them. 'Mum, I need you.'

She prayed for the relief of tears, but she'd forced them back too well earlier in the day and they refused to come now. All she could do was press her face to the pillow and count the minutes as the clock ticked the night away.

CHAPTER THREE

JAZ let herself into the bookshop at eight-thirty sharp on Monday morning. She could hear Connor... She cocked her head to one side. She could hear Connor *and* his men hammering away upstairs already.

She locked the front door and headed out the back to the kitchenette. After a moment's hesitation, she cranked open the back door to peer outside. Connor's van—in fact, two vans—had reversed into the residential parking spaces behind the shop, their rear doors propped wide open. Someone clattered down the wooden stairs above and Jaz ducked back inside.

Through the window above the sink, she stared at the sign-writing on the side of the nearest van as she filled the jug—'Clara Falls Carpentry'. A cheery cartoon character wearing a tool belt grinned and waved.

A carpenter. Connor?

Had he painted those signs on the vans?

He was obviously very successful, but did it make up for turning his back on his art, his talent for drawing and painting?

There's nothing wrong with being a carpenter.

Of course not.

And Connor had always been good with his hands. A blush stole through her when she remembered exactly how good.

She jumped when she realised that water overflowed from the now full jug. She turned off the tap and set about making coffee.

Upstairs the banging continued.

Ignore it. Get on with your work.

She had to familiarise herself with the day-to-day running of the bookshop. Managing a small business wasn't new to her—she and her good friend Mac ran their own very exclusive tattoo parlour in Sydney. But she'd been relying on the fact that she'd have staff who could run her through the bookshop's suppliers, explain the accounting and banking procedures… who knew the day-to-day routine of the bookshop.

A mini-office—computer, printer and filing cabinet—had been set up in one corner of the stockroom. The computer looked positively ancient. Biting back a sigh, she switched it on and held her breath. She let it out in a whoosh when the computer booted up. So far, so good.

A glance at her watch told her she had fifteen minutes until she had to open the shop. She slid into the chair, clicked through the files listed on the computer's hard drive and discovered…

Nothing.

Nothing on this old computer seemed to make any sense whatsoever.

She dragged her hands back through her hair and stared at the screen. Maybe all that insomnia was catching up with her. Maybe something here made sense and she just couldn't see it.

Maybe returning to Clara Falls was a seriously bad idea.

'No!' She leapt out of her chair, smoothed down her hair and gulped down her coffee. She'd open the shop, she'd ring the local employment agency…and she'd sort the computer out later.

Without giving herself time for any further negative thoughts, she charged through the shop, unlocked the front door and turned the sign to 'Open'. She flicked through the *Yellow Pages*, found the page she needed, dialled the number and explained to the very efficient-sounding woman at the other end of the line what she needed.

'I'm afraid we don't have too many people on our books at the moment,' the woman explained.

Jaz stared at the receiver in disbelief. 'You have to have more than me,' she said with blunt honesty.

'Yes, well, I'll see what I can do.' The woman took Jaz's details. 'Hopefully we'll have found you something by the end of the week.'

End of the week!

'Uh…thank you,' Jaz managed.

The woman hung up. Jaz kept staring at the receiver. She needed staff now. Today. Not perhaps maybe in a week.

'What's up?'

The words, barked into the silence, made her start. Connor!

She slammed the phone back to its cradle, smoothed down her hair. 'Sorry, I didn't hear the bell above the door.'

The lines of his face were grim, his mouth hard and unsmiling. She fancied she could see him wishing himself away from here. Away from her.

Which was fine. Excellent, actually.

'I asked, what's up?'

No way. She wasn't confiding in him. Not in this lifetime. He wasn't her knight. He wasn't even her friend. He was her builder. End of story.

Derisive laughter sounded through her head. She ignored it.

He was hot.

She tried to can that thought as soon as she could.

'Nothing's up.'

He wouldn't challenge her. She could tell he wanted out of here asap. Only a friend would challenge her—someone who cared.

'Liar.' He said the word softly. The specks of gold in his eyes sparkled.

She blinked. She swallowed. 'Is this a social call or is there something I can help you with?' The words shot out of her, sounding harder than she'd meant them to.

The golden highlights were abruptly cut off. 'I just wanted to let you know that your things arrived safely yesterday.'

'I…um… Thank you.' She moistened her lips, something

she found herself doing a lot whenever Connor was around. She couldn't help it. She only had to look at him for her mouth to go dry. He started to turn away.

'Connor?'

He turned back, reluctance etched in the line of his shoulders, his neck, his back. Her heart slipped below the level of her belly button. Did he loathe her so much?

She moistened her lips again. His gaze narrowed in on the action and she kicked herself. If he thought she was being deliberately provocative he'd loathe her all the more.

She told herself she didn't care what he thought.

'I'm going to need some of my things. I only brought enough to tide me over for the weekend.' She shrugged, apologetic.

Why on earth should *she* feel apologetic?

His gaze travelled over her. She wore yesterday's trousers and Saturday's blouse. She'd shaken them out and smoothed them the best she could, but it really hadn't helped freshen them up any.

Pride forced her chin up. 'There's just one suitcase I need.' It contained enough of the essentials to get her through. 'I'd be grateful if I could come around this evening and collect it.'

'What's it look like?'

'It's a sturdy red leather number. Big.'

'The one with stickers from all around the world plastered over it?'

'That's the one.' She had no idea how she managed to keep her voice so determinedly cheerful. She waited for him to ask about her travels. They'd meant to travel together after art school—to marry and to travel. They'd planned to paint the world.

He didn't ask. She reminded herself that he'd given all that up. Just like he'd given up on her.

Travel? With his responsibilities?

He'd made his choices.

It didn't stop her heart from aching for him.

She gripped her hands behind her so she wouldn't have to acknowledge their shaking. 'When would it be convenient for me to call around and collect it?'

His eyes gave nothing away. 'Have you booked into Gwen's B&B?'

She nodded.

'Then I'll have it sent around.'

She read the subtext. He didn't need to say the words out loud. It would never be convenient for her to call around. She swallowed. 'Thank you.'

With a nod, he turned and stalked to the door. He reached out, seized the door handle…

'Connor, one final thing…'

He swung back, impatience etched in every line of his body. A different person might've found it funny. 'You and your men are welcome to use the bookshop's kitchenette and bathroom.' She gestured to the back of the shop. The facilities upstairs sounded basic at best at the moment—as in non-existent. 'I'll leave the back door unlocked.'

He strode back and jammed a finger down on the counter between them. 'You'll do no such thing!'

'I beg your pardon?'

'People don't leave their back doors unlocked in Clara Falls any more, Jaz.'

They didn't? She stared back at him and wondered why that felt such a loss.

'And you, I think, have enough trouble without inviting more. Especially of that kind.'

She wanted to tell him she wasn't having any trouble at all, only her mouth refused to form the lie.

'Fine, take the key, then.' She pulled the keys from her pocket and rifled though them. She hadn't worked out what most of them were for yet.

'Here, this one looks a likely candidate.' She held one aloft, sidled out from behind the counter and strode all the way through the shop to the back door again. She fitted the key in the lock. It turned. She wound it off the key ring and shoved it into Connor's hand. 'There.'

'I—'

'Don't let your dislike of me disadvantage your men. They're working hard.'

She refused to meet his gaze, hated the way the golden lights in his eyes were shuttered against her.

'I wasn't going to refuse your offer, Jaz.'

That voice—measured and rhythmic, like a breeze moving through a stand of radiata pine.

'We'll all welcome the chance of a hot drink and the use of that microwave, believe me.'

Amazingly, he smiled. It was a small one admittedly, wiped off his face almost as soon as it appeared, but Jaz's pulse did a little victory dance all the same.

'Do you have a spare? You might need it.'

He held the key between fingers callused by hard work, but Jaz would've recognised those hands anywhere. Once upon a time she'd watched them for hours, had studied them, fascinated by the ease with which they'd moved over his sketch pad. Fascinated by the ease with which they'd moved across her body, evoking a response she'd been powerless to hide.

A response she'd never considered hiding from him.

She gulped. A spare key—he was asking her about a spare key. She rifled through the keys on the key ring. Twice, because she didn't really see them the first time.

'No spare,' she finally said.

'I'll have one cut. I'll get the original back to you by the close of business today.'

'Thank you. Now, I'd better get back to the shop.' But before she left some imp made her add, 'And don't forget to lock the door on your way out. I wouldn't want to invite any trouble, you know.'

She almost swore he chuckled as she left the room.

* * *

At ten-thirty a.m., a busload of tourists descended on the bookshop demanding guidebooks and maps, and depleting her supply of panoramic postcards.

At midday, Jaz raced out to the stockroom to scour the shelves for reserves that would replenish the alarming gaps that were starting to open up in her *Local Information* section. She came away empty-handed.

She walked back to stare at the computer, then shook her head. Later. She'd tackle it later.

At three-thirty a blonde scrap of a thing sidled through the door, barely jangling the bell. She glanced at Jaz with autumn-tinted eyes and Jaz's heart practically fell out of her chest.

Was this Connor's daughter?

It had to be. She had his eyes; she had his hair. She had Faye's heart-shaped face and delicate porcelain skin.

Melanie—such a pretty name. Such a pretty little girl.

An ache grew so big and round in Jaz's chest that it didn't leave room for anything else.

'Hello,' she managed when the little girl continued to stare at her. It wasn't the cheery greeting she'd practised all day, more a hoarse whisper. She was glad Connor wasn't here to hear it.

'Hello,' the little girl returned, edging away towards the children's section.

Jaz let her go, too stunned to ask her if she needed help with anything. Too stunned to ask her if she was looking for her father. Too stunned for anything.

She'd known Connor had a daughter. She'd known she would eventually meet that daughter.

Her hands clenched. She'd known diddly-squat!

Physically, Melanie Reed might be all Connor and Faye, but the slope of her shoulders, the way she hung her head, reminded Jaz of…

Oh, dear Lord. Melanie Reed reminded Jaz of herself at the

same age—friendless, rootless. As a young girl, she'd crept into the bookshop in the exact same fashion Melanie just had.

Her head hurt. Her neck hurt. Pain pounded at her temples. She waited for someone to come in behind Melanie—Connor, his mother perhaps.

Nothing.

She bit her lip. She stared at the door, then glanced towards the children's section. Surely a seven-year-old shouldn't be left unsupervised?

If she craned her neck she could just make out Melanie's blonde curls, could see the way that fair head bent over a book. Something in the child's posture told Jaz she wasn't reading at all, only pretending to.

She glanced at the ceiling. Had Connor asked Melanie to wait for him in here?

She discounted that notion almost immediately. No way.

She glanced back at Melanie. She remembered how she'd felt as a ten-year-old, newly arrived in Clara Falls. She took in the defeated lines of those shoulders and found herself marching towards the children's section. She pretended to tidy the nearby shelves.

'Hello again,' she started brightly. 'I believe I know who you are—Melanie Reed. Am I right?'

The little face screwed up in suspicion and Jaz wondered if she'd overdone the brightness. Lots of her friends in Sydney had children, but they were all small—babies and toddlers.

Seven was small too, she reminded herself.

'I'm not supposed to talk to strangers.'

Excellent advice, but… 'I'm not really a stranger, you know. I used to live here a long time ago and I knew both your mum and your dad.'

That captured Melanie's interest. 'Were you friends?'

The ache inside her grew. 'Yes.' She made herself smile. 'We were friends.' They'd all been the best of friends once upon a time.

'I can't remember my mum, but I have a picture of her.'

Jaz gulped. According to Frieda, Melanie had only been two years old when Faye had left. 'I…uh…well… It was a long time ago when I knew them. Back before you were born. My name is Jazmin Harper, but everyone calls me Jaz. You can call me Jaz too, if you like.'

'Do you own the bookshop now?'

'I do.'

Melanie gave a tentative smile. 'Everyone calls me Melanie or Mel.' The smile faded. 'I wish they'd call me Melly. I think that sounds nicer, don't you?'

Jaz found herself in total agreement. 'I think Melly is the prettiest name in the world.'

Melanie giggled and Jaz sat herself down on one of the leatherette cubes dotted throughout the bookshop for the relief of foot-weary browsers. 'Now, Melly, I believe your dad is going to be at least another half an hour.'

Melanie immediately shot to her feet, glanced around with wild eyes. 'I'm not supposed to be here. You can't tell him!'

Yikes. 'Why not?'

'Because I'm supposed to go to Mrs Benedict's after school but I hate it there.'

Double yikes. 'Why?'

'Because her breath smells funny…and sometimes she smacks me.'

She smacked her! Jaz's blood instantly went on the boil. 'Have you told your daddy about this?'

Melly shook her head.

'But Melly, why not?'

Melly shook her head again, her bottom lip wobbled. 'Are you going to tell on me?'

Jaz knew she couldn't let this situation go on, but… 'How about I make a deal with you?'

The child's face twisted up in suspicion again. 'What?'

'If you promise to come here after school each afternoon this week, then I won't say anything to anyone.' At least Melly would be safe here.

Melanie's shoulders relaxed. 'Okay.' She shot another small smile at Jaz. 'It's what I always do anyway.'

'There, that's settled then.' Jaz smiled back at her. She figured it would only take her a day or two, till Thursday at the latest, to convince Melanie to confide in Connor.

And she wouldn't like to be in Mrs Benedict's shoes once he found out she'd been smacking his little girl.

'Who picks you up from Mrs Benedict's? Daddy?'

'Yes, at five o'clock on the dot at Mrs Benedict's front gate,' Melly recited.

Jaz glanced at her watch. 'That's nearly an hour away. You know what, Melly? In celebration of making my very first new friend in Clara Falls, I'm going to close the shop early today and walk with you to Mrs Benedict's.'

Melly's eyes grew round. 'I'm your friend?'

'You bet.'

Then Melly beamed at her, really smiled, and the ache pressed so hard against the walls of Jaz's chest that she thought it'd split her open then and there.

Jaz found Connor leaning against the shop front when she arrived at eight-fifteen on Tuesday morning. He held out the key she'd given him yesterday. 'I had a spare one cut. Sorry I didn't get it back to you yesterday.'

She reached out, closed her fingers around it. It still held warmth from his hand. 'Thank you.'

He looked exactly as the radio weatherman had described the weather that morning—cold and clear with a chill in the air, blue skies hinting at the warmth to come later in the day. She didn't know about the warmth to come.

'You closed the shop early yesterday.'

No judgement, just an observation. He looked tired.

Something inside her softened to the consistency of water or air…marshmallow.

Not marshmallow! She didn't do marshmallow any more.

But that weariness…it caught at her.

He and Faye had only lasted two years.

Had Connor married Faye on the rebound?

The thought had never occurred to her before. But that marriage… It had happened so fast…

Her knees locked. No! She would not get involved in this man's life again. She would not give him the power to destroy her a second time.

But that weariness…

She hadn't noticed it yesterday or on Saturday. All she'd noticed then was his goldenness. The goldenness might've dimmed, but that didn't make him any less appealing. With his hair damp from a recent shower, the scent of his shampoo enhanced rather than masked the scent of autumn that clung to him.

She tried to pinpoint the individual elements that brought that scent to life, hoping to rob it of its power. A hint of eucalyptus, recently tilled earth…and fresh-cut pumpkin. Those things together shouldn't be alluring. It didn't stop Jaz from wanting to press her face against his neck and gulp in great, greedy breaths.

Good Lord. Stop it!

'I closed fifteen minutes early. I had things to do.'

She wondered if she should tell him about Melanie.

She recalled the way Melly's face had lit up when Jaz had declared them friends and knew she couldn't. Not yet. If Melly hadn't confided in Connor by the end of the week, though, she would have to.

'Have you found new staff yet?' Connor all but growled the words.

Jaz unlocked the door, proud that her hand didn't shake, not even a little. 'I'm working on it.'

'Will someone be in to help today?'

'Perhaps.'

He followed her into the bookshop. 'Perhaps! Do you think that's good enough?'

'I don't think it's any of your concern.'

He followed her all the way through to the kitchenette.

'Coffee?'

Idiot. Mentally she kicked herself. Coffee was way too chummy.

Relief didn't flood her, though, when he shook his head. Work boots thumped overhead and an electric saw rent the air. 'Sorry. I hope we're not disturbing you too much.'

'Not at all.' That didn't bother her in the slightest. Seeing Connor every day…now that was tougher.

Don't go there.

'What time do you start work?' she asked, because it suddenly seemed wise to say something, and fast.

'Seven-thirty.'

She swung around from making coffee. 'Yet you didn't knock off yesterday till just before five?'

One corner of his mouth kinked up as if he'd read the word *slave-driver* in big letters across her forehead. 'My apprentices knocked off at three-thirty.'

But he'd hung around at least an hour longer?

'Look, Connor, you don't need to bust a gut getting the work done in double-quick time, you know. If it takes an extra week or two…' She trailed off with a shrug, hoping she looked as nonchalant as she sounded. He really should be at home spending time with Melly.

His jaw tightened. 'I said it would be completed asap and I meant it. I at least have employees to help me.'

He planted his legs, hands on hips, and Jaz's saliva glands suddenly remembered how to work. Heavens, Connor Reed was still seriously drool-worthy.

'What do you mean to do about it?' he demanded.

She stepped back. Stared. Then she shook herself. He meant her staffing problem.

Of course that was what he meant.

'Get straight to work. That's what I mean to do. I have oodles to get through today.' She wanted to spend between now and nine o'clock trying to coax the secrets out of that ancient computer, particularly the ones that would point her in the direction of her suppliers.

After she'd walked Melly to Mrs Benedict's front gate this afternoon, she'd return and see what else she could coax from it.

Just for a moment, gold sparked from the brown depths of Connor's eyes. 'Have you settled in at Gwen's? Are you comfortable there?'

'Very comfortable, thank you.'

Not true. Oh, her room and en-suite bathroom, the feather bed, were all remarkably comfortable. Gwen's reception, though, hadn't been all Jaz had hoped for.

She made herself smile, saluted Connor with her mug of coffee. 'Now, if you'll excuse me, I have work to do.' Then she fled to the stockroom before those autumn-tinted eyes saw the lies in her own.

The computer did not divulge her suppliers' identities. It didn't divulge much of anything at all. Who on earth was she supposed to phone, fax or email to order in new books? She started clicking indiscriminately on word documents but none of them seemed to hold a clue. Before she had a chance to start rifling through the filing cabinet, it was time to open the shop.

Business wasn't as brisk as it had been the previous day, but she still had a steady stream of customers—all tourists. As she'd had to do the previous day, whenever she went to the bathroom she hung a 'Back in five minutes' sign on the door.

She breathed a sigh when it was time to close the shop and walk Melly the five blocks to Mrs Benedict's front gate.

'Melly, why don't you want to tell your dad that you're unhappy at Mrs Benedict's?'

Melly stopped skipping to survey Jaz soberly. 'Because Daddy has lots of worries and Mrs Benedict is his last hope.' She leaned in close to confide, 'I know because I heard him say so to Grandma. There's no one else who can look after me and I'm too little to stay at home alone.'

'I think your happiness is more important than anything else in the world to your Daddy.' She waited and watched while Melly digested that piece of information. 'Besides,' she added cheerfully, 'there's always me. You're more than welcome to hang out at the bookshop.'

Melly didn't smile. 'Grandad's picking me up today. I stay with him and Grandma on Tuesday nights.'

'That'll be nice.'

Melly didn't say anything for a moment, then, 'Grandma thinks little girls should wear dresses and skirts and not jeans. I don't have any jeans that fit me any more. Yvonne Walker thinks skirts are prissy.'

'Yvonne is in your class at school?' Jaz hazarded.

'She's the prettiest girl in the whole school! And she has the best parties.' Melly's mouth turned down. 'She didn't invite me to her last party.'

Jaz's heart throbbed in sympathy.

'But if she could see my hair like this!'

Melly touched a hand to her hair. Jaz had pulled it up into a ponytail bun. It made Melly look sweet and winsome. 'I'll do it like that for you any time you like,' she promised.

Melly's eyes grew wide.

'And you know what else? I think if you asked your daddy to take you shopping for jeans, he would.'

Jaz waited on the next corner, out of sight, until Melly's grandfather had collected her, then walked back to the shop and installed herself in front of the computer.

She turned it on and stroked the top of the monitor, murmured 'Pretty please,' under her breath.

Above her a set of work boots sounded against bare floorboards, the scrape and squeal of some tool against wood. She glanced up at the ceiling. Why wasn't Connor at home with Melly? Why was he here, working on her flat, when he could be at home with his daughter?

She glanced back at the computer screen and shot forward in her seat when she realised the text on the screen was starting to break up. 'No, no,' she pleaded, placing a hand on either side of the monitor, as if that could help steady it.

Bang! She jumped as a sound like a cap gun rent the air. Smoke belched out of the computer. The screen went black.

'No!'

No staff and now no computer?

She shook the monitor, slapped a fist down hard on top. Nothing.

She sagged in her chair. This couldn't be happening. Not now. *Not now.*

Don't panic.

She leapt to her feet and started to pace. *I won't let you down, Mum.*

The filing cabinet!

With a cry, she dropped to her knees and tried to open the top drawer. Locked. She fumbled in her pockets for the keys. Tried one—didn't fit. Tried a second—wouldn't turn. Tried a third…

The drawer shot open so fast it almost knocked her flat on her back. She rifled through the files avidly. She stopped. She rifled through them again…slowly…and her exultation died. Oh, there were files all right, lots of files. But they were all empty.

She yanked open the second drawer. More files, very neatly arranged, but they didn't contain a damn thing, not even scrap paper. Jaz pulled out each and every one of them anyway, just to check, throwing them with growing ferocity to the floor.

Finally, there were no more to throw. She sat back and stared at the rack and ruin that surrounded her. Maybe Richard had taken the files for safekeeping?

She smoothed down her hair, pulled in a breath and tried to beat back her tiredness.

No, Richard wouldn't have the files. He'd have given them back to her by now if he had.

Maybe her mother hadn't kept any files?

That hardly seemed likely. Frieda Harper had kept meticulous records even for the weekend stall she'd kept at the markets when Jaz was a teenager.

Jaz rested her head on her arm. Which meant Dianne or Anita—or both of them together—had sabotaged the existing files.

'What the bloody hell is going on in here?'

Jaz jumped so high she swore her head almost hit the ceiling. She swung around to find Connor's lean, rangy bulk blocking the doorway to the kitchenette. Her heart rate didn't slow. In fact, her pulse gave a funny little jump.

'Don't sneak up on a person like that!' Hollering helped ease the pulse-jumping. 'You nearly gave me a heart attack!'

'Sorry.' He shoved his hands in his pockets. 'I thought I was making plenty of noise.' His gaze narrowed as it travelled around the room, took in the untidy stack of files on the floor. 'What are you doing?'

'Having a clean out.' She thrust her chin up, practically daring him to contradict her.

For a moment she thought the lines around his mouth softened, but then she realised the light was dim in here and she was tired. She was probably only seeing what she wanted to see.

His nose wrinkled. 'What's that smell?'

'I was burning some incense in here earlier,' she lied.

He stared at her. She resisted the urge to moisten her lips. 'I have a question about a wall,' she said abruptly, gesturing for him to follow her through to the bookshop and away from eau de burning computer.

She was lying through her teeth.

Man, he had to give her ten out of ten for grit.

Keeping one eye on her retreating back, Connor bent to retrieve a file. Empty. Like its counterparts, he guessed, air whistling between his teeth as he flung the file back on the top of the pile.

He glanced at the computer. He knew the smell of a burning motherboard. He'd told Frieda months ago she needed to upgrade that computer. He dragged a hand through his hair, then followed Jaz out into the bookshop.

'This wall here…' She pointed to the wall that divided the kitchenette from the bookshop.

He had to admire her pluck. But that was all he'd admire. He refused to notice the way her hair gleamed rich and dark in the overhead light—the exact same colour as the icing on Gordon Sears's chocolate éclairs. He refused to notice how thick and full it was either or how the style she'd gathered it up into left the back of her neck vulnerable and exposed.

He realised she was staring at him, waiting. He cleared his throat. 'I wouldn't advise building bookshelves on that wall, Jaz.' He rapped his knuckles against it. 'Hear how flimsy it is?'

She stared at him as if she had no idea what he was talking about. 'I can strengthen the wall if you like.' But it'd cost and it'd take time…time she wouldn't want to waste waiting for work to be done if he had her pegged right. 'I could write you up a quote if you want.' What the hell. He'd do the job for cost.

'I don't want bookshelves there. I just want to know if you're doing anything to this wall when you start work down here?'

'No.' One section of floorboards needed replacing and a couple of bookcases needed strengthening, but not the walls.

'So I'm free to paint it?'

'Sure.' He frowned. 'But surely it'd be wiser to wait until all the work is finished, then paint it as a job lot.'

She stared at him. Her eyes were pools of navy a man could drown in if he forgot himself. She moistened her lips—lush, soft lips—and Connor tried not to forget himself.

'I don't mean that kind of painting, Connor.'

It took a moment for her words to make sense. His head snapped back when they did.

She stared at the wall and he knew it wasn't pale green paint she saw.

'I mean to paint a portrait of my mother here.' She turned, a hint of defiance in her eyes, but her whole face had come alive. So alive it made him ache.

A memorial to Frieda? He wanted to applaud her. He wanted to kiss her. He needed his head read. 'Do you mean to start it tonight?'

'No, but I might prime the wall tomorrow.'

For Pete's sake, did she mean to work herself into the ground? 'I thought you'd be back at Gwen's by now.'

'Hmm, no.'

Something in her tone made his eyes narrow. 'Why not?' Jaz and Gwen had been great pals.

She didn't look at him. She cocked her head and continued to survey the wall.

He resisted the urge to shake her. 'Jaz?'

'I think the less Gwen has to see of me, the happier she will be.'

He'd considered Richard's suggestion that Jaz stay at Gwen's an excellent one at the time. He'd thought it'd give Jaz a friend, an ally. He'd obviously got that wrong…and he should've known better. 'Sorry.' The apology dropped stiff from his lips. 'My fault.'

She glanced over her shoulder. 'I hardly think so.'

'I should've thought it through. Gwen…she was pretty cut up when you left. She wouldn't speak to me for months. She kept expecting to hear from you.'

Jaz stiffened, then she swung around, closed the gap between them and gripped his forearms. 'What did you just say?'

Her scent assaulted him and for a moment he found it impossible to speak. Her face had paled, lines of strain fanned out from her eyes. He couldn't remember a time when she'd looked more beautiful. The pressure of her hands on his arms increased, her grip would leave marks, but he welcomed the bite of her nails on his skin.

'She thought you were friends, Jaz. She cared about you.' After him and Faye, Gwen and Richard had been Jaz's closest friends. 'Then you left and she never heard from you again. You can guess how she took that.'

Air hissed out between her teeth. She dropped his arms and stepped back, her eyes wide, stricken—an animal caught in the headlights of an oncoming truck; something wild and injured trying to flee. Without a thought, he reached for her. But she pulled herself up and away, drew in a breath, and he watched, amazed, as she settled a mask of cool composure over her features. As if her distress had never been there at all.

Hell! That couldn't be healthy. He dragged a hand back through his hair, surprised to find that it shook. His heart hammered against his ribcage and he cursed himself for being a hundred different kinds of fool where this woman was concerned.

'Well—' she smiled brightly '—that's me done for the day.' The knuckles on her hands, folded innocuously at her waist, gleamed white. 'So, if you'll excuse me…'

'No!' He cleared his throat, tried to moderate his tone. 'I mean…' Ice prickled across his scalp and the back of his neck. Was it something like this that had tipped Frieda over the edge? 'I mean, where are you going?'

Her eyes had gone wide again. This time with surprise rather than… He didn't know what name to give the expression he'd just witnessed—shock, pain, grief?

'Why, to Gwen's, of course. I have an apology to make.' Sorrow stretched through the navy blue of her eyes. 'I can't believe how shabbily I've treated her. It—'

She waved a hand in front of her face, as if to dispel some image that disturbed her, and he suddenly realised what it was he'd seen in her eyes—self-loathing. She'd never considered herself worthy of his love, or of Faye, Gwen and Richard's friendship, had she?

Why was he only seeing that now?

She glanced at her watch. 'Where's the best place to buy a bottle of wine at this time of night? And chocolate. I'll need chocolate.'

'The tavern's bottle shop will still be open.'

'Thank you.'

She smiled at him and he could see that concern for herself, for the bookshop, had been ousted by her concern for Gwen. He didn't know why that should touch him so deeply. 'Can I give you a lift?'

She snorted. 'Connor, it's a two-minute walk. Thanks all the same, but I'll be fine.'

She stared up at him. He stared back. The silence grew and she moistened her lips. 'I'll see you later then.'

He nodded, dragged in a breath of her scent as she edged past him, then watched as she let herself out of the shop and disappeared into the evening.

He turned to stare at the wall she meant to paint.

With a muffled oath, he strode into the storeroom, disconnected the computer and tucked it under his arm.

He told himself he'd do the same for anyone.

CHAPTER FOUR

AT LUNCHTIME on Wednesday a group of teenagers sauntered through the bookshop's door and it immediately transported Jaz back in time ten years.

Oh, dear Lord. Had she ever looked that...confrontational? She bit back a grin. All of them, boys included, wore tip-to-toe black, the girls in stark white make-up and dark matt lipstick. Between the five of them they had more body piercing than the latest art-house installation on display at the Power House Museum. Their Doc Marten boots clomped heavily against the bare floorboards.

Jaz stopped trying to hold back her grin. She shouldn't smile. They were probably skiving off from afternoon sport at Clara Falls High. But then...Jaz had skived off Wednesday afternoon sport whenever she could get away with it too.

'If there's anything I can help you with, just let me know,' she called out.

'Cool,' said one of the girls.

'Sweet,' said one of the boys.

Jaz went back to studying the book she'd found in the business section half an hour ago—*Everything You Need To Know About Managing a Bookshop*. So far she'd found out that she needed a new computer and an Internet connection.

One of the girls—the one who'd already spoken—seized a book and came up to the counter. 'Every week, I come in here to drool over this book. I can't afford it.'

It was a coffee table art book—*Urban Art*. Exactly the same kind of book Jaz herself had pored over at that age.

'Look, we know the people who used to work here quit.' The girl ran her hands over the cover, longing stretched across her face. 'If I worked here, how many hours would it take me to earn this book?'

Jaz told her.

'Will you hire me? My name is Carmen, by the way. And I'm still at school so I could only work weekends, but… I'll work hard.'

Jaz wanted to reach out and hug her. 'I'm Jaz,' she said instead. They probably knew that already but it seemed churlish not to introduce herself too. 'And yes, I am looking for staff—permanent, part-time and casual.' At the moment she'd take what she could get. 'How old are you, Carmen?'

'Sixteen.'

'I would love to hire you, but before I could do that I would need either your mum or dad's permission.' No way was she going to cause *that* kind of trouble.

Five sets of shoulders slumped. Jaz's grew heavy in sympathy.

'I hate this town,' one of them muttered.

'There's never anything to do!'

'If you look the least bit different you're labelled a trouble-maker.'

Jaz remembered resenting this town at their age too for pretty much the same reasons. 'You're always welcome to come and browse in here.' She motioned to the book on urban art.

'Thanks,' Carmen murmured, but the brightness had left her eyes. She glanced up from placing the book back on its shelf. 'Is it true you're a tattoo artist?'

'Yes, I am.' And she wasn't ashamed of it.

'And are you running drugs through here?'

What? Jaz blinked. 'I could probably rustle you up an aspirin if you needed one, but anything stronger is beyond me, I'm afraid.'

'I told you that was a lie!' Carmen hissed to the others.

'Yeah, well, fat chance that my mum'll let me work here once she catches wind of that rumour,' one of the others grumbled.

The teenagers drifted back outside.

Drugs? Drugs! Jaz started to shake. Her hands curved into claws. Just because she was a tattoo artist that made her a junkie, or a drug baron?

She wished Mac could hear this.

The whole town would boycott her shop if those kinds of rumours took hold. Very carefully, she unclenched her hands. She drummed her fingers against the countertop for a moment, a grim smile touching her lips. Very carefully, she smoothed down her hair. Her smile grew. So did the grimness.

She hooked the 'Back in five minutes' sign to the window, locked the door and set off across the street. 'You'll enjoy this,' she said, without stopping, to Mrs Lavender, who sat on her usual park bench on the traffic island. She reminded herself to walk tall. She reminded herself she was as good as anyone else in this town. Without pausing, she breezed into Mr Sears's shop with her largest smile in place and called out, 'Howdy, Mr Sears! How are you today? Aren't we having the most glorious weather? Good for business, isn't it?'

Mr Sears jerked around from the far end of the shop and his eyes darkened with fury, lines bracketing his mouth, distorting it.

'I'll take a piece of your scrumptious carrot cake to go, thanks.'

The rest of the bakery went deathly quiet. Jaz pretended to peruse the baked goodies on display in their glass-fronted counters until she was level with Mr Sears. 'If you refuse to serve me,' she told him, quietly so no one else heard her, 'I will create the biggest scene Clara Falls has ever seen. And, believe me, you *will* regret it.' Her smile didn't slip an inch.

Mr Sears seized a paper bag. He continued to glare, but he very carefully placed a piece of carrot cake inside it. It was a trait Jaz remembered, and it brought previous visits rushing back. He'd always treated his goods as if they were fine porcelain. For some reason that made her throat thicken.

She swallowed the thickness away. 'Best bread for twenty miles, my mother always used to say,' she continued in her bright, breezy, you're-my-long-lost-best-friend voice. A voice that probably carried all the way outside and across to where Mrs Lavender sat grinning on her park bench.

Carmen emerged from the back of the bakery. 'Hey, Dad, can I…' She stopped dead to stare from her father to Jaz and back again. She swallowed, then offered Jaz a half-hearted smile. 'Hey, Jaz.'

'Hey, Carmen.' Carmen was Gordon Sears's daughter? Whew! His glare grew even more ferocious. She grinned back. *That* was too delicious for words. 'And I'll take a loaf of your famous sourdough too, Mr S.'

He looked as if he'd like to throw the loaf at her head. He didn't. He placed it in a bag and set it down beside her carrot cake. His fingers lingered on the bag, as if in apology to it for where it was going.

Jaz grinned and winked as she paid him. 'It's great to be back in town, Mr S. You have a good day now, you hear?'

He slammed her change on the counter.

'And keep the change.'

She breezed back outside.

To slam smack-bang into Connor. His hands shot out to steady her. His eyes danced with a wicked delight that she feared mirrored her own. 'Lunchtime, huh?'

'That's right. You too?'

'Yep.'

His grin widened. It made her miss…everything.

No, it didn't! She stepped away so he was forced to drop his hands. 'I'd…er…recommend the carrot cake.'

'The carrot cake, huh?'

'That's right.' She swallowed. 'Well… I'll catch ya.' Oh, good Lord. Had she just descended into her former teenage vernacular? With as much nonchalance as she could muster, she stalked off.

His laughter and his hearty, 'Howdy, Mr S,' as he entered the bakery, followed her up the street, across the road and burrowed a path into her stomach to warm her very toes.

She unlocked the bookshop door, plonked herself down on her stool behind the sales counter and devoured her piece of carrot cake. For the first time in her life, Mr Sears's baked goods didn't choke her. The carrot cake didn't taste like sawdust. It tasted divine.

When she closed her eyes to lick the frosting from her fingers all she saw was Connor's laughing autumn eyes, making her feel alive again. In the privacy of the bookshop, she let herself grin back.

An hour after she'd last seen him, Connor stormed into the bookshop with a computer tucked under one arm and the diminutive Mrs Lavender tucked under the other.

Jaz blinked. She tried to slow her heart rate, did what she could to moderate the exhilaration pulsing through her veins. Just because she was back in Clara Falls didn't mean she and Connor were…anything. In fact, it meant the total opposite. They were…nothing. Null and void. History. But…

No man had any right whatsoever to look so darn sexy in jeans and work boots. Thank heavens he wasn't wearing a tool belt. That would draw the eye to…

No, no, no. Jaz tried to shoo that image right out of her head.

Connor set the computer on the counter. Jaz glanced at it, then back at him. She moistened her lips, realised his gaze had narrowed in on that action and her mouth went even drier. 'I know the question is obvious, but…what is that?'

'This is a computer I'm not using at the moment and is yours on loan until you get a chance to upgrade the shop's computer. This—' he pulled a computer disk from his pocket '—is the information my receptionist—the receptionist that I didn't fire and who is a whiz at all things computer—managed to save from your old hard drive. Including several recently deleted files.' He set the disk on top of the computer. 'She's hoping it will go some way to making amends for any previous inconvenience she's caused you.'

Jaz stared at him, speechless.

'And this—' he placed his hands on Mrs Lavender's shoulders '—is Mrs Lavender who, if you remember, owned the bookshop before your mother. A veritable fount of information who is finding herself at a bit of a loose end these days, and who would love to help out for a couple of hours a day, if you're agreeable.'

Agreeable? Jaz wanted to jump over the counter and hug him!

'Gives me a front row seat for watching all the drama. I'll enjoy seeing Gordon Sears brought down a peg or two.' Mrs Lavender's dark eyes twinkled.

Jaz slid out from behind the counter and wrapped her arms around the older woman. Over the top of Mrs Lavender's head, she met Connor's eyes. 'I don't know how to—'

'How's Gwen?'

She straightened and smiled, smoothed down her hair. 'Great.' The word emerged a tad breathy, but Connor was looking at her with such warmth that for a moment she didn't know which way was up.

'Gwen is great.' Gwen had accepted her apology. They'd shared the bottle of wine, they'd eaten the chocolate and they'd forged the beginnings of a new friendship.

He reached out, touched her cheek with the back of one finger. 'Good.' Then he stepped back and shoved his hands into his pockets. 'Time for me to get back to work. I'll see you ladies later.'

He turned, left the shop and disappeared. Only then did Jaz realise he hadn't given her time to thank him. He hadn't given her time to refuse his kindness either. She reached up to touch the spot on her cheek where his finger had lingered for the briefest, loveliest moment.

'Come along, Jaz. We've no time for mooning.'

Mooning? Who was mooning? 'I'm not mooning!'

She gulped. Mrs Lavender was right. She had no time for mooning. Absolutely no time at all.

But that afternoon, before it was time to close the shop and walk Melly home, Jaz's painting supplies were delivered to the bookshop. Connor must've searched through her boxes until he'd found everything she'd need to paint her portrait of Frieda.

She carried the box through to the stockroom, rested her cheek against it for a moment, before setting it to the floor and walking away. It didn't mean anything.

'Have you thought any more about telling your daddy about Mrs Benedict?' Jaz asked Melanie as she walked her to Mrs Benedict's front gate that afternoon.

The child drew herself up as if reciting a lesson. 'I'm not to worry Daddy about domestic matters. He has enough to worry about.'

'Domestic matters?'

'It means household stuff, money and babysitters,' Melly said, rattling each item off as if she'd learned them by heart. 'I checked,' she confided. 'So I'd get it right.'

'Did Daddy tell you not to worry him about domestic matters?' No matter how hard she tried, Jaz could not hear those words emerging from Connor's mouth.

'Grandma did.'

Jaz wondered if she'd go to hell for pumping a child so shamelessly for information. It wasn't for her own benefit, she reminded herself. It was for Melanie's. She wanted the child safe and happy. She couldn't even explain why, except she saw her younger self in Melanie.

That and the fact that Melanie was Connor's child. The kind of child she'd once dreamed of having with Connor.

Which made her sound like some kind of sick stalker! She wasn't. She just wanted to do something…good.

'I think your daddy would be very sad to hear you say that.'

'Why?'

'I think he'd be very interested in everything you do and think, even the domestic ones.'

'Nuh-uh.' The child stuck her chin out and glared at the footpath. 'He was supposed to take me out on the skyway on Saturday, but he didn't coz he had to work.'

Connor had broken a date with his daughter to work on the sign for Jaz's shop!

'Grandma made me promise not to nag him to take me Sunday because she said he'd be tired from working so hard and would need to rest.'

'That was very thoughtful of you.'

Melly glanced up, spearing Jaz with a gaze that touched her to the quick. 'I don't think he needs to work so hard, do you?'

Jaz thought it wiser not to answer that question. 'Perhaps you should tell him you think he's working too hard.'

Melanie shook her head and glanced away. Jaz wondered what else Grandma had made Melanie promise.

'Order, everyone. Order!'

Connor winced. Gordon Sears had a voice that could cut through rock when he was calling a meeting to order. Connor shifted on his seat. Beside him, Richard half-grinned, half-grimaced in sympathy.

'Now, are we all agreed on the winter plantings for the nature strip?'

There were some mutterings, but a show of hands decided the matter. Connor marvelled that it could take so long to decide in favour of hyacinths over daffodils. Personally, he'd have chosen the daffodils, but he didn't much care. It certainly hadn't warranted half an hour's heated debate.

He glanced at his watch. It was almost Mel's bedtime. He hoped his father was coping okay. He tapped his foot against the floor. He didn't like leaving Mel with his parents two nights running. With his mother mostly confined to a wheelchair these days, he considered it too much work for his father. But Russell Reed adored his granddaughter. Mel put a bounce in the older man's step. Connor couldn't deny him that.

When they'd heard Connor was thinking of attending this evening's town meeting, they'd insisted Mel spend the night with them. He bit back a sigh. It was probably for the best. He'd miss reading Mel her bedtime story, but it had started to become all too apparent that Mel hungered for a female influence in her life—a female role model. He'd seen the way she watched the girls at school with their mothers and his heart ached for her.

He was hoping his own mother's presence would help plug that particular hole. At least it gave Mel a woman to confide in.

She needs a younger woman. He pushed that thought away. Two women had left him without backwards glances. He wasn't going through that again, and he sure as hell wasn't risking his daughter's heart and happiness to some fly-by-night. He and Mel, they'd keep muddling along.

'Now, to the last item on the agenda.'

That rock-cracking voice had Connor wincing again. Richard rolled his eyes at Mr Sears's self-importance. Connor nodded in silent agreement.

'Now, I believe most of you will agree with me when I say we most certainly do not want a tattoo parlour polluting the streets of Clara Falls. Those of you who are in favour of such an abomination, please put forward your arguments now.'

Mr Sears glared around the room. Connor shifted forward on his seat, rested his arms on his knees. This was the reason he'd come tonight.

Nobody put forward an argument for a tattoo parlour in Clara Falls, and Connor listened with growing anger to the plan outlined by Gordon Sears to halt the likelihood of any such development occurring in the future.

Finally, he could stand it no longer. 'I don't know if this has escaped everyone's notice or not,' he said, climbing to his feet, 'but you can't block a non-existent development.'

Mr Sears puffed up. 'That's just semantics!'

'No,' Connor drawled. 'It's law.'

'This town has every right to make its feelings known on the subject.'

Connor planted his feet. 'If you approach Jaz Harper with this viciousness—'

'No names have been mentioned!' Mr Sears bluffed.

'No names have been mentioned, but everyone in this room knows exactly who you're talking about. Jaz Harper has made no move whatsoever to set up a tattoo parlour in Clara Falls. She's come back to run her mother's bookshop. End of story.'

He glanced around the room. Some people nodded their encouragement. Others shifted uneasily on their seats as their gazes slid away. Bloody hell! If Jaz were susceptible to the same kind of depression that had afflicted Frieda then…then she wouldn't need the likes of Gordon Sears banging on her door and shoving a petition under her nose.

'Connor is right.' Richard stood too. 'Last time I checked, this country was still a democracy. If you approach *my client*,' he stressed those two words, 'with a petition or with any other kind of associated viciousness—' he borrowed the term from Connor, but Connor didn't mind '—I will take out a harassment suit on her behalf. And, what's more, I'll enjoy doing it. She's a local businesswoman who is contributing to the economy of this town and we should all be supporting her.'

'I'll second that!' Connor clapped Richard on the back. Richard clapped him back. They both sat down. He watched with grim satisfaction as Gordon Sears brought the meeting to a close in double-quick time.

Mr Sears approached him as he and Richard stood talking by their cars. Connor could sense the anger in the older man, even though he hid it well. 'If any such proposal does go forward to the local council, I want you both to know that I will use every means in my power to block it.'

'I hope you're talking about legal means,' Richard said smoothly.

'Naturally.' Mr Sears lifted his chin and glared at Connor. 'I should've known you'd take her side.'

Connor planted his feet. 'This isn't about sides. It's about keeping Clara Falls as the kind of place where I'm happy to raise my daughter. A place not blinded by small-minded bigotry.'

'Ah, your daughter…yes.'

His smirk made the muscles of Connor's stomach contract.

'I take it that you are aware Melanie has been seen leaving the bookshop with Jaz Harper every afternoon this week?'

She what?

Mr Sears laughed at whatever he saw in Connor's face. 'But, then again, perhaps not.' He strolled off, evidently pleased with the bombshell he'd landed.

'There'll be a perfectly reasonable explanation,' Richard said quietly.

'There'd better be. And I mean to find out what it is.' Now. 'Night, Richard.'

'Night, Connor.'

Connor climbed into his car and turned it in the direction of Frieda's Fiction Fair.

He eased the car past the bookshop at a crawl. A light burned inside, towards the rear of the shop. His lips tightened. She was there. He swung his car left at the roundabout and headed for the parking space behind her shop.

He let himself in with the key Jaz had given him. 'Hello?' He made his voice loud, made sure it'd carry all the way through to the front of the shop. He rattled the door and made plenty of noise. He had no intention of startling her like he had last night.

'Through here,' Jaz called.

He followed the sound of her voice. Then came to a dead halt. She'd started her picture of Frieda.

She was drawing!

He reached out and clamped a hand around the hard shelf of a bookcase as the breath punched out of him. *She looked so familiar.* A thousand different memories pounded at him.

She'd sketched in the top half of Frieda's face with a fine pencil and the detail stole his breath. He inched forward to get a better view. Beneath her fingers, her mother's eyes and brow came alive—so familiar and so…vibrant.

Jaz had honed her skill, her talent, until it sang. The potential he'd recognised in her work eight years ago—the potential anyone who'd seen her work couldn't have failed to recognise—had come of age. An ache started up deep down inside him, settled beneath his ribcage like a stitch.

He wanted to drag his gaze away, but he couldn't.

He found his anger again instead. What the hell was Jaz doing with his little girl? Why had Mel been seen with her every afternoon this week? And why hadn't Mrs Benedict informed him about it?

His hands clenched. He'd protect Mel with every breath in his body. Mel was seven—just a little girl—and vulnerable… And in need of a mother.

He ignored that last thought. Jaz Harper sure as hell didn't fit that bill.

Jaz exhaled, stepped back to survey her work more fully, then she growled. She threw her pencil down on a card table she'd set up nearby—it held a photograph of Frieda—then swung around to him, her eyes blazing. 'I'm grateful for what you did earlier in the day—the loan of the computer, Mrs Lavender et cetera. You left before I could thank you. So…thank you. But you obviously have something on your mind now and you might as well spit it out.'

'I mean to.' He planted his feet, hands on hips. 'I want to know what the hell you've been doing with my daughter every afternoon this week?'

The words shot out of him like nails from a nail gun, startling him with their ferocity, but he refused to moderate his glare. If she'd so much as harmed one hair on Mel's head, he'd make sure she regretted it for the rest of her life.

'Did you hear this from Melanie?'

'Gordon Sears,' he growled.

Jaz's lips twisted at whatever she saw in his face. Lush, full lips. Lips he—

No. He would not fall under her spell again. He wouldn't expose Mel to another woman who'd run at the first hint of trouble.

'Still jumping to conclusions, Connor?'

Her words punched the air out of his body.

'What on earth do you think I've been doing with her?' She planted her hands on her hips—a mirror image of him—and matched his glare. 'What kind of nasty notions have been running through your mind?'

Nothing specific, he realised. But he remembered the gaping hole Jaz had left in his life when she'd fled Clara Falls eight years ago. He wouldn't let her hurt Mel like that.

'One more day,' she whispered. 'That's all I needed with her—one more day.' She said the words almost to herself, as if she'd forgotten he was even there.

'One more day to do what?' he exploded.

She folded her arms, but he saw that her hands shook. 'You haven't changed much at all, have you, Connor? It seems you're still more than willing to believe the worst of me.'

Bile burned his throat.

'I needed one more day to convince her to confide in you, that's what.'

To confide in him... Her words left him floundering. 'To confide what?'

'If you spent a little more time with your daughter, then perhaps you'd know!'

'If I...' His shoulders grew so tight they hurt. 'What do you know about bringing a child up on your own?' About how hard it was. About how the doubts crowded in, making him wonder if he was doing a good job or making a hash of things. About how he'd always be a dad and never a mum and that, no matter how nurturing and gentle he tried to be, he knew it wasn't the same.

'I…nothing.' Jaz took a step back. 'I'm sorry.'

The sadness that stretched across her face had his anger draining away, against his will and against his better judgement. She turned away as if to hide her sadness from him.

'Are you going to tell me what's been going on?' To his relief, his voice had returned to normal.

She started gathering up her pencils and placing them back in their box. 'I don't suppose you'd trust me for just one more day?'

'No, I wouldn't.' He tried to make the words gentle. He had to bite back an oath when she flinched. 'I won't take any risks where Mel's concerned. I can't.'

She smiled then and he saw the same concern she'd shown for Gwen last night reflected in her eyes now. His chest started to burn as if he'd run a marathon. If Jaz had gleaned even the tiniest piece of information that would help him with Mel…Mel, who'd gone from laughing and bright-eyed to sober and withdrawn in what seemed to him a twinkling of an eye.

Mel, who'd once chattered away to him about everything and nothing, and who these days would only shake her head when he asked her if anything was wrong.

'Mel has been coming to the bookshop after school instead of Mrs Benedict's.'

'Do you know why?'

'I…yes, I do.' She hesitated. 'May I ask you a question first?'

His hand clenched. He wanted his bright, bubbly daughter back—the girl whose smile would practically split her face in two whenever she saw him. He'd do anything to achieve that, pay any price. Even if that meant answering Jaz's questions first. He gave a short, hard nod.

'Why is Melly going to Mrs Benedict's after school? Please don't get angry again, but…if you start work at seven-thirty most mornings, surely you should be able to knock off in time to collect Melly from school at three-thirty? Obviously I don't know your personal situation, but it looks as if you're doing well financially. Do you really need to work such long hours?'

No, he didn't.

She frowned. 'And who looks after Melly in the mornings before school?'

'The school provides a care service, before and after school.'

She didn't ask, but he could see the question in her eyes—why didn't he use that service instead of sending Mel to Mrs Benedict's?

'You don't want to tell me, do you?'

What the hell...? That mixture of sadness and understanding in her voice tugged at him. It wouldn't hurt to tell her. It might even go some way to making amends for bursting in here and all but accusing her of hurting Mel.

He raked a hand back through his hair. 'We had a huge storm on this side of the mountain two and a half months ago. It did a lot of damage—roofs blown off, trees down on houses, that kind of thing. The state emergency services were run off their feet and we jumped in to help. We're still getting through that work now. At the time it seemed important to secure people's homes against further damage, to make them safe again...liveable. But it did and does mean working long hours.' He hated to see people homeless, especially families with small children.

'And you feel responsible for making things right?'

He didn't know if that was a statement or a question. He shrugged. 'I just want to do my bit to help.'

'Yes, but don't you think you need to draw the line somewhere? There are more important things in life than work, you know.'

A scowl built up inside him. Did she think work counted two hoots when it came to Mel? Mel was his life.

Jaz thrust her chin out. 'You worked on my sign last Saturday instead of taking Melanie on the skyway. You broke a date with your daughter to work on my stupid sign.'

'You didn't think that sign so unimportant at the time!'

Guilt inched through him. He had cancelled that outing with Mel, but he'd promised to take her to the skyway the next day instead. She'd seemed happy enough with that, as happy as she seemed with anything these days. Except…

He frowned. When Sunday had rolled around Mel had said she didn't want to go anywhere. She'd spent the day colouring in on the living room floor instead.

He should've taken her on the Saturday—he should've kept his promise—but when he'd found out Jaz was expected to arrive in Clara Falls that day, he hadn't been able to stay away. At the time he'd told himself it was to get their initial meeting out of the way, and any associated unpleasantness. As he stared down into Jaz's face now, though, he wondered if he'd lied.

He pulled his mind back. 'It's not just the work. Mel needs a woman in her life. She's—'

He broke off to drag a hand down his face. 'I see the way she watches the girls at school with their mothers.' It broke his heart that he couldn't fill that gap for her. 'She hungers for that…maternal touch.'

Jaz frowned. Then her face suddenly cleared. 'That's what Mrs Benedict's about. She's your maternal touch!'

He nodded. 'She came highly recommended. She's raised five children of her own. She's a big, buxom lady with a booming laugh. A sort of…earth mother figure.'

'I see.'

'I thought that, between her and my mother, they might help fill that need in Mel.'

Scepticism rippled across Jaz's face before she could school it. 'What?' he demanded. From memory, Jaz had never liked his mother.

'Melanie doesn't like going to Mrs Benedict's.'

'She hasn't said anything to me!'

Jaz twisted her hands together again. 'Apparently Mrs Benedict has been smacking her.'

CHAPTER FIVE

'SHE'S what?' Connor reached out and gripped Jaz's shoulders. 'Did you say *smacking her*? Are you telling me Mrs Benedict is *hitting* my daughter?'

'You're hurting me, Connor.'

He released her immediately. And started to pace.

'Relax, Connor, Melly is—'

'Relax? Relax!' How the hell could she say that when—

'Melanie is safe. That's all that matters, right? You can tackle Mrs Benedict tomorrow. Flying off the handle now won't solve anything.'

She had a point. He dragged in a breath. But when he got hold of Mrs Benedict he'd—

'Working out what's best for Melanie is what's important now, isn't it?'

'She's not going back to that woman's place!'

'Good.'

He dragged in another breath. 'So that's why she's been coming here?'

'Yes.'

'And you've been walking her to Mrs Benedict's front gate each afternoon?'

'Yes.'

'And trying to talk her into confiding in me?'

'Yes.'

He ground his teeth together. 'Thank you.'

'It was nothing.'

She tried to shrug his words off, but her eyes were wide and blue. It wasn't nothing and they both knew it.

He unclenched his jaw. 'Do you have any idea why Mel didn't want to confide in me?'

Jaz hesitated again. 'I…'

She did! She knew more about what was going through his daughter's head than he did.

She eyed him warily. 'Will you promise not to shout any more?'

Did she think he'd lash out at her in his anger? He recalled the way he'd stormed in here, and dragged a hand down his face. 'I'll do my best,' he ground out.

'It seems that because you're working so hard, your mother is concerned about your…welfare.'

He frowned. 'I don't get what you're driving at.'

She moistened her lips. He tried to ignore their shine, their fullness…and the hunger that suddenly seized him.

'It seems your mother has been lecturing Melly not to bother you with her troubles when you're so obviously busy with work.'

He gaped at her. No! He snapped his jaw shut. 'You never did like my mother, did you?'

'No, Connor, that's not true, but she never liked me. And in hindsight I can't really blame her. She could hardly have been thrilled that the rebellious Goth girl was going out with her son now, could she?'

His mother had always been…overprotective.

'Look, I'm not making this up.'

He didn't want to believe her…but he did.

She grimaced. 'And, for what it's worth, I think your mother is well-intentioned. She is your mother, after all. It's natural for her to have your best interests at heart.'

'She should have Mel's best interests at heart.' He collapsed onto one of the leatherette cubes. Mel needed a woman in her life, but the two he'd chosen had let her down badly.

And so she'd latched onto Jaz?

What a mess.

This wasn't his mother's fault. It wasn't even Mrs Benedict's fault, though he'd still have some choice words for her when he saw her tomorrow. This was his fault. He hadn't wanted to acknowledge it before and he didn't want to acknowledge it now, but Mel needed a younger woman in her life. Not two women who were at least fifty years older than her.

But Jaz?

'Don't look like that,' Jaz chided. 'This isn't the end of the world. So you knock off from here in time to collect Melly from school for the rest of the week. That's no big deal.'

'It'll put work on the flat back by a day.'

She shrugged again. 'Like I said—no big deal.'

'She didn't confide in me!' The words burst from him, but he couldn't hold them back. Mel had refused to confide in him, but she'd confided in Jaz?

Jaz!

'So you work on winning back her trust. On Saturday you take her out on the skyway. Tell her she looks so pretty you're going to call her Princess Melly for the day and that her every wish is your command.'

He stared at her and he couldn't help it—a grin built up inside him at the image she'd planted in his mind…and at how alive her face had become as she described it. Who called Jaz Princess Jaz? Who tried to make her dreams come true?

He wondered if she'd like to come out on the skyway with him and Mel on Saturday? He wondered if—

Whoa! He pulled back. No way. He was grateful for the insights she'd given him, but not that grateful. Mel might need a younger woman in her life, but Jaz Harper wasn't that woman.

Jaz's smile faltered. 'You want me to butt out now, don't you?'

'Yes.' There was no sense in trying to soften his intentions.

'I see.'

He felt like a heel. He didn't want to hurt her feelings, but he would not—could not—let her hurt Mel. He hardened his heart. 'I don't want you involved in my daughter's life.'

'Good!' Her eyes flashed. 'Because I don't want to be involved in any part of your life either.'

He didn't want what had happened to Frieda happening to Jaz either, though. The thought had him breaking out in a cold sweat. 'I didn't mean that to sound as rotten as it did. It's just…you tell me you're only here for twelve months.'

She folded her arms. 'That's right.'

He swore he glimpsed tears in her eyes. 'Bloody hell, Jaz. If you're only here for twelve months, I don't want Mel getting attached to you. She'll only be hurt when you leave. She won't understand.'

'I hear you, all right!'

Yep, definitely tears. 'Look, I didn't understand when you left eight years ago and I was eighteen. What hope does a seven-year-old have?'

Her jaw dropped and that old anger, the old pain, reared up through him. 'Hell, Jaz! You left and you didn't even tell me why!'

She'd hurt him. Eight years ago, she'd hurt him. She could tell by his pallor, in the way his eyes glittered. In the way the tiredness had invaded the skin around his mouth.

But he'd married Faye so quickly that she'd thought…

She gulped. 'Darn it all, Connor, I was only going to be gone for three months.'

'Three months!' His jaw went slack. His Adam's apple worked. 'Three months?' he repeated before he tensed up again. 'Where the hell did you go? And why didn't you tell me?'

His pain wrapped around her with tentacles that tried to squeeze the air out of her body. She had to drag in a breath before she could speak. 'You have to understand, I was seriously cut up that you thought I could ever cheat on you.'

He hadn't given her a chance to explain at the time. He'd hurled his accusations with all the ferocity of a cornered, injured animal—even then she'd known it was his shock and pain talking, the unexpectedness of finding her at the Hancocks' house, because she had lied about that.

'Stop playing games, Jaz.' He spoke quietly. 'I *know* you were cheating on me with Sam Hancock.'

A spurt of anger rippled through her, followed closely by grim satisfaction. She wanted—no, *needed*—him to keep his distance. If he thought she was the kind of woman who'd cheat on him and still lie about it eight years later, he'd definitely keep his distance.

She was not travelling to hell again with Connor Reed. It had taken too long to get over the last time. He hadn't trusted her then and he didn't trust her now. He'd jumped to conclusions back then and, on this evening's evidence, he still jumped to conclusions now. So much for older and wiser!

'Does it even matter now?' she managed in as frigid a tone as she could muster.

'Not in the slightest. I understand why people cheat. That's not the issue.'

She didn't bother calling him a liar. There didn't seem to be any point. Perhaps it didn't make an ounce of difference to him now anyway.

'What I don't understand is why people run.' He stabbed a finger at her. 'What I don't get is why you left the way you did.'

The flesh on her arms grew cold. If Faye had deserted him too without an explanation…

Was an overdue explanation better than no explanation at all? One glance into his face told her the answer. She pulled in a breath and did what she could to ignore the sudden tiredness that made her limbs heavy. 'Let's just take it as a given that I was in a right state by the time I got home that night, okay?' It made her sick to the stomach just remembering it.

'Fine.' The word emerged clipped and short.

'My mother calmed me down.' Eventually. 'And, bit by bit, got the story out of me.'

'And?' he said when she stopped.

'Did you know that my mother didn't approve of our relationship?'

He blinked and she laughed. Not a mirthful laugh. Definitely not a joyful one. 'I know—funny, isn't it? The rest of the town thought it was me—the rebel Goth girl—leading clean-cut Connor Reed astray.'

'I thought she liked me!'

'She did. But she thought we were too young for such an intense relationship. She was worried I'd put all my dreams on hold for you.'

She could see now that Frieda Harper had had every reason to be concerned. Jaz had been awed by Connor's love—grateful to him for it, unable to believe he could truly love a girl like her. And she'd hidden behind his popularity, his ease with people, instead of standing on her own two feet. Frieda had understood that.

'She asked me to go away from Clara Falls for three months. She begged me to.'

Connor's face had gone white. Jaz swallowed. 'She told me that you and I needed time out from each other, to gain perspective.' And Jaz had been so hurt and so…angry. She'd wanted Connor to pay for the things he'd said. 'She told me that if you really loved me, you'd wait for me.' And Jaz had believed her. 'I went to my aunt's house in Newcastle for three months.' And she'd counted down every single day.

She lifted her head and met his gaze. 'But you didn't wait for me.'

His eyes flashed dark in the pallor of his face. 'Are you trying to put the blame back on me?'

'No.' She shook her head, a black heaviness pressing down on her. 'I'm simply saying you didn't wait.'

He flung an arm in the air. 'I thought you were gone for ever! I didn't think you were ever coming back.'

He'd jumped to conclusions. Again. 'You didn't bother looking for me!'

He took several paces away from her, then swung back. 'Three months?' He stabbed an accusing finger at her. 'You didn't come back!'

The space between them sparked with unspoken resentments and hurts.

Jaz moistened her lips and got her voice back under control. 'The day before I was due to come home, my mother rang. She told me Faye was pregnant and that you were the father. And that you were engaged.'

Connor dragged both hands back through his hair. He collapsed to the leatherette cube as if he'd lost all strength in his legs. Jaz leant heavily against the wall by the unfinished portrait of her mother.

She reached up to touch it, then pulled her hand away at the last moment. She glanced back at Connor. 'You have to see that I couldn't come back once I'd heard that.'

'Why not?'

'There'd be no chance for you and Faye to sort things out if I'd done that.'

She didn't mean to sound arrogant, but it was the truth. For good or ill, she and Connor would've picked straight up where they'd left off—in each other's arms.

He shot to his feet. 'Am I supposed to take that as some kind of noble gesture on your part?'

That tone would've shrivelled her eight years ago. It didn't shrivel her now.

'Noble? Ha!' She glared at him. 'I can't see there's much of anything noble in this entire situation.' She pushed away from the wall. 'But a baby was going to be involved and…and I wasn't going to interfere with that.'

His glare subsided. He bent at the waist, rested his hands on his knees and didn't say anything.

'But how could you?' Her voice shook. 'How could you

sleep with my best friend? Faye, of all people!' The pain of that still ran deep. 'Why Faye?'

Very slowly, he straightened. The emptiness in his eyes shocked her. 'Because she reminded me of you. I was searching for a substitute and she was the nearest I could find.'

The breath left her body. She fell back against the wall. She couldn't think of a single thing to say.

What was there to say? It was all history now. It was too late for her and Connor.

The silence stretched—eloquent of the rift that had grown between them in the intervening years. Connor finally nodded. 'Goodnight, Jaz.' And he made for the door.

For a moment she still couldn't speak. Then, 'If you tell Melly I broke her confidence…it will hurt her.'

He stopped, but he didn't turn around.

'I don't think she deserves that.'

He seemed to think about that and then he nodded. 'You're right.' He took one further step away, stopped again…and then he turned. 'Do you seriously think that, given more time, she would've confided in me?'

'I'm convinced of it.' She tried to find a smile. 'Wait and see. She still might yet.'

She thought he might say something more, but he didn't.

'By the way, did you know that Carmen Sears is looking for an after school job?'

He frowned. 'Why are you telling me this?'

'She'd make a great babysitter for Melanie.'

'But she's—'

He broke off and Jaz couldn't stop her lips from twisting. 'Yes, she's a rebel Goth girl. *And* she seems like a nice kid. Just thought you might be interested, that's all.'

He stared at her for a long moment. 'Why did it take you so long to come back?'

The tone of his voice gave nothing away, and for a brief moment a sense of loss gaped through her. She shrugged and strove for casual. 'Pride, I guess, and resentment at the way things turned out. I was angry with you and Faye. I was angry with my mother. I wanted to forget.'

She shrugged again. She had a feeling she might be overdoing the shrug thing but she couldn't seem to help it. 'In the end it became a habit.' A habit that had broken her mother's heart.

She lifted her chin. 'Goodnight, Connor.'

First thing Thursday morning, Mrs Lavender put Jaz to work changing the book display in the front window. Jaz had a feeling it was a ploy to stop her from fretting about their lack of customers.

'It hasn't been changed in nearly two months. Look, we've all these lovely new bestsellers…and it'll be Mother's Day in a couple of weeks. It needs sprucing up!'

A shaft of pain speared straight into Jaz's heart at the mention of Mother's Day. She kept her chin high, but Mrs Lavender must've seen the strain in her face because she stilled, then reached out and touched Jaz's hand. 'I'm sorry, Jazmin, that was thoughtless of me.'

'Not at all.' She gulped. She would not let her chin drop. 'I'm the one who didn't come back for the past eight Mother's Days. I have no right to self-pity now.' Oh, she'd sent flowers, had phoned, but it wasn't the same.

'You have a right to your grief.'

Jaz managed a weak smile, but she didn't answer. She deserved to spend this coming Mother's Day burning with guilt.

She made Mrs Lavender a cup of tea, noticed Connor's truck parked out the back, and the burning in her chest increased ten-fold.

'Have you looked these over, Jaz?'

Jaz had just climbed out of the window, pleased with her brand new display. She glanced over Mrs Lavender's shoulder. 'Oh, those.' A printout of the sales figures for the last three months. A weight dropped to her shoulders and crashed and banged and did what it could to hammer her through the floor. 'Appalling, aren't they?'

'You have to turn these around, and fast.' There was no mistaking Mrs Lavender's concern. 'Jaz, this is serious.'

'I…' She was doing all she could.

Mrs Lavender tapped her pen against the counter, ummed and ahhed under her breath. Then her face suddenly lit up. 'We'll have a book fair, that's what we'll do! It'll stir up some interest in this place again.'

'A book fair?'

'We'll get in entertainment for the kiddies, we'll have readings by local authors… We'll have a ten per cent sale on all our books. We'll get people excited. We'll get people to come. And, by golly, we'll save this bookshop!'

Jaz clutched her hands together. 'Do you think it could work?'

'My dear Jazmin, we're going to have to make it work. Either that or make the decision to sell up to Mr Sears.'

'No!' She cast a glance towards the back wall and the unfinished portrait of Frieda. 'I'm not selling to him.' She hitched up her chin. 'We'll have a book fair.'

She and Mrs Lavender spent the rest of the morning planning a full-page advertisement in the local newspaper. They discussed children's entertainment. Jaz started to design posters and flyers. They settled on the day—the Saturday of the Mother's Day weekend.

If the book fair didn't work…

Jaz shook her head. She refused to think about that.

At midday Mrs Lavender excused herself to go and sit on her usual park bench to torment Boyd Longbottom.

'What's the story with you and Boyd Longbottom, anyway?' Jaz asked.

'He was a beau of mine, a long time ago.'

Jaz set her pen down. 'Really?'

'But when I chose my Arthur over him, he swore he'd never speak to me again. He's kept his word to this very day.'

'But that's awful.'

'He never left Clara Falls. He never married. And he's not spoken to me again, not once.'

'That's...sad.'

'Yes, Jaz, it is.' Mrs Lavender opened her mouth as if she meant to say more, but she shut it again. 'I'll see you tomorrow.'

At quarter past twelve Connor jogged across the street to Mr Sears's bakery. On his way back he stopped right outside the bookshop window to survey the new display.

Jaz stood behind one of the bookcases she was tidying and watched him. Her heart squeezed so tight the blood rushed in her ears.

Turn your back. Walk away.

Her body refused to obey the dictates of her brain.

At least close your eyes.

She didn't obey that order either. She remembered how she and Connor had once shared their drawings with each other, offering praise or criticism, suggestions for improvements. She searched his face. Did he like her display?

She couldn't tell.

He didn't lift his eyes and search for her inside the shop.

Eventually he turned and strode away. The tightness around Jaz's heart eased, but nothing could expand to fill the gap that yawned through her.

At a touch after three-thirty the phone rang. Jaz pounced on it, eager to take her mind off the fact that Melly wasn't here. She'd known Melly wouldn't show up here today. Just as she knew Melly wouldn't show up here tomorrow...or any other day from now on.

She didn't know why it should make her feel lonely, only that it did.

'Hey, mate!' Her business partner's voice boomed down the line at her. 'How're you doing?'

'Mac!' She grinned. 'Better now that I'm talking to you. How are Bonnie and the kids?'

'They send their love. Now, tell me, has the town welcomed you back with open arms?'

'Yes and no. Business could be a lot better, though. I'm not getting any local trade.'

'Are they giving you a hard time?'

'Well, there is a rumour that I'm the local drug baron.'

His laughter roared down the line, lifting her spirits. 'What? Little Ms Clean-as-a-Whistle Jaz Harper?' He sobered. 'I bet that's doing wonders for business.'

'Ooh, yeah.'

'Listen, mate, I have a job for you, and I have a plan.'

Her smile widened as she listened to his plan.

CHAPTER SIX

'OKAY, Princess Melly—' Connor held the door to Mr Sears's bakery open '—what is your pleasure?'

Mel's eyes danced. It gladdened Connor's heart.

'Princess Melly wants a picnic!'

'Where…at the park? Or perhaps at one of the lookouts?' He cocked his head to one side. 'On the skyway?' They'd already been back and across on the skyway twice this morning.

Over the course of the morning Mel had laughed with her whole self, and it made things inside him grateful and light. She'd retreated into her shell a couple of times, but so far she'd come peeping back out again.

Jaz had been right. The Princess Melly thing was working a treat. It had disarmed his daughter almost immediately—that and the skyway rides. Not to mention the jeans-buying expedition. Mel had only requested one pair of jeans, but it had suddenly occurred to Connor that she didn't have any—at least, none that fitted her any more. They'd bought three pairs. Mel had near burst with excitement over that one. She wore a pair now.

'A picnic in the botanic gardens,' Princess Melly announced.

'Excellent.' Connor rubbed his hands together, walked her up and down the length of the counter to eye all of Mr Sears's goodies. It was only a touch after eleven o'clock but, given the amount of energy they'd expended already, coupled with the plans he could see racing through Mel's mind, he figured she might need refuelling. 'What should we take on our picnic?'

She stared up at him with big liquid eyes—identical to his, so he was told. He didn't believe it. His eyes couldn't melt a body like that.

'Princess Melly would like a sausage roll now—' she slipped her hand inside his, as if he might need some extra persuasion '—which will spoil her lunch, you know?'

'It will?' He tried to figure out where she was going with this.

'Which means we can just have apple turnovers and lemonade for lunch.'

Connor grinned. Mel's smile slipped. 'Excellent idea,' he assured her. 'Apple turnovers for lunch it is.'

Once in the proverbial blue moon wouldn't hurt, would it?

Her smile beamed out at him again.

Heck, no, it couldn't hurt anything. Still…responsible adult instincts kicked in. 'I am afraid, though, that your humble servant—' he touched his chest '—has a voracious appetite. Would it be permissible for him to order egg-and-lettuce sandwiches to take on the picnic, do you think?'

She nodded solemnly, but her eyes danced. Connor placed their order and they sat at a table in the front window to munch their sausage rolls and sip hot chocolates.

The roar of motorbikes interrupted them mid-bite. They both swung to stare out of the window. Motorbikes—big, black, gleaming Harley-Davidsons—trawled up the street, chrome and leather gleaming in the sun. There had to be at least a dozen bikes, most with pillion passengers…and all the riders wore black leather. Connor blinked, and then he started to laugh, deep and low, and with undeniable satisfaction. The roar and thunder abated as the bikes found parking spaces down either side of the street. All of the leather-clad visitors made a beeline for Jaz's bookshop.

His gut clenched when Jaz danced out to meet them. He thought a blood vessel in his brain might burst when the biggest and burliest of the visitors swung her around as if she didn't weigh any more than a kitten, rather than five feet ten inches of warm, curvaceous woman. When the burly visitor placed her back on the ground, he kissed her on the cheek.

Kissed her! Something dark and ugly pulsed through him.

Jaz hadn't mentioned being involved with anyone in Sydney, but then they hadn't really discussed what she'd been doing since she'd left.

'Daddy?'

He glanced down to find Mel staring at his mangled sausage roll.

He tried to loosen his grip around it, tried to grin. 'Oops, I obviously don't know my own strength.'

Melly giggled.

Connor wiped his hand on a paper serviette and glanced back out of the window. He couldn't stop a replay of all the kisses he and Jaz had shared eight years ago from playing through his mind now—all of them, in all of their endless variety.

He couldn't remember kissing her on the cheek too often.

On the cheek!

That hadn't been the kiss of some lover impatient to see his girlfriend after a week of enforced separation. Connor couldn't explain the rush of relief that poured into him. Actually, he could explain it, but he wouldn't. Not to himself. Not to anyone.

Some of Jaz's friends followed her into the bookshop. Others broke into groups of twos and threes to stroll down whichever side of the street seemed to take their fancy, for all the world like idle tourists. Which was probably what they were. They didn't wear bike gang insignias on their leather jackets. They were probably a bunch of people who shared a passion for bikes. He'd bet they were carpenters and bookshop owners and bakers like him and Jaz and Mr Sears.

He cast a glance around the bakery. He wasn't the only one transfixed. The arrival of over a dozen bikes in town had brought the conversation in the bakery to a screaming halt. Mr

Sears's face had turned the same colour as the icing on his Chelsea buns—pink. Bright pink.

Connor grinned. After the way Mr Sears had treated her this past week, Jaz deserved her revenge. He enjoyed the beauty of her payback. Not that it would boost her popularity rating as far as the rest of the town was concerned. Already an assortment of tourists and locals were surreptitiously returning to their cars and driving away—intimidated by the combination of loud motorbikes and leather.

Then suddenly Jaz was standing outside the Sears's bakery without any of her friends in tow and Connor cursed himself for the distraction that had cost him the treat of watching her stride across the road, head held high and shoulders thrown back. Her eyes met his through the plate glass and that thing arced between them—a combination of heat and history.

The bell above the door tinkled as she entered. 'Hello, Connor.'

'Hello, Jaz.'

She swung away from him abruptly to smile at Mel—an uncomplicated display of pleasure that kicked him in the guts. 'Melly! How are you?'

Melly leaned towards her. 'I'm Princess Melly today.'

Jaz let loose a low whistle. 'Hardly surprising. You do look as pretty as a princess today, you know?'

'Daddy says I look as pretty as a princess every day.' But she said the words uncertainly.

Jaz bent down. 'Princess Melly, I think your daddy is right.' Then she winked. 'By the way, I love the jeans.'

Mel beamed. Connor's gut clenched in consternation. As if she sensed that, Jaz straightened. 'I'd love to stay and chat, but I have visitors to get back to. You have fun today, okay?'

Mel nodded vigorously. 'We will.'

'Hey, Carmen. Howdy, Mr S.' Jaz boomed this last.

Mr Sears raced down to the end of the counter where Jaz stood, the end nearest Connor and Mel. 'What are you doing?'

he demanded in an undertone. 'Trying to chase all of Clara Falls' business out of town?'

'I have nearly twenty people for morning tea.' She didn't lower her voice. 'Which, at least for your bakery, Mr S, is going to be *very* good business. I'll take one of your large carrot cakes, a strawberry sponge and...what would you suggest? A chocolate mud cake or a bee sting?'

Connor couldn't resist. 'Go with the orange and poppy seed, Jaz. It can't be beat.'

She swung around to stare at him. That warmth arced between them again. The colour in her cheeks deepened. Connor's groin kicked to life. She swung back to Mr Sears. 'The orange poppy seed it is.'

Every single one of Mr Sears's muscles—at least those from the waist up that Connor could see—bunched. If steam could've come out of his ears, Connor was guessing it would've. And yet he placed each of the three cakes in a separate cardboard box with the same care and reverence mothers showed to newborn babies.

But when he placed them on the counter for Jaz to collect, he leaned across and grabbed her wrist. Connor pushed his chair back and started to rise.

'If the tone of this town is brought down any further,' Mr Sears hissed, 'you'll ruin the lot of us. And it'll be all your doing.'

'No, it'll be yours,' she returned, as cool as the water in the Clara Falls themselves.

With one twist, she freed her wrist. Connor sat back down. She didn't need his help.

'I run a bookshop, Mr S, and I need to attract customers from somewhere. Until my bookshop starts securing its usual level of trade, and the rumours about drugs trafficking start dying down, I'm afraid you'll have to get used to my weekend visitors. They have bikes and will travel. They believe supporting independent bookshops is a good cause.' She hitched her head in the direction of the door. 'Believe me, this lot is only the tip of the iceberg.'

Mr Sears drew back as if stung.

She sent him what Connor could only call a salacious wink. 'Your call, Mr S.' She lifted the cakes and all but saluted him with them. 'Mighty grateful to you. Have a great day now, you hear? I'll be back later to grab afternoon tea for the hordes. Who knows how many extra bodies could show up between now and then? And those Danish pastries look too good to resist.' With that she swept out of the shop.

A buzz of conversation broke out around the tables the moment the door closed behind her. Connor watched every step of her progress with greedy delight as she returned to the bookshop. She walked as if she owned the whole world. It was sexy as hell. You had to hand it to her. The lady had style.

'Jaz is my friend,' Mel said, hauling his attention back.

He sobered at that. He didn't want his daughter getting too attached to Jaz Harper. It wouldn't do her any good. Just like it hadn't done him any good.

'Stop!'

Luckily Connor had already slowed the car to a crawl in expectation of the approaching pedestrian crossing when Mel shouted, because he planted his foot on the brake immediately.

'What?' He glanced from the left to the right to try and discover what it was that had made Melly shout. Katoomba's main street was crowded with shoppers and tourists alike—a typical Saturday. He couldn't see anything amiss. She couldn't want more food, surely? They'd not long finished their sausage rolls and hot chocolates.

'Jaz just went in there with two of her friends.'

He followed the direction of Mel's finger to Katoomba's one and only tattoo parlour.

Mel lifted her chin. 'I want to go in there too.'

He hesitated. He played for time. He edged the car up to the pedestrian crossing, where he had to wait for pedestrians...and more pedestrians. 'What about the botanic gardens and our picnic?'

'Something is wrong.' Melly's bottom lip wobbled and his gut twisted. 'She looked sad and she's my friend and she made me feel better when I was sad.'

Her bottom lip wobbled some more. He gulped. 'When were you sad?'

'Last week.'

'Why were you sad?'

Would she tell him? He held his breath. The pedestrian crossing cleared and he pushed the car into gear and started moving again.

'Because Mrs Benedict smacked me.'

Connor slid the van into a free parking space and tried to unclench his hands from around the steering wheel. That still had the power to make his blood boil…

But Mel had confided in him!

'You won't ever have to go back to Mrs Benedict's again, okay, sweetheart?'

Mel's eyes went wide, then opaque. Connor couldn't read her face at all. He didn't know if she was about to throw a temper tantrum or burst into tears. 'You said I was Princess Melly today.'

The whispered words speared straight into him. 'You are, sweetheart.'

'And that my every wish was your command.'

'Yep, that's right.' If she didn't want to talk about this, then he wouldn't force her.

'Then I want to see Jaz!'

He was hers to command. But how could he explain that neither one of them had the right to command Jaz?

Why was Jaz sad?

The thought distracted him. Perhaps that was why Mel's escape plan succeeded because, before he realised what she meant to do, she'd slipped off her seat belt, slid out of the car and raced back down the street towards the tattoo parlour.

'Bloody hell!'

Connor shot out of the car after her. He fell through the front door of the tattoo parlour in time to see Mel throw her arms around Jaz's waist as Jaz emerged from the back of the shop.

'What's this?' Jaz hugged Mel back but she glanced up at Connor with a question in her eyes.

'I'm sorry.' He shrugged and grimaced. Mel clung to Jaz like a limpet and an ache burned deep down inside him. 'She got away from me. She saw you and thought you looked sad.' He didn't know what else to say because it suddenly hit him that Mel was right—something was wrong. Jaz was sad. He didn't know how he could tell. Nothing in her bearing gave it away.

Two men emerged from the back of the shop—one of them the man who'd kissed Jaz on the cheek earlier. She smiled at them weakly and shrugged, much the same way he just had to her. 'This is my friend, Melly...and her father Connor. This is Mac and Jeff.'

They all nodded to each other, murmured hellos.

'Melly saw me and wanted to say hello.' She knelt down to Mel's level. 'I am a bit sad, but I promise I'm going to be all right, okay?'

Mel nodded. 'Okay.'

'Now, if you'll excuse me—' Jaz rose '—I have some work to do.'

Connor saw the question forming in Mel's eyes and wanted to clamp a hand over her mouth before she could ask it.

'Are you going to tattoo someone?'

Jaz glanced briefly at him, then back to Mel. 'Yes.'

He wondered why she sounded so reluctant to admit it. One thing was clear—she did not want them here.

Her sadness beat at him like a living thing. He remembered what had happened to Frieda. *She has her friends.*

'Can I watch?'

Jaz crouched back down to Mel's level. 'I don't think that's a good idea, Melly, and—'

'I don't mind.' The man called Jeff spoke quietly, but somehow his words filled the entire room.

'Are you getting the tattoo?' Mel breathed, awe audible in every word.

'I'm getting a picture of my little girl tattooed here.' Jeff touched a hand to the top of his left arm.

'Where is she? Can we play?'

He shook his head. 'She's a long way away.'

Melly bit her lip. 'Is it going to hurt?'

'Yes.'

'Will it help if I hold your hand?'

'Yes, it will.' With a glance at Connor, Jeff picked Melly up in his great burly arms. Connor sensed that with just one word or look from him, Jeff would release Mel in an instant, but something in the man's face and manner, something in the way Jaz regarded him, held Connor still.

Then they all moved to the back of the shop.

The tattoo took nearly two hours. Connor had never seen anything like it in his life. Beneath Jaz's fingers, a young girl's face came alive.

This wasn't just any simple tattoo. It was an indelible photograph captured on this man's arm for ever.

It was a work of art.

Mel watched Jaz's movements quietly, solemnly. She held Jeff's hand, stroked it every now and again. Finally she moved to where Connor sat, slid onto his lap and rested her head against his shoulder. He held her tight, though for the life of him he couldn't explain why. Her relaxed posture and even breathing eventually told him she'd fallen asleep.

At last, Jaz set aside her tools and stretched her arms back above her head. She held up a mirror for Jeff to view the finished tattoo. 'Thank you,' he said simply.

Jaz leant across then and placed a kiss in the centre of Jeff's forehead. 'May she live in your heart for ever,' she whispered.

That was when Connor realised why he held Melly so tight.

That tattoo wasn't a work of art. It was a memorial.

'Cherish her,' Jeff said with a nod at the sleeping child.

'I will,' he promised.

Then Jeff left the room, closely followed by Mac, and Connor expelled one long breath. He reached out and touched Jaz's hand. 'That was the most amazing thing I've ever seen.' He didn't smile. He couldn't. But he wanted her to know how much he admired her skill and generosity.

When she turned, he could see the strain the last two hours had put on her—the overwhelming responsibility to do her absolute best work, not to make a mistake. It showed in her pallor, the lines around her eyes and mouth.

He adjusted the child in his arms, rose and put one arm around Jaz's shoulders. 'Let me take you home.'

For a moment he thought she would lean into him, but then she stiffened and edged away. 'Mac will take me home, thanks all the same. Enjoy the rest of your day, Connor.'

Before she could move fully away, Melly stirred, unwrapped an arm from around her father's neck and wound it around Jaz's. It brought Jaz in close to Connor again—her arm touching his arm, his scent clogging her senses. The more of him she breathed in, the more it chased her weariness away.

'That was way wicked!' Melly said.

A spurt of laughter sprang from Jaz's lips at the sheer unexpectedness of Melly's words. She tried to draw back a little to stare into Melly's face. Melly wouldn't let her draw back any further than that. 'Where did you pick up that expression?'

'Carmen Sears. She looked after me for a couple of hours yesterday and I think she's way wicked too.'

Jaz grinned. She couldn't help it. Although she kept her gaze on Melly's face, from the corner of her eye she could see Connor's lips kick up too. Her heart pounded against the walls of her chest as if her ribcage had shrunk.

'Can we go on our picnic now, Daddy?'

'Your wish is my command.'

'I want Jaz to come on our picnic too.'

Jaz stiffened. She tried to draw away but Melly tightened her hold and wouldn't let her go. Oh, heck! Connor had told her he didn't want her as part of Melly's life. She should imagine that included attending picnics with her.

'Princess, your wish is *my* every command,' Connor started.

'You're going to say no.'

Melly's bottom lip wobbled. It wouldn't have had such a profound effect on Jaz if she hadn't sensed Melly's valiant effort to hide it. Connor's Adam's apple bobbed.

'Sweetheart, Jaz isn't anyone's to command. She's her own princess. We don't have the right to tell her what to do.'

Mel leaned in close to her father and whispered, 'But Jaz might like to come.'

He hesitated. He nodded. Then he smiled. 'I guess you'd better ask her, then.'

'Princess Jaz, would you like to come on a picnic with us?' She turned pleading eyes on Jaz. 'Please?'

Thank you, Connor Reed! So she had to play bad guy, huh? She wondered if she could lie convincingly enough not to hurt Melly's feelings. The hope in the child's face turned Jaz's insides to…marshmallow.

'I would love to come on a picnic with you, Princess Melly…' That wasn't a lie. 'But I'm very tired.' That wasn't a lie either. 'And I really should get back to the bookshop.' That was only half a lie.

'But you're still sad!'

Melly's grip eased, but she didn't let go. Her bottom lip wobbled again, making Jaz gulp. If Melly cried…

'Please come along with us, Jaz.'

Connor's voice, warm and golden, slid through to her very core. Her decidedly marshmallow core.

'I'd like you to come along too.'

She had to meet his gaze. Those words, that tone, demanded it. Her breath hitched. His autumn-tinted eyes tempted her…in every way possible.

She shouldn't go.

He couldn't really want her to tag along.

'Bonnie and Gail have the shop under control,' Mac said from the doorway. 'Go on the picnic, Jaz, it'll do you good.'

Three sets of eyes watched her expectantly. 'I…' Exhilaration raced through her veins. 'I think a picnic sounds perfect.'

'Good.'

If anything, Connor's eyes grew warmer.

Oh, dear Lord. What had she just agreed to?

Melly struggled out of her father's arms to throw her arms around Jaz's middle. 'Yay! Thank you.'

She smoothed Melly's hair back behind her ears. 'No, sweetheart, *thank you* for inviting me along. It'll be a real treat.'

She glanced up at Connor and for some reason her tongue tried to stick fast to the roof of her mouth. 'I'll…umm…just go grab my things.'

In the end, Melly decided it was too far to go to the botanic gardens and chose a picnic spot near Katoomba Cascades instead. Jaz couldn't remember a time when egg-and-lettuce sandwiches or apple turnovers had tasted so good.

After they'd eaten, they walked down to the cascades. The day was still and clear and cool. Jaz drank in the scenery like a starving woman. She hadn't forgotten how beautiful the mountains were, but her recollections had been overshadowed by…other memories.

Melly's chatter subsided abruptly when they returned to the picnic area. She stared at the children playing in the playground—two swings, a tiny fort with a climbing frame and a slippery dip—and the hunger in her face made Jaz's heart twist.

Melly swung around, her gaze spearing straight to Jaz's, a question in her eyes that brought Jaz's childhood crashing back—the crippling shyness…the crippling loneliness.

She made herself smile, nodded towards the playground. 'Why don't you go over and make friends?' Then she remembered Connor. Not that she'd ever forgotten him. 'We don't have to go home yet, do we?'

'This is Princess Melly day.' He spread his arms as if that said it all.

Jaz wished he hadn't spread his arms quite so wide or in that particular fashion. If she took just one step towards him she'd find herself encompassed by those arms.

A small hand slipped inside Jaz's, hauling her back. Melly stared up at her with such trust in her autumn-tinted eyes—eyes the spitting image of Connor's—that it stole her breath.

'But what do I say?' Melly whispered.

Jaz dropped her duffel bag to the grass and knelt down beside Melly. She took a second look at the children playing in the playground. Tourists. 'I think you should go over and say: Hello, I'm Melly and I live near here. Where do you live? And then…' Jaz racked her brain. She remembered her own childhood. She could sense Connor watching them intently, but she did what she could to ignore him for the moment. 'Remember that story we read—was it Tuesday or Wednesday? The one with the wood sprites and the water nymphs.'

Melly nodded.

'Well, perhaps you could tell them about the wood sprites and water nymphs that live in the Katoomba Cascades.' She nodded her head in the direction of the cascades. 'I'm sure they'd love to hear about that.'

Melly's face lit up. 'Can I go play, Daddy?'

He spread his arms again. It made Jaz gulp. 'Is your name Princess Melly?'

Melly giggled and raced off.

Connor lowered himself to the grass beside Jaz, stretched out on his side. 'Thank you.'

'I…' Her tongue had gone and glued itself to the roof of her mouth again.

'You said exactly the right thing.' He frowned. 'How'd you do that?'

Her tongue unglued itself. 'Why, what would you have said?'

'I'd have probably told her to just play it by ear.'

Jaz shook her head. 'I remember what it was like to be Melanie's age…and shy. I'd have wanted some clear instructions or suggestions about how to get the initial conversation started. You can play it by ear after that.'

Connor watched Melly. 'It seems to be working.'

Warmth wormed through her. 'I'm glad. She's a delightful little girl, Connor. You must be very proud of her.'

He glanced up at her. 'I am.'

She gripped her hands together. 'I'm sorry I came along today,' she blurted out. But it was partly his fault. He'd caught her at a weak moment.

He shot up into a sitting position. 'Why?' he barked. 'Haven't you had a nice time?'

'Yes, of course, but…' She stared back at him helplessly. 'But you didn't want me as part of Melly's life, remember? I was supposed to keep my distance.' She lifted her hands, then let them fall back to her lap. 'But I didn't know how to say no to her.' She glared. 'And you didn't help.'

She didn't know if it was a grimace or a smile that twisted his lips. 'She wanted you to come along so badly. I didn't know how to say no to her either.'

What about him? Had he really wanted her to come along?

She halted that thought in its tracks. She didn't care what Connor wanted.

'I seem to recall you saying you didn't want me as part of your life either.'

She wrinkled her nose. 'That was just me wanting to say something mean back to you.' It had been about erecting defences.

'It wasn't mean. It was you telling the truth, wasn't it?'

She had no intention of letting him breach those defences. 'Yes.' She pulled in a breath. 'There's a lot of history between us, Connor.'

He nodded.

'And I have no intention of revisiting it.'

'History never repeats?' he asked.

'Something like that.'

'For what it's worth, I think you're right.' He was quiet for a long moment, his eyes on Melly. 'It doesn't mean you and Mel can't be friends, though, does it?'

She blinked. 'But you didn't want me to…'

'For better or worse, Melly likes you, she identifies with you.' He met her gaze head-on. 'But can you promise me that you won't leave again the way you did the last time?'

'Yes, I can promise that.' She'd grown up since those days. 'It's funny, you know, but it's nice to be back.' She gestured to the view spread out before them. 'I've missed all this. When I do get the bookshop back on its feet, I mean to come back for visits.'

She'd promised Gwen.

She'd promise Melly too.

'I have no intention of hurting your little girl, Connor.'

'I know that.'

She turned and stared back out at the view.

CHAPTER SEVEN

THE hunger in Jaz's face as she stared out over the valley made Connor's gut clench.

This was her home. She might not be ready to admit that to herself yet, but the truth was as clear to him as the nose on her face…and the fullness of her lips.

He tried to drag his mind from her lips, from thoughts of kissing her. Jaz had made her position clear—there would be no him and her again.

He didn't know why that should make him scowl. It was what he wanted too.

No, he wanted to kiss her. He was honest enough to admit that much. But she was right. There was no future for them.

But now that she was back in Clara Falls, she shouldn't have to leave in twelve months' time. Not if she didn't want to.

He thought back to Mac—the cheek kisser; Mac of the tattoo parlour. He rolled his shoulders. 'You're good with kids.' Did she plan to have children of her own?

She turned back. He could tell she was trying to hold back a grin. 'You sound surprised.'

'Guess I've never really thought about it before.' He paused. 'You and Mac seem close.'

Her lips twisted. She all but cocked an eyebrow. 'We are. He and his wife Bonnie are my best friends.'

He felt like a transparent fool. He rushed on before she

could chide him for getting too personal. 'What are your plans for when you return to your real life in the city?'

She blinked and he shrugged, suddenly and strangely self-conscious—like Mel in her attempts to make new friends. 'You said that returning to run the bookshop was a temporary glitch.'

'It is.'

She eased back on her hands, shifted so she no longer sat on her knees, so she could stretch the long length of her legs out in front of her. Without thinking, he reached out to swipe the leaves from her trouser legs.

She stiffened. He pulled his hand back with a muttered, 'Sorry.'

'Not a problem.'

Her voice came out all tight and strangled. Oh, yeah, there was a problem all right. The same problem there had always been between them—that heat. But it hadn't solved things between them eight years ago and it wouldn't solve anything now.

He just had to remember not to touch her.

'Your plans?' he prompted when she didn't unstiffen.

'Oh, yes.' She relaxed. She waved to Melly on the slippery dip. She didn't look at him; she stared out at the view—it was a spectacular view. He didn't know if her nonchalance was feigned or not, but it helped ease the tenseness inside him a little—enough for him to catch his breath.

He made himself stare out at the view too. It *was* spectacular.

Not as spectacular—

Don't go there.

'I mean to open an art gallery.'

He stared at her. Every muscle in his body tensed up again. 'An art gallery?' An ache stretched through him. He ignored it. 'But don't you run a tattoo parlour?'

'And a bookshop,' she reminded him.

She smiled. Not at him but at something she saw in the middle distance. 'Mac and I financed the tattoo parlour together, but Mac is the one in charge of its day-to-day running. I'm more of a…guest artist.'

The thought made him smile.

'I'm pretty much a silent partner these days.'

'Perhaps that's what you need at the bookshop—a partner?'

She swung around. 'I hadn't thought of that.' Then, 'No.' She gave a decisive shake of her head. 'The bookshop is all I have left of my mother.'

'And you don't want to share?'

Her eyes became hooded. 'It's my responsibility, that's all.' She turned back to the view.

'So the art gallery, that would be your real baby?'

She lifted one shoulder. 'I guess.'

'Where are planning to set it up?'

'I'd only just started looking for premises when Mum—' She broke off. His heart burned in sympathy.

'I found wonderful premises at Bondi Beach.'

Despite the brightness of her voice, her pain slid in beneath his skin like a splinter of polished hardwood. He wanted to reach for her, only he knew she wouldn't accept his comfort.

He clenched his hands. 'Bondi?' He tried to match her brightness.

'Yes, but I'm afraid the rent went well beyond my budget.'

'I bet.' It suddenly occurred to him that the rents in the Blue Mountains weren't anywhere near as exorbitant as those in the city.

'An art gallery…' He couldn't finish the sentence. All the brightness had drained from his voice. He could see her running this hypothetical gallery, could almost taste her enthusiasm and drive. He could see her paintings hanging on the walls. He could—

'Which brings me to another point.' She turned. Her eyes burned in her face as she fixed him with a glare. 'You!'

He stared back. Somewhere in the background he heard Melly's laughter, registered that she was safe and happy at the moment. 'Me?' What had he done?

She dragged her duffel bag towards her. The bag she'd refused to leave in the car. The one she hadn't allowed him to carry for her on their walk. She'd treated it as if it contained something precious. He'd thought it must hold her tattooing gear. He blinked when she slapped something down on his knees.

A sketch pad!

Bile rose up through him when she pushed a pencil into his hand. 'Draw, Connor.'

Panic gripped him.

She opened the sketch pad. 'Draw,' she ordered again.

She reached over and shook his hand, the one that held the pencil, and he went cold all over.

'No!'

He tried to rise, but she grabbed hold of his arm and wouldn't let it go.

'I don't draw any more,' he ground out, trying to beat back the darkness that threatened him.

'Nonsense!'

'For pity's sake, Jaz, I—'

'You're scared.'

It was a taunt, a challenge. It made him grit his teeth together in frustration. His fingers around the pencil felt as fat and useless as sausages. 'I gave it up,' he ground out.

'Then it's time you took it back up again.'

Anger shot through him. 'You want to see how bad I've become, is that what this is about?' Did she want some kind of sick triumph over him?

Her eyes travelled across his face. Her chin lifted. 'If that's what it takes.'

Then her eyes became gentle and it was like a punch to the gut. 'Please?' she whispered.

All he could smell was the sweet scent of wattle.

He gripped the pencil so hard it should've snapped. If she wanted him to draw, then he'd draw. Maybe when she saw how ham-fisted he'd become she'd finally leave him in peace. 'What do you want me to draw?'

'That tree.' She pointed.

Connor studied it for a moment—its scale, the dimensions.

They settled automatically into his mind. That quick summing up, it was one of the things that made him such a good builder. But he didn't deceive himself. He had no hope of being a halfway decent artist any more.

It didn't mean he wanted Jaz forcing that evidence in front of him. She sat beside him, arms folded, and an air of expectation hung about her. He knew he could shake her off with ease and simply walk away, but such an action would betray the importance he placed on this simple act of drawing.

He dragged a hand down his face. Failure now meant the death of something good deep down inside him. If Jaz sensed how much it meant—and he had the distinct impression she knew exactly what it meant—he had no intention of revealing it by storming away from her. He'd face failure with grace.

Maybe, when this vain attempt was over, the restlessness that plagued him on bright, still days would disappear. His lips twisted. They said there was a silver lining in every cloud, didn't they?

Just when he sensed Jaz's impatience had become too much for her, he set pencil to paper.

And failed.

He couldn't draw any more. The lines he made were too heavy, the sense of balance and perspective all wrong...no flow. He tried to tell himself he'd expected it, but darkness pressed against the backs of his eyes. Jaz peered across at what he'd done and he had to fight the urge to hunch over it and hide it from her sight.

She tore the page from the sketch pad, screwed it into a ball and set it on the ground beside her. Sourness filled his mouth. He'd tried to tell her.

'Draw the playground.'

He gaped at her.

She shrugged. 'Well...what are you waiting for?' She waved to Melly again.

Was she being deliberately obtuse? He stared at the playground, with all its primary colours. The shriek of Melly's laughter filled the air, and that ache pressed against him harder. In a former life he'd have painted that in such brilliant colours it would steal one's breath.

But that was then.

He set pencil to paper again but his fingers refused to follow the dictates of his brain. He'd turned his back on art to become a carpenter. It only seemed right that his fingers had turned into blocks of wood. Nevertheless, he kept trying because he knew Jaz didn't want to triumph over him. She wanted him to draw again—to know its joys, its freedoms once more…to bow to its demands and feel whole.

When she discovered he could no longer draw, she would mourn that loss as deeply as he did.

When he finally put the pencil down, she peeled the page from the sketch pad…and that drawing followed the same fate as its predecessor—screwed up and set down beside her.

'Draw that rock with the clump of grass growing around it.'

He had to turn ninety degrees but it didn't matter. A different position did not bring any latent talent to the fore.

She screwed that picture up too when he was finished with it. Frustration started to oust his sense of defeat. 'Look, Jaz, I—'

'Draw the skyway.'

It meant turning another ninety degrees. 'What's the point?' he burst out. 'I—'

She pushed him—physically. Anger balled in the pit of his stomach.

'Stop your whining,' she snapped.

His hands clenched. 'You push me again…'

'And you'll what?' she taunted.

He flung the sketch pad aside. 'I've had enough!'

'Well, I haven't!' She retrieved the sketch pad and slapped it back on his knees. 'Draw the skyway, Connor!'

Draw the skyway? He wished he were out on that darn skyway right now!

His fingers flew across the page. The sooner this was over, the better. He didn't glance at the drawing when he'd finished. He just tossed the sketch pad at Jaz, not caring if she caught it or not.

She did catch it. And she stared at it for a long, long time. Bile rose from his stomach to burn his throat.

'Better,' she finally said. She didn't tear it from the sketch pad. She didn't screw it up into a ball.

'Don't humour me, Jaz.' The words scraped out of his throat, raw with emotion, but he didn't care. He could deal with defeat but he would not stand for her pity.

In answer, she gave him one of the balled rejects. 'Look at it.'

He was too tired to argue. He smoothed it out and grimaced. It was the picture of the playground. It was dreadful, horrible…a travesty.

'No,' she said when he went to ball it up again. 'Look at it.'

He looked at it.

'Now look at this.' She stood up and held his drawing of the skyway in front of her.

Everything inside him stilled. It was flawed, vitally flawed in a lot of respects, and yet… He'd captured something there— a sense of freedom and escape. Jaz was right. It was better.

Was it enough of an improvement to count, though?

He glanced up into her face. She pursed her lips and surveyed where he sat. 'This is all wrong.' She tapped a finger against her chin for a moment, then her face cleared. She seized her duffel bag. 'Come with me.'

She led him to a nearby stand of trees. He followed her. His heart thudded in his chest, part of him wanted to turn tail and run, but he followed.

'Sit there.'

She pointed to the base of a tree. Its position would still give him a good, clear view of Melly playing. Melly waved. He waved back.

He settled himself against the tree.

'Good.' She handed him the sketch pad and pencil again. She

pulled a second sketch pad and more pencils from her bag and settled herself on the ground to his left, legs crossed. She looked so familiar, hunched over like that, Connor thought he'd been transported back eight years in time.

She glanced across at him. 'Bend your knees like you used to do…as if you're sitting against that old tree at our lookout.'

Our lookout. Richardson's Peak—out of the way and rarely visited. They'd always called it *their lookout.* He tried to hold back the memories.

Jaz touched a hand to the ground. 'See, I'm sitting on the nearby rock.'

It wasn't rock. It was grass, but Connor gave in, adjusted his back and legs, and let the memories flood through him. 'What do you want me to draw?'

'The view.'

Panoramas had always been his speciality, but he wasn't quite sure where to start now.

He wasn't convinced that this wasn't a waste of time.

'Close your eyes.'

She whispered the command. She closed her eyes so he closed his eyes too. It might shut out the ache that gripped him whenever he looked at her.

It didn't, but her voice washed over him, soft and low, soothing him. 'Remember what it was like at the lookout?' she murmured. 'The grand vista spread out in front of us and the calls of the birds…the scent of eucalyptus in the air…'

All Connor could smell was wattle, and he loved it, dragged it into his lungs greedily.

'Remember how the sun glinted off the leaves, how it warmed us in our sheltered little spot, even when the wind played havoc with everything else around us?'

His skin grew warm, his fingers relaxed around the pencil.

'Now draw,' she whispered.

He opened his eyes and drew.

On the few occasions he glanced across at her, he found her

hunched over her sketch pad, her fingers moving with the same slow deliberation he remembered from his dreams.

Time passed. Connor had no idea how long they drew but, when he finally set aside his pencil, he glanced up to find the shadows had lengthened and Jaz waiting for him. He searched the picnic ground for Melly.

'Just over there.' Jaz nodded and he found Melly sitting on the grass with her new friends.

'Finished?' she asked.

He nodded.

'May I see?'

She asked in the same shy way she'd have asked eight years ago. He smiled. He felt tired and alive and…free. 'If you want.'

She was by his side in a second. She turned back to the first page in the sketch pad. He'd lost count of how many pictures he'd drawn. His fingers had flown as if they'd had to make up for the past eight years of shackled inactivity.

Jaz sighed and chuckled and teased him, just like she used to do. She pointed to one of the drawings and laughed. 'Is that supposed to be a bird?'

'I was trying to give the impression of time flying.'

'It needs work,' she said with a grin.

He returned her grin. 'So do my slippery dips.'

'Yep, they do.'

The laughter in her voice lifted him.

'But look at how you've captured the way the light shines through the trees here. It's beautiful.'

She turned her face to meet his gaze fully and light trembled in her eyes. 'You can draw again, Connor.'

Her exultation reached out and wrapped around him. *He could draw again.*

He couldn't help himself. He cupped one hand around the back of her head, threaded his fingers through her hair and drew her lips down to his and kissed her—warm, firm…brief. Then he released her because he knew he couldn't take too much of that. 'Thank you. If you hadn't badgered me…' He gestured to the sketch pad.

She drew back, her eyes wide and dazed. 'You're welcome, but—' she moistened her lips '—I didn't do much.'

Didn't do much.

'You had it in you all the time. You just had to let it out, that's all.' She reached up, touched her fingers to her lips. She pulled them away again when she realised he watched her. Her breathing had quickened, grown shallow. She lifted her chin and glared at him. 'If you ever turn your back on your gift again, it will desert you. For ever!'

He knew she was right.

He knew he wanted to kiss her again.

As if she'd read that thought in his face, Jaz drew back. 'It's getting late. We'd better start thinking about making tracks.'

She didn't want him to kiss her.

He remembered all the reasons why he shouldn't kiss her.

'You're right.'

He tried to tell himself it was for the best.

Jaz found Connor sitting on the sales counter munching what looked like a Danish pastry when she let herself into the bookshop at eight o'clock on Monday morning.

'Hey, Jaz.'

She blinked. 'Hello.'

What was he doing here? Shouldn't he be upstairs working on her flat? The absence of hammering and sawing suddenly registered. Her heart gave a funny little leap. 'Is my flat ready?'

'We're completing the final touches today and tomorrow, and then it'll be ready for the painters and carpet layers.'

She'd already decided to paint it herself. It'd give her something to do. Funnily enough, though, considering how she'd expected her time in Clara Falls to drag, this last week had flown.

She'd have the carpet laid in double-quick time. She wasn't spending winter in the mountains on bare floorboards. Once her furniture was delivered from Connor's, she could paint and decorate the flat in her own good time.

She edged around behind the counter to place her handbag in one of the drawers and tried to keep Connor's scent from addling her brain. Handbag taken care of, she edged back out again—his scent too evocative, too tempting. It reminded her of that kiss. That brief thank you of a kiss that had seared her senses.

Forget about the kiss.

'Did you want me for something?'

His eyes darkened at her words and her mouth went dry. He slid off the counter and moved towards her—a hunter stalking its prey. He wore such a look of naked intensity that... Good Lord! He didn't mean to kiss her again, did he? She wanted to turn and flee but her legs wouldn't work. He reached out...took her hand...and...

And plonked a paper bag into it.

'I thought you might like one.'

Like one...? She glanced into the bag. A pastry—he'd given her a pastry. In fact, he'd handed her a whole bag full of them. 'There's at least a dozen pastries in here.'

'Couldn't remember what filling you preferred.'

She almost called him a liar. Then remembered her manners. And her common sense. Who knew how much he'd forgotten in eight years?

But once upon a time he'd teased her about her apple pie tastes. She wished she could forget.

Her hand inched into the bag for an apple Danish. She pulled it back at the last moment. 'I don't want a pastry!'

She wanted Connor and his disturbing presence and soul-aching scent out of her shop. She tossed the bag of Danishes onto the counter with an insouciance that would've made Mr Sears blanch. 'Why are you here, Connor? What do you want?'

'I want to thank you.'

'For?'

'For your advice to me about Melly. For making me draw again.'

He'd already thanked her for that—*with a kiss!*

She didn't want that kind of thanks, thank you very much. Her heart thud-thudded at the thought of a repeat performance, calling her a liar.

'I think I've made a start on winning back Mel's trust.'

'If Saturday's evidence is anything to go by, I think you're right.' And she was glad for him.

Glad for Melly, she amended.

Okay—she shifted her weight from one foot to the other, slid her hands into the pockets of her trousers—she was glad for both of them, but she was gladder for Melly.

'Look, Jaz, I've been thinking…'

Her mouth went dry. Something in his tone… 'About?'

'What if you didn't leave Clara Falls at the end of this twelve months?'

Her jaw dropped.

He raised both hands. 'Now hear me out before you start arguing.'

She supposed she'd have to because she appeared to have lost all power of speech.

'What if you opened your art gallery in the mountains? It has two advantages over the city. One—lower rents. And two—you'd get the passing tourist trade.' He spread his arms in *that* way. 'Surely that has to be good.'

Of course it was good, but—

'There's an even bigger tourist trade in Sydney,' she pointed out.

'And you'll only attract them if you find premises on or around the harbour.'

She could never afford that.

'What's more, if you settle around here you'll be close to the bookshop if you're needed, and it's an easy commute to the city on the days you're needed in at the tattoo parlour.'

He spread his arms again. 'If you think about it, it makes perfect sense.'

'No, it doesn't!'

He didn't look the least fazed by her outburst. 'Sure it does. And, Jaz, Clara Falls needs people like you.'

She gaped at him then. 'It's official—Connor Reed has rocks in his head.' She stalked through the shop to the kitchenette. 'People like me?' She snorted. 'Get real!'

'People who aren't afraid of hard work,' Connor said right behind her. 'People who care.'

'You're pinning the wrong traits on the wrong girl.' She seized the jug and filled it.

He leant his hip against the sink. 'I don't think so. In fact, I know I'm not.'

She would not look into those autumn-tinted eyes. After a moment's hesitation, she lifted a mug in his direction in a silent question. Common courtesy demanded she at least offer him coffee. After all, he had supplied the pastries.

'Love one,' he said with that infuriating cheerfulness that set her teeth on edge.

He didn't speak while she made the coffees. She handed him one and made the mistake of glancing into those eyes. Things inside her heated up and melted down, turned to mush.

No mush, she ordered.

That didn't work so she dragged her gaze away to stare out of the window.

'Clara Falls needs you, Jaz.'

'But I don't need Clara Falls.'

He remained silent for so long that she finally turned and met his gaze. The gentleness in his eyes made her swallow.

'That's where I think you're wrong. I think you need Clara Falls as much as you ever did. I think you're still searching for the same security, the same acceptance now as you did when you were a teenager.'

Very carefully, she set her coffee down because throwing it

all over Connor would be very poor form…and dangerous. The coffee was hot. Very hot. 'You have no idea what you're talking about.'

'You might not want to admit it, but you know I'm right.'

'Garbage! You're the guy with rocks in his head, remember?'

'Frieda knew it too. It's why she wanted you to come back.'

Her mother's name was like a punch to the solar plexus. She wanted to swing away but there wasn't much swinging room in the kitchenette, and to leave meant walking—squeezing— past Connor. If he tried to prevent her from leaving, it would bring them slam-bang up against each other—chest-to-chest, thigh-to-thigh. She wasn't risking that.

She tossed her head. 'How do you know what my mother thought?'

He glanced down into his coffee and it hit her then. 'You…the pair of you talked about me…behind my back?'

'We'd have been happy to do it to your face, Jaz, if you'd ever bothered to come back.'

Guilt swamped her. And regret. How could she have put her mother through so much? Frieda had only ever wanted Jaz's happiness. Jaz had returned that love by refusing to set foot back in Clara Falls. She'd returned that love by breaking her mother's heart.

Connor swore at whatever he saw in her face. He set his mug down and took a step towards her. Jaz seized her coffee, held it in a gesture that warned him he'd wear it if he took another step. 'Don't even think about it!' If he touched her, she'd cry. She would not cry in front of him.

He settled back against the sink.

'I know I am responsible for my mother's death, Connor. Rubbing my nose in that fact, though, hardly seems the friendly thing to do.'

Frown lines dug furrows into his forehead, drew his eyebrows down low over his eyes. 'What the hell…! You are not responsible for Frieda's suicide.'

He believed that, she could tell. She lifted her chin. He could believe what he liked. She knew the truth.

He straightened. 'Jaz, I—'

'I don't particularly want to talk about this, Connor. And, frankly, no offence intended, but nothing you say will make the slightest scrap of difference.'

'How big are you going to let that chip on your shoulder grow before you let it bury you?'

'Chip?' Her mouth opened and closed but no other words would emerge.

'Fine, we won't talk about your mother, but we will talk about Clara Falls and the possibility of you staying on.'

'There is no possibility. It's not going to happen so just give it a rest.'

'You're not giving yourself or the town the slightest chance on this, Jaz. How fair is that?'

Fair? This had nothing to do with fair. This had to do with putting the past behind her.

'Have you come back to save your mother's shop? Or to damn it?'

How could he even ask her that?

'You need to start getting involved in the local community if you mean to save it. Even if you are only here for twelve months.'

She didn't have to do any such thing.

'The book fair is a start.'

He knew about—?

'You've done a great job on the posters.'

Oh, yes.

'But you need to let the local people see that you're not still the rebel Goth girl.'

Darn it! He had a point. She didn't want to admit it but he did have a point.

'You need to show people that you're all grown up, that you're a confident and capable businesswoman now.'

Was that how he saw her?

She dragged her hands back through her hair to help her think, but as Connor followed that action she wished she'd left her hands exactly where they were. Memories pounded at her. She remembered the way he used to run his fingers through her hair, the way he'd massaged her scalp, how it had soothed and seduced at the same time. And being a confident and capable businesswoman didn't seem any defence at all.

'The annual Harvest Ball is next Saturday night. I dare you to come as my date.'

He folded his arms. His eyes twinkled. He looked good enough to eat. She tried to focus her mind on what he'd said rather than...other things. 'Why?' Why did he want to take her to the ball?

'It'll reintroduce you to the local community, for a start, but also...it occurred to me that while it's all well and good for me to preach to you about staying here in Clara Falls and making it a better place, I should be doing that too. I think it's time Mr Sears had some competition for that councillor's spot, don't you?'

She stared at him. 'You're going to run for town councillor?'

'Yep.'

Being seen with her, taking her to the ball, would make a definite statement about what he believed in, about the kind of town he wanted Clara Falls to be. Going to the ball would help her quash nasty rumours about drugs and whatnot too.

'Our going to the ball...' she moistened her lips '...that would be business, right?'

She'd made her position clear on Saturday during the picnic. He'd agreed—history didn't repeat. For some reason, though, she needed to double-check.

'That's right.' He frowned. 'What else would it be?'

'N...nothing.'

The picture of Frieda she'd started on the bookshop's wall grew large in her mind. The darn picture she couldn't seem to finish. *Have you come back to save your mother's shop? Or to damn it?*

She wanted to save it. She had to save it.

She shot out her hand. 'I'll take you up on that dare.'

He clasped her hand in warm work-roughened fingers. Then he bent down and kissed her cheek, drenched her in his scent and his heat. 'Good,' he said softly. 'I'll pick you up at seven next Saturday evening.'

'Well—' she reclaimed her hand, smoothed down the front of her trousers '—I guess that's settled, then. Oh! Except I'm going to need more of my things.' Something formal to wear for a start and her strappy heels.

'Why don't I run you around to my place after work this afternoon and you can pick out what you need?'

'Are you sure?' She wasn't a hundred per cent certain what she meant by that only…she remembered the way he hadn't wanted her at his home last week. She added a quick, 'You're not busy?'

'No. And I've arranged for Carmen to mind Mel for a couple of hours this afternoon.'

Had he been so certain she'd say yes?

You did say yes.

She moistened her lips again. 'Thank you, I'd appreciate that.'

She didn't bother trying to stifle the curiosity that balled inside her. She just hoped it didn't show. It didn't make any sense, but she was dying to know where Connor lived now. Not that it had anything to do with her, of course.

Of course it didn't.

'I'll pick you up about five-fifteen this afternoon.'

Then he was gone.

Jaz reached up and touched her cheek. The imprint of his lips still burned there. A business arrangement, she told herself. That was all this was—a business arrangement.

Jaz slipped into the car the moment Connor pulled it to a halt outside the bookshop. At precisely five-fifteen.

'Hi.'

'Hi.'

That was the sum total of their conversation.

Until he swung the car into the drive of Rose Cottage approximately three minutes later and turned off the ignition. 'Here we are,' he finally said.

She gaped at him. She turned back to stare at the house. 'You bought Rose Cottage?'

Most old towns had a Rose Cottage, and as a teenager Jaz had coveted this one. Single-storey sandstone, wide verandas, established gardens, roses lining the drive, picket fence—it had been her ideal of the perfect family home.

It still was.

And now it belonged to Connor? A low whistle left her. Business must be booming if he could afford this. 'You bought Rose Cottage,' she repeated. He'd known how she'd felt about it.

'That's right.' His face had shuttered, closed.

Had he bought it because of her or in spite of her?

'Your things are in there.'

She dragged her gaze from the house to follow the line of his finger to an enormous garage.

He wasn't going to invite her inside the house?

She glanced into his face and her anticipation faded. He had no intention of inviting her inside, of giving her the grand tour. She swallowed back a lump of disappointment…and a bigger lump of hurt. The disappointment she could explain. She did what she could to ignore the hurt.

'Shall we go find what you need?'

'Yes, thank you, that would be lovely.'

She followed him into the garage, blinked when he flicked a switch and flooded the cavernous space with stark white light. Her things stood on the left and hardly took up any space at all. 'All I need is—'

She stopped short. Then veered off in the opposite direction.

'Jaz, your stuff is over here!'

She heard him, but she couldn't heed his unspoken command. She couldn't stop.

Her feet did slow, though, as she moved along the aisle of handmade wood-turned furniture that stood there—writing desks, coffee tables, chests. She marvelled at their craftsmanship, at the attention paid to detail, at the absolute perfection of each piece.

'You made these?'

'Yes.'

The word left him, clipped and short.

He didn't need to explain. Jaz understood immediately. This was what he'd thrown himself into when he'd given up his drawing and painting.

'Connor, you didn't give up your art. You just…redirected it.'

He didn't say anything.

'These pieces are amazing, beautiful.' She knelt down in front of a wine rack, reached out and trailed her fingers across the wood. 'You've been selling some of these pieces to boutiques in Sydney, haven't you?'

'Yes.'

'I came across a piece similar to this a couple of years back.' She forced herself upright. If she'd known then that Connor had made it she'd have moved heaven and earth to buy it.

'I went into that shop in my lunch hour every day for a week just to look at it.'

His face lost some of its hardness. 'Did you buy it?'

'No.' It had been beyond her budget. 'I couldn't justify the expense at the time.'

She sensed his disappointment, though she couldn't say how—the set of his shoulders or his lips, perhaps?

'Mind you,' she started conversationally, 'it did take a whole week of lecturing myself to be sensible… and if it had been that gorgeous bookcase—' she motioned across to the next piece '—I'd have been lost…and horrendously in debt. Which is why I'm going to back away from it now, nice and slow.'

Finally he smiled back at her.

'My things!' She suddenly remembered why they were here. 'I'll just grab them and get out of your hair.'

He didn't urge her to take her time. He didn't offer to show her any of the other marvels lined up in the garage. She told herself she was a fool for hoping that he would.

CHAPTER EIGHT

WHEN Jaz opened the door to him on Saturday evening, Connor's jaw nearly hit the ground. She stood there in a floor-length purple dress and he swore he'd never seen anything more perfect in his life. The dress draped the lines of her body in Grecian style folds to fasten between her breasts with a diamanté brooch. It oozed elegance and sex appeal. It suited the confident, capable businesswoman she'd become.

Ha! No, it didn't. Not in this lifetime. That dress did not scream professional businesswoman. The material flowed and ran over her body in a way that had his hands itching and his skin growing too tight for the rest of his body. It definitely wasn't businesslike. What he wanted to do to Jaz in that dress definitely wasn't businesslike.

He had to remind himself that the only kind of relationship Jaz wanted with him these days was businesslike.

He had to remind himself that that was what he wanted too.

'Hi, Connor.'

Gwen waved to him from the end of the hallway. It made him realise that he and Jaz hadn't spoken a word to each other yet. He took in Jaz's heightened colour, noted how her eyes glittered with an awareness that matched his own, and desire fireballed in his groin. If they were alone, he'd back her up against a wall, mould each one of her delectable curves to the angles of his body and slake his hunger in the wet shine of her lips.

No, he wouldn't!

Bloody hell. *Get a grip, man. This is a business arrangement.* He tried to spell out the word in his head—B-U-S… It was a sort of business arrangement, he amended. He wanted to help Jaz the way she'd helped him. He wanted to prove to her that Clara Falls was more than Mr Sears and his pointed conservatism. He wanted her to see the good here—the way Frieda had. Instinct told him Jaz needed to do at least that much. If she wanted to leave at the end of twelve months after that, then all power to her.

He glanced down into her face and tried to harden himself against the soft promise of her lips…and the lush promise of her body.

Gwen strode down the hallway. 'Are you okay, Connor?'

He realised he still hadn't uttered a word. 'Uh…' He cleared his throat, ran a finger around the inside collar of his dress shirt. 'These things cut a man's windpipe in two. I feel as trussed up as a Sunday roast.'

'You look damn fine in it, though.'

'You're looking pretty stunning yourself,' manners made him shoot back at her. In truth, with Jaz in the same room he barely saw Gwen. He had a vague impression of red and that was about it.

Jaz folded her arms and glared at him. Man, what had he done now? He turned back to Gwen. 'Who's your date tonight, then?'

Gwen shook her head. 'I'm going stag this year. I don't want to be shackled to any man. Not when there'll be so many eligible males to choose from this evening.'

Fair enough. 'Need a lift?'

'No, thank you. I mean to be fashionably late.'

'Do you expect me to be shackled to you all evening?' Jaz demanded.

He stiffened. Yes, dammit!

He rolled his shoulders. No, dammit.

So much for relaxation. 'We arrive together. We leave together.

We eat together. First dance and last dance.' He rattled each item off. They were non-negotiable as far as he was concerned. 'Fair enough?' he barked at her. They'd settle this before they left.

She didn't bat an eye. 'Fair enough,' she agreed.

The pulse at the base of his throat started to slow. He found he could breathe again. He meant to negotiate more than two dances out of her, come hell or high water. He meant to hold her in his arms, enjoy the feel of her, safe in the knowledge that nothing could happen in such a public place.

He turned to find Gwen staring at him with narrowed eyes. He gulped. 'I…er…want her to schmooze,' he tried to explain.

'I just bet you do,' she returned with evil knowingness.

'I…' He couldn't think of a damn thing to say.

Jaz jumped in. 'Did you know that Connor is planning to challenge Gordon Sears for the town councillor position at the next election?'

Gwen's jaw dropped. 'Are you serious? But you're not some power-hungry nob.'

'No, he's not.' Satisfaction threaded through Jaz's voice. 'Which should make him the perfect candidate, don't you think?'

He stood a little straighter at her praise, pushed his shoulders back.

'It at least makes him better than Gordon Sears, but enough of that.' Gwen dismissed the subject with a wave of her hand. 'Make Jaz's day and tell her the move is complete.'

'It's all done.' His men had moved Jaz's things out of his garage and into her flat today. He hadn't helped move those things. Whenever he'd driven into the garage, walked through the garage, walked past the garage, and saw her things there, he'd had an insane urge to go through them to try and discover a clue as to how she'd spent the last eight years. He hadn't. He wouldn't. But he'd put himself out of temptation's way today and had taken Mel for a hot chocolate and another skyway ride instead. 'You can move in and start unpacking as early as tomorrow if you want.'

When he'd driven the van into the garage this afternoon and found all her things gone, it had left a hole inside him as big as the Jamison Valley. Why?

Because you're an idiot, that's why. Because you still want her.

He ground his teeth together. He'd made a lot of mistakes in the last eight years, but he wasn't making that one. Not again. He would not kiss Jaz. He would not make love to Jaz. He would not get involved with Jaz.

Never again.

He had to think of Mel. His daughter already adored Jaz more than he thought wise. He didn't want Mel thinking of Jaz as anything other than a friend.

It would be hard enough for Mel to cope with Jaz leaving in twelve months' time, let alone…

He ran a finger around the inside of his collar again. Let alone anything more. End of story.

'I'll move into the flat on Monday,' he heard Jaz tell Gwen. 'I'm hoping business will be brisk in the bookshop tomorrow.'

She was working tomorrow? They'd better not make it a late night then. His jaw tightened. Not that he'd intended on making it a late night.

He tried to get his brain onto business and away from the personal. 'How are the new staff members working out?' She'd spent the last four days training staff the recruitment agency in Katoomba had sent her.

'So well that I'm planning on taking Monday and Tuesday off to unpack and set the flat up properly. I'll only be a shout away if needed.'

'Good. It's about time you stopped working so hard and took a couple of days off. If you're not careful you'll make yourself ill.'

Her eyes widened and he thrust his hands in his pockets with a scowl. That comment had been way too personal. He started to spell *businesslike* out in his mind again.

Speculation fired to life in Gwen's face. She raised an

eyebrow at Jaz. Jaz pressed her lips together and gave one tight shake of her head. Connor adjusted his tie. It seemed a whole lot tighter now than it had when he'd left home.

Gwen laughed. 'You two give off as much heat as you ever did.'

His collar tightened until he thought he'd choke. Jaz's eyes all but started from her head.

Jaz swung to him. 'Speaking of heat…'

He wondered if he'd ever breathe again.

'…is the town hall still heated? Or should I change into something warmer? Something with longer sleeves?'

'Don't change!' The words burst out of him with revealing rapidity.

He coughed and quickly overrode Gwen's triumphant 'Aha!'

He rapped out, 'It gets uncomfortably warm in the town hall. You'll be grateful for those short sleeves once the dancing starts.'

'Okay.' She gazed at him expectantly for a moment, then finally sighed. 'I'll get my handbag and wrap and then we can leave.'

The town hall was festooned with ribbons and pine cones, with fragrant boughs of eucalyptus. Beneath it all, Connor could smell the tantalising scent of wattle. He and Jaz paused as they crossed the threshold, and Connor had to bite back a grin when one section of the hall—Gordon Sears and his set—broke off their conversation around a table of hors d'oeuvres to turn and stare.

Actually…gaped summed it up more accurately.

Beside him, Jaz stiffened and he drew her hand into the crook of his arm, folded his hand over it and tried to convey to her that she wasn't alone. He hadn't brought her here to feed her to the lions. Her hand trembled beneath his, but she lifted her chin and planted a smile on her face, held herself tall and erect. That simple act of courage warmed him, made him stand taller and prouder too.

'I think it's safe to say that we've given them something to talk about for the rest of the night,' she quipped.

He released her hand to seize two glasses of champagne from the tray of a passing waiter and handed her one. 'Whereas we won't spare them another thought for the rest of the evening.'

She touched her glass to his. 'I'll drink to that.'

Her hair framed her face in a feathery style that highlighted high cheekbones and long-lashed eyes. He wanted to reach out and touch that hair, to run his fingers through it, cup a hand around the back of her head and draw her in close to—

He snapped upright, glanced around the room.

'Who should we schmooze with first?' she asked.

'This way.' With his hand in the small of her back, he turned her towards a knot of people on the opposite side of the room and tried to ignore the way the heat from her body branded his fingertips as it seeped through the thin material of her dress. With half a growl, he dragged his gaze from the seductive sway of her hips. That was when he saw Sam Hancock.

Sam Hancock without a date!

Sam and his sister hadn't sold the family home when their father had died, although neither one of them lived in Clara Falls now. They used the house as a weekender. Obviously Sam had decided to grace Clara Falls with his presence this particular weekend.

'Connor?'

Jaz's soft query drew him back, her blue-green eyes fathomless.

'I just saw your old friend Sam Hancock.' The observation didn't come out anywhere near as casual as he meant it to.

She stared at him. 'Did you want to go over and say hello?'

She'd promised to leave with him at the end of the night. He held fast to that. He tried to relax his hold on his champagne flute. She didn't crane her neck over his shoulder to catch a glimpse of Sam. She didn't push her glass of champagne into his hand and rush off to embrace her former lover. The tightness in his chest eased a fraction.

Which sent warning bells clanging through him. He didn't

want Jaz for himself, but he didn't want other men having her either?

Or was it just Sam Hancock?

He tested the theory, tried to imagine Jaz with some other man in the room—any man. His teeth ground together. No, it wasn't just Sam Hancock.

Charming. He was a dog in the manger.

Only…he did want her for himself, didn't he?

'Connor!'

He snapped to.

'I thought we were supposed to be schmoozing. Stop glaring around the room like that. You won't win any votes with that look on your face.'

He laughed. He didn't mean to, but her words—the scolding—the warmth deep down in her eyes eased his tension. 'Come and meet the Barries.' He'd enjoy the night for what it was and nothing more.

Connor found that he did enjoy the evening. Jaz conversed easily with everyone he introduced her to. The Jaz of old hadn't had that kind of confidence or social poise. The Jaz of old would've held back and spent most of the night hiding behind him. The Jaz of old had been nothing more than a girl. This Jaz—the here and now version—was a strong, confident woman. Something told him she'd earned that self-possession.

It made her ten times more potent.

She ate dinner at the table beside him. They danced the first dance… and the second… and Connor almost breathed a sigh of relief when she excused herself to go and powder her nose. He needed oxygen—big time.

It didn't stop him from watching her as she made a circuit around the room, though. Along the way, people stopped her. Here and there, she stopped of her own accord. Then she stopped by Sam Hancock, who was sitting on his own, and Connor gripped a handful of linen tablecloth. Sam leapt to his feet and said something that made her laugh. She said something back that made him laugh. Then she kept walking.

She kept walking.

He released the tablecloth. If he hadn't been sitting he'd have fallen.

It hit him then—Jaz hadn't flirted with a single man here tonight. Frieda would've flirted with every man in the room. He saw the defence behind that tactic now too—by flirting with every man present, Frieda had managed to keep them all at arm's length. About the only man she hadn't flirted with was Gordon Sears.

His heart started to burn. Jaz was not made in the same mould as her mother. Had he got it wrong eight years ago?

He remembered the sight of her in Sam Hancock's arms, the words she'd uttered that had damned her. They still proved her guilt, her infidelity.

But, suddenly, he found he wasn't quite so sure of anything.

Jaz returned from the powder room to take her seat at the table beside Connor again. All the other couples from their table were dancing. She gulped. She prayed Connor wouldn't ask her to dance again. She wasn't sure how much more of that she could take, especially now they'd dimmed the lights.

'Enjoying yourself?'

'Yes.' And she meant it. 'It's been lovely meeting up with people again.'

He set a glass of punch down in front of her. 'Non-alcoholic,' he said before she could ask. 'I know you're working tomorrow.'

'Thank you.'

She didn't reach out for the drink because her fingers had gone suddenly boneless. He looked so sure and…male in his dinner suit. His body had grown harder in the eight years she'd been away. His shoulders had become broader, his thighs more powerful. And he still created an ache of need deep down inside her like he'd always done.

She hoped he wouldn't push the stay-in-Clara-Falls-for-ever-and-make-it-your-home thing again. She couldn't stay for ever in the same town as Connor Reed. It just wouldn't work.

One corner of his mouth kinked up but it didn't warm his eyes. 'You've schmoozed beautifully.'

She raised her eyes at the edge in his voice. 'Is that supposed to be a compliment?' she asked warily.

He frowned. 'Yes.'

'Sorry.' She hadn't meant to misinterpret his mood. 'I am having fun, but this really isn't my favourite kind of do.'

'What is?'

'Beer and pizza nights.' She sighed in longing. A beer and pizza night with a bunch of her friends would go down a treat at the moment.

Connor grinned and this time the gold flecks in his eyes came out to play. 'Well, there's not a soul in this room who'd sense you'd rather be anywhere else this evening. You've charmed everyone you've met.'

She smiled at that. 'Wonders will never cease, huh? The rebel Goth girl developing a few social graces after all.'

'It's quite a change, Jaz, even you have to admit that. Where did you go when you decided not to come back to Clara Falls? What did you do? How did you manage the…transformation?'

Jaz realised she'd been waiting for him to ask that question all night. 'After I left my aunt's I went to the airport, directly to the airport, I didn't pass go and I didn't collect two hundred dollars.'

He stared at her. Jaz shrugged. 'I went to America.'

He leant forward. 'Why America?'

She'd wanted to run as far away as possible. She'd wanted to start over in a place that didn't know her. And she'd needed to make a grand gesture. 'Would you believe me if I said— because I was young and stupid?'

He smiled. 'Young, yes, but never stupid.'

He was wrong about that. 'I strode into the airport and

decided I was going to Europe or America. The travel agent must've thought me mad…or a criminal. I just asked for the first flight out. And that's how I ended up in LA with next to no money, no job and nowhere to stay. Believe me, that makes a girl start thinking on her feet pretty fast.'

'What did you do?'

'Rented a dingy hotel room for a week, bought a sketch pad and charcoals and spent the week drawing portraits of tourists on the beach and charging them five dollars a pop. That's where Carroll Carson found me. He's *the* big-name tattoo artist on the west coast.' She shrugged. 'He took me under his wing, offered me an apprenticeship. I was lucky.'

She glanced across at him and something inside her shifted. Perhaps Mrs Lavender had been right and Jaz had done the right thing leaving Clara Falls all those years ago. If she hadn't left, she'd have spent her life living in Connor's shadow, grateful to him for loving a misfit like her.

She wasn't a misfit. She'd earned her place in the world. She didn't need any man to make that right.

'Faye was a one-night stand.'

The admission shot out of Connor like bullets from a gun, and with as much impact. All Jaz could do was stare. She wanted to tell him it wasn't any of her business.

'A one-night stand?' Her voice came out hoarse and raspy.

He scratched a hand back through his hair. 'Faye was the one who told me about you and Sam Hancock.'

Her jaw dropped. Surely Faye hadn't thought—

'You'd left. We both missed you like the blazes. We drank too much and…'

He trailed off with a shrug. She was glad he didn't go into details.

'The next day I told her that it had been a mistake. That it couldn't happen again.'

Jaz stared at him, shook her head, tried to comprehend what he was telling her. 'How did she take that?'

'Not well.'

Had Faye been in love with Connor all along? The thought made her feel suddenly ill. 'Why are you telling me this?' She found herself on her feet, shaking with…she wasn't sure what—more regrets? She didn't have room for any more of those.

Connor stood too. 'I just wanted you to know the truth, that's all.'

The gold sparks in Connor's eyes, their concern, reached out and wrapped her in their warmth. The same way his arms had wrapped around her when they'd danced. It had near sent her pulse sky-rocketing off the charts.

She pulled back. There was no future for her and Connor. There was no point wondering what it would be like to rest her head against his shoulder or to nuzzle her face against his neck, to slip her hand beneath his shirt and trace the contours of muscle and sinew honed by hard physical labour.

There might not be any point to it, but she couldn't seem to stop imagining it.

'Hey, guys, having fun?'

Gwen, cheeks flushed from dancing, bore down on them.

'Absolutely,' Jaz managed.

'You bet,' Connor said. 'You look as if you're slaying them in the aisles.'

Jaz ground her teeth together.

'Are you drinking that?' Gwen pointed to the glass of punch.

Jaz handed it to her. 'Help yourself.'

'Thanks.' She drained it dry. 'Ooh, look, there's Tim Wilder. I'll catch you both later.'

'You bet. Go knock him dead.'

That was Connor again.

'Are you okay?' he asked when he turned back to Jaz.

She slammed her hands to her hips. Connor backed up a step. 'You have that itching for a fight look plastered all over your face. What have I done this time?'

'It's what you haven't done. Or, more precisely, what you

haven't said. Is there something wrong with my appearance?' she demanded.

He shoved his hands in his pockets. 'No.' He shifted his feet. 'Why?'

'Because you've told every woman you've met this evening how lovely or stunning or wonderful she looks. Every woman, that is, except me!'

A grin spread across his face, slow and sure. His shoulders lost their tightness. He moved in closer, crowding her with his heat, his scent…their history. He angled his body towards hers in a blatant invitation she wanted to accept.

'Does my opinion matter so much to you, Jaz?'

'No, of course not,' she snapped, angry with herself. 'Put it down to a moment of feminine insecurity.'

She tried to move past him but his arm snaked out and caught her around the waist, drew her back against his heat and his hardness. With agonising slowness and thoroughness, he splayed his hand across her stomach. Low down across her stomach. She bit back a whimper. If he moved that hand, if he moved so much as his little finger, she'd melt in his arms where she stood.

'You don't have any reason whatsoever for insecurity, Jazmin.'

His breath touched her ear. She closed her eyes. He'd only ever called her Jazmin when they'd made love. And in the eight long years since she'd left here, she'd never had another lover. Not one. Trembling shivers that started at her knees and moved upwards shook her body, betraying her need.

'But if I start telling you how sexy you look in that dress, how wearing your hair like that highlights your eyes and how the gloss on your lips makes my mouth water…then that might lead to me telling you how I want to tear that dress from your body and make love to you all night long—fast and frantic the first time, slow and sensual the second time, watching every nuance in your face the third time.'

She couldn't find her voice. Her breath came in short shallow gulps.

'But, given the circumstances, that might not be wise.'

No, not wise at all.

He pulled her more firmly against him until she couldn't mistake the hardness pressing against the small of her back. 'I burn for you as much as I ever did, Jazmin.'

His teeth grazed her ear. She moaned.

'I can feel that same need burning in you. I can feel your body trembling for me. I want to take you home and make love to you. Now. Just say the word,' he murmured against her ear, 'and we're out of here. Say it!' he ordered.

Yes! To spend a glorious night of pleasure and freedom in Connor's arms. Yes! To touch him as her fingers and lips burned to do, to scale the heights with him and...

No.

Her heart dropped. She gulped. She peeled his fingers from her stomach, one by one, and stepped away. 'And what happens tomorrow, Connor?' She turned to face him. 'And the day after that?' Did he think they could just pick up where they'd left off?

The flush of desire in his eyes didn't abate. 'We—'

'What happens the next time you find me with another man in a situation you can't account for? Are you going to fly off the handle and accuse me of cheating on you again?'

His head snapped back.

'You didn't trust me then and you don't trust me now.' More importantly, she didn't trust herself. Who would she hurt the next time he broke her heart?

There wouldn't be a next time!

She had no intention of losing her heart to him ever again. No man was worth that kind of pain. 'If you'll excuse me, I'm in serious need of a glass of punch.'

She turned and stalked off in the direction of the refreshments table and she didn't wait to see if he followed. From the evidence she'd seen, he'd need a moment to himself.

She helped herself to punch, started to raise the glass to her lips, when Gordon Sears bore down on her.

'I've been looking for you everywhere, Jaz.'

She loathed his fake jovial tone, the smirk on his face. She ignored the headache pounding at her temples to inject a false brightness of her own. 'Why's that, Mr S? Did you want to ask me to dance?'

'No, just wanted to give you advance warning that I'll be serving papers on your solicitor come Monday morning.'

Her stomach started to churn. 'What kind of papers?'

'No doubt you're aware that I lent your mother fifty thousand dollars?'

Punch sloshed over the side of her glass.

Satisfaction settled over his face. 'No?' he said. 'That was remiss of her.'

'I don't believe you,' she whispered. Why would Frieda borrow money from this man?

'She needed it to buy the bookshop.' He rubbed his hands together, his smile widening. 'And now I'm calling in that debt. Pay up within seven days or the bookshop is mine.'

Fifty thousand dollars! She didn't have that kind of money. He had to be bluffing.

He had to be bluffing!

Oh, Mum. Why? To lure me back to Clara Falls? I wasn't worth it.

'Is there a problem?' Connor demanded, striding up and placing himself between Jaz and Mr Sears.

Mr Sears threw his head back and laughed. 'Not for much longer.' With that, he swaggered off.

Connor's brows drew down low over his eyes. 'What was that all about?'

'Just Mr Sears trying to cause trouble as usual.' But her voice shook.

His eyes narrowed. 'Has he succeeded?'

She lifted her chin, forced her shoulders back. 'Of course not.' She glared at him. 'But why couldn't this have just been a beer and pizza night, huh?' She could do with a fat-laden pepperoni pizza right now, washed down with an ice-cold beer. It might help her think.

It might help her sleep.

Connor frowned. 'Are you feeling okay, Jaz?'

'I'm perfect,' she snapped.

He stared down at her for a long moment. 'You look beat. Are you ready to leave?'

She gave a fervent nod. 'Yes, please.'

CHAPTER NINE

JAZ stood outside the door of her upstairs flat and turned the key over and over in her hand. She tried to regulate her breathing, her heart rate.

With an impatient movement, she shoved the key in the lock, but she didn't turn it. She drew back again to twist her hands together. *Jeez Louise!*

She'd made excuses whenever Connor had asked her if she wanted to inspect the flat. Same with the carpet-layers. And the men who'd fitted the blinds and light-fittings. She couldn't make any more excuses. What on earth would she say to Gwen if she delayed moving into the flat any longer—*I don't want to enter the place where my mother lost all of her hope?*

It wouldn't do.

But she still didn't move forward to open the door.

'Hello, Jaz.'

She jumped and swung around, clutching her heart. 'Connor!' She gulped. 'I…um…didn't hear you.'

He stood two steps below the landing. Wooden steps. *Rickety* wooden steps. She had a feeling that she really ought to have heard him.

He didn't point out that his work boots must've made plenty of noise. He stared at the closed door and then at her. 'Are you okay?'

'Of course I am.'

'Then what are you doing?'

'I was just about to go into the flat, that's all.'

In one hand he held a large parcel wrapped in brown paper. She wondered what it was. She wondered what he could be doing here with it. She brightened. Perhaps he hadn't finished work on the flat after all and still had one or two things to install? It'd give her a legitimate excuse to race back to Gwen's B&B.

'Housewarming gift,' he explained, gesturing to it.

Darn!

Then she remembered her manners. 'That's nice of you, Connor. But you certainly didn't have to go to any trouble.'

'No trouble.'

He glanced at the door again, then back at her. 'Besides, I wanted to.'

For a moment his eyes burned and she recalled with more clarity than she could've thought possible the feel of his hand on her abdomen when it had rested there on Saturday night, his breath against her neck.

'Are you going to open the door?'

She gulped and swung back to the door. 'Yes, of course I am.' But she didn't reach out and unlock it.

Connor moved up the final two steps with a grace she'd have appreciated all the more if her heart hadn't tried to dash itself against her ribs.

'I knew there was a problem when you kept making excuses not to inspect the flat.'

'No problem. I just trusted your workmanship. That's all.'

'Your mother didn't die inside there, you know, Jaz.'

'I know that!' Her mother had died later at the hospital. 'Like I said, there's no problem.'

He ignored that. 'Okay, the way I see it, I can either pick you up and physically carry you inside…'

Good Lord, no. Bad, bad idea. She didn't want him touching her.

Yes, you do, a little voice whispered through her.

Fine, then. She didn't want what it might lead to.

Are you so sure?

She ignored that. 'Or?'

'Or I can watch your back while you go first.'

That didn't fill her with a great deal of enthusiasm either.

'Or I can go first.'

She met the amber and gold flecks in his eyes. He hadn't stated the obvious—that he could leave. She should tell him to go.

'If I go first I can give you the grand tour. I can point out the work the guys and I have done. You can ooh and ahh over all the improvements.'

She moistened her lips, then nodded. 'I'd…um…appreciate that.'

'I want you to be the one to unlock the door, Jaz.'

She gulped again. His eyes held hers—steady…patient. She didn't glance at the door again. She kept her gaze on his face and soaked up all his warmth and strength. With fingers that shook, she reached out and unlocked the door.

Connor smiled. She wished she could smile back, but she couldn't. He moved past her, gathered her hand inside his and led her into the flat.

'As you can see, the flat is a gun-barrel affair.'

His matter-of-fact tone soothed her.

'This door is the only entrance and exit to the flat. So if a fire ever starts down this end and you're at the other end, you'll need to climb out the front windows onto the shop awning and swing down to the street from there.'

'Just call me Tarzan,' she muttered.

He grinned and, although she couldn't grin back, it eased some of the tightness in her chest.

He gestured to the left. 'We ripped the old bathroom out and replaced it.'

She stuck her head around the door—black and white tiles. 'Nice.'

'This is the kitchen. Another rip-out-and-replace job.'

The hallway opened out into a neat kitchen. Connor and his men had done a nice job. She ran her free hand across a kitchen cupboard, a countertop. Her other hand felt warm and secure in Connor's.

'Very nice,' she managed.

They didn't stop to study it any further. Connor tugged her up the three steps that led into the enormous combined dining and living area, towed her into the centre of the room and then dropped her hand. Jaz turned on the spot. Even with all her boxes piled up in here, she could make out that the proportions of the room were generous.

Perfect for dinner parties.

And beer and pizza evenings.

Some more of that soul-sickening tension eased out of her.

'Why don't you go explore further?'

He smiled that steady, patient smile and his strength arced across the space between them to flood her. With a nod, she followed a short passageway to the two bedrooms—a small one on the left and a large bright one at the front that held her bed, wardrobe and dressing table. Light poured in at two large windows. She leant on the nearest windowsill and stared out at the vista spread before her—a glorious view of Clara Falls' main street, framed by the mountains in the background.

Her mother had lived in this flat without proper heating, without a working gas stove and with rotting floorboards in one section of the living room because of a leak in the roof, not to mention the wood rot in the kitchen and bathroom. Yet…

Jaz's lips curved up. Her mother would've thought that a small price to pay for this view.

Frieda would also have loved the wood-panelled walls and pressed tin ceilings. She'd have been happy here.

Relief hit Jaz then—lovely, glorious relief. She dropped to her knees by the window, lifted her face to the sun and murmured a prayer of thanks. She hadn't come upstairs once in the last two weeks, afraid that the despair that must've enveloped her mother would still hang heavy and grim in these rooms. She'd expected it to taunt her, berate her…sap her of her energy and her determination.

She'd welcomed every delay—first by the carpet layers, then by the firm who'd measured the flat for blinds and curtains, and then the gas board. Even this morning—after she'd rung Richard to warn him of Mr Sears's threats—she'd hung around and dithered in the shop until her staff had shooed her out with promises to call her if she was needed.

But the air didn't press down on her with suffocating heaviness, punishing her for not coming home sooner. It didn't silently and darkly berate her for abandoning her mother. She opened her eyes. The mid-morning sunlight twinkled in at the windows and the flat smelt fresh and clean and full of promise.

She pushed herself to her feet and glanced out of the window at Mr Sears's 'baked-fresh-daily' country bakery and resolve settled over her shoulders.

She had boxes to unpack.

'Connor?'

He hadn't followed her into the bedroom, and the click of the front door told her he'd just left.

She stared down the empty corridor and her heart burned. He'd sensed the demons that had overtaken her. He'd helped her face them…and then he'd left? Just like that? He hadn't let her thank him.

The housewarming gift!

She raced back out to the living room and tugged off the brown paper wrapping. She sat back on her heels and stared. Her throat thickened and she had to swallow.

He'd given her the handmade wine rack she'd admired so much that day in his garage.

With a hand that shook, she reached out and ran a finger across the smooth wood. 'Thank you,' she whispered into the silence.

* * *

Jaz hadn't thought to check if the electricity had been connected to the flat until shadows started to lengthen around her. She glared at the light switch on the wall, but she didn't reach out to switch it on and see. She glared around the kitchen. She'd made progress today—good progress.

For all the good it would do her.

Richard had called her an hour ago—Mr Sears's claim was legitimate. Jaz had to find fifty thousand dollars in the next seven days or lose the bookshop.

A knock sounded on the door and Jaz raced to answer it, welcoming the interruption. 'Mrs Lavender! What are you doing here? Come in.'

Mrs Lavender tsk-tsked. 'You'll ruin your eyesight, Jazmin Harper!' She moved past Jaz, flicked on the light and bathed the kitchen in a warm glow. 'That's better. Now, I can't stay. I just wanted to bring you up some supplies.'

The older woman's thoughtfulness touched her. 'You didn't need to go to any trouble.'

'No trouble, dear. It's just some coffee, a carton of milk and a loaf of bread. Oh, and some eggs,' she said, pulling the items out of a muslin bag. 'Now, don't work too late and don't forget to eat.'

'I won't,' Jaz promised. On impulse, she reached out and hugged the older woman. 'Thank you.'

She saw Mrs Lavender out, then came back in and stared up at the kitchen light sending out its golden glow.

'It's a good sign,' she announced to a pile of empty boxes in the corner. 'It's a good sign,' she said to the jug, filling it. She needed all the good signs she could get.

'Oh, stop talking to yourself and go make your bed!'

She flicked on every light as she went. She made her bed, straightened the bedside tables. She hunted out her bedside clock, a couple of paperbacks and a framed photograph of Frieda.

Now it looked as if someone lived here.

Hands on hips, she surveyed the room and decided the dressing table would look better on the opposite wall. She set her shoulder against it, out-of-all-proportion grateful for castor wheels. The dressing table moved an inch, then stuck fast. She tried hauling it towards her instead. Same result. With a grunt she managed to pull it out from the wall, and reached behind to investigate.

'Darn.' A panel of wood was wedged between wall and dressing table. It must've fallen off the wall. Biting back a very rude word, she pulled it out and set it aside, shoved her dressing table into its new location with more speed than grace, then turned to assess the damage.

Connor had said the bedrooms in the flat were structurally sound. That all they'd need was a coat of paint…and new carpet…and new blinds and curtains. 'What do you call this?' she grumbled. Then remembered she wasn't supposed to be talking to herself.

She tried to fit the panel back to the wall.

She didn't try biting back that very rude word when the panel fell off the wall again.

She seized it in both hands and held it like a club. She could tattoo big, burly men without batting an eyelash. She could do a pretty good Carly Simon rendition on karaoke nights, but home maintenance?

Very carefully she set the panel of wood on the floor, hauled in a deep breath and massaged her temples. For reasons of personal pride, it had become important to fix this slim panel of wood back to the wall. She needed to work out how piece A fitted into piece B. It took her all of five seconds to realise she'd need a torch.

'At least I have one of those.'

She rushed out to the living room to rifle through boxes, and forgot to berate herself for talking out loud. 'Aha!' She held the torch aloft in triumph. 'Yes!' The battery even worked.

She raced back to the bedroom and studied the piece of wood panelling thoroughly, and then the wall. What she needed to do was—

Something glittered in the gap in the wall. Jaz squinted, adjusted the torch. An old Christmas shortbread tin?

She hesitated for only a moment before pushing her hand through the hole. 'But if anything black and hairy so much as touches me…'

Her fingers closed around the tin and she drew it out. She set it on the floor and stared at it. 'Wouldn't I love to find fifty thousand dollars inside you,' she murmured.

She reached out, ran her fingers across the tin's lid—remarkably dust-free. She shone her torch into the wall cavity—*not* remarkably dust-free.

She clambered to her feet, tucked the tin under her arm and went to make herself a cup of coffee.

She sipped her coffee on the steps between the kitchen and living room and surveyed the tin. 'If this were a novel, I really would find fifty thousand dollars in you, you know? And, as we are sitting above a bookshop…' She lifted a hand, then let it fall. 'All I'm trying to say is, if you'd like to come to the party I don't have any complaints.'

She set her mug down and pulled the tin towards her. 'With my luck it'll be a bomb,' she grumbled.

She hauled the lid off.

She stared.

And then she smiled.

Letters. Letters addressed to Frieda Harper, tied in pink ribbon and scented with rose petals. 'Oh, Mum—' she sighed '—who'd have guessed you had such a romantic streak?'

She untied the ribbon, lifted the first letter from the pile, eased it out of its envelope and unfolded it.

My beloved Frieda.

Oh, how beautiful. Jaz's hand went to her chest. She turned the letter over, searching for the signature, the name of her mother's admirer, and—

No!

She abandoned the letter to tear open the next one…and the

one after that…until she'd checked them all. They all bore the same signature.

She pinched herself. She started to laugh. She leapt to her feet and danced around the room. 'We've saved the bookshop, Mum!'

The tin didn't hold fifty thousand dollars. It held love letters addressed to her mother from Gordon Sears.

Gordon Sears!

If the contents of these letters became public, his credibility would be ruined in Clara Falls for ever.

She swept the letters and the tin up, along with her still-warm cup of coffee, and raced out of the flat and downstairs to the bookshop to address the portrait of Frieda on the wall. The one she hadn't finished yet. Couldn't finish.

That didn't stop her talking to it. 'Look!' She held the letters up for Frieda to see. 'I don't know if you meant for me to find these, Mum, but you didn't destroy them so…' She hauled in a breath and tried to contain her excitement. 'They couldn't have come at a better time. I can save the bookshop with these.'

For the first time she found she could smile back at the laughing eyes in Frieda's portrait.

She set her mug on the floor, opened the tin and started reading the letters out loud to her mother. 'I would've only been eleven when you received this one.'

But, as she continued to read, her elation started to fade. 'Oh, Mum…' She finished reading the third letter, folded it and slipped it back into its envelope. She settled herself on the floor beneath her mother's portrait. 'He must've loved you so very much.'

Her triumph turned to pity then, and compassion. Very slowly she eased the tin's lid back into place, pulled it up to her chest and hugged it.

That was how Connor found her half an hour later.

'Am I interrupting anything?'

'No.' She eased the tin back down to her lap.

'I saw the light on and it reminded me that I hadn't returned your key.'

She studied his face as he settled on the floor beside her. She snorted her disbelief at his excuse. 'Richard's spoken to you, hasn't he? Isn't there such a thing as a professional code of privacy in this town?'

'All he said was that you might need a friend this evening, nothing else.'

'Oh.'

'You haven't finished Frieda's portrait yet.'

She couldn't. She didn't know why, but she just couldn't. 'I've been busy.'

She had a feeling he saw through the lie.

'Want to tell me what's going on?'

'Why not?' She didn't bother playing dumb. 'It'll be common knowledge around town soon enough.' She leant her head against the wall. 'My mother borrowed fifty thousand dollars from Gordon Sears. He's calling the debt in.'

'Fifty thousand dollars!' Connor shot forward. 'Are you serious?'

She nodded. 'And no,' she added, answering the next question in his eyes, 'I don't have access to that kind of money. But I do have an appointment with the bank manager first thing tomorrow.'

She dragged a hand down her face. She didn't want to think what would happen if the bank refused her the loan.

Sympathy and concern blazed from Connor's eyes. It bathed her in a warmth she hadn't expected. If felt nice having him sit here on the floor beside her like this—comforting. Perhaps Richard was right and she did need a friend. Maybe, given enough time—and with a concerted effort on her part to ignore the attraction that simmered through her whenever she saw him—she and Connor could be friends.

'Thank you for stopping by and making sure I was okay. I do appreciate it.' Perhaps they were friends already?

'You're welcome.'

She met his eyes. Their gold sparks flashed and glittered and tension coiled through her—that tight, gut-busting yearning she needed to find a way to control. Finally, as if he too could no longer bear it, his gaze dropped to the tin in her lap and she could breathe again.

He nodded towards it. 'What have you got there?'

Without a word, she passed the tin across to him, watched the expressions that chased themselves across his face as he opened it and read the top letter.

'Bloody hell, Jaz! Do you know what this means?' He held the letter up in his long work-roughened fingers, leaning forward in his excitement. 'This is your bargaining chip. Show these to Gordon Sears and he will definitely come to some agreement with you about paying back the loan. They're pure gold!'

'Yes.'

He stilled, studied her face. 'You're not going to use them, are you?'

'No.'

'But…'

She sympathised with the way the air left his lungs, the way he sagged back against the wall to stare at her as if he couldn't possibly have heard her properly.

'I'm not going to use these letters to blackmail Mr Sears.' She couldn't use them.

She tried to haul her mind back from thoughts of dragging Connor's mouth down to hers and kissing him until neither one of them could think straight. Which would be a whole lot easier to do if the scent of autumn hadn't settled all around her, making her yearn for the impossible.

'Why not?'

She took a letter from the tin. *'My beloved Frieda,'* she read. *'All my love…forever yours.'* She dropped it back into the tin. The action sent his scent swirling around her all the more. She breathed it in. She couldn't do anything else. 'To use that as blackmail would be to desecrate something very beautiful. I won't do it.'

She gestured to the unfinished portrait above them. 'My

mother wouldn't want me to do it.' She wanted to make Frieda proud of her, not ashamed.

Connor stared at her for a long time and those beautiful broad shoulders of his bowed as if a sudden weight had dropped onto them. His mouth tightened, the lines around it and his eyes became deeper and more pronounced. His skin lost its colour. His autumn eyes turned as bleak as winter.

Her heart thudded in sudden fear. 'Connor?'

'You didn't cheat on me eight years ago, did you, Jaz? I got it wrong. I got it all wrong.'

Her skin went cold, then hot. She hunched her knees up towards her chest and wrapped her arms around them. 'No, I didn't cheat on you.'

She hadn't thought he could go any paler. She'd been wrong. She wanted to reach out a hand and offer him some kind of comfort but she was too afraid to. She'd always known it would rock him to his foundations if he ever discovered the truth. She recognised the regret, the guilt, the sorrow that stretched through his eyes. Recognised too the self-condemnation, the belief in the inadequacy of any apology he tried to offer now.

She should've stayed eight years ago. She should've stayed and fought for him.

She couldn't change the past but...

'What time is it?'

He glanced at his watch, stared at it for an eternity, then shook himself. 'It's only half past six.'

'Is your car out the back?'

He nodded.

'C'mon then.' She rose. 'There's something I want to show you.'

He followed her outside, waited for her to lock the bookshop, then led her to his car. 'Where to?' he asked, starting the engine.

'Sam Hancock's.'

He swung to face her but he didn't say anything. Did he think she meant to punish him? He set his shoulders, his mouth a grim line and she could almost see a mantle of resolve settle over him as he started the car. He intended to endure whatever she threw at him.

Oh, Connor. I don't want to hurt you any more. I want you to understand and find peace, that's all.

They didn't speak as he drove the short distance to Sam's house. Nor did they speak as she led the way to the front door. Sam had told her on Saturday night that he was here for the next week.

'Hi, Sam,' she said when he answered the door. 'You told me the other night that I was welcome to come around and view my handiwork if I wanted. Is now a convenient time?'

'Absolutely.' With a smile, he ushered them into the house and led them through to the main bedroom, gestured to the life-size painting on the wall. 'I'll leave you to it. Yell if you need anything.'

Jaz murmured her thanks but barely managed to drag her gaze away from Connor as he studied the picture she'd painted of Lenore Hancock eight years ago. 'This is Sam's mother,' she said because she had to say something.

'Yes.' He moved closer to it to study it more carefully.

'This is where I first understood the power of my talent.'

He turned to meet her gaze and she shrugged. 'I hadn't fully comprehended the effect something like this could have. It frightened me.'

He gestured to the wall too, but he didn't glance back at the picture. His eyes remained glued to her face. 'How did this come about?'

'Sam's dad developed dementia and started walking the streets at all times of the day and night searching for Lenore. She'd died a couple of years before him, you see.'

'So you drew her on the wall for him?'

'Yes.'

'Why didn't you tell me?'

'Because Sam and his sister asked me to keep it a secret.'

His hands clenched. 'Even from me?'

She wanted to reach out and wipe the anguish from his eyes. 'Sam and his sister didn't want to put their father into a nursing home, but they both had to work and the nurse who came for a few hours every day was finding him harder and harder to deal with. The fewer people who knew, the fewer people who could interfere.'

She pulled in a breath. She owed him the whole truth. 'What I felt for you, Connor…it scared me too. Some days I thought you would swallow me whole. I needed to find my own place in the world that was separate from yours.' And she'd found it in the worst way possible. 'Though it never occurred to me that you could misconstrue…'

He stepped back, his lips pressed together so tightly they almost turned blue. Her stomach turned to ash. Could he even begin to understand her insecurity back then?

He swung away to stare at the picture again. 'Did it work? Did they have to put Mr Hancock into a nursing home?'

'It worked better than any of us had dreamed.' She bit her lip, remembering the evening they'd unveiled the finished portrait to Mr Hancock. 'When he saw the picture, he pulled up a chair and started talking to her. I'll never forget his first words. He said—*Lenore, I've been looking for you everywhere, love. And now I've found you.*' It had damn near broken her heart. She'd had to back out of the room and race outside.

Connor swung around as if he sensed that emotion close to the surface in her now. 'That's the same night I found you with Sam, isn't it?'

She hesitated, then nodded.

'Mr Hancock's reaction, it freaked you out, didn't it? It wore you out the same way that tattoo you did for Jeff wore you out.'

'Yes.' The word whispered out of her.

'And Sam was trying to comfort you.'

Her throat closed over. She managed a nod.

'When you said—*I loathe this thing and I love it too, but whatever I do I can't give it up*—you were talking about your ability to draw people so well, so accurately, and not about your relationship with Sam.'

Her head snapped up. 'Is that what you thought?' She stared at him in shock.

'I should have believed in you.'

Yes, he should've. 'I should have stayed and made you listen.'

Eight years ago, she'd been too afraid to stay and fight for him.

'God, Jaz, I'm sorry!' He reached out one hand towards her, but he let it drop before it could touch her. 'Is it too late to apologise?'

She smiled then. 'It's never too late to apologise.' She had to believe that.

'Then I'm sorry I jumped to conclusions eight years ago. I'm sorry I accused you of cheating on me. I'm sorry for hurting you.'

A weight lifted from her. 'Thank you.'

He reached for her then and she knew he meant to fold her in his arms and kiss her.

She wanted that. She wanted that more than she'd ever wanted anything.

She took a step back. Her heart burned. Her eyes burned. 'It's not too late for apologies, but it is too late for hope. We can't turn time back. I'm sorry, Connor, but it's too late for us.'

He stilled. He dragged a hand back through his hair, his mouth grim. 'Do you really believe that?'

The words rasped out of his throat, raw, and Jaz wanted to close her eyes and rest her head against his shoulder. She stiffened her spine and forced herself to meet his gaze. 'Yes, I do.' Because it was true.

His mouth became even grimmer. 'Does this mean we can't be friends?' she whispered. She could at least have that much, couldn't she?

The mouth didn't soften. The gold highlights in his eyes didn't sparkle. 'Is that what you want?'

'Yes.' For the life of her, though, she couldn't manage a smile.

'Friends it is.'

He didn't smile either.

'C'mon.' He took her arm. 'I'll take you home.'

CHAPTER TEN

CONNOR showed up the next day for her appointment at the bank.

'What on earth…' she started.

'Friends?' he cut in, his mouth as grim as it had been last night.

'Yes, but—'

'Then trust me.'

Something about his grimness made her nod and back down. She didn't need a knight in shining armour, but it was nice knowing Connor was on her side all the same.

She got the loan. Connor told the bank manager he'd take his business—his not inconsiderable business—elsewhere if they refused her the loan. He'd have even gone guarantor for her but she put her foot down at that. The terms of the loan would stretch her resources, the bookshop would need to make a profit—and soon—all plans for an art gallery had to go on hold… But she got the loan.

'Anything else I can help with?' Connor asked once they were standing out on the footpath again.

'Well, now, let me see…' She smiled. She wanted to see the golden highlights in his eyes sparkling. She wanted to see him smile back. 'I don't have anyone lined up to man the sausage sizzle on Saturday.'

This Saturday. The Saturday of the book fair.

The book fair that now had to do well.

Very well.

'Done. I'll be there.'

He turned and strode away. No sparkling. No smiling.

She spent the rest of the week trying to lose herself in the preparations for the book fair. She double-checked that the authors and poets lined up for the Saturday afternoon readings were still available. She double-checked that the fairy she'd hired to read stories to the children hadn't come down with the flu, and that the pirates she'd hired to face-paint said children hadn't walked the plank and disappeared.

She double-checked that the enormous barbecue she'd hired would still arrive first thing Saturday morning, and that the butcher had her order for the umpteen dozen sausages she'd estimated they'd need for the sausage sizzle.

She would not let anything go wrong.

She couldn't afford to.

She didn't double-check that Connor would still man the sausage sizzle, though.

That didn't mean she could get him out of her mind.

Alone in her flat each night, she ached to ring him.

To say what?

Just to find out if he's okay.

Oh, for heaven's sake. Get over yourself. Connor has not spent the last eight years living in the past…or fleeing from it. Of course he's okay.

His men finished work on the bookshop in double-quick time…and Connor was so okay he didn't even bother coming around to check up on it.

Gritting her teeth, she wrote a cheque and posted it.

She tried to sleep but, as usual, insomnia plagued her.

By closing time on Friday afternoon, she was so wound up she didn't know if she wanted to bounce off walls or collapse into a heap.

'You're driving your staff insane, you know that?' Mrs Lavender observed.

'I'm not meaning to.' Jaz twisted her hands together and

glanced out of the window. She was always glancing out of the window. What for? Was she hoping for a sight of Connor? She dragged her gaze back.

Mrs Lavender's eyes narrowed. 'What happened to the woman who strode down the street with purpose and determination?'

'I'm still that same woman.'

'Are you? It seems to me you spend more time hand-wringing and…and mooning, these days.'

Jaz exhaled sharply. 'I'll wear the hand-wringing, but not the mooning!'

She wasn't mooning.

Was she?

She gulped. Had she let her feelings for Connor undermine her purpose?

A pulse behind her eyes hammered in time with the heart that beat against her ribs. She could not let anyone, not even Connor—especially not Connor—distract her from making her mother's dream a reality.

She nodded slowly. The hammering eased. 'You're right.' She glanced out of the window, not looking for Connor, but towards Mr Sears's bakery. As if on cue, Connor drove past with Melly in the car. Jaz refused to follow the car's progress. She didn't speak again until the car was lost from her line of sight.

'There's something I need to do,' she said with sudden decision. She didn't want to put it off any longer.

'I'll close the shop for you.'

'Thank you.'

Jaz raced upstairs, grabbed the tin of letters. Then she set off across the road to Mr Sears's 'baked-fresh-daily' country bakery.

She didn't enter the shop with a booming, Howdy, Mr S. She waited quietly to one side until he'd served the two customers in front of her, and only when they were alone did she approach the counter.

'I found something that belongs to you.' She handed him the tin, then stepped back.

Mr Sears frowned, glowered…lifted the lid of the tin…and his face went grey. The skin around his eyes, his mouth, bagged. Some force in his shoulders left him. Jaz wondered if she should race around the counter and lead him to a chair.

'What do you want?' The words rasped out of him, old-sounding and wooden. With both hands clasped around the tin, he leant his arms against the counter. Not to get closer to her, but to support himself.

'Peace,' she whispered.

He met her gaze then. He nodded. Finally he said, 'How much?'

It took her a moment to decipher his meaning. Her head snapped back when she did. He thought she wanted money?

'Or have you already given copies to the local newspapers?'

'I am my mother's daughter, Mr Sears.' She lifted her chin. 'Did my mother ever *once* threaten you with those?'

She nodded towards the letters. He didn't say anything.

'I haven't made copies, I haven't photographed them and I haven't shown them to any gossip columnists.'

She watched the way his lips twisted in disbelief and swore she would never let love tear her up, screw up her thinking, twist her, like it had in the past. Like it was doing now to Mr Sears.

'Once upon a time you loved my mother a great deal. She kept your letters, which tells me she must've loved you too. Now that she's dead they belong to you, not to anybody else.' She took a step back from the counter. 'I did not come back to Clara Falls to make my mother ashamed of me, Mr Sears.'

She turned around and walked away, knowing he didn't believe her. For the next month…three months…perhaps for the rest of his life, Gordon Sears would pick up the local paper with the taste of fear in his mouth. He'd watch for thinly dis-guised snickers and people falling silent whenever he walked into a room.

Until he let go of his fear, he would find no peace.

Until she let go of her fear, neither would she.

Her feet slowed to a halt outside the bookshop's brightly lit window with its colourful display of hardbacks, the posters advertising tomorrow's book fair.

Her fear.

It wasn't the fear of the bookshop failing—though, with all her heart, she needed to make that dream a reality for her mother. No, it was the fear that a true, passionate love—like the love she and Connor had once shared—would go wrong and once again she'd become bitter and destructive, hurting, even destroying, the people she most loved.

She rested her head against the cold glass. Once she'd reconciled herself to the fact that love was closed to her—love, marriage…and children. Once she'd managed that, then perhaps she'd find peace.

Jaz was awake long before she heard the tapping on the front door of her flat at seven-thirty the next morning.

At six o'clock, and over her first cup of coffee, she'd pored over the day's programme. Even though she'd memorised it earlier in the week. Then she'd started chopping onions and buttering bread rolls for the sausage sizzle. She was counting on the smell of frying onions to swell the crowd at the book fair by at least twenty per cent. Who could resist the smell of frying onions?

And who could be tapping so discreetly on her front door, as if they were worried about disturbing her, this early in the morning?

Unless the barbecue and hotplate had arrived already.

She wondered if Connor would show up and man the sausage sizzle as he'd promised.

Of course he would. Connor always kept his promises.

She tried to push all thoughts of him out of her head as she rushed to answer the door.

'Melly!'

Melly stood there, hopping from one foot to the other as if

her small frame could hardly contain her excitement. 'Did I wake you up?'

'No, I've been up for ages and ages.'

Jaz ushered her into the flat, patted a stool at the breakfast bar and poured her a glass of orange juice. 'What are you doing here?'

Melly clutched a crisp white envelope in one hand and she held it out to Jaz now. 'I had to show you this.' She grinned. She bounced in her seat.

Jaz took the envelope and read the enclosed card, and had a feeling that her grin had grown as wide as Melly's. 'This is an invitation to Yvonne Walker's slumber party tonight!'

Melly nodded so vigorously she almost fell off her stool. Jaz swooped down and hugged her. 'Sweetheart, I'm so happy for you.'

'I knew you would be. I wanted to come over yesterday to tell you, but Daddy said you were busy.'

Did he? 'I…er…see.'

Melly bit her lip. 'Are you busy now?'

'Not too busy for you,' she returned promptly.

Melly's autumn-brown eyes grew so wide with wonder Jaz found herself blinking madly.

'Then…then can you do my hair up in a ponytail bun this afternoon? I…I want to look pretty.'

'Absolutely, and you'll knock their socks off,' Jaz promised. But…

'Daddy knows you're here now, though, doesn't he?'

Melly shook her head. 'He was sleeping and I didn't want to wake him up. He was awake most of last night.'

Jaz wondered why. Then she stiffened. Good Lord! If Connor woke and found Melly gone…

Melly bit her lip again. 'Are you cross with me?'

'No, of course not, Melly, it's just… How would you feel if you woke up and couldn't find Daddy anywhere in the house?'

'I'd be scared.'

'How do you think Daddy will feel if he wakes up and he can't find you?'

Melly's eyes went wide again. 'Will he be scared too?'

Jaz nodded gravely. 'He'll be very, very worried.'

Melly leapt down from her stool. 'Maybe he's not awake yet and if I run home really, really fast…'

Jaz prayed Connor hadn't woken yet. She grabbed her car keys. 'It'll be quicker if I drive you.'

She cast a glance around at all the preparations she'd started, then shook her head. It'd only take a minute or two to see Melly home safe. She had plenty of time before the book fair kicked off at ten.

She gulped. Lord, if Connor woke and couldn't find Melly…

'Hurry, Jaz! I don't want to worry Daddy.'

Jaz stopped trying to moderate her pace. She grabbed Melly's hand and raced for the door. She released Melly to lock the door behind them and, when she turned back, Melly had already started down the stairs. Jaz had almost caught up with her when a voice boomed out, 'Melanie Linda Reed, you are in so much trouble!'

Connor! He'd woken up.

At the sound of his voice Melly swung around and Jaz could see the child's foot start to fly out from beneath her. It would send her hurtling head first down the rest of the stairs. Jaz lunged forward to grab the back of Melly's jumper, pulling the child in close to her chest. She tried to regain her balance but couldn't quite manage it and her left arm and side crashed into the railing, taking the brunt of the impact.

She gritted her teeth at the sound of her shirt sleeve tearing. Exhaled sharply as pain ripped her arm from elbow to shoulder. Struggled to her feet again.

Connor was there in seconds, lifting Melly from her arms and checking the child for injury.

'Is she okay?' Jaz managed.

He nodded.

'We were trying to get home really fast,' Melly said with a

sob. 'Jaz said you'd be really, really worried if you woke up and couldn't find me. I'm sorry, Daddy.'

Jaz wanted to tell him to go easy on Melly, but her arm was on fire and it took all her strength to stay upright.

'We'll talk about it later, Mel, but you have to promise me you'll never do that again.'

'I promise.'

'Good. Now I want to make sure Jaz didn't hurt herself.'

Jaz gave up trying to stay upright and sat.

Connor set Melly back down and they turned to her as one. As one, their eyes widened.

Jaz tried to smile. 'I think I scratched my arm.' She couldn't look at it. She could do other people's blood, but her own made her feel a bit wobbly.

And she knew there was blood. She could feel it.

'You're bleeding, Jaz.' Melly's eyes filled with tears. 'Lots!'

It didn't mean she wanted it confirmed.

'What was it, Connor? A rusty nail?'

He glanced at the railing above, narrowed his eyes, then nodded.

'Brilliant! So now I'll have to go and get a tetanus shot.' It was the day of the book fair. She didn't have time for tetanus shots. *Oh, Mum, I'm sorry.*

Connor kicked the railing. 'I'm going to replace this whole damn structure! It's a safety hazard.' Then he took her arm in gentle fingers and surveyed it.

Melly sat down beside Jaz and stroked her right hand. 'You saved my life,' she whispered in awe.

That made Jaz smile. She squeezed the child's hand gently. 'No, I didn't, sweetheart. I saved you from a nasty tumble, that's all.'

'I'm sorry, Jaz, but I think you're going to need more than a tetanus shot.'

She gulped. 'Stitches?'

He nodded.

'But…but I don't have time for all this today.' The book fair! 'Can't we put it off till tomorrow? Please?'

'It'll take no time at all,' he soothed as if to a frightened child. He brushed her hair back from her face. 'Mel and I will take you to the hospital in Katoomba and they'll have you fixed up within two shakes of a lamb's tail, I promise.'

He looked so strong and male. Jaz wanted to snuggle against his chest and stay there.

'Daddy is a really good hand holder, Jaz. You will hold Jaz's hand, won't you, Daddy?'

'I will,' he promised.

It reminded Jaz that she should at least look brave for Melly's sake. 'No time at all, you say?'

'That's right.' He slipped an arm around her waist. 'Come on, I'll help you to the car.'

She had no choice but to submit. *Oh, Mum, I'm sorry.*

They were at the hospital for four hours.

Four hours!

Connor wanted to roar at the staff, he wanted to tear his hair out…he wanted to take away Jaz's pain.

He paced. He called his father to come and collect Melly. He rang Mrs Lavender to tell her what had happened. He held Jaz's hand.

Until they took her away and wouldn't let him go with her.

He replayed over and over in his mind that moment when Jaz had thrown herself forward to save Mel from harm. He'd been a bloody fool to roar at Mel like that, but he'd been so darn relieved to find her…

Over and over he relived his fear of that moment when he'd thought both Mel and Jaz would fall headlong down those stairs together.

One certainty crystallised in his mind with a clarity that made his hands clench. From now on, he wanted to keep Jaz from all harm. For ever.

It wasn't too late for them. It couldn't be!

Finally Jaz reappeared. She had some colour in her cheeks again and a bandage around her upper arm. She smiled at him as if she sensed his worry and wanted to allay it. 'Right as rain again, see.' She held up a piece of paper. 'I just need to get this prescription filled and then we can go.'

The nurse accompanying Jaz folded her arms. 'And what else did the doctor say, Ms Harper?'

'I'll have something to eat when I get home, I promise.'

'You'll do no such thing.' The nurse transferred her glare to Connor. 'You will take her down to the cafeteria and you won't let her leave until she's had a sandwich and an orange juice, you hear?'

'Yes, ma'am.'

'But the book fair—'

'No arguments,' he told Jaz. They'd follow the doctor's orders. 'You've been here four hours; another twenty or so minutes won't make any difference.'

She glared at him. 'You said two shakes of a lamb's tail.' She snorted. He couldn't really blame her. When her shoulders slumped he wanted to gather her in close and hold her.

He didn't. He took her for a sandwich and an orange juice.

They sat outside at a table in the sun because Jaz said she'd had enough of being cooped up indoors. He pulled his sweater over his head and settled it around her shoulders. A bolt of warmth shot through him when she pulled the sweater around her more securely and huddled down into its warmth. He found himself fighting the urge to warm her up in a far more primitive manner.

'How are you feeling?' he asked when she'd finished her sandwich.

'Actually, as good as new.'

He raised a sceptical eyebrow.

'It's true! I mean, the arm is a bit sore, but other than that...I'm relieved, if the truth be told.'

'Relieved!'

'From the looks on your and Melly's faces, I thought at the very least I was going to need twenty stitches.'

'How many did you get?'

'Three.'

'Three! I thought—'

'You thought I was going to lose my arm.'

He threw his head back and laughed with sheer relief. 'You really are feeling all right?'

'I am.'

'Good. Then I can do this.'

He leaned over and kissed her, savoured all of her sweet goodness with a slowness designed to give as much pleasure as it received. When her lips trembled beneath his, it tested all of his powers of control.

He drew back and touched a finger to her cheek, smiled at the way her breath hitched in her throat. 'I love you, Jaz.'

The words slid out of him as natural as breathing. Then he bent his head and touched his lips to hers again.

CHAPTER ELEVEN

'WHAT on earth…?'

Jaz pushed against him so violently she'd have fallen off her seat if he hadn't grabbed her around the waist to hold her steady.

'What do you think you're doing?' She leapt right out of his arms and stood trembling, facing him.

He'd have laughed out loud at her words if the expression on her face hadn't sliced him to the marrow. 'I thought that was kind of obvious.' He tried to grin that grin—the one that she'd told him eight years ago could make her knees weak. The grin that kicked up one corner of his mouth and said he couldn't think of anything better on this earth than making love with her.

The grin wasn't a lie. He couldn't think of anything he'd rather do.

She stared at his mouth and took a step back, gripped her hands together. 'This can't happen!'

He rose too, planted his feet. He wanted to fill her field of vision the way she filled his. 'Why not?'

'What do you mean, why not? You… I…' She snapped her mouth shut, dragged in a breath and glared. 'You know why not.'

Her voice trembled. It made him want to smile, to haul her into his arms…to cry.

'Nope, can't say I do.' He shook his head. 'I loved the girl you were eight years ago, and I love the woman you are now even more. I don't get why we can't be together.'

Her eyes grew wide and round. For a brief moment her whole body swayed towards him and a fierce joy gripped him. He'd win her round yet. 'There's nothing to stop us from being together, Jaz. Nothing at all.' He'd prove it to her. He took a step towards her, reached out his hands…

Jaz snapped back, away from him. 'I already told you. It's too late!'

Frustration balled through him. And fear. He couldn't lose her a second time. He couldn't.

'When are you going to stop running?'

'Running?' She snorted. 'I'm not running. I came back to Clara Falls, didn't I? And I'm not leaving until my mother's bookshop is back on its feet. Doesn't seem to me that there's much running away involved in any of that.'

At the mention of the bookshop, though, a spasm of pain contracted her nostrils, twisted her mouth. The bookshop. He thought back to the darn loan with its outrageous interest rate that she'd lumbered herself with. He'd have given her the money if she'd let him. He'd have offered to lend it to her, but he'd known she'd have refused that too.

Something told him she would not survive the closure of the bookshop. Financially, she couldn't afford it. Emotionally…a cold chill raised the hairs on the back of his neck.

'Why is the bookshop so important, Jaz?'

Her eyes darkened. Not for the first time, he noticed the circles beneath them. 'Making it a success…it's the only thing left that I can do for my mother.'

It all clicked into place then. He should've realised it right from the start. Her return to Clara Falls; it wasn't about pride or revenge. It wasn't about showing the town she was better than they'd ever given her credit for. It was about love. This woman standing in front of him had only ever been about love.

And yet she held herself responsible for her mother's death. She'd healed all the dark places inside him. He wanted to heal the dark places inside her too. 'When are you going to stop punishing yourself and let yourself be happy?'

'I can't,' she whispered.

The pain in her voice tore at him. 'Why not?' He kept his voice low, but something in her eyes frightened him. He wanted to reach for her but he knew that would only make her retreat further. He clenched his hands and forced them to remain by his sides.

'When you thought I'd cheated on you, it broke my heart, Connor.'

A weight pressed down on his chest, thinning his soul. He deserved her resentment. He sure as hell didn't deserve her forgiveness. And yet he'd thought... 'I've tried to apologise, Jaz. I'm sorrier for that mistake than I can find the words for. If I could turn time back...'

'I know, and it's not what I mean. We both made mistakes we're sorry for. It's...' She broke off to pull his sweater more tightly around her body as if she were cold and couldn't get warm, no matter how hard she tried. 'I became a different person afterwards, that's what I'm trying to tell you. I became bitter and hard, destructive.'

She met his eyes, her own bleak but determined. Bile filled his mouth, his soul.

'I'm not saying I blame you for that because I don't. It wasn't your fault. It was mine. I turned into the kind of person who refused to come back to Clara Falls even though my mother begged me to, even when I knew how much it would mean to her. Can you believe that?'

She gave a harsh laugh. He closed his eyes.

'I may as well have handed my mother that bottle of sleeping pills with my own hands.'

His eyes snapped open. 'You can't believe that!'

Her hands shook. 'But I do.'

'You can't hold yourself responsible for another person's actions like that, Jaz.'

'If I'd come home, I'd have seen how things were. I could've helped. I could've saved her.' She whispered the last sentence.

Then she threw her head back and her eyes blazed. 'But I didn't because I'd turned into some unfeeling monster. That's why there's no future for me and you, Connor. I can't risk loving like that ever again. Who will I hurt or destroy the next time love fails me, huh?'

His mouth had gone dry. 'Who says it will fail?'

She stared back at him—wounded, tired…resolute. 'I'm sorry, Connor, but that's one gamble I'm not prepared to take.'

His stomach…his heart…his whole life, dropped to his feet at the note of finality in her voice. She was wrong, so wrong to exile herself from love like this.

To exile him!

He'd imagined her in his arms so fully and completely, and for all of time. To have her snatched back out of them now was too much to bear. This woman standing in front of him was all about love…but she'd exempted herself. And that meant she'd barred him from love too because he would never settle for second best again. For him, anyone but Jaz Harper was second best.

'According to your philosophy then, I'd better not have the gall to go falling in love again.'

Her jaw dropped, but then she pressed her lips together into a tight line. Pain rolled off her in waves. It took all of his strength not to reach for her and do what he could to wipe that pain away.

'I mean, what if I let jealousy get the better of me again for even half a second? Given my past form, I quite obviously have no right messing with women's hearts.'

She pressed the heels of her hands to her eyes. He hated the defeated slope of her shoulders, the way she seemed unable to throw her head back when she pulled her hands away. 'That's not what I meant and you know it.'

'You said the only thing left that you could do for your mother was to save the bookshop. You're wrong. The best gift you could give Frieda is to live your life fully and without fear…to finally let love back into your life. You don't get it, do you, Jaz? Frieda never wanted you to come back to Clara Falls for her own comfort or peace of mind. She wanted you to come back for yours!'

He watched her try to take in the meaning of his words.

'Do you think she'd be pleased by what you are doing to yourself now?'

She paled.

'Do you think she'd be proud of you?'

She just stared back at him, frozen, and he wondered if he'd pushed her too far. All he wanted to do was drop to his knees in front of her and beg her to be happy.

She took a step away from him. 'Take me home, please, Connor.'

She wouldn't meet his eyes and his heart froze over. 'I'm supposed to be running a book fair. I need to see if I can manage to salvage something from this day.'

And then she turned away and Connor knew that was her final word. His words hadn't breached the walls she had erected around herself.

He'd failed.

They made the fifteen-minute journey from Katoomba hospital to Clara Falls in silence. Jaz's heart hurt with every beat it took, as if someone had taken a baseball bat to it. A pain stretched behind her eyes and into eternity.

The force of Connor's words still pounded at her and she could barely make sense of anything. She'd thought she'd started to put things right, to make things better. Except…

Connor loved her.

One part of her gave a wild, joyful leap. She grabbed it and pulled it back into line. She and Connor?

No.

She forced herself to swallow, to straighten in her seat. They'd reach Clara Falls' main street any moment now.

She realised she still clutched Connor's sweater around her like an offer of comfort. She inhaled one last autumn-scented breath, then folded it neatly and set it on the seat beside her.

She tried to ready herself for the sight of a closed bookshop and no customers, for fairies and pirates who would rightly demand payment anyway. She tried to push to the back of her mind how much money she'd plugged into advertising, on orders for sausages and hiring barbecue plates. She tried to think of ways she could allay the disappointment of the authors and poets who'd promised her their time free of charge this afternoon as a favour to their community.

From the corner of her eye, she saw Connor glance at her. 'You think that Mrs Lavender and co have had to cancel the book fair, don't you?'

She ached to reach out and touch his shoulder, to tell him she'd never meant to hurt him. She didn't. It wouldn't help. 'Yes.'

He frowned. 'Why? Do you think you're that indispensable?'

'Of course not!'

She didn't think she was indispensable to him at all. He'd find someone else to love. One day. And she wanted him to. She gritted her teeth. She meant it. She did. He deserved to be happy.

She reminded herself they were talking about the bookshop. 'Mr Sears will have found a way to sabotage the fair.' And without her there to run the gauntlet…

Her stomach roiled and churned as they turned into Clara Falls' main street.

There weren't as many tourists down this end of the street as usual. Even though the day was disgustingly bright and sunny. Her mouth turned down. She wished for grey skies and hail. Somehow that would make her feel better.

But the sun didn't magically stop shining and rain and huge balls of ice didn't pour down from the sky. She bit back a sigh and kept her eyes doggedly on the streetscape directly beside her.

As they moved closer towards the bookshop, Jaz wanted to close her eyes. She didn't. But she didn't move her eyes past the streetscape directly beside her either. She would not look ahead. She didn't have the heart for that.

She didn't have the heart to glance again at Connor either.

She wished the car would break down. She wished it would come to a clunking halt and just strand her here in the middle of the road, where she wouldn't have to move until it was closing time in Clara Falls.

It didn't happen. The car kept moving forward. Jaz kept her eyes on the view beside her. A few more tourists appeared. At least it wasn't only her shop that was doing poorly today.

Then the scent of frying onions hit her.

Onions!

She slid forward to stare out through the front windscreen.

People.

Oodles and oodles of people. All mingling and laughing out the front of her bookshop.

Connor pulled the car to a halt and a cheer went up when the townsfolk saw her.

A cheer? For her?

Her jaw went slack when she saw who led the cheer.

Mr Sears!

Not only did he lead the cheer but he manned the barbecue hotplate full of sausages too. Carmen grinned and waved from her station beside him. Somehow, Jaz managed to lift her hand and wave back.

Just as many people—perhaps more—were crammed inside the bookshop. It was so full it had almost developed a pulse of its own. She recognised two staff members amid all the chaos, caught sight of a fairy and couldn't help wondering where the pirates had set up for the face painting.

She turned to stare at Connor. 'But what…?'

He didn't smile. He just shrugged. 'Why don't you hop out here? I'll park the car around the back.'

She didn't want to get out of the car. She didn't want to leave him like this. She'd hurt him and…

And she couldn't help him now.

She slid out of the car and stood on the footpath, watched as the car drew away. Only then did she turn back to the crowd and wondered what she should tackle first.

Not what, but who. With a sense of unreality, she made her way through the crowd to Mr Sears. 'I…' She lifted her hands, then let them drop. 'Thank you.' Somehow that seemed completely inadequate.

'No.' He shook his head. 'Thank you.'

And then he smiled. She wondered if she'd ever really seen him smile before.

'In this town, Jaz, we pull together.'

'I… It means a lot.' She found herself smiling back and that didn't seem completely inadequate. It felt right.

She glanced around and what she saw fired hope in her heart. *Oh, Mum, if you could only see this.* She swung back to him. 'What can I do?'

'Carmen and I have things sorted out here for the moment, don't we, Carmen?'

The teenager's eyes danced. 'Aye, aye, Captain.' She saluted her father with the tongs and her sense of fun tugged at Jaz.

He pointed to the door. 'You'll find Audra Lavender and Boyd Longbottom directing proceedings inside.'

She went to turn away, then swung back. 'Did I just hear you say Mrs Lavender *and* Boyd Longbottom?'

'That's right.' He winked. 'I think you'll find it's a day for miracles.'

She started to grin. 'I think you must be right.' She turned and headed for the door.

'Jaz, dear.' Mrs Lavender beamed when she saw her. 'I hope your poor arm is okay.'

'Yes, thank you. It's fine.'

Mrs Lavender had set up two sturdy card tables against the back wall in preparation for the cheese and wine Jaz had ordered for the afternoon readings. She'd pushed the leatherette cubes against the walls and into the spaces between the bookcases. It would leave a circle of space around the authors as they gave their readings. Perfect.

'And the authors can use these tables for signings afterwards, you know, dear. I mean, once the crowd hears our three guests, they're going to want to buy the books. And yes, we do have plenty in stock,' she added when Jaz opened her mouth.

Jaz closed it again, noticed Boyd Longbottom sorting bottles of wine in the stockroom and nodded towards him. 'How?' she whispered.

'I said to him this morning—"Boyd Longbottom, I need help with our Jazmin's book fair and I don't know who else I can ask."'

Jaz's eyes widened. 'It was that easy?'

'Well, now, he did say—"If you agree to have dinner with me tonight then I'm all yours, Audra Lavender." And he said it so nice like. A lady shouldn't turn down a nice offer like that, should she?'

'Of course not.'

Jaz couldn't help thinking back to the way Connor had told her he loved her—as if he couldn't help but say it; as if there hadn't been another thought in his head.

Jaz leant forward and clasped Mrs Lavender's hand. 'I'm pleased for you.'

The older woman's eyes turned misty. 'Thank you, dear. Boyd and I, we've wasted enough time now, I think.'

Jaz straightened and her heart started to thump, but she wasn't sure why. She searched the room for Connor but couldn't see him anywhere. He was the usual reason her heart rate went haywire.

'Mrs Lavender, thank you for everything you've done today. I...'

'Did you really think we'd leave you in the lurch?'

'I certainly didn't expect you to take so much upon yourselves.'

'Why not?'

Jaz stared, and then didn't know quite what to say.

'You've given an old woman a new lease of life. You've

given your staff a fun and harmonious working environment. This book fair, it's galvanised us, made us work together. You've made us feel as if we matter.'

'But you do!'

'Precisely, Jazmin Harper. We all matter. Even you.'

Before Jaz could respond, Mrs Lavender rushed on, 'And I don't know what you did to charm Mr Sears, but it was well done. The moment he saw Boyd and I wrestling with the barbecue, he was across the road like buckshot. He started directing and things just fell into place.'

'I'm very grateful.'

'Jazmin, dear, you're one of us. We look after our own.'

Jaz felt the walls of the community wrap around her and it felt as good as she'd always imagined it would.

'I…well, now that I'm here, what can I do?'

'Mingle. Chat and charm. Bask in the glow of the fair's success. And take care of that arm. Everything else has been taken care of. We know where to find you,' she added when Jaz opened her mouth to argue. 'If we need to.'

Jaz had to content herself with that. She mingled. She chatted. As she moved about the room, it occurred to her that she felt comfortable here—here in Clara Falls, of all places. More comfortable than she had ever felt anywhere in her life before.

'Your mother would've enjoyed this,' Mr Sears said, coming up beside her as the guest authors prepared themselves for the readings.

The scent of frying onions still seasoned the air. She glanced out of the window behind her. Connor had taken over the sausage sizzle. A pulse fluttered in her throat. She had to swallow before she could speak. 'Yes, she would've had a ball.'

Mr Sears followed her gaze. He turned back to her. 'Don't make the same mistakes Frieda and I made.'

'Which was?' She held her breath. It was none of her business but…

He stared back at her. 'I loved your mother from the first

moment I clapped eyes on her.' His lips tightened briefly. 'I understood why she wouldn't get involved with me when I was married. But when my wife died…'

Mrs Sears had died over ten years ago, when Carmen and her brother were just small children.

'I didn't understand why she wouldn't take a chance on us then. I knew she loved me.'

'Didn't she ever tell you why?'

He was quiet for a long moment. 'She said we couldn't be together until all the children were grown up. She said her reputation would make things too difficult for them.'

Jaz's jaw dropped.

'And I took that to mean that she cared more about what people thought than she cared about me.'

He broke off for a moment, then pulled in a breath. 'I wanted the bookshop so badly because I suspected the letters were in the building somewhere. And I wanted it because it was part of her. I treated you very badly, Jazmin. I'm sorry.'

'Apology accepted,' she said without hesitation. 'But, speaking of the bookshop, I am looking for a business partner.'

His eyes suddenly gleamed. 'The two of us could make Frieda's dream a reality.'

She nodded.

'We'll talk about this further.'

She smiled. 'That's what I was hoping you'd say.'

He sobered again. 'I let my disappointment that Frieda wouldn't marry me turn my love into something ugly and twisted.' He reached out, touched her hand briefly. 'Don't you go and make the same mistake.'

Then he was gone.

Jaz's heart pounded and burned. She turned to the partially completed portrait of Frieda on the back wall for guidance. *Oh, Mum, what do I do?*

The partially completed portrait didn't give her so much as a hint or clue.

Perhaps if Jaz could finish it…but she couldn't seem to bear to.

It wasn't that she couldn't bear to. She simply couldn't do it—it was as plain as that. Something blocked her, something stood between her and her ability to find and execute that final essence of Frieda.

Would Frieda want her to take a chance on Connor?

She glanced out of the window again. Sun glinted off his hair and yearning gripped her. But…

No! Fear filled her soul. She couldn't risk it; she just couldn't. She'd won more today than she had ever expected. She had to content herself with that. It would have to do.

The rest of the afternoon breezed along without so much as the tiniest push from Jaz. Everyone agreed that the author readings were a huge hit—not least the authors, who must've sold dozens of their books between them.

Connor packed up the sausage sizzle and disappeared. Jaz did her best not to notice.

Just when she thought the day was starting to wind down, a new buzz started up. Connor stood at the back of the room, in the same spot the guest authors had, calling for everyone's attention.

Jaz blinked and straightened. She chafed her arms and tried to look nonchalant.

'As most of you know, today wouldn't have been possible if it wasn't for one special lady—Jaz Harper.'

She gulped, tried to smile at the applause that broke out around her.

'Jaz returned to Clara Falls to honour her mother's memory, and to make her mother's final dream a reality. I can't tell you all how glad I am to see the town come out in such numbers to support her.'

Jaz noticed then that most of the tourists had wandered off—they'd probably left after the readings. The people who were left were almost all locals.

Connor gestured to the partially completed portrait on the

wall behind him. 'As you can see, Jaz means to leave a lasting memorial of her mother here in Clara Falls. It only seems fitting that the grand finale to the day should be Jaz putting the finishing touches to her mother's portrait. If you agree, put your hands together and we'll get her up here to do exactly that.'

No way! He couldn't force her hand this way. She wouldn't do it. She *couldn't* do it.

But a path had opened up between her and Connor and everyone was clapping. Some people cheered, yet others stomped their feet, and Jaz had no choice but to move forward.

'What is this?' she hissed when she reached him. 'Payback?'

'Just finish the damn picture, Jaz.'

His voice was hard, unrelenting, but when she glanced into his face the gold highlights in his eyes gleamed out at her. 'Connor, I can't.' She was ashamed at the way her voice wobbled, but she couldn't help it.

He took her hands in his. 'What is it you focus on in the photographs that you turn into tattoos? What is it that you see in those photographs of people you don't know, but capture so completely that you bring tears to the eyes of their loved ones?'

She searched his eyes. 'Details,' she finally whispered. She focused on the details—one thing at a time, utterly and completely.

'Will you trust me on this?'

She stared at him for a long moment, then nodded. 'Yes.'

He wouldn't lead her astray on something so important. Even though she had hurt him. She knew that with her whole heart. He would try to help her the way she'd helped him.

He handed her the photograph of her mother. 'Forget that she's your mother, forget that you ever knew her, and focus only on the details.'

She stared at the photograph. The details. Right.

Then he handed her a paintbrush. 'Paint, Jaz.' Only then did she notice that he'd already arranged her paints about her.

Jaz painted. The scent of autumn engulfed her and she painted.

She'd finished the eyes and nose, the brow and the wild hair already. Now she focused on the mouth—the lips wide open in laughter, creases and laughter lines fanning out from the corners. She focused on the strong, square jaw with its beauty spot, then the neck and the shoulders.

She lost herself in details.

As always happened, when Jaz finished the last stroke she had no idea how much time had passed. She set her paintbrush down and stepped back, and the room gave a collective gasp. Jaz heard it for what it was—awe. It meant she'd done a good job.

She couldn't look yet. She needed all those details to fade from her mind first.

She pressed the heels of her hands to her eyes, unutterably weary. Strong arms went around her and drew her in close, soaking her in their warmth and strength. She wanted to shelter in those arms—Connor's arms—for ever. He'd remained standing behind her the entire time she'd painted, his presence urging her on, ordering her to stay focused. And she had.

But she couldn't stay here in his arms. At least, not for ever. She'd already made that decision—she couldn't afford to let the worst of her nature free in the world again.

But, before she was ready to let him go, he was putting her from him. 'Are you ready to see it?'

She pulled in a shaky breath, managed a nod. He eased her back towards the crowd, then slowly turned her around to face her finished artwork.

Jaz stared. And then she staggered as the impact of the portrait hit her. She'd have fallen flat on her face if Connor hadn't kept an arm around her.

Frieda laughing in the sun.

Her mother stood in front of her laughing, filled with happiness and goodwill and her own unique brand of fun, and Jaz ached to reach out and touch her. *This* was how Frieda would want Jaz to remember her. *This* was how Frieda would want everyone to remember her.

Oh, Mum, I loved you. You did know that, didn't you?

Yes. The word drifted to her on an autumn-scented breeze and suddenly her cheeks were wet with all the tears she hadn't yet shed. The tightness in her chest started to ease.

Oh, Mum, what do I do?

No answer came back to her on a breeze—autumn-scented or otherwise, but the answer started to grow in Jaz's heart the longer she stared at Frieda's portrait.

Be happy. That was what her mother would say. It was all that Frieda had ever wanted for her.

Did she dare?

She scrubbed the tears from her cheeks with hands that shook, then turned to face the hushed crowd that stood at her back. 'I want to thank you all for coming here today—for supporting me and Frieda and the bookshop. If she could, I know my mother would thank you too.' She paused, dragged in a breath. 'I came back to Clara Falls with a grudge in my heart, but it's gone now. I've finally realised my true home is here in Clara Falls and—' she found herself smiling '—it's good to be back.'

The crowd broke into a loud round of applause. Mr Sears brought it back under control after what seemed like an age. 'Okay, folks, that's officially the end to the book fair...' he sent Jaz a sly look '...for this year, at least.'

Good Lord!

She thought about it. An annual event? The idea had merit.

'Now, there's still plenty of cleaning up to be done,' Mr Sears continued, 'so those of you who are willing to stick around...'

Jaz couldn't help but grin as he took control.

Connor touched her arm. 'Jaz. I... It's time I headed off.'

The golden lights in his eyes had disappeared. Leaving? But...no! She didn't want him to go.

Her mouth went dry. *She didn't want him to go.* It hit her then. Denying herself the chance of building a life with Connor, of being with him—that was hurting her just as much as his lack of faith in her had eight years ago.

Did that mean she'd turn back into that desperate, destructive person she feared so much?

She all but stopped breathing. Her fingernails bit into her palms. She hunched into herself and waited for the blackness, the anger, to engulf her again…and kept waiting.

She lifted her head a little, dragged in a shaky breath, and counted to three. She lifted her head a little higher, and slowly it dawned on her. The blackness—it wasn't coming back.

She'd learned from the mistakes of the past.

She was stronger, older, wiser.

She wasn't afraid any more!

She wanted to dance. To sing and dance and—

She glanced into Connor's face and the singing and dancing inside her abruptly stopped. Had she left it too late? Had Connor finally run out of patience…and love?

She glanced at Frieda's portrait, then back at Connor.

'I love you.' She said the words as simply and plainly as he had to her earlier in the day. She didn't know if it was too late to say them or not. She only knew she had to say them.

Connor froze. He backed up a step. 'What did you just say?'

She grew aware that the people nearest to them had turned to stare. She leaned in close to him and whispered the words again. 'I love you, Connor.'

He threw his head back, his eyes blazed. 'Are you ashamed of your feelings or something?'

'No, I'm not ashamed that I love you, Connor.' She said the words, loud and proud. 'It's just that guys aren't as gushy-gushy as girls and I thought you might like to have this conversation in private, that's all.'

He just stared at her. He didn't move. He didn't say anything. He had to have heard her. She'd said it three times!

'It's customary for the boy to kiss the girl at this point,' Mrs Lavender pointed out. 'And if that is your intention, Connor Reed, then I definitely suggest you find yourself some privacy.'

Her words acted on him like magic. He grabbed Jaz's hand,

pulled her through the stockroom, out through the kitchenette and all the way outside. He dropped her hand again and swung around to stare at her.

'You're not kissing me yet,' Jaz couldn't help but point out.

'Not yet.' He pointed a finger at her. It shook. 'You say that you love me.'

'Yes.'

'Why the change of heart?'

'It's not really a change of heart. I've always loved you.' The way she sensed he'd always loved her.

'What made you change your mind about taking the risk?'

'Frieda.' She said her mother's name simply. 'I couldn't finish her portrait because I was blocked. I was blocked because you were right. I wasn't living my life the way she'd have wanted. When I looked at the finished portrait I finally realised what she'd want me to do.'

He frowned. 'To tell me you love me?'

'To be happy,' she corrected softly. 'And being with you is what makes me the happiest.'

His eyes darkened with intent then. Her pulse leapt. He moved towards her…

It started to rain.

'I don't believe this,' Jaz murmured under her breath. 'Not now!'

She glanced from the sky with its lowering clouds to Connor. 'We could…er…always go up to my flat.'

The gold highlights in his eyes glittered. He reached out and captured her chin in his strong callused fingers. 'If you invite me up there, Jaz, I won't be leaving any time soon.'

A thrill shot through her. The rain continued to fall around them. 'Where's Melly?' she managed.

'With my parents. My father is going to drop her off at Yvonne's party tonight.'

Jaz stared up at the rain again, then back at Connor. 'So you don't have anywhere you need to be tonight?'

'No.'

'Then…'

'Then…?' he mimicked.

Jaz groaned. 'Kiss me, Connor.'

He did.

When he lifted his head, long moments later, she could hardly breathe let alone stand. 'Come on.' When the strength returned to her limbs, she grabbed his hand and headed up the stairs and to her flat.

Connor took the keys from her fingers and turned her to face him, heedless of the rain. 'I'm not prepared to lose you a second time, Jaz. I want you to know that this—' he nodded at the door '—is for keeps. I need to know that you feel the same way.'

Her heart expanded until she thought it might burst. 'For keeps,' she whispered. She'd never been surer of anything in her life. It made a mockery of all her previous doubts.

'For ever?' he demanded.

'And ever,' she agreed.

He rested his forehead against hers. 'I love you with all that's in me, Jaz Harper. Promise me you will never run away again. I don't think I could bear it.'

His eyes darkened with remembered pain. She reached up and brushed his hair from his forehead. 'I promise.' Then she kissed him with all the love in her heart.

They were both breathing hard when she drew back.

'In return,' he rasped, holding her gaze, 'I swear to you that I will always listen to you. I won't jump to stupid conclusions.'

'I know,' she said. But it suddenly occurred to her that, even if he did, they were both stronger now. Together, they could overcome anything.

She didn't know why, but she found herself suddenly laughing in his arms, so glad to be near him and loving him, revelling in the freedom of it.

'What do you young people think you're doing up there?' Mrs Lavender called from below, her voice tart with outrage.

'Don't you know it's raining? Get inside with you before you catch your deaths!'

'Better do what the lady says,' Connor said with a lazy grin, unlocking the door.

Jaz's heart leapt. 'Absolutely,' she agreed, the breath catching in her throat.

He held his hand out to her. She placed hers in it. Together they stepped over the threshold.

OUTBACK BACHELOR

BY
MARGARET WAY

Margaret Way, a definite Leo, was born and raised in the subtropical River City of Brisbane, capital of the Sunshine State of Queensland. A Conservatorium-trained pianist, teacher, accompanist and vocal coach, she found her musical career came to an unexpected end when she took up writing—initially as a fun thing to do. She currently lives in a harbourside apartment at beautiful Raby Bay, a thirty-minute drive from the state capital, where she loves dining *al fresco* on her plant-filled balcony, overlooking a translucent green marina filled with all manner of pleasure craft: from motor cruisers costing millions of dollars, and big, graceful yachts with carved masts standing tall against the cloudless blue sky, to little bay runabouts. No one and nothing is in a mad rush, and she finds the laid-back village atmosphere very conducive to her writing. With well over one hundred books to her credit, she still believes her best is yet to come.

PROLOGUE

THE night before she was to make her sad journey back to Djinjara, after a self-imposed absence, Skye's dreams were filled with vivid childhood memories of life on the great station. Those had been the halcyon days when Djinjara had been the centre of her universe, the days before she had become overpowered by the McGoverns, cattle barons prominent among the nation's great landed families. Broderick McGovern had been master of Djinjara when she had been growing up; a man with tremendous obligations and responsibilities, greatly respected by all. Keefe, his elder son, had been the heir. Scott, next in line, the difficult one, burdened with sibling rivalry issues, always making it his business to stir up discord. Rachelle, the youngest, was rather good at stirring up trouble herself, but happily for the McGovern dynasty Keefe was everything he was supposed to be. And much more.

By the time she was five she had fallen totally under his spell. She couldn't imagine life without Keefe in it! A deprived child, struggling with the loss of a mother and a mother's love and guidance, she found Keefe to be a source of continual comfort, delight and admiration. He commanded her world. It was a role her hard-working, grieving father didn't seem able to fill. At least not for a long time. Skye's father, Jack McCory, was a man who had never come to terms with losing his beautiful young wife Cathy in childbirth. Thereafter, he lamented it would never have happened only Cathy had insisted on having her child on the station instead of at Base Hospital.

By such decisions was our fate determined.

In her early years Skye couldn't understand her father's deep melancholy, neither as a child could she be expected to, though she always tried to ease it by being a good girl and putting her mind to her lessons at the station school. Her teacher, Mrs. Lacey, always embarrassed her, instructing the other children, offspring of station employees, *"Let Skye be an example to you!"*

With Mrs. Lacey, an excellent teacher, she could do no wrong.

"Why shouldn't she praise you?" Keefe commented lazily when she complained. *"You're one bright little kid. And you're really, really pretty!"* This with a playful tug on her blonde curls. Keefe was six years her senior. From age ten he had been sent as a boarder to his illustrious private school in Sydney. The times he was home on vacation were, therefore, doubly precious to her.

Times changed. People changed with them. It wasn't unusual for the bonds of childhood not to survive into adulthood. By the time Keefe became a man he was no longer the Keefe who had laughed at her, listened to her, tolerated her showing-off, taken her up on his shoulders while she squealed her pleasure at the top of her lungs. The *adult* Keefe not only filled her with awe, he came close to daunting her. Even when he was looking straight at her she imagined he was looking *through* her. Something absolutely fundamental between them had changed. What made it all that much harder to bear was it seemed to happen overnight.

Their respective roles became blindingly clear.

She could never, not *ever*, enter Keefe McGovern's adult world.

Despite her strenuous efforts to distance herself, and make her own way in life, Keefe continued to live on in her mind and her dreams. He was her shooting star, with all a star's grandeur. Not with the best will in the world could she change that. Obsessions, unlike many friendships, remained constant.

It had been devastation of a kind after she had made the break to go to university. It had become very important for her to separate herself from the McGoverns. Separate from Keefe, her hero. Even the thought made her weep, but her tears fell silently down the walls of her heart.

Keefe! Oh, Keefe!

Had *it* really happened those few years ago, or had she imagined it all? *Remember.* Oh, yes it had happened.

No young men she had met thereafter—and she had met many who were attracted to her—could measure up to Keefe. Now twenty-four she was making a success of her life even if she continued to feel deeply obligated to the McGoverns. Their interest in her had secured her bright future. McGovern money had paid for her expensive education. Her father explained years later that Lady McGovern, grandmother to Keefe, Scott and Rachelle, had insisted that fact be keep quiet.

"Skye is not to know. But she's such a clever child she must be given the best possible chance in life."

Although Lady McGovern had always been a majestic figure, as aloof as royalty, in all truth she had been oddly protective of a lowly employee's young daughter. That alone had caused the ever-deepening rift between Rachelle and herself. Rachelle had a jealous nature. She loved both her brothers, but it was Keefe she adored. It was Keefe's attention Rachelle always fought for.

If it were true that some mothers couldn't give up their sons to girlfriends and wives, it was equally true that some sisters were unwilling to take a back seat in their brother's affections. Rachelle hung in there, determined Skye would never be allowed to stake a claim on the family. Skye was always *"the pushy little daughter of—can you believe—a station hand? Always trying to ingratiate yourself with our family."* Reading between the lines, that meant Rachelle's adored brother, Keefe. These were just a couple of the insults Rachelle tossed off like barbed arrows.

Over time, the insults worsened.

"You're to be pitied. You may be chocolate-box pretty, but you're so disadvantaged by your background. You'll never be accepted into our world. So don't even try!" The tone Rachelle employed was so caustic she might have been trying to skin the younger girl alive. Skye learned early in life all about jealousy. It was to her credit such jealousy hadn't crushed her. Rather, the reverse. She learned to stand up for herself. McGovern wealth, status and their pastoral empire gave them uncommon power. They certainly had power over her. Even in her dreams Keefe and Djinjara didn't let go.

As she lay sleeping on that heated and stormy November evening, with the air-conditioner running full blast, she became trapped in that idyllic past as images began to flood her mind. So vivid were they, they brought into play all five of her senses. She could actually *smell* things, *feel* things, *hear* things, *taste* things. She could *see* all the rich colours, observe the legions of tiny emerald and gold budgies that flew overhead in their perfect squadron formations. It was stunning how clearly she was able to open a window on the past, a traveller in time…

She was five and back on Djinjara. Her father Jack was then a Djinjara stockman, later a leading hand, rising to overseer by the time she was ten. It was around about puberty that life abruptly became *different*. Suddenly out of nowhere she felt the weight of strange longings; an urgency and a hunger for sight and sound of Keefe, a pressing need for his company. She only saw him when they came together in the school vacations. It was way too long in between. What she was feeling, had she known it, was desire, but she was too young to recognise it. That was as well, for it was ill advised. Whatever Skye desired, it was never going to happen. Her intuitive response was to modify her warm, open manner to avoid embarrassing herself and, God forbid, Keefe.

In the academic year following her twelfth birthday she was stunned to learn she was to be sent away to Rachelle's prestigious girl's school. She had never thought such a thing could happen. The fees alone were way, way beyond her father's modest means; the choice of such a college not even considered by a parent in Jack McCory's position in life. This was a school for the social elite.

It took Skye years to find out the McGoverns had paid the fees. But back then, to make her father proud, she had worked very hard, graduating five years later with a top score. That score had enabled her to go to the university of her choice and study law. Her driving interest had become women's affairs. She wanted to be in a position to help women facing serious legal problems, especially women facing such problems alone.

In her dream that hot, humid night, she was a child again, standing transfixed, holding fast to Keefe's hand. They were looking out on an enchanted world of wildflowers. Never in her short life had she seen such an extraordinary spectacle! It was so beautiful it made her heart ache.

"The miracle after years of drought!" Keefe's voice lifted on a note of pride and elation. *"The desert wildflowers have arrived,*

little buddy!" He often called her "little buddy" in those days. It was like real affection flowed between her and this Outback prince. That year, when she turned five, the flowers were out in their millions. They came in the wake of a major cyclone in the tropical Far North. The run-off floodwaters poured in great torrents down the interior's Three Rivers System. They reached right into the Red Heart, spilling out of the infinite maze of intricate, interlocking waterways of the Channel Country, bringing great rejoicing even though station after station was left stranded in an inland sea.

In her dream, the flowers blazed their way across the great golden spinifex plains, climbed the fiery red pyramids of the sand dunes, spread right to the feet of the distant hills that always appeared to her child's eye like ruined castles full of mystery and past splendours. The flowers were dazzling white, bright yellow, all the pinks and oranges, mauve into violet, vibrant reds, their colours dancing in the breeze. They were the loveliest creations she had ever seen, their beauty hazy under the golden desert sun.

"Thought you might like to see them." Keefe smiled down at her, pleased with her evident excitement, an excitement he shared. Marvellously handsome and clever, he was home for the long Christmas-New Year vacation.

"Oh, Keefe, it's *magic*!" She clapped her hands, transported out of herself with joy. Even at that age she felt deeply. *"Thank you, thank you, for bringing me."*

"No need to thank me. I knew how much you'd love it. You're our little Outback princess."

In retrospect it was a very strange thing for him to say, though as a five-year-old she accepted it as a joke. In return she gave him her purest little girl smile, thrilled and excited he had thought of her. Really, she was just another little kid on the station, yet he had actually come in search of her, taking her up before him on his beautiful, fleet-footed thoroughbred mare,

Noor, one of the finest in Djinjara's stables. Keefe could ride her. Keefe could ride anything. He was tall for his age, with the promise of attaining over six feet in manhood.

In her dream he was holding firmly to her hand lest she run excitedly into the shimmering sea of paper daisies that could easily shelter a dragon lizard that might not take kindly to being disturbed. Keefe was there to protect her as well as show her the wild flowers. He was no ordinary boy. He didn't look it. He didn't sound it. Even then he had been one of those people with enormous charisma. And why not? He was Keefe McGovern, heir to Djinjara.

Her father was often required to go away on long musters, leaving Skye for days, sometimes weeks. She was almost an orphan, except everyone on the station looked out for her. She even had a nanny called Lena, a gentle, mission-educated aboriginal lady appointed by Lady McGovern, stern matriarch of the family. When her father was away on those long musters Lady McGovern allowed her and Lena to stay at the Big House. That was the name everyone on the station called Djinjara homestead. It was a *palace*, so grand and immense! She and her dad lived in a little bungalow that would have just about fitted into Djinjara's entrance hall. Her dad had impressed on her that it was a "great honour" to be allowed to stay at the Big House. So she had to be a good girl.

It was easy. No one upset or frightened her. Well…Rachelle did, but she was finding her way around that. There was something nasty about Rachelle, two years her senior. But even though she was little, Rachelle didn't intimidate her. It was her duty to be a good, brave girl and not worry her father, who worked so hard.

In her dreamscape she was weaving her small fingers in and out of Keefe's strong brown hand. *"I really love you, Keefe."*

He smiled, his light eyes like diamonds against his tanned skin. *"I know, little buddy."*

"Will you marry me when I grow up?"

At this point Skye woke abruptly. It was then the tears came.

CHAPTER ONE

FOLLOWING instructions, she took a domestic flight to Longreach, where she was to be met by Scott who would fly her back to the station. She was none too happy about that. She hadn't forgiven Scott. And she had tried.

The news of Broderick McGovern's death had been broken to her by her father, who had worshipped the man. A short time later the news broke on radio, T.V. and the Internet. Broderick McGovern, billionaire "Cattle King", had been killed in a helicopter crash while being ferried to a McGovern outstation on the border of the Northern Territory. He, the pilot and another passenger, a relative and federal politician, had been killed when the helicopter, flown by an experienced pilot, simply "fell out of the sky", according to a lone witness who had been rounding up brumbies at the time.

No one had been prepared for this violent assault by Fate.

Keefe McGovern, 30, Broderick McGovern's elder son, was now master of Djinjara, the historic Outback station. Mr McGovern could not be reached for comment. The family was said to be in total shock. Broderick McGovern had only been 55 years of age.

Such had been his stature, not only as one of the country's richest men, a philanthropist and premier cattle producer, that the Prime Minister announced with genuine regret, *"This is a man who will be sorely missed."*

Skye stood under a broad awning, waiting for Scott to arrive. Scott was another one who had a hold on her memory. She wondered if he had matured at all since she had last seen him; wondered if his fierce jealousy of his older brother had abated over time. Both Scott and Rachelle were very much affected by having a brother like Keefe. Instead of making their own mark, they chose to remain in Keefe's long shadow. Scott, who had been trained in the cattle business and played an active role, sadly lacked Keefe's extraordinary level of competence, let alone the leadership qualities necessary in a man who had to run a huge man-orientated enterprise. Still he raged, secretly secure in the knowledge he would in all probability never be called upon. Rachelle, the heiress daughter, made no effort at all to find her own niche in the world. She preferred to live on Djinjara and take numerous holidays at home and abroad whenever she found herself bored.

To Skye it was an empty, aimless life. She had no idea what would have happened had Scott been his father's heir instead of Keefe. Instead, Scott and Rachelle acted as if their lives had been mapped out for them.

Goodness, it was hot! Far, far hotter than it ever was in sub-tropical Brisbane, but this was the dry heat of the Outback. Oddly its effects on her were invigorating. She had grown up in heat like this. Even the slight breeze was bringing in the familiar, tantalising scent of the bush. She drew in a breath of the aromatic fragrance, trying to calm herself and unravel the tight knots in her stomach. It wasn't easy, returning to Djinjara, but it was unthinkable not to attend Broderick McGovern's funeral. He had always been kind to her and to her father, who was in genuine mourning.

It wasn't the time to wish it was Keefe who was coming for

her. She knew perfectly well Keefe wouldn't be able to get away. He had taken on his dead father's mantle. But she still had many reservations about Scott. He had always been a chameleon when they had been growing up. Sometimes he had been fun, if a bit wild, other times a darkness had descended on him. He idolised his brother. No question. But to Scott's own dismay he'd had to constantly battle a sometimes overwhelming jealousy of Keefe, the heir. It had made him angry and resentful, ready to lash out at everyone on the station who couldn't answer back without the possible risk of getting fired. That included her father who felt pity for Scott McGovern, the classic second string with all its attendant problems.

When Scott was in his moods, especially as he grew older, station people learned to steer clear of him until the mood passed. Skye in later years realised she was perhaps the only one who had missed out for the most part on Scott's sharp, hurtful ways. It had taken a while for her to become aware that Keefe had always appeared to keep a pretty close eye on them.

Why?

She had found out. And a lot sooner than she had ever imagined. When she had been around sixteen and Scott almost twenty he had fancied himself either in love with her or determined to take advantage of her. Either way, it was the cause of an ongoing simmering tension between the two brothers. One that stemmed from a single violent confrontation.

Over her.

All these years later, Skye remembered that traumatic episode as though it were yesterday…

As she stepped into the deep emerald lagoon, catching her breath at its coldness, Skye became aware someone was watching her. She spun about, calling, "Who's there?"

She wasn't nervous. She felt perfectly safe anywhere on the station. She knew everyone and everyone knew her. There wasn't a soul on the station who hadn't kept an eye on her as she was growing up. They had all known her beautiful mother. They worked alongside her father. The entire station community had as good as adopted her. No one would harm her. She called again, startling a flock of sulphur-crested, white cockatoos that set up a noisy protest. A few seconds later, lanky Scott appeared. He had the McGovern height but not Keefe's great shape. He was dressed in his everyday working gear—skin-tight jeans, checked cotton shirt, riding boots. His hat was tipped down over his face. He had the McGovern widow's peak that looked so dramatic on his older brother but vaguely sinister on him.

"Why didn't you speak?" she asked in surprise. How long had he been watching her from the cover of the tree—three minutes, four? She had stripped down to her turquoise and white bikini, leaving her clothes neatly folded on the sand.

He didn't move. Didn't respond. He remained where he was at the top of the sloping bank, the loose sand bound by a profusion of hardy succulent-type plants with pockets of tiny perfumed white and mauve lilies in between.

"Scott?" she questioned, shading her eyes with her hand. "Is something wrong?"

Suddenly he smiled, spread out his long arms, then half ran, half skidded, like they had done when they had been kids, down the bank to the golden crescent of sand. "Boy, oh, boy, you should get a look at yourself," he whooped. "That's some bikini, girl!"

It wasn't the words, normal enough, but the way he said them that caused her first ever flurry of unease. "Like it?" She answered in a deliberately casual voice, nothing that could remotely sound like a come-on in her tone. "It's new." This was Scott. This was a McGovern. Much was expected of them.

"You have a beautiful body, Skye, baby," he drawled, his

eyes moving very slowly and insolently over her. "Beautiful face. That blonde mane of hair and those sparkly blue eyes!"

He moved closer, tossing his wide-brimmed hat away. "I'm coming in."

She wanted to shout, No! Some expression on his face was causing her alarm. Instead she managed, "Don't, Scott."

For answer he began to strip off his shirt. "Don't tell me what I can and can't do, Skye McCory."

It sounded remarkably like a threat. That put the fight into her. "Well, you'll have to swim alone," she announced crisply. "I'm coming out. I have things to do."

"What things?" He spoke disparagingly, sounding a bit too much like his sister for comfort. "Don't try to disappear on me," he warned.

Now he was stripping off his jeans.

A voice inside told her things had changed. In his briefs, she couldn't avoid seeing he was sexually aroused. Immediately she decided to change tack and strike out for the opposite bank. What then? She was a good swimmer with a lot of pace. Scott was coming after her. What was his plan, to trap her? Not only cold water washed over her. She felt the icy finger of panic. She couldn't help knowing males got intense pleasure from looking at her these days. Even her friends at boarding school teased her all the time about the crushes their brothers had on her.

She reached the jade shallows, pulling herself up out of the water, her heart banging against her ribs. Swiftly she shook back her long hair. It had come free of its plait. Where to now? Take one of the trails?

Scott pulled himself out of the water seconds after her, his grin tight. "What's the matter with you?" he challenged.

She put her arms around herself, shielding her small breasts, their contours enhanced by the snugly fitting bra top from his view. "What's the matter with you is more to the point?" she said sharply. "You're upsetting me, Scott." Indeed, he was changing her perception of him.

His answer was to lurch towards her, fixing her with a look that dismayed her. He easily pinned her wrists, because he was very much taller and stronger. "I want to kiss you. I want you to kiss me back."

Part of her brain searched for words to stop him but couldn't find them. He was overstepping the boundaries and he knew it. "Are you mad?" She got ready to aim a well-deserved kick at his groin. She was an Outback-bred girl. She knew all the ways a lone woman could defend herself.

"Mad for you." There was the fierce glow of lust in his eyes.

She looked around her quickly. On this side of the lagoon the trees grew more thickly. There was sunlight coming in streams through the canopy, lighting up the trails taken by horses and riders. This particular lagoon was her favourite swimming spot, one of many on the vast station, but today the whole magnificent wild area seemed threatening and deserted. "Take a deep breath, Scott," she cautioned, wishing Keefe would miraculously ride that way. "Stop this now."

"Stop what?" He leaned closer to her.

"What you think you've started. It's not on. So get yourself together. Remember who you are."

Scott set his jaw, his handsome face turning grim. "I'm not Keefe. Is that it? I'll never be Keefe. Keefe is the one you want." His grip on her wrists became punishingly hard as his pathological jealousy grew.

She responded with heat. "You're hurting me, Scott." She wasn't about to show her fear. She stood her ground, even if inwardly she cringed.

Abruptly he released her, but just as she relaxed, one of his hands reached out to caress her breast. He wasn't toying with her. He was dead serious.

She flung herself backwards and dashed a tear from her eye. Surely she wasn't crying? She never cried. A small fallen branch lay on the sand. She bent sideways to pick it up. If she had to defend herself, she would. She knew with Scott in this mood something bad could happen to her.

He found it too easy to create fear in her. Scott appeared to be enjoying her efforts at evasion. "Give up," he advised with a brittle laugh. "I'm really mad about you, Skye. That's what I'm tryin' to tell you. Don't you care?"

There was a hard knot at the base of her breastbone. "I care that you're making a huge mistake, Scott." Her voice was tight with strain. "You're my friend. You're Scott. You can't be anything more to me."

He struck like lightning. She landed a stinging lash on his arm. The tanned skin reddened immediately but he didn't look at the welt, or appear to feel it. No matter how much she wished otherwise, there was no mistaking her imminent danger and his raw intent. Scott meant to have his way. Kiss her? Or take her forcibly? Anything was possible. Who was she to him anyway? Only the overseer's daughter. Dozens of girls would gladly have swapped places with her, no matter the risk. Scott McGovern mightn't be his brother, but he was still a great catch.

"Now, what makes you think that?" he asked with slow menace. "I tell you, Skye, you've turned into the sexiest thing on two legs."

I'm scared but I can't show it.

Find me, Keefe. Find me.

She concentrated on sending her message out into the great plains. "This isn't going to work, Scott. You'd better find someone else."

"I don't want anyone else." He cut her off with a chopping motion of his hand. "And when I make up my mind, I don't change it."

"Then go to hell!" she shouted, adrenalin flooding into her blood. *"You're acting like a bully and a coward."*

It was a mistake.

Scott reached for her, wrapping one arm around her. *"This can work, Skye if you let it."*

"No. No. And no!" She fought back, digging in her nails.

"Too ordinary for you, am I? I'm not Keefe."

She threw back her head. *"Keefe would never force a woman,"* she cried with utter conviction.

"Wouldn't have to, would he? You'd let him take you in a minute!" There was rage and bitter resentment in Scott's blue eyes as he repeated his resentment of his older brother. He went to kiss her and she turned her face, both of them recoiling abruptly as a familiar voice came from behind them in a barely contained roar of ferocity.

"What the hell is going on here?"

Keefe's tall, wide-shouldered, lean figure came stalking along the narrow sunlit corridor. His body language was wrathful. He looked blazingly angry, angrier than Skye could ever have imagined. Keefe was famous for keeping his cool.

Now it was Scott's turn to be intimidated. Instead of attempting an answer, he appeared ludicrously shocked, while Skye found herself moaning her relief. With no thought to her actions, she ran to Keefe's side, grasping his hard, muscled arm, feeling the heat of rage sizzle off his skin.

"Okay, I guess I know what was happening," he rasped, shoving Skye bodily behind him. *"You can't help yourself, can you, Scott? The only thing that concerns you is getting what you want."*

"And I would have got it if you hadn't turned up. Skye has the hots for me."

"Believe that, and you'll believe anything," Keefe bit off with disgust. He closed the short distance to where his brother

stood, grabbing hold of his bare shoulder with such force Scott winced. "Goddammit, Scott," Keefe groaned in a kind of agony. "I'm repulsed by you. Where's your sense of decency? Your sense of honour?

"You got the lot," Scott retorted with sudden venom, trying unsuccessfully to break his brother's iron grasp. "You want her yourself."

Keefe's expression was daunting. "What you're saying is what I want, you must take for yourself."

"Well, she is one alluring little chick!"

That was when Keefe hit him. Scott dropped to the sand with blood streaming from his nose. He tried to get up, fell back again, moaning. "Can't say I didn't have that coming," he wailed, as unpredictable as ever.

"You bastard!" Keefe raged with a mix of horror and regret. "You never can deal with the consequences of your actions. Why do you let your dark side take you under?'

Skye, who had been frozen to the spot, now rushed to Keefe's side. She had to make an attempt to allay his rage. "Don't hit him again, Keefe. Please. Nothing happened."

"Keep out of this," Keefe warned, with the blackest of frowns. "Get dressed and go home."

His anger sparked an answering anger in Skye. "Don't treat me like a child."

He turned on her, his silver-grey eyes so brilliant they bored right into her. "A child?" he ground out. "You're no longer a child, Skye. You're a woman, with all a woman's power. My brother isn't such a monster."

"She's temptation on legs," Scott offered from his prone position on the sand. To his mind that exonerated him from all blame.

"Shut up!" Keefe violently kicked up the sand near him,. "Apologise to Skye. Tell her you were acting crazy. Tell her such

a thing will never happen again. And it won't, believe me. This is your one and only warning. You'll have me to deal with."

Scott wilted beneath his brother's fury and disgust. *"You won't tell Dad,"* he choked, his hand pressed to his bleeding nose.

"Dad?" Keefe roared. *"Apologise to Skye. How could you begin to betray her trust?"*

Shaking all over, Skye fervently wished for her clothes, which were lying in a tidy pile on the opposite bank. As it was, she had to stand there, receiving the attention she didn't want. Her brief bikini barely covered her. Even now she couldn't believe what Scott had done. A woman's beauty came with inherent dangers. Beauty brought fixations and unwelcome attention. The last thing in the world she wanted was to rouse the brute in a man. Now Scott! She had never dreamed she would be in this position, coming between the two brothers. She was the innocent party here, yet Keefe appeared to be so furious with her she might as well have been as guilty of wrongdoing as Scott.

Scott took the opportunity to stagger to his feet, gingerly feeling his jaw. Pain lanced up into his head. *"I'm sorry, Skye,"* he mumbled. *"You know a lot about me so you know from time to time I run off the rails. I would never hurt you. I just wanted a kiss."*

"A kiss and the rest!" Keefe shouted, hooked into his rage.

"You sure pack a punch, Keefe. You really hurt me." Unbelievably Scott appeared to be feeling sorry for himself.

"You're lucky I didn't pummel you into the ground," Keefe cried.

"Damn! Damn everything," Scott moaned. *"So what am I supposed to do now, avoid her?"*

"What you're supposed to do is what you've been reared to do. Treat Skye—all women—with respect. You think Dad would be angry? What about Gran? She'd have you horsewhipped."

"She would, too." Scott suddenly grinned.

"Oh, please, please, stop," Skye begged.

Only then did Keefe turn to stare at her. "Are you okay?"

She was caught in that diamond-hard star, so fierce she almost felt terror. "I told you. He didn't touch me." All she wanted was for this dreadful episode to be over.

Keefe's laugh was a rasp. "Only because I turned up. I'll never know why I came this way. I thought I heard you calling me."

She had been.

The part of him beyond reason had clearly heard her.

A few minutes elapsed before a small airport runabout swept into sight. It pulled up beside her and the driver got out, coming around the rear of the vehicle. Skye gave a convulsive gasp. Some emotions were so extreme they couldn't be put to rest.

Keefe.

The world she had tried hard to build up for herself started to disintegrate and turn to rubble.

All you've got to do is breathe in and breathe out. Breathe in. Breathe out.

It was the voice of reason, only it took several seconds before she could even swallow. Inside she felt a piercing thrill of the old excitement. Outside a near-paralysis. Focusing hard, she drew a deep calming breath into her lungs. It didn't quell the clamour. Her nerves were bunched tight. How did she hide her enormous vulnerability when it was pitted against a towering wave of pleasure?

He was even more handsome in maturity, but harder, tougher, severe of expression. All traces of that wonderful tenderness had gone. Some might say his arresting good looks were a bit on the intimidating side, given the air of gravitas and authority he projected. She knew strangers had sometimes mistaken that aura for arrogance. They were wrong. It was Keefe's heightened sense of responsibility, of being who he was, instilled in him from childhood. He looked stunningly fit from a lifetime of hard physical activity. His darkly tanned skin glowed richly. His thickly curling sable hair worn longer than was usual—hairdressers were few and far between in the bush—was swept back from his forehead in the manner of some medieval prince. Strong and distinctive as his features were, they were dominated by his remarkable wide-set eyes. They were a mesmerising silver-grey, brilliant, crystal clear, yet impossible to read.

He didn't smile. Neither did she.

The air crackled as it did when an electrical storm approached. They stood there studying one another in silence. Skye felt a deep, sharp sadness. As for Keefe, she couldn't read him. As in everything, for so long now, he was an enigma. He had distanced himself from her as she had distanced herself from him. But what did he *really* want of her? What did she want of him? What were the changes each one of them saw in the other? She was ill prepared for this confrontation. Had she known Keefe was to come for her, she could have worked on some defence strategy.

Don't kid yourself, girl. Such a strategy doesn't exist.

There was always drama around the McGoverns. Instead of Scott, Keefe had appeared. The man she dreamed about, so often and so vividly, that it was as if he was in bed with her. He was dressed in a khaki bush shirt with epaulettes and buttoned-down pockets, close-fitting jeans, beaten-copper-buckled leather belt, glossy riding boots on his feet. Everyday wear, but quality all the way. There was something utterly compelling about a splendid male body, she thought raggedly, the height, the width of shoulder, the narrowness of waist and hip descending into long, long straight legs.

"It's good to see you, Skye." Finally he spoke. "Weren't waiting long?"

She readied herself. His voice, like the rest of him, carried a natural command. It had become more and more like his father's; the timbre deep and dark, the accent polished and slightly clipped. "No more than five minutes," she said with admirable composure. She had to force the adrenalin rush down. "I wasn't expecting you, Keefe. I was told Scott was coming."

"Well, *I'm* here," he said, looking directly into her eyes.

He was so beautiful! All strength and sinew with an intense sexual aura. Her entire body leapt to vivid life, sparks coursing like little fires along her veins. What she felt for Keefe couldn't be easily governed. Even her nerves were like tightly strung wires humming and vibrating inside her. How long had it been since she had felt this mad surge of excitement? Not since the last time she had been with him. Years of loving Keefe. Years of unfinished business. It was like they were tied together against their wills. She pulled in a deep breath, keeping her tone neutral.

"And thank you. I appreciate it." No way could she betray the tumult in her heart. "I'm so very sorry about your father, Keefe. I know how hard it must be for you."

His glittering gaze moved to the middle distance. "Forgive me, Skye. I can't talk about it."

"Of course not. I understand."

"You always did have more sensitivity than anyone else," he commented briefly, reaching for her suitcase. It was heavy—she had packed too much into just one case—but he lifted it as though its weight was negligible. "We'd best get away. As you can imagine, there's much to be done at home."

She shook her head helplessly. "You didn't *have* to come for me, Keefe."

He paused to give her another searing glance. "I *did*."

Ah, the heady magnetism of his gaze! She moved quickly, letting her honey-blonde hair cascade across one side of her face. Anything to hide the wild hot rush of blood. She opened the pas-

senger door, then slid into the seat. All the years she had spent
mounting defences against Keefe…!

You still have no protection.

Their flight into Djinjara couldn't have been smoother. Keefe
was an experienced pilot. But, then, his skills were many, all burnished to a high polish. He had been groomed from childhood
to take over leadership from his father.

They were *home*.

Djinjara was still—would always be—the best place in the
world. The vastness, the freedom, the call of the wild. There was
a magic to it she had never found in the city, for all the glamour
of her hectic life there. She had made many friends. Some of them
in high places. She was asked everywhere. She had a stack of
admirers. She knew she was rated a fine, committed advocate.
Her clients trusted her, looked to her to get them through their
difficult times. Her career was on the up and up. Yet, oddly,
though she had hoped to gain great satisfaction from it all, that
hadn't happened. Sometimes she felt disconnected from her city
life. Other times she felt disconnected from everything.
Successful on the outside, when she allowed herself time for in-
trospection, she felt curiously *empty*. Starved of what she really
wanted.

Such was the pull of love; the elation, the sense of comple-
tion in being with Keefe. But along with it went long periods of
loneliness.

On the ground, beneath a deliriously blue sky, she marked the
familiar spectacular flights of birds, the shadows beneath the
rolling red sand dunes that stretched across the vast plains. The
sands were heavily embossed with huge pincushions of spinifex
scorched to a dark gold; in the shimmering distance the purple of
the eroded hills with their caves and secret, crystal-clear water-
holes.

Skye drew the unique pungent aromas of the bush into her lungs, realising how much she had missed Djinjara. The mingling wind-whipped scents, so aromatic like crushed and dried native herbs, to her epitomised the Outback. She had a very real feel for the place of her birth, even though her mother had died here giving her life. Not everyone fell under the spell of the bush but Djinjara, from her earliest memories, had held her captive.

They were met by her father. He had been lolling against a station Jeep, a tall whipcord-thin man with a lived-in, interesting sort of face and love for his daughter shining out of bright blue eyes.

"Skye, darling girl! It's marvellous to see you." Jack rushed forward, his hard muscled arms wide stretched in greeting.

"Marvellous to see *you*, Dad." Skye picked up her own pace, meeting up with her father joyously. She went into his embrace, kissing his weathered mahogany cheek. He smelled of sunlight, leather and horses. "I've missed you *so* much."

"Missed you." Jack looked down into his daughter's beautiful face, revelling in her presence, the glorious grace of her. She was so like his beloved Cathy. The way she smiled. The way she *shone*.

"Sad about Mr McGovern," Skye spoke in a low voice.

"Tragic!" her father agreed, dropping his arms as Keefe, who had given father and daughter a few moments alone, came towards them.

Keefe was a stunning-looking man by any standard, Skye thought. Quite unlike any other man she had ever seen. "I'll take you up to the house first, boss," Jack called. "Then I'll drop Skye off."

"Fine," Keefe responded. The force field around him was such it drew father and daughter in. "I know you'll want to

spend this first night together, Jack. You must have much to catch
up on—but I thought as the bungalow is on the small side, Skye
might be more comfortable up at the house for the rest of her
stay." He looked from one to the other. "It's entirely up to you."

Skye's heart leapt, then dropped like a stone. She had no
stomach for the rest of the family, other than Lady McGovern.
"I'll stay with Dad," she answered promptly, "but thank you for
the kind thought, Keefe." Despite herself, a certain dryness crept
into her tone.

"You might want to change your mind, my darling," Jack said
wryly, looking at his beautiful daughter. He was immensely
gratified she wanted to stay with him, but worried the bungalow
really *was* too small.

"Well, see how it goes," Keefe clipped off.

"It's very good of you, Keefe." Jack looked respectfully
towards the younger man.

"Not at all." Keefe turned his splendid profile. "My grandmother will want to see you, Skye."

"Of course." She couldn't miss out on an audience with
Lady McGovern, who would be devastated by the loss of her
son. Pity rushed in. Besides, she could never forget what she
owed the McGoverns for what they had done for her. Albeit
without her knowledge.

Jack watched on, sensing an odd tension between the boss
and his daughter. It hadn't always been like that. Skye had
adored Keefe all the time she had been growing up. Keefe had
been there for her, like an affectionate and protective big brother.
It was only half a joke, suggesting Skye might change her mind.
His beautiful girl, his princess, belonged in a palace, not a
bungalow. Keefe was right. The bungalow wasn't a fitting place
for her now she had grown into a lovely accomplished woman.
A lawyer no less! At home in her city world. His Skye, far more
than the caustic Rachelle, the McGovern heiress, looked and

acted the part, Jack thought with pride. Skye's beauty and her gifts came from her mother. They certainly didn't come from him. He was just an ordinary bloke. He still couldn't believe Cathy, who had come into his life as Lady McGovern's young visitor, had fallen in love with him and, miracle of miracles, agreed to marry him. It had been like a fairy-tale. But, like many a fairy-tale, it had had a tragic end.

CHAPTER TWO

GRIEF was contagious. The faces of the hundreds of mourners who attended Broderick McGovern's Outback funeral showed genuine sadness and a communal sense of loss. There was no trace of mixed emotions anywhere. This was a sad, sad day. He had been a man of power and influence, but incredibly he had gone through life without attracting enemies. The overriding reason had to be that he had been a just man, egalitarian in his dealings; a man who had never wronged anyone and had never been known to go back on his word. Broderick McGovern had been a gentleman in the finest sense of the word.

All the men and most of the women, except for the elderly and the handful of young women who were pregnant, had elected to make the long walk from the homestead to the McGovern graveyard set down in the shadow of a strange fiery red sandstone monolith rising some hundred feet above the great spinifex plain. The McGovern family from the earliest days of settlement had called it Manguri, after one of the tribal gods. The great sandstone pillar did, in fact, bear a remarkable resemblance to a totem figure, only Manguri was the last remaining vestige of a table-topped mountain of pre-history.

Like all the desert monoliths, Manguri had the capacity to change colour through the day, from the range of pinks commencing at dawn, to the fiery reds of noon, to the mauves and the amethysts of evening. It was a fascinating phenomenon. Generations of McGoverns had been buried in Manguri's shadow. Curiously, Skye's own mother was buried in an outlying plot when the custom was for station employees right from the early days to be buried at another well-tended graveyard. In the old days there had been some talk of Cathy being distantly related to Lady McGovern. The rumour had never been confirmed. Certainly not by the McGoverns. As a lawyer, Skye could have checked out her mother's background had she so chosen. Instead, she found herself making the conscious decision *not* to investigate her mother's past. She didn't know why, exactly, beyond a powerful gut feeling. Was she frightened of what she might find? She would admit only to an instinctive unease. Her father had always said her mother had been an orphan Lady McGovern had taken an interest in. Much like her own case.

She wasn't the only young person on the station the McGoverns had sent on to tertiary education either. Most of the sons and daughters of station employees elected to live and work on Djinjara. It was home to them. They loved it and the way of life. But others, of recent times, all young men of exceptional academic ability, had been sent on to university by the McGoverns. One was a doctor in charge of a bush hospital. The others were engineers working in the great minefields of Western Australia.

All three were present today.

Keefe had made it perfectly plain she was expected to come up to the house afterwards, even if her father was not. Jack held an important position as overseer but he knew and accepted his place in the social scheme of things. It was the last thing Skye wanted to do, but her father had urged her and she was painfully aware of her obligations. The scores of ordinary folk who had made the long hot overland trek in a convoy of vehicles were being catered for in huge marquees set up within the extensive grounds of the home compound. The more important folk, the entire McGovern clan, fellow cattle barons and pastoralists along with their families, and a large contingent of VIPs crowded their way into Djinjara's splendid homestead, which had grown over the years since the 1860s when Malcolm James McGovern, a Scottish adventurer of good family, had established his kingdom in the wilds. Oddly, Djinjara with its fifty rooms looked more like an English country mansion that anything else, but Malcolm was said to have greatly admired English architecture and customs and had kept up his close ties with his mother's English family. The bonds remained in place to the present day. Lady McGovern was English, and a distant relative. She had come to Australia, a world far removed from her own, as Kenneth McGovern's—later Sir Kenneth McGovern—bride. In her new home, despite all the odds, she had thrived. And, it had to be said, *ruled*.

Try as she did to move inconspicuously about the large reception rooms and the magnificent double-height library, Skye was uncomfortably aware that a great many people were looking at her. Staring really. She had to contend with the fact she would never melt into a crowd. Not with the looks she had inherited from her mother. Some people she recognised from her childhood but she wasn't sure if they recognised her. Others acknowledged her with genuine warmth and kindly expressed admiration for her achievements. She was dressed in traditional black but she couldn't help knowing black suited her blonde colouring. She had discarded the wide-brimmed black hat that had protected her face and neck from the blazing sun, but she still wore her hair in a classic French pleat. As a hairstyle it looked very elegant, but the pins were making her head ache.

She had sighted Scott with a dark-haired young woman always at his side. She was rather plain of face, conservative in her dress for her age—the black dress was slightly too large for her—but she had a look of intelligence and breeding that saved the day. Jemma Templeton of Cudgee Downs. Skye hadn't seen her for a few years but she was aware Jemma had always had a crush on Scott. Rachelle, stick thin, fine boned and patrician-looking—the McGoverns were a very good-looking family—kept herself busy moving from group to group, carrying her responsibilities, it could be said, to the extremes. Rachelle was more about form than feeling. Doing what was expected. The show of manners. She had never shown any to the young Skye. Skye knew Rachelle had spotted her but had determined on not saying hello unless forced into it. Rachelle didn't have *friends*—hadn't even at school. As a McGovern she only had minions.

I bring out the worst in her, Skye thought regretfully. And there's nothing I can do about it. Rachelle will never make peace with me. She resents me bitterly. And it's all about Keefe.

She turned away just as a rather dashing young man with close-cropped fair hair rushed to stand directly in front of her, obscuring her view. "Skye, it is you, isn't it?" he burst out with enthusiasm. "Of course it is! Mum said it was. That blonde hair and those blue eyes! You're an absolute knockout!"

Skye had to smile at such enthusiasm. "Why thank you, Robert." Robert Sullivan was one of the McGovern clan, the grandson of one of Broderick McGovern's sisters. He had had three. There had been a younger brother too. But he had died tragically when he had crashed his motorbike on the station when he was only in his early twenties. "You look well yourself. It's been a long time." The last time she had seen Robert had been at a McGovern family Christmas Eve party some years back.

"Too long." He gave an exaggerated moan. "I say, why don't

you come and sit with me? I'll find somewhere quiet. Look at this lot!" His hazel glance swept the room. "They're knocking back food and drink like it was a party. Terrible about Uncle Brod."

"Indeed it is," Skye lamented. "He always seemed so indestructible. The family will miss him greatly." She broke off as her eyes fell on Lady McGovern, who was seated in an antique giltwood high-backed chair not unlike a throne. She was indicating with a slight movement of her hand that she wanted Skye to come over. "Rob, would you excuse me one moment?" she said, placing a hand on Robert's jacket sleeve. "Lady McGovern is beckoning me. I haven't had a chance to offer my condolences as yet."

"Tough old bird," Robert murmured, with not a lot of liking but definite respect. "Not a tear out of her. Stiff upper lip. Straight back. Father was a general, don't you know?"

"Yes, I do," Skye answered a trifle sharply. Robert's words had annoyed her. "Because Lady McGovern doesn't cry in public, it doesn't mean she's not crying inside, Robert. I know she will be grief stricken even if it's her way not to show it."

"Okay, okay." Robert held up placating hands. "Training and all that. She's always made me feel as though I'm not quite up to scratch. Of course, no one *could* be beside Keefe. Come back to me when you've finished paying your respects. I want to hear all about what you've been doing, you clever girl! Mother is very impressed. She spotted you the instant you walked into the room. You *do* stand out. 'Why, that's little Skye McCory all grown up! And she looks simply stunning! One would never know she had such a humble start.'"

Skye hadn't forgotten how patronising the McGoverns were.

"There you are, my dear," Lady McGovern said, indicating with her heavily be-ringed hand an empty chair beside her. Lady

Margaret McGovern was a diminutive woman but she had enormous presence. Even at eighty it was easy to see she once had been a beauty. The bone structure was still there. Her skin stretched very tight over those bones was remarkably soft and unlined.

Skye obeyed. "I'm so very sorry, Lady McGovern," she murmured as she sat down. "I couldn't get to you before with so many people wanting to offer their condolences. I know how much pain you're in. I feel so sad myself. Mr McGovern was a wonderful man. He was always very kind to me."

"Who could not be?" Lady McGovern said. She took Skye's two hands in her own, her face carefully in control of emotions. "Welcome home, Skye."

It was so unexpected, so enormously comforting, that tears sprang to Skye's eyes. *Home?* With an effort of will she forced the tears away. Too many people were watching.

"Let me look at you," Lady McGovern said, turning her full scrutiny on Skye. "You're even more beautiful than your mother. But the colour of your hair is *exactly* the same. The same radiant blue eyes full of expression. She would have been very proud of you."

"Oh, I hope so!" Skye released a fluttery breath. "But I wouldn't be where I am today without *you*, Lady McGovern. I will never forget that."

"Enough of the Lady McGovern!" The old lady spoke as if she were heartily sick of the title. "I want you to call me Margaret, or Lady Margaret if you feel more comfortable with that. Margaret is my name. It's a name long in my own family. I would like you to use it. I rarely hear it any more. It's Gran and Nan, Aunt and Great-Aunt and, I dare say, the Old Dragon. Don't try to tell me you can't do it. I look on you as family, Skye."

That touched a finger to an open wound. Some things would

seem to be hidden, but they couldn't be hidden for ever. "I've always felt something of it," she confessed. "But why? Can't you tell me?" The plea came straight from the heart. "Who *was* my mother really? I never knew her, which is the tragedy of my life. Dad always said she was an orphan." Skye's frown deepened. "He said she spoke beautifully. Not an educated Australian accent, but an English voice. Like you. Was she English?" There was something in Lady McGovern's fine dark eyes that was making Skye very uneasy.

"As a solicitor, Skye, you've made no attempt to trace your mother's background?" Lady McGovern asked with a grim smile. Could it be pain or disapproval?

"Very oddly, *no,* Lady Margaret." Now that she had said it, "Lady Margaret" came surprisingly easily to her tongue.

"You had concerns about what you might find?" Again the piercing regard.

Skye shook her head. "After all, my mother had a connection to you." Though she didn't expect to be answered, Skye prepared herself for whatever might come.

In vain. "I was very fond of her," Lady McGovern said briefly, then changed the subject. "Your use of my name comes sweetly to my ear. Kindly continue to use it, no matter what. I'm fully aware my granddaughter has always been jealous of you. Jealous of Keefe's affection for you. That is her nature. She's going to find it very hard to find a husband if she's expecting someone like Keefe to come along. It won't happen."

"No," Skye agreed quietly. "Rachelle loves both her brothers, but she adores Keefe."

"Exactly." Lady McGovern brushed the topic aside. "I want you to know Cathy herself chose your father."

"But of course!" Skye was startled. "She fell in love with him." She knew she was supposed to hold her tongue but it got away from her. "But how did they find the opportunities to meet? She stayed at the house on her visits. My father at the time was a stockman. Times have changed somewhat, but there was a huge social divide."

"Of course," Lady McGovern acknowledged, as if the divide was still firmly in place. "Nevertheless, Cathy knew Jack McCory was the man for her. And a fine man he is too. He mourns your mother to this day. As do I. Let's not talk any more about this, Skye. It upsets me. I don't know if Jack ever told you, but Cathy knew the baby she was carrying was a girl. She had the name Skye already picked out for you. And doesn't it suit you! Somehow she knew you would have her beautiful sky-blue eyes."

Skye stayed a few minutes more talking to Lady McGovern, but it was obvious others wanted the opportunity to express a few words of sympathy to the McGovern matriarch. She no sooner moved away than Robert Sullivan made a bee-line to her side.

"I don't really know why but you and my great-aunt look more comfortable together than she and Rachelle," he announced. "Why is that, do you suppose?"

"I have no idea, Robert," she responded calmly.

"Neither do I. Just one of those quirky things." Robert took her arm and began to lead her away. "Look, how long are you staying?" He stared down at her smooth honey-blonde head.

"No more than a week." Actually, she had weeks of her leave left. "I only came for the funeral."

"But we've got to meet up." Robert spoke with extraordinary determination. "I've thought of asking Keefe if I can spend a little time here. I'm sure he won't mind. The house is big enough to billet an army."

"But won't you be expected back home?" Robert worked for his father, a well-known pastoralist running both sheep and cattle on a large property on the Queensland/New South Wales border.

"I could do with a break. I'll check it out with Dad. He was as impressed with you as Mother. I want you to come over and say hello. That's if I can find them in this crush. Even in this huge house there's hardly room to move. And just look at Keefe!"

Look at him! Skye couldn't drag her eyes off him. Everything about him pierced her to the heart.

"The minute he enters the room, he's the stand-out figure," Robert said with undisguised envy. "And it's not just his height. He really takes the eye. He's a man with power. And money. Poor old Scott is still as jealous of him as he ever was. Scott really ought to go away and make a life for himself. Rachelle, too, though she spends plenty of time in Sydney and Melbourne."

"I see Scott with Jemma Templeton," Skye sidetracked. She didn't want to discuss Rachelle. "What I remember of Jemma is good."

"But isn't she plain?" Robert groaned, with a pitying look in his eyes. "Talk about a face like a horse!"

"A particularly well-bred one." Skye's eyes were still on Keefe's tall, commanding figure. He looked beyond handsome in his formal funeral attire. "I don't consider Jemma plain at all. She has a look of breeding and intelligence.'

"I suppose. But I bet she'd love to be pretty. And you *are* being kind. I suppose a woman as beautiful as you can afford to be kind. Poor old Jemma must be nuts if she's looking to land Scott. She's mad about him, poor thing!" Robert rushed on with characteristic candour. "Who knows why. Doesn't say much for her intelligence in my book. Scott is trouble. It's the way he goes off like an out-of-control rocket from time to time."

"Whatever, he's always got a whole string of girls after him."

"And Keefe?" Couldn't she control her tongue?

Robert didn't appear to notice the tautness of her tone. "Who knows what's on Keefe's mind?" he mused. "A couple of stayers are hanging in there. Fiona Fraser and Clemmie Cartwright.

You remember them. My money's on Fiona. She's swanning around somewhere. She's stylish, well connected, knows the score, sharp as a tack but beneath that she's the worst of things— a snob."

"And you're not?" Skye gave him a sweetly sarcastic smile.

"Of course I'm not!" He denied the charge. "Mum is, maybe. Clemmie is nicer, totally different, but I don't believe she can fit the bill.'

"Surely it's all up to Keefe?"

"Maybe he hasn't found the woman to measure up?" Robert pondered. "He's a great guy, don't get me wrong. I admire him enormously. I'm not in his league. None of us are, for that matter. The guy's a prince!"

He's always been a prince. My prince.

By late afternoon everyone, with the exception of a few relatives who were staying overnight, had made their way home in the private planes and the charter planes that had been dotted all over the airfield, the half-dozen helicopters, bright yellow like bumblebees, and the convoys of vehicles that would make the return journey overland. Skye, who had returned to Lady McGovern's side as requested, found herself one of the last to leave. She had made her way to the entrance hall when Rachelle suddenly confronted her, a smile on her lips, her eyes cold and flat.

"So, Skye! Sorry I didn't get a minute to speak to you earlier. How are you?"

"I'm well, thank you, Rachelle." Skye spoke gently. "Please accept my condolences. The manner of your father's premature death was terrible. I know you will miss him greatly."

"Of course. He was a great man," Rachelle said stiffly. "How long exactly are you staying?" As usual she was talking down to Skye.

"A few days."

"I'm sure Gran asked you to come up to the house," Rachelle challenged. "To stay, I mean."

"Both Lady Margaret and Keefe invited me but I'm quite happy staying with my father. I won't get in your way, Rachelle, if that's what's bothering you."

Rachelle's face took on an expression of extreme hauteur. "You couldn't bother me if you tried. And I certainly don't like the way you refer to my grandmother as Lady Margaret. She's Lady McGovern to you."

"Why don't you check with your grandmother?" Skye said quietly, preparing to move on. "It was she who asked me to call her that."

Rachelle's dark eyes held a wild glare. "I don't believe you."

Skye ignored her, continuing on her way. On this day of days Rachelle, incredibly, was looking for a fight.

She hadn't been at the bungalow ten minutes before she heard footsteps resounding on the short flight of timber stairs. They didn't sound like her father's. Not at all. They sounded like… She hurried to the front door, gripped by tension. The door wasn't shut. She had left it open to catch a breeze. The bungalow had ceiling fans, but no air-conditioning.

To her complete shock, Keefe stood there, his brilliant eyes stormy. He had changed out of his funeral attire into riding gear. "I tried to catch you at the house," he bit off, almost accusingly, 'but you were pretty quick to get away."

A flicker of temper, born of high emotion, flashed over her face. It had been *the* most dreadful day. "Let me stop you there, Keefe. I was one of the last to leave. Your grandmother didn't want me to stray too far from her side. I don't really know why." She broke off, her eyes filling with apprehension. "Is something the matter?" she asked quickly. "Surely not her?" Lady McGovern was eighty years old.

"No, no." Swiftly he reassured her. "She's retired, of course. Losing Dad has robbed her of all vigour. She was in fine form up until then. But God knows what will happen now! She's lost two sons. And a husband."

"I know," Skye said sadly. "In one way she has lived a life of privilege, but she has suffered a lot. Losing a child must be the greatest loss a woman can ever know." Her head was aching so much she ripped at the pins in her hair, pulling them out one by one and setting them down on the small table by the door. Afterwards she shook her hair free with a sigh of relief, letting it settle into shining masses around her face and shoulders.

"Sometimes you're so beautiful I can hardly endure looking at you," Keefe said abruptly. He reached out suddenly for a handful of her hair, twining it around his hand, pulling on it slightly to draw her closer to him.

"You haven't had to endure me of late," she reminded him with a flare of bitterness.

"Your decision." His tone was just as harsh. He released the silky swathe of her hair. "Can you do something for me, Skye?"

She relented. She had to on this day of days. "Of course I can." She could see the pressure that had been building in him all day. There was a faint pallor beneath his tan. Another sign of his anguish.

"Then get out of that dress." His tone was so short it sounded like an order. "I have the most desperate need to get away from the house. Put your riding gear on. Don't tell me you didn't bring it. I need to ride off some of this torment. It's all been such a nightmare. Dad gone. The memory of that last morning. So businesslike, so matter-of-fact. I never got a chance to tell him how much I loved him, admired and respected him. He was my role model."

"Keefe, he *knew*!" She wanted desperately to touch him but held herself back with an effort of will. "You're everything he wanted and needed in his son, his successor. He knew the empire he built was safe with you. He never mentioned your name without it ringing with love and pride."

He turned his dark head away, his skin drawn taut over his chiselled bones. "Do what I ask. I want to gallop until I drop."

"Why *me*?" She issued it like a challenge. "You have a brother, a sister, yet you come looking for me."

"Of course, *you*," he responded roughly. "Who else?"

It was mutual validation of sorts. "I don't understand you, Keefe," she said on a note of despair. "You push me away. You draw me back in. You make life a heaven and a hell."

"Maybe I only feel complete when you're around." He turned to her with intensity. "I missed you. You didn't come."

That almost sent her over the edge. "You surely didn't think I was about to forgive you for breaking my heart?" she cried fiercely. "You showered me with affection, Keefe. As a child, as an adolescent. You made sure I was never lonely. Your kindness and your patience. It's all etched into my memory. You might have been years and years older instead of only six. Then I grew up. And you took it all away. But not before you took *me*." Her blue eyes blazed.

Colour rose in a tide under his bronzed skin. "It was what *you* wanted." He grasped her by two arms, agony in his expression. "What *I* wanted. Neither of us could stop it. Neither of us tried. It was like it was ordained. Knowing your body meant everything in the world to me, Skye. Don't ever forget it, or downgrade it. It was another stage in our incredible bonding. The intimacy. I have a sister who's struggled all her life with jealousy of you. Consider her feelings for a moment. It was *you* I loved. *You*, Skye. You were so full of life and fun and endless intelligent questions. You *sparkled*. I love Rachelle. She's family. We share the same blood but, terrible to say, often times I don't *like* her."

"And you think you should?" Skye asked a little wildly. "Rachelle was never nice to me. Not for one single minute. She let her jealousy eat her up. Anyway, it's not unusual not to like someone in your family, though I didn't have one, except Dad. Thing is, we can't pick our families. We can't always like them."

"I guess." A muscle throbbed along his jaw. "I have to contend with Scott's jealousy as well. The two of them, my sister and my brother, ruining their lives with jealousy and resentment. Neither of them will find a life for themselves. Rachelle won't consider getting herself a job. There are things she could do, but she's falls back on her trust fund. Who knows what Scott's thought processes are? I've offered him Moorali Downs. It's a chance for him to find his feet. But no! It's all about focusing his weird enmity on me."

"Maybe if he falls in love?" Skye suggested, feeling his distress and frustration. "Finds the right girl? Marries her?"

Keefe laughed grimly. "Scott's fantasy is all about *you*."

That hit her like a blow "But surely he's forgotten me." Her expression revealed she was shocked and appalled. "I saw him with Jemma. She's a very nice young woman."

"Who is wasting her time." Keefe rejected that solution with a kind of anger. "I like Jemma too. She'll make some lucky man a fine wife but it won't be Scott. Scott's choice has to be *my* choice. Scott will always want the woman *I* want. As Gran once said, 'Scott wants to be *you,* Keefe'. That's his huge problem in life. Sibling rivalry is part of Scott's deepest being."

"Then that's a hell of a thing," she said. "Maybe he needs professional help."

"You think he doesn't realise it?" Keefe spoke with a mix of anger and sorrow. "Scott *does* have an insight into his own behaviour. He *knows* what drives him. The tragedy is he doesn't want to change things."

"So this is what it always comes to. I shouldn't have come

back." Skye was painfully convinced it was so. "There's no place for me here, Keefe. I only make matters worse. Remember who I am."

His eyes flashed like summer lightning. "Who you are? I'll tell you. You're a beautiful, bright, accomplished woman. What more do you want? I don't give a damn that you were raised as Jack McCory's little motherless daughter. Jack is a good man. But who in God's name was your mother? That's the real question."

Her head shot up, all sorts of alarms going off. "What do you mean?"

"Why don't you have the courage to allow your concerns—our concerns—to leap to the centre?"

"I have no idea what you mean." She did. There were critical parts of her mother's life that were totally unknown.

"You do," he flatly contradicted, "but I can't handle it now. Take that black dress off, though heaven knows it makes your skin and your hair glow. Leave a note for Jack. Say you've gone riding with me. He'll understand."

"Of course he will!" She cut him off with something of his own clipped manner. "He's my father."

CHAPTER THREE

BIRDS shrieked, whistled, zoomed above their heads, filling the whole world with a wild symphony of sound. They had left the main compound far behind, driving the horses, initially unsettled and hard to saddle, at full gallop towards the line of sandhills, glowing like furnaces in the intermittent, blinding flashes of sun. Aboriginal chanting so ghostly it raised the short hairs on the nape at first floated with ease across the sacred landscape. Now the sound was fading as they thundered on their way.

From time to time crouching wallabies and kangaroos lifted their heads at their pounding progress, taking little time to get out of the way of the horses. Manes and tails flowing, they raced full pelt across the plains, their hooves churning up the pink parakeelya, the succulent the cattle fed on, and sending swirls of red dust into the baked air.

The heat of the day hadn't passed. It had become deadly. Thunderclouds formed thick blankets over a lowering sky. But as threatening as the sky looked—a city dweller would have been greatly worried they were in for an impending deluge—Skye, used to such displays, realised there might be little or no rain in those climbing masses of clouds. A painter would have inspiration for a stunning abstract using a palette of pearl grey, black, purple and silver with great washes of yellow and livid green.

Probably another false alarm, she thought, not that she cared if they got a good soaking. Any rain was a blessing. Her cotton shirt was plastered to her back. Sweat ran in rivulets between her breasts and down into her waistband. There could be lightning. There was a distant rumbling of thunder. She had seen terrifying lightning strikes. A neighbouring cattle baron had in fact been killed by a lightning strike not all that many years previously. Yet oddly she had no anxiety about anything. She was with Keefe.

Half an hour on, as if a staying hand had touched his shoulder, Keefe reined in his mount. Skye did the same. Riders and horses needed a rest. In a very short time the world had darkened, giving every appearance of a huge electrical storm sweeping in. It confirmed to her distressed mind this had been a very sad day. Wasn't that the message being carried across the vast reaches of the station by an elaborate network of sand drums? The chanting and the drums acted as powerful magic to see *Byamee,* Broderick McGovern, safely home to the spirit world.

Keefe took the lead, in desperate need of the quiet secrecy and sanctuary of the hill country. He loved and respected this whole ancient area, with all its implications. The ruined castles with their battlements had a strange mystique, an aloofness from the infinite, absolutely level plains country. It was as though they were secure in the knowledge it was *they* that had been there from the Dreamtime, created by the Great Beings on their walkabouts. The hill country exerted a very real mystical force that had to be reckoned with. Many a Djinjara stockman, white or aboriginal, had over the years claimed they had experienced psychic terror in certain areas, a feeling of being watched when there was no other human being within miles. Keefe knew of many over time, including the incredibly brave explorers, who had tasted the same sensation around the great desert monuments that had stood for countless aeons, especially the Olgas, the aboriginal *Katajuta.* Ayer's Rock, *Uluru,* sacred to the desert tribes, was acknowledged as having a far more benign presence, whereas the extraordinary cupolas, minarets and domes of *Katajuta* projected a very different feeling.

They dismounted, their booted feet making deep footprints in the deep rust-red loam. They saw to the horses, then began moving as one up a sandstone slope to where stands of bauhinia, acacia, wilga and red mulga were offering shade. The powerful sun was sending out great sizzling golden rays that pierced the clouds and lit up the desert like some fantastic staged spectacle.

Skye knew this place well. She had been here many times, mostly with Keefe, at other times on her own to reflect and wonder. This was *Gungulla:* a favourable place. A place of permanent water and a camping spot for white man and aborigine alike. Up among the caves there were drinking holes in the form of big rock-enclosed bowls and basins. There was bush tucker too, all kinds of berries and buds packed with nutrition. One could survive here. She turned to witness a thrilling sight. The summits of the curling, twisting, billowing clouds were rimmed with orange fire.

Keefe had pulled a small blanket from his pack, letting it flap on the wind before spreading it on the sand beneath the clump of orchid trees. He looked up at Skye, standing poised above him, twirling a white bauhinia blossom with a crimson throat in her hand. She had picked the orchid-like flower off one of the trees as she had passed beneath. Keefe indicated that she should sit beside him. She did so, feeling a blend of longing and trepidation. Immediately the little sandhill devil lizards scurried for cover.

"I can't get my head around the fact my father is dead." Keefe spoke in an intense voice. "He was only in his mid-fifties. No great age these days. There's Gran eighty. Dad was *needed.*"

Sympathy and understanding were in her blue eyes. "His

death has put a huge burden on you, Keefe. I know that. You thought you would have more years to grow into the job but the truth is you're ready. You can be at rest about that."

"Well, I'm not!" He wasn't bothering to conceal his grief from her. This was Skye. He was letting it out. "The numbers of us killed in light plane crashes!"

She couldn't argue with that. "But it can't prevent you from flying. Out here flying is a way of life. You were able to come for me."

He made a short bitter sound, more a rasp than a laugh. "I'd come for you no matter what."

She had to press her eyes shut. Block him out. "Don't fill my head with impossible dreams, Keefe." Goaded, she pitched the bauhinia blossom aside. He had hurt her so deeply the wounds would never heal. Yet here she was again defying all common sense.

"Do you dream of me?" he asked abruptly.

It took her breath.

"I dream of *you*," he said, lying back on the rough grey blanket and staring up at the sky.

She looked down at his dark, brooding face. "If we weren't who we are, would you marry me?" How absurd could she get? She waited. He didn't speak so she answered her own question. "I think not." All these years wasted. Only they were unforgettable years. She would remember them to her last breath.

"Who *are* we exactly?" Abruptly he pulled her down to him in one swift, fluid motion.

She allowed him to do it even when she knew she could ill afford the least sign of surrender. To prove it, high emotion kicked in in a heartbeat. Keefe's sexual magnetism was unquestioned, and so proprietorial. He knew he owned her. That alone aroused a certain female hostility. Being *owned* was wrong. "Are you saying there are secrets, Keefe?" She turned on her side to challenge him. They were so close, the pain was scarcely to be borne. Whatever had happened between them, they could never truly lose the old unifying bond. In his own way he needed her. But never as much as she needed him. There was nothing really normal about their relationship, she thought.

Again he didn't speak. Groaning with frustration, she flung her arm across his hard, muscled chest, feeling the rhythmic thud of his heart beneath her hand. Sometimes she thought she would simply expire with the pain of loving Keefe, when there seemed to be no resolution to the matter. It was here, almost this very spot, where he had first made love to her. Taken her virginity. Captured her heart. Held it so fast he had denied her the freedom to enjoy another lover for a long time. Even then, those few relationships had never taken real shape. There was no one like Keefe. The way he made love to her. The things he did. The things he said. It was magic and music. Unforgettable.

"Secrets, yes," he muttered. With a strong arm he fitted her body to him, as though her proximity gave him all the comfort this world could offer. "But does every secret need to be told?"

Her vulnerable flesh was pulsing with desire, causing deep knife-like sensations in her groin. He hadn't asked a rhetorical question. He needed an answer. "You're saying not every secret needs to be exposed to the light? Are you worried I'm *family,* Keefe?" Finally she threw her hidden anxieties into the ring.

"Isn't that the fear locked away in your own Pandora's box?" he countered, a correspondingly sharp note in his voice. "Let it out and who knows what will happen? Family!" he groaned. "There's nothing *family* about the way I feel about you."

Such an admission, yet she had a fierce desire to lash out at him. "*Feel,* certainly. Never *act* on those feelings. They could be taboo." Why not hurt him as he always managed to hurt her? "Just give me a simple answer. What *do* you feel?" She stared at him with her black-fringed radiant blue eyes.

He brushed the question aside as if she had wasted her breath asking it. "Is that some kind of a joke? Neither of us can let go of the other. More to the point, I need to ask, is it a safe time for you?" There was a great urgency in him she couldn't fail to miss.

"Safe?" She considered that with a brittle laugh. "No time is safe with you." She didn't think she could withstand the heat of his scrutiny. "Oh, Keefe!" Her breast rose and fell with her deep troubled sigh. Impossible to sustain the illusion she was her own woman. She was a woman who couldn't let go. Worse, he wouldn't *let* her go.

He shifted position, half pinning her beneath his powerful body but withholding most of his weight. "I want to make love to you. Tell me you'll let me?" The very first sight of her at the airport had triggered a desperate need in him for the mind-bending pleasure of knowing her body again. He needed her to lessen the pain of this dreadful chaotic day. Make it bearable.

"It's always what *you* want," she said. "Shades of the old *droit de seigneur!*" Tears sparkled in her eyes.

"Never heard of it," he darkly mocked, lifting skeins of her golden hair then letting them slide through his fingers. "I said, only if *you* want it."

"What a concession, Keefe!" Hostility was coming off her like steam. She knew it had its genesis in status. His. Hers. Though successive generations were easing up on the status war. Once it would have been considered a disgrace for the scion of a great pastoral family to become involved with the daughter of a lowly employee. But *she* was an educated woman living in the twenty-first century. She could take her place anywhere. Except, it seemed, at Djinjara.

"Do I want it?" She considered his question bleakly. With a tremendous effort of will she exerted enough strength to break free of him. High time she made it perfectly plain she was her own woman. "Do you really believe I'm happy to think of myself as a woman possessed?" A high flush of colour had come to her cheeks.

"Possessed and possessing," he answered bluntly. His hand, with a life of its own, moved up to caress her breast, shaping its contours within his palm, his thumb teasing the berry-ripe nipple. "I can feel your heart racing. It beats for *me*."

The truth of it cut her to the bone. One had an intellectual life. And one had an emotional life. Sometimes the two were at war. "So arrogant!" she lamented. "I exist only to worship at your feet?" Deliberately she removed his hand from her breast. She knew about love. She knew about total seduction. He had long since mastered the art.

"Maybe I am arrogant," he agreed flatly. "Maybe that's what you do to me, Skye."

He resumed his position, in all probability waiting for her to come round. Instead, she sat rigid with self-control, watching an eagle hawk swoop on its prey. "Are you ever going to free me, Keefe?" she asked eventually. "Or are you just holding onto me until you find someone else?"

He didn't appear to be listening to her. As though what she was saying made no sense to him. "This is almost the precise spot where I first made love to you," he said in a quiet, serious voice, an element of—was it regret?—in his tone.

"The heir to Djinjara having sex with the young daughter of a station employee."

Again he didn't choose to hear her. "The world was perfect that day. You made me feel like a titan. Capable of taking on the world. Sweet, funny little Skye with her ceaseless questions grown into a beautiful woman."

"You always took the time to answer those questions."

"They were always so intelligent. You had a great thirst for knowledge."

Her released breath had a soft, shaken sound. "You were so kind to me in those days. Then overnight you drew back. You kept your distance. "

His handsome features tightened. "What would you have had me do? Keeping a distance between us was the only course open to me."

"Of course." There was brittle acceptance in her tone. "Keefe McGovern and Skye McCory. What a no-no! That was never going to work." Her gaze went beyond him. "It's going to storm."

He didn't move. "Right this minute I don't care if we're heading for Armageddon. I want to *crush* you. You won't let me. I want to take every little particle of you into me."

"That would seem to be our misfortune," she said with the greatest irony.

"I call it destiny." Abruptly he sat up. "I've missed you so much, Skye. You were supposed to come in August."

To be here with him, remote from everyone and everything, and hold herself aloof was an excruciating test of her resolve. "And sow more discord?" she challenged. 'No, Keefe, I couldn't. What was the point? Besides, you might have found yourself a fiancée by then."

His expression hardened. "Be damned to that! Haven't you forgotten something?"

"And what is that?" She spoke in a strung-out voice, knowing she was coming close to tumbling over the edge.

"*You're* the only woman I want."

The admission was like a blinding illumination.

Isn't that your lifetime passion? said the voice in her head. *To be Keefe's woman?*

When she spoke she spoke sadly. "The things you say are enough to blow my mind. *I'm* the only woman you want? If that's true—if I can possibly believe you—what in heaven or hell is wrong with us both?"

"Nothing good, it seems." On a wave of agitation he reached out to pull her back into his arms.

He was strong….so strong…the male scent of him the most powerful aphrodisiac. Pride made her put up a struggle of sorts, her blonde head lolling away from him, her eyes glistening with tears. Was there something missing in her that left her so vulnerable?

"Skye, please. Don't fight me," he begged.

"Can't you see I *must*?" She had to find it within herself to pull back from this point of no return.

"No, *don't*!" He lowered his head, hungrily covering her mouth with his own. His tongue lapped the moistness that slicked her full lips like it was the most luscious of wines. "Don't, don't, don't!"

Her heart contracted; her senses reeled. Desire came at her in an annihilating rush. This was black magic at its highest level. Keefe was the magician, ready to transport her to a different world. All she had to do was give herself up to his stunning sexual supremacy. His hands were moving down over her body. Soon she would stop thinking altogether. Mind and body would become two entirely separate regions.

Only…she couldn't shed all her painful memories like a snake shed its skin. Memories had the power to come crashing through. She wanted him desperately—she was *starving* for what only he could give her—yet she gathered herself sufficiently to pull away. Perhaps she should have pulled away that *first* time. Said *No, Keefe*, instead of *Yes, Keefe* and saved herself a whole world of pain. Memory opened up like a book…

Second-year exams were over. She thought she had done well. She had promised her closest girlfriend Kylie Mitchell—a fellow law student—she would spend part of the long summer vacation with her and her family at their beautiful beach hide-away on one of the Great Barrier Reef islands, but she was to spend Christmas and the New Year with her father. He was so looking forward to seeing her it was impossible to disappoint him, even if she knew she was going back into the lion's den. She hadn't forgotten Scott's near-assault on her. Mercifully it had never been repeated. In his heart Scott knew his brother would destroy him if he ever hurt her. From her sixteenth year, she had become off limits to Scott and his attentions. But from that day on she had never trusted him. On the surface they managed to get by quite well. There were pleasantries and jokes, but Skye thought she always saw at the back of Scott's eyes a familiarity bordering on insolence that exposed what was really at his heart.

Scott still fancied her. The only thing that stopped him from doing something about it was fear of swift retribution from his brother. From time to time Skye had rather horrible nightmares about Scott coming after her. Then, when it seemed he was about to physically overcome her, Keefe was always there to rescue her.

Keefe, her knight in shining armour. Only *confusion* reigned. Keefe remained her knight, but his whole attitude towards her had changed. It was as though she had lost her sweet innocence and turned into some sort of siren. In short, Keefe kept her at a distance. Just as he made sure his brother maintained a safe distance from her, he maintained that distance himself. What had happened that summer years ago had caused Keefe to shut a door on her.

A big Christmas Eve party was being held at the House. Lady McGovern herself had issued Skye an invitation.

"I won't take no for an answer, Skye,' she said, gauging from the expression on Skye's face she was about to make some excuse. "Your father won't mind in the least. You're a beautiful, clever young woman. A credit to us all. Quite a few young members of the family will be here. You'll enjoy yourself. Have you something pretty to wear?"

Luckily the perfect get-out had been handed to her on a plate. "Nothing to wear to a party, Lady McGovern, I'm afraid. You must excuse me, but thank you so much for thinking of me. I know you'll understand I'd feel awkward and out of place in the one dress I've brought with me. It's a cotton sundress. I'm sure Rachelle and her cousins will be beautifully turned out."

"So they will," Lady McGovern agreed with an unsmiling nod. Rachelle's cousins, all from wealthy families, were out earning their own money, carving out careers, not relying on trust funds like Rachelle. Nothing she said made any difference to her granddaughter. Rachelle lacked drive. Worse, she had no sense of reality. Her feet didn't even touch the ground. That's what wealth did to some people. Why bother earning money when you had plenty? Here in front of her was young Skye McCory—the image of her mother—taking up life and developing her character. At the end of Skye's first year of law she was among the top five students. Lady McGovern fully expected she would repeat or even gain standing when the results for year two were posted in the New Year.

"Don't worry about that," she said, fixing Skye with her regal stare. "I took the opportunity of having something appropriate for you to wear sent in from Sydney. Think of it as an extra Christmas present." Djinjara's staff were given suitable Christmas presents. It was a long-standing tradition, as was their big New Year's Eve party held in the Great Hall. "Come along with me and I'll show it to you." The civility of the tone didn't conceal the fact it was an order. "Shoes to match so don't worry about them either. I have countless evening bags. I'm sure you can pick out something from among them."

Skye, at twenty, felt overwhelmed. "But Lady McGovern—"

"No buts about it!" The old lady turned on her, her tone so sharp it was like a rap over the knuckles. "Come along now."

Skye knew better than to argue.

As always, Rachelle was on hand to upset her.

She was almost at the front door when Rachelle tore down the grand staircase. "What have you got there?" she demanded, her dark eyes riveted to the long, elegant box in Skye's hands with its distinctive packaging and label.

Normally poised in the face of Rachelle's obvious dislike, Skye felt acute embarrassment. Colour swept hotly into her cheeks. "Lady McGovern has been kind enough to give me my Christmas present," she said.

"A dress?" Rachelle's upper-crust voice rose to a screech. "How come you rate a dress from Margaux's?" She advanced on Skye, looking shocked to her roots. Margaux's was arguably Sydney's top boutique, carrying designer labels from all over the world.

"Yes, a dress, Rachelle." Skye was recovering somewhat. "I'm thrilled."

"So you should be!" Rachelle's tone lashed. "Gran hasn't asked you to come to the Christmas Eve party surely?"

Skye held her temper. "She has. I'm sorry if this upsets you, Rachelle. I'll endeavour to keep out of your way."

Rachelle's face registered a whole range of emotions, fury uppermost. "I don't believe this!" she cried. "How could Gran do this to me?" Her eyes abruptly narrowed to slits. "I believe you begged her for an invitation. That's it, isn't it? You'd have the hide!"

"Wrong again." Skye shook her blonde head. "If you ask your grandmother, you'll learn the truth. But do remember to ask nicely. You're losing all your manners."

"I hate you, Skye McCory." As if she needed to, Rachelle laid it on the line. A McGovern to a McCory. A McGovern with a streak of vengeance.

"You have no right to," Skye replied, keeping her tone level, although she felt sick to her stomach. She was sick of Rachelle's drama. In fact, she wanted to pitch the elegant box at this appalling young woman's head.

She had to walk away.

Right now.

The McGoverns still had her in their power, even if she was subsidising her own way with two part-time jobs. Beggars couldn't be choosers. But she had long since made the vow she would repay every last penny she owed them, even if it took years.

Surely her skin had never looked so luminous? Her thick, deeply waving honey-blonde hair formed a corona around her excited flushed face, animated to radiance. She couldn't help but be thrilled by the way she looked. She had never expected to own a dress like this. Not for years yet, and then she would have to be earning a darned good salary. It was gossamer light, the most beautiful shade of blue that, like magic, turned her eyes to blue-violet. The fabric was silk chiffon, with jewelled detailing, the bodice strapless, draped tightly around her body to the hips, from where it fell beautifully to just clear of her ankles. Her evening sandals—like the dress a perfect fit—were silver, as was her little evening bag that inside bore a famous Paris label.

"Oh, my darling girl, aren't *you* dolled up!" her father exclaimed in pride and pleasure when she presented herself for his inspection. "You look every inch a princess! I'm enormously proud of you, Skye. If only your mother was here to share this moment!"

Always Cathy, her mother. For her father there had never been any other woman. "I'm enormously proud of *you*, Dad," she

countered, giving him a hug. "I suppose we'd better get going."
Her father was to drive her up to the homestead, which was
blazing with light.

"You enjoy yourself, hear me," her father urged as she
alighted from the station Jeep. "Don't let that Rachelle get under
your skin. Poor girl has problems."

Skye, blessed with a generous heart, hoped Rachelle would
one day solve them.

Days later she was still in a daydream, her head crammed with
the long silent looks Keefe had given her that splendid Christmas
Eve. All the other looks and stares. Many had looked for a very
long time at Skye McCory in their midst, but the close attention
had slid off her like water off a duck's back. What she hadn't
realised was she had the arresting air of someone not conscious
of her own beauty. Her looks were simply a part of her. Part of
her genetic inheritance. She wasn't and never would be burdened
by personal vanity. Rachelle of the patrician features was a
beauty. But Rachelle brought to mind the old saying that beauty
was only skin deep. Far better a beautiful nature. A beautiful
nature could not be ravaged by time.

But the way *Keefe* had looked at her! It had made her feel rap-
turous, yet madly restless, like her body was a high-revving
machine. Not like the old days when she had still been a child.
Like a *woman*. A woman he desired. Her own feelings were still
locked in the realms of dreams, but Keefe had looked at her as
if *anything* were possible. He was the Prince who could claim
his Cinderella. For Cinderella she was. At least to the
McGoverns. That evening had been the most disturbing, the
most exciting night of her life. She didn't think her memories
would ever fade.

Had Keefe forgiven her for having distracted his brother?
Lord knew, it hadn't been deliberate. Did he finally understand

that? She had given Scott not the slightest encouragement. It was Scott who had had the willful drive to take what he wanted. With Keefe, it was like the start of something quite new and wondrously strange. A wonderful, sumptuous, brilliant night of tens of thousands of glittering stars and the Southern Cross hanging overDjinjara's huge tiled roof. Some memories lasted for ever.

She took her camera out to the sandhills. She had become very interested in photography since attending university. Her friend, Ewan, a fellow law student, had introduced a few of the others to the art form, fanning their enthusiasm to the point they had all pored over the various magazines on the market once they had moved past the basic techniques. The best magazines had taught her how to get great outdoor shots. She had quickly moved onto the intermediate level, such was her eye and her interest.

"You have an amazing talent, Skye!" Ewan had said, quite without envy. He had a big talent himself. "You're a born photographer. You should give up law."

"As though I could find work as a photographer!" she had scoffed. "If I'm so good, why don't you all chip in and buy me a decent camera?" Of course she had been joking but to her shocked delight Ewan had run around with the hat, raising close to eight hundred dollars with a very nice contribution from a top woman lecturer who admired Skye's work.

Skye had read up on all the great photographers, including Ansel Adams, recognised as one of the finest landscape photographers of all time. Landscape had been what she was particularly interested in. Considering where she had been born and lived, the savagely beautiful Channel Country, the home of the nation's cattle kings, was high up on her list of must-take photographs. She had thought she might even be able to make a bit of a name for herself, but she wasn't all that hopeful. Ewan, now, was far more interested in people. He had taken numerous photographs of her, which had captured her essence, according to her friends. The only time she had ever turned Ewan down had been when he had wanted to photograph her nude. Not that the shots wouldn't have been tasteful. Ewan was dead serious about his work. It was just that she was too darned modest—modesty, had she known it, was part of her charm—and she had been worried where the photographs might eventually turn up. Ewan had already been offered a showing at one of the small but interesting galleries.

That afternoon she had taken herself out to the hill country with her brand-new camera. In a year she had raised enough money on her own to trade in the camera her friends' generosity had bought her for the next model. The new camera had many extras, options and problem-solving capabilities. It had already augmented her natural ability to capture just the image she was striving for. She was starting to think of herself as a photographic artist seriously setting about taking impressions of her own country. On Djinjara there were countless special locations. Even then one needed patience for just the right light, just the right shot. She intended to wait it out to capture the amazing vibrance of an Outback sunset. City people didn't realise the fantastic range and depth of colour or the three-dimensional nature of the clouds. Outback sunsets and sunrises were overwhelmingly beautiful. In them one could see the hand of God.

Of special interest to her were the ghost gums. What wonderful trees they were, with their pure white silky-to-the-touch boles. They made such a brilliant contrast to the rich red soil and the bright violet-blue sky. She was lying on her back, trying to get as low as possible so she could get in as much as she could of the trees and their wonderful sculptural branches

That was the way Keefe found her. He must have spotted the

station Jeep at the base of the foothills and followed her trail. He knew about her burgeoning interest in photography but he hadn't as yet seen her work. She and Keefe were separated these days, weren't they? But in their own way they remained tied.

It was really strange, the connection. A silver cord that could never be cut.

"Won't be a minute," she said, trying to bring full concentration back to her shot. She had been thinking so much about Keefe lately she had almost driven herself crazy.

"Take your time." With a faint sigh he lowered his lean frame onto a nearby boulder. Curiously it was shaped like a primitive chair, the back and the seat carved and smoothed to a high polish over aeons.

"I was hoping to take a few shots of the sunset," she explained, beginning to get up. "Djinjara's sunsets are glorious."

He stood immediately, put out a hand, helped her to her feet.

Skin on skin. For a disconcerting moment it was almost as though he had pressed her hand to his lips. How susceptible was the flesh! It had been a blazingly hot day so she was wearing brief denim shorts and a pink cotton shirt tied loosely at the waist over one of her bikini tops. Quite a bit of her was on show. She wasn't supposed to be on show, was she?

"You're really into this, aren't you?" he asked, a trace of the old indulgence in his voice.

"Love it," she said, whisking a long shining wave of her hair off her flushed face. She had tied it back in a ponytail but the wind had gone to work on the neat arrangement. "It would take a lifetime but one of my ambitions is to photograph as much as I can of our great untouched land," she confided, knowing he would understand. No one loved the land more than Keefe. The land was a passion they shared. "I can't wait for the miracle of the wildflowers."

"Your special time," he said.

His diamond-bright eyes moved to rest on her with such an unsettlingly tender expression that her body might have been a long-stemmed blossom.

"*Our* special time." She managed a smile, tingling to the tips of her fingers. "I loved every moment I spent with you as a child. But those were the halcyon days, weren't they? We've moved on."

"*You've* moved on," he said, a touch grimly. "*I'm* still here."

"You wouldn't be anywhere else," she scoffed.

"Don't you miss it?" He leaned into the boulder with a characteristically elegant slouch. Keefe had such grace of movement. He had discarded his wide-brimmed hat, his luxuriant black hair thick and tousled, his darkly tanned skin glittering with the lightest sweat.

"Of course I miss it!" she said fervently, betraying her sense of loss. "I'll probably miss it all my life."

"So what's your life going to be, Skye?" he questioned, his eyes a sharply observant silver.

"I haven't figured that out yet." Immediately she was on the defensive.

"Well, you're only twenty." He shrugged. "But you must have a whole string of admirers by now?"

"No more than you," she shot back.

"Now you're being ridiculous."

"I'm not being ridiculous at all," she said heatedly. "What about Fiona Fraser? She stayed glued to your side at the party. Then there's Clementine. I like Clemmie. Your second cousin Angela has become very glamorous. And she's a gifted pianist."

"So she is," he nodded. "A conservatorium graduate. Angela is a city girl."

"Here we go!" she answered breezily. "That counts *her* out, then. City girls are trouble. So we're back to Fiona."

"*You're* back to Fiona, and I thought you were a hell of a lot smarter. I'm twenty-six years old, Skye. Twenty-six to your twenty. I have no thought of marriage on my mind."

"As yet. You have to be aware you're one of the biggest catches in the country.' It came to her that she was deliberately winding him up. It was really crazy of her, wanting to pick a fight.

"Then you know way more than I do." He dismissed that impatiently. "I'm the guy who's being groomed to one day take over not only a cattle empire but Dad's numerous business interests as well. We've been diversifying for a long time now."

"No one ever said the McGoverns weren't smart." She made a wry face, one hand making a move to button up her shirt. Only it was too darned obvious. The bikini top was pretty skimpy. Not that Keefe was looking at her in *that* way. The sad thing was he could arouse her most potent, erotic feelings with a single glance.

She wanted…wanted… What *did* she want? She was still a virgin. No frustration attached to that state. She had plenty of friends. Male and female. It was simply that no young man she had met had come close to measuring up to Keefe. That was the pity of it.

A pity beyond all telling is hid in the heart of love. Blake, his "Songs of Innocence". She felt like an innocent, a babe in the woods.

There was a frown on Keefe's dynamic face as he watched her. "Don't you feel safe here, Skye?" he asked.

The seriousness of his tone cut across her reverie. "What a question!" Her hand dropped to her side. Why was she so nervous of revealing her body to Keefe? She was oblivious to all the stares she received whenever she visited a beach. Then she thought: *It's Keefe! It's always Keefe.*

Dusk was closing in. Shrieking, the legions of birds were starting to home into the density of trees that lined the maze of watercourses, lagoons, swamps and creeks on the station. It was an awe-inspiring sight, the sheer numbers.

"Answer it," Keefe said in a firm voice.

She stared at him. "You sound stressed."

"Maybe I am." He swatted at a dragonfly with iridescent wings. It seemed bent on landing on his head. "Scott won't bother you," he said, his expression formidable.

Scott? Scott wasn't even an afterthought. "I'm not worried about Scott, Keefe," she assured him quickly. "We're getting along. You warned him off. He heeded your message. You love your brother, don't you?"

He plunged an impatient hand through his hair, fingers splaying into the distinctive McGovern widow's peak. "Of course I do," he said edgily. "But like you I know he has a callous streak. I don't want to see that turned on women."

"Of course not!" She couldn't control a shudder, acutely aware he was monitoring her every movement and expression. "Is he interested in Jemma Templeton?" She knew for a fact Jemma had always had a crush on Scott.

"Why do you want to know?" His silver eyes blazed.

She swallowed at his tone. It was so clipped it provoked a flash of anger. "No particular reason," she answered shortly. "Just making conversation. *I* have no interest in Scott, Keefe. Take my word for it. "

It's you I love.

"Sometimes I get so tired of it all." Unexpectedly he made the admission. "Not the job. I can handle that. Handle the lot." He paused, studying her closely. "Nothing is the same between us, is it, Skye? The ease has gone with the wind."

He hadn't moved, yet she felt she had been taken into a passionate embrace. "You sound like you're grieving for what we lost." Despite that and the angst of his tone, she had an escalating sense of excitement, so intense she knew it was carrying her close to peril.

His silver eyes blazed. "If I touch you I'll make love to you. Do you *know* that?"

He had said it yet she seemed hardly able to take it in. Even her heart rocked in shock.

"No answer?"

She began to shiver in the dry heat. How *could* she answer? She needed time to react to the pulverising shock. Besides, his tone seemed as much savage as sensual, as though he had found himself unwillingly caught in a dilemma.

"Here in the shadow of the sand dunes with all the Dreamtime gods around us," he intoned. "I'm convinced this is a sacred place. That's one reason why I'd like to spread a blanket on the sand, take you down on it. You've always been little Skye to me. Now you've become pure desire." He spoke with such intensity his luminous eyes had darkened to slate grey. "I didn't tell you how beautiful you looked in your blue dress the other night."

Her stomach was churning, her limbs seized by trembling. Yet incredibly she said, "Maybe your eyes told me." Even her body was swaying towards him like a flower swayed towards the sun.

"Eventually I was bound to give myself away," he said, a twist to this mouth. "I'm sure I'll remember how you looked that night to the end of my days. No one wears the colour blue like you do."

Whatever he *said*, he wore the demeanour of a man who was in the process of making a hard decision. A decision he meant to stick by come what may. "I don't want to leave you here." He turned his head abruptly, his tone a shield. "It's getting late. You can come back tomorrow if you like. There's always another sunset."

"It's okay, I'll stay." He was hurting her, punishing her. For what? Growing up? Turning into a desirable woman? She could see the pulse drumming away in his temple.

"It's *me*, isn't it, Keefe?" She took a hesitant step towards him, her blue eyes full of entreaty. "*I'm* the one causing you tension. You don't really want me here. I've turned from your 'little buddy' into a woman, thus an unwanted distraction."

The air between them fairly crackled. "You want me to tell you that?" he challenged roughly. "Well, I *can't*. I do want you here, but my job is to *protect* you. It's always been my job. Gran really suffered when your mother died. Did you know that?"

Skye shook her head helplessly. Why was he going off at a tangent? And now? "No, I didn't," she admitted. "If she suffered, she must have loved my mother?"

"*Love.*" He reached for her in a blind rush, hauling her right into his arms.

His grip was so powerful, so *perfect,* she felt as weightless as a china doll.

Breathe, Skye. Breathe. Her emotions were running so high, her response so headlong, it was possible she could pass out.

"*God!*" he breathed, turning up his head to the cobalt dome of the sky. It sounded to her ears like a cry for help. Like he knew he shouldn't do this. Whatever the desire he felt for her—she couldn't help but be aware of his arousal—he felt compelled not to give in to it. "We have to go. Really, we have to go." His grip eased abruptly so she could move.

Only she couldn't. She wanted to stay there with him for the rest of her life. Even if it sounded as if his heart was being torn out of him. That gave her wild hope. "No, stay here with me," she begged. Where had that alluring tone of voice come from? She had never used it before.

From the heart.

Unable to control the mad urge that had come upon her, she brought up her arms to lock them around his neck. The thought of having power over him was absolutely dizzying. She heard him groan like a man ensnared in some inescapable golden net.

"What are you *doing* to me, Skye?" he muttered. "You *know* what will happen?"

"So?" Her eyes were devouring each separate feature of his face. The set of his extraordinary eyes. The arch of his black brows that formed such a stunning contrast. His tanned skin bore a prickle of dark beard. And, oh, his *mouth*! That wide, strong, sensual mouth, the outline so cleanly cut it might have been chiselled.

"You're a virgin?" He looked down into her eyes, his hands spreading out over her back burning through the cotton.

"I am." Her voice was scarcely above a whisper.

"You wouldn't lie to me."

It was a statement, not a question. Was he that sure of her? So aware she had an emotional dependency on him? "Are *you* lying in some way to me now, Keefe? Tormenting me? Or are you promising to take me where you believe I want to go?"

His handsome face showed stress. "Let me try."

All nature seemed to be listening. Even the birds, though they wheeled overhead, gave no cries to stay her. She should be listening too. Not making it so easy for Keefe to win her over. *"You?"* she questioned. "The never-puts-a-foot-wrong Keefe McGovern to cut loose with Jack McCory's daughter?"

"The more I try, the fiercer the longing gets." Keefe's answer was harsher than he had intended but he felt himself on a knife edge. Attraction this strong, this elemental rendered a man nearly powerless. Slowly he closed his roughened hands around the satin-smooth planes of her face, caressing her cheekbones as he would caress an exquisite piece of porcelain.

It was too much for Skye. Little silver sparks were dancing wildly in her breast. She had to close her eyes to contain the powerful shooting sensations. Excitement that had started as a dull roar was turning into a raging flame. If there was a taboo, it was about to be broken…

In the next breath she felt his mouth, warm and lushly *male,* come down over hers. He tasted wonderful! Delectable! She could scarcely get enough of him. Her knees were buckling from the sheer weight of emotion. She had to cling to him, throw her arms around his waist to anchor her to the ground. Sexual desire—no it was much more: an undying *passion*—was mounting at such a rate it had become a turbulent flood of hunger ready to surge over her and take her under. Keefe did things better than anyone. Better than anyone *could.*

Keefe drew her lips up with his own, taking deeply erotic exploratory breaths, sipping and sucking at the sweet nectar within, while he continued to hold her against him with unknowing strength. The intimacy was so intense it was almost unbearable. The light clear pure bonds of childhood had turned into an adult force so powerful it was intimidating. He had always looked at her with such fondness, like a much-loved little cousin, with respect for her high intelligence. How, then, could he allow himself to become a threat to her? Worse, possibly destroy what they had?

"Is it wrong to go from protector to lover?" he asked, never more serious in his life. He drew back quickly so he could search her face. He couldn't believe how beautiful she looked, or how highly aroused. Her beauty and desirability leapt at him.

He had to bend low to hear her whispered answer. "Couldn't we see it as entirely natural?" she asked. He was so absolutely perfect to her in every way. No one could replace him.

"Then God will forgive me," Keefe answered in a strange near-mystical tone. What had befallen him had befallen her.

Kismet.

Skye allowed her heavy lids to fall shut. She felt as though Heaven had given her permission to allow ascendancy to the blind yearning she felt. This moment in time had been accorded her. Therefore she had to seize on it, feeling like a mortal maiden about to couple with a young god.

CHAPTER FOUR

The Present

HER father sat down to a dinner with a sad and haunted look in his eyes. The colour was a bright blue like hers but they were a different shape.

"I'm glad you went riding with Keefe," he said, picking up his knife and fork. "He mightn't have shown it but he was really labouring to get through today."

"I know, Dad." For a moment she wondered if denying Keefe the comfort of her body was not a failure on her part. For his part, he had accepted her decision and moved on.

"This looks great, love!" Jack praised the unfamiliar dish.

Skye had to smile. He was her dad. He was forever praising her. Everything she did was just great.

"Thai stir-fried beef with a few vegetables and noodles. Hope you like it."

"I like anything you make," he told her, quite unnecessarily. "How did you turn into such a good cook?"

"I took lessons in the city," she said, forking a slice of bell pepper. "Everyone should be able to cook. I enjoy cooking. I'm quite domesticated, really."

"You know what? So was your mother!" The sad expression

lifted like magic. "Cathy was a bonzer little cook. Very fancy. Presented a meal beautifully. Not like your poor old dad. It's steak and chips mostly and lashings of tomato sauce. At least the steak is prime Djinjara beef. Tender enough to melt in your mouth." Jack paused, to look directly into his daughter's eyes. "I thought I spotted a bit of tension between you and Keefe when you arrived. I was pretty keyed up myself."

"Why wouldn't you be?" she replied gravely. "Mr McGovern's death came as a terrible shock. As for Keefe and me, nothing is as easy as the old days, Dad. They're gone. We're adults now. I have to accept it. Keefe is Keefe, Master of Djinjara and everything else besides. It's a huge job he's taken on. In many ways it's been unfair. There's always been great pressure on Keefe. Little or no pressure on Scott. All Rachelle has to do is marry more money."

"She won't be an easy target," Jack pronounced. "Keefe will have been left in charge of the McGovern Trust. No fortune-hunter will get past him."

"Well, I don't wish any bad experience on Rachelle," Skye said. "You'd think she'd interest herself in one or other of the McGovern enterprises. I'm sure she'd make a good business-woman if she tried."

Jack looked unconvinced. "Very unpleasant young woman, I'm sorry to say." Jack was never the one to talk badly of anyone. "No one likes her. She's an outstanding example of a first-class snob, when Keefe, the heir, is anything but. Don't worry about Keefe, love. I know what he means to you. He's up to the job. Count on it. I've never seen a man prouder of his son than Mr McGovern was of Keefe."

"True, but he had *two* sons, Dad," Skye felt obliged to point out. "Perhaps without meaning to Mr McGovern, while lavishing his love and pride on Keefe, turned Scott into a bitter young man." She pondered that a moment, then rejected it. Broderick McGovern had loved both his sons.

"No, dear." Jack McCory shook his head. "Scott sprang from his poor mother's womb, bitter."

"Seems like it!" Skye gave a regretful sigh. "Still, many gifts and attributes were showered on Keefe at birth. Not the other son."

"Not simply the luck of the draw, Skye. Mr McGovern did love Scott. He worried about Scott's mood changes. Scott was given every opportunity to make a success of himself with that job on Moorali. It would have been a big leg up. He turned it down flat. Both Scott and Rachelle take after the mother's family, the Crowthers. Mrs McGovern was never really at home on Djinjara, although as a Crowther she was Outback born and raised. Rachelle is like her, in looks as well."

"I barely remember her," Skye said. "Lady McGovern has always ruled. I must have been ten or eleven when Keefe's mother died. Melanoma wasn't it?"

Jack nodded.

Skye set down her knife and fork seeing an opening. "We never talk about *my* mother, Dad. There's only one *good* photograph of her in the house."

"And aren't you the image of her!" Jack exclaimed. "Even then I couldn't take it out for years and years. The pain of loss was too great. That's the danger in giving your heart away."

Gently she touched his hand. "Dad, I understand the pain—"

"No, darlin', you *don't*," Jack said with conviction. "You only *think* you know. One has to experience the death of that beloved person to know the total devastation. I wouldn't wish it on anyone."

"Of course not." Skye felt chastened, but determined to persevere. "Lady McGovern avoids the whole subject, as you do. It's like venturing into dangerous territory, but you must understand, Dad, there are things I want to know, things it's taken me far too long to ask." Like who *exactly* was my mother? That was the issue Keefe had referred to as a "Pandora's box".

Jack's head shot up. "Oh, darling girl, I'm sorry. I'm just plain selfish," he apologised. "All I've thought of is my own pain, my own loss. You'll have to forgive me. The worst of the pain—the most brutal, heart-wrenching grief—has eased. A man couldn't continue to live with it. But I can never forget. I loved my Cathy with all my heart. She died giving me the best and most beautiful daughter in the whole wide world."

Skye's eyes filled with tears. She rose from her chair to put her arms around her father's shoulders, kissing his weathered cheek. "All right, Dad, we won't talk now. Finish your meal. There's coconut ice cream with lime and ginger syrup for later. Maybe when we have our coffee you'll feel able to answer just a few of my questions."

Jack had his work cut out, giving his daughter a smile. When all was said and done there was a great deal about his beautiful Cathy *he* didn't know. Cathy had been such a private person not even he had been able to intrude.

Skye returned to her chair feeling a prickling of unease. If her mother had been a member of Lady McGovern's family in England—maybe extended family—what relationship did she herself bear to the McGovern family? According to legend, her mother was the daughter or niece of a friend of Lady McGovern's. No one knew exactly, it was all terribly vague. Deliberately vague. But why?

She was soon to discover her father knew amazingly little about his beautiful young wife's background....

"I married Cathy because I loved her, not because of any background," he said, resting back in his armchair. "She was like an angel from Heaven, bringing glory into my life. I couldn't *believe* it when she consented to marry me."

Skye had no difficulty accepting that. Wasn't her own situation with Keefe a reversal of the situation that had existed between her father and mother; the social divide which would have been far greater in their day? Then there was the issue regarding her mother's exact connection to the McGoverns. "But how did the relationship grow, Dad?" she asked, covering her bewilderment. "You were a stockman at the time. She was a guest of Lady McGovern. How could it be? Where did you meet? How often? How long did it take you to fall in love?" She knew from her father's expression that the whole topic was causing him distress, but she felt driven to continue.

"Me?" Jack's eyebrows shot up. "Why, the instant I laid eyes on her! And she *knew*. I must have given myself away that very day. She was so beautiful, so fresh and sweet. Nothing stuck-up about her. She was someone who spoke to everyone on the station. Everyone loved her. That love has been passed on to you. When I was out of it with grief, there was always someone keeping an eye on you. Lady McGovern placed you in Lena's care."

"And wonderful she was to me too!" Skye was still in contact with Lena, who now lived with a family in Alice Springs.

Jack nodded. "True blue was Lena. I tried once to get her to talk—fill me in about Cathy and her connection to the family—but Lena wouldn't open up. Still, I think Lena knew a lot."

"About what, specifically?" Maybe she could get more information out of Lena than her father if she tried?

"Oh, an amazing amount of stuff," Jack said, looking like he wanted to terminate the whole conversation. "I guess we should have had this discussion years ago, but in all truth, love, I never did know a lot. Cathy wouldn't talk about her past. She'd started a new life. With me. Whatever she wanted I went along with. So in a way I'm accountable for her death."

"No, Dad, *no!*" Skye protested strongly. "You have to stop all that. It was a tragedy."

"Yes, a tragedy," Jack groaned. "She died in my arms. My

little Cathy. Do you suppose it could have been because you arrived early?"

This was way beyond Skye. There had never been any mention that she had been a premature baby. All her life she had enjoyed excellent health. Unease struck harder.

"Who attended the birth? Who was the doctor, the midwife, whatever?"

Jack's face was showing strain. "Tom Morris. A good bloke, a good doctor. He's dead now, Tom."

"Who called him?"

Jack looked stunned. "Why, Lady McGovern got him here fast. He was flown in. I remember him saying practically right off he had concerns."

"Why didn't she go to hospital?"

"She didn't *want* to," Jack said broken-heartedly. "She was adamant about it. She was happy to be on Djinjara. She loved it here. She loved being with me. *'You're my minder, Jack,'* she used to say with a laugh. I minded her. Yes, I did. Until the end. I don't know what her reasons were for leaving her own people. All I know is she found sanctuary with Lady McGovern. Lady McGovern used to talk to Cathy like she was her own child. Of course she wasn't. But I wouldn't be surprised to hear there was some blood connection."

"You don't know?"

"No, I don't, love." Jack shook his head. "And I wouldn't dare ask the old lady."

So her father had lived with his own demons. High time for her to face up to her own. Lady McGovern would know the truth. Probably she was the only one living who did. But she had the dismal notion Lady McGovern wasn't about to help anyone out. Bizarre as it sounded, even Broderick McGovern might never have known a great deal about Cathy. He would have been married by then with a wife and children.

Time to visit her mother's grave. Then time to go back to her city life. Back to the life she had forged for herself. She had to confront the fact the same aura of unease regarding her background surrounded Keefe as it did her. Maybe the crucial bits that were missing explained why neither of them seemed able to move forward. Only Lady McGovern knew exactly what had happened all those years ago…

She took one of the horses to the McGovern graveyard, tethering the mare in the shade of the massive desert oaks. A huge wrought-iron fence enclosed the whole area, the iron railings topped by spikes. The gates were closed, but unlocked. She opened one side and walked through, shutting it with a soft clang behind her. This was the McGovern graveyard, scrupulously tended, with generations of McGoverns buried here. Everywhere there were markers and plaques, tall urns, a few statues. A classical-style white marble statue of a weeping maiden marked the grave of the wife of the McGovern founding father.

What was her mother doing, lying here among the McGoverns? She had asked Lady McGovern once when she had been about twelve and had failed to get any answer whatever. Just a stern silence. She had never asked again. Broderick McGovern's grave as yet had no headstone. No one had expected him to die so prematurely, leaving his son at barely thirty to take up the reins.

She had brought flowers with her. Not from the home gardens, though she could have asked and been given as many armfuls as she wanted. Instead, she had broken off several branches of pink and white bauhinia, arranging them in a sheaf. Oddly, although the cemetery wasn't a cheerful place, it wasn't depressing either. Surrounded by such incredible empty *vastness*, in the distance the ancient temples of the sandhills glowing an orange-red flame, it wasn't difficult to get one's own life into perspective.

Her mother's grave was marked by a child-sized white marble angel with outspread wings. The inscription read:

Catherine Margaret McCory, 1964-1986.
Do not stand at my grave and weep
I am not there

Silently she mouthed several more lines of the famous bereavement poem. She knew them by heart. All around her the silence was absolute except for the soft tranquil swish of the desert breeze. For an instant she fancied the breeze very sweetly kissed her cheek. Perhaps it was a greeting from her mother? Why not? It was hard to believe one simply ceased. There was mind, spirit. Only the body was consigned to the ground.

Cathy could well be in the thousand winds that blew, the swift uplifting rush of birds, the soft stars that shone at night. Though the stars that shone in their billions over Djinjara were ten times more brilliant than city-soft.

"Where are you, Cathy?" Without being aware of it Skye spoke aloud. "*Who* are you?" She desperately needed reassurances. Tears for what might have been pooled in her eyes. She bent to place the bauhinia branches, weighed down by exquisite blossom, on the white stone. There were so many mysteries in life. She couldn't seem to get to the bottom of the mystery of her own family. Had her mother lived she could have bombarded her with questions and got answers. She had always been a questioning child. Now it seemed her mother's short life had been defined by her death.

She paid her respects at Broderick McGovern's resting place then made her way slowly along the gravelled path to the tall gates. Along the way she passed a brilliant bank of honeysuckle that adorned one side of the fence, pausing to draw in the haunting perfume. Life might be many things, she thought, but in the end it all came down to one thing. Great or small, the body returned to dust. She chose to believe the soul roamed freely...

Just as she reached the gate, a station Jeep pulled up so hard it raised a great swirl of red dust and fallen dry leaves. Deliberate, Skye thought. Rachelle was at the wheel. Resolutely Skye turned to face her. She could hardly remount and gallop away. Unpleasant and abrupt as Rachelle was, this was Djinjara. Rachelle was a McGovern. She had to be accorded respect.

Rachelle was out of the vehicle with the speed of a rocket being fired. She was dressed in a cream silk shirt and jodhpurs, riding boots on her feet when it was well known Rachelle didn't particularly enjoy riding, though she was competent, as expected of a McGovern.

"What are you doing here?" Rachelle whipped off her big black designer sunglasses.

"I wonder you ask, Rachelle," Skye managed a quiet answer. "My mother is buried here."

"Highly unusual, I'd say." There were shadows under Rachelle's fine dark eyes. She looked faintly ill and nerve-ridden. Yet even in the tranquillity of the graveyard, with her father laid to rest not far away, Rachelle couldn't rein in her dislike and resentment.

"You should speak to your grandmother some time," Skye suggested. "She was very fond of my mother. My mother could only have been buried here with her approval."

"It's all seriously odd," Rachelle said, a vein throbbing in her temple. "That's all I can say. Your mother should be all but forgotten. *You* didn't know her. We were only little kids when she died yet we can't seem to get rid of her. Or *you* either."

Skye gave the other woman a saddened look. "Why do you hate me so much, Rachelle?"

Rachelle looked back with huge disbelief. "You don't know?" she hooted. "You robbed me of my brother for years and years of my life."

"No."

"You *did.*"

"Maybe he saw *you* weren't going to be my friend?"

"*Please!* You could never be numbered among my friends."

"Where *are* all your friends, Rachelle?" Skye retorted, suddenly firing up. "You didn't have any at school. I'm fairly modest by nature but you might recall *I* did. I was also head girl in my final year."

"How impressive!" Rachelle sneered. "Who knows why Gran wanted you there in the first place. I guess she had to be fond of your mother. Who was she anyway? Over twenty years have gone by and Gran won't say a word about her. "

Wasn't that the truth! "You surely must know if she was a relative? One of Lady McGovern's relatives in England?" Skye challenged, so desperate for clues she would ask even Rachelle.

Rachelle's outraged expression rejected that. "I'd have a heart attack if I thought you and I were related," she snapped off. "Your mother was just some stray Gran befriended. I don't know from where. Like I care!"

"But you *do* care."

It had got to the stage where they all cared. "Nonsense!" Rachelle's cry was a near shriek. "You're the bane of my life, Skye McCory."

"Sounds like you should get a life," Skye advised, turning away.

"Keefe might have loved you when we were kids," Rachelle called after her. "But he doesn't love you now. *You'll* never get him. That's what he told me, I swear. Though I expect that cuts your heart to ribbons. You love him. Don't think I'm a fool. You've always loved him. But nothing will ever happen between you and him. Keefe has his life planned differently. He's way out of your league."

Skye had to wait until the initial shock had worn off. "Where did you learn to be such a terrible snob, Rachelle?" she asked quietly enough, though Rachelle's words had landed like punches.

"It's called knowing who you *are*," Rachelle explained with a lofty tilt of her chin. "I'm a McGovern. You're Jack McCory our overseer's kid. He's a real rough diamond, isn't he, your dad?"

Skye felt heat burn up her veins. *Steady. Steady.* She got herself under control. "He could teach *you* some manners," she answered with cool disdain. "I can see there's never going to be a way for us to start over, Rachelle. In a way, I'm sorry about that. I know you're not good at taking advice, but if I were you I'd jettison the bitterness and save your sanity. Hatred and jealousy hold bad karma."

"Bad karma?" Rachelle's laugh held more than a hint of ferocity. "Tell me about it! And what's this with Rob? He only stayed over thinking he could hang around you. Except Keefe put a sock in it and set him to work. Using Rob as a back-up, are you, dear? Can't have Keefe. Scott isn't interested. Maybe Robbie will do?"

Introducing Cousin Robert at this point caught Skye by surprise. She hadn't laid eyes on Rob since the day of the funeral.

"Well?" Rachelle gave Skye a disgusted look.

"Sorry, I need time to digest that, Rachelle. Rob is nice. I like him. But I have no romantic interest in him whatever."

"Maybe not but you do need a leg up in the world. A Sullivan would certainly do. But there again too much of a reach." Rachelle laughed with bitter triumph. "You're nothing but—"

She broke off hastily as a tall shadow fell. Both young women turned round to see Keefe standing barely a few feet away. How had he moved so silently? Skye marvelled. It didn't seem possible. But, then, Keefe managed to do some pretty incredible things.

"Is this really the place to have an argument?" he asked tersely, his light eyes blazing from one young woman to the other.

"Not an argument, Keefe." Colour flooded Rachelle's pale face. "I was laughing."

Keefe's expression would have daunted anyone. "If that was a laugh, Rachelle, you'd never get me to join in. Why are you always attacking Skye? Is it ever going to end? Skye has no interest in Rob. It's Rob who is out of his depth."

"Please, Keefe! Don't go on," Skye implored, seeing all Rachelle's bravado drain out like her life's blood. "Rachelle is very stressed. We all are. I came to pay my respects to your father and visit my mother's grave. I'll go now."

"Believe me, that's for the best," said Rachelle hoarsely, no more able to control herself than a two-year-old. "This is family. This is the family cemetery. I have fresh flowers in the Jeep for Dad. Are you going to join me, Keefe?" She swung her dark head to appeal to her brother.

"Yes," he returned sombrely, speaking directly to Skye. "No matter what happens, life goes on. We need to round up the best of the brumbies in the morning. We badly need a few more working horses. I thought you'd like to come along."

Rachelle moved closer to her brother. "Count me in. I'd like to come."

"I thought you regarded herding brumbies as a bad idea?" Keefe countered, looking down at his sister.

"Maybe I want to rediscover the thrill."

"Then I have to warn you, you might be sore and sorry the next day."

"What about *her*?" Rachelle countered, wearing a huge frown.

"Even you will have to admit Skye's a far better rider than you, Rachelle," Keefe said, keeping his tone level. "Also she keeps up with her riding when she's back in the city. I can't think when you last went out for a gallop, even if you do like to wear riding clothes. But I will say they suit you."

"I can keep up," Rachelle maintained stoutly. "I'll take one of the horses out this very afternoon. Give it a workout."

Keefe didn't answer, but turned back to Skye. "I'd like to make a pre-dawn start. Okay with you?"

The least contact with Rachelle left Skye feeling frayed. "Keefe, I think I'll pass," she told him quietly.

"You amaze me!" There was a satiric inflection in his voice. "Besides, you *can't* pass. I've counted you in."

They saddled up when Minghala, the dawn star, hung high in the east. It was still dark and the air was a good ten degrees cooler than it would be in only a few hours' time.

Keefe, sitting tall in the saddle, looked across to Skye. "Stick with me," he said.

"You got it, boss!" she mocked, touching a finger to the brim of her Akubra.

"You don't want to?" There was a twist to his mouth.

"It used to be much the best place to be." Their relationship was highly sexual but the strong attachment was also non-sexual. Their liking for each other, the interests they shared, their love of the land. It would always hold them together.

"Don't talk like it's history," he said.

And an odd history it was too! Swiftly she changed the subject. "I see you've allowed Rob to come along?' She looked towards the group of other riders. Rob Sullivan was a fine horseman and an excellent polo player. He often played on Keefe's team.

"Actually, Rob *begged* to come along," Keefe stressed. "He'll be an asset. I don't know about Rachelle." Rachelle made up the rest of the party along with three of the station's top aboriginal stockmen. All three had great tracking eyes—tracking was essential, demanding considerable skill—and a wonderful way with horses. One of them, Jonah, was manoeuvring his gelding back and forth in a parody of herding cattle. Everyone was mounted, circling the forecourt, getting the frisky horses under control.

"So where are we heading?" Skye could feel the build-up of excitement.

Keefe rode alongside her. "The mob has been spotted drinking near Jinjin Swamp. They could have moved on but some of the mares are carrying foals. That will slow them down."

"So who's the kingpin these days?" she asked, watching a very impatient-looking Rachelle scolding the horse she was riding. The mare *was* acting up a little, but there was no doubt Rachelle's bad mood was communicating itself to the animal.

"Still Old Man Mooki," Keefe said, lifting an arm and gesturing to the north-west to mark their start. "He's still capable of impregnating the mares and he's still full of fight. Mooki is as wily as they come. He's no use to us, of course, but there are ten or twelve decent-looking colts running with him. We're after them."

"How many in the mob?" She looked towards the horizon, now washed with ever-expanding bands of pearl grey, pink and lemon.

"Around thirty last time we checked. I know you're good at this, but don't take any chances."

She responded to the seriousness of his tone. "I won't."

"You might keep an eye on Rachelle from time to time. I've asked Rob to do the same. He's got one hell of a crush on you, by the way, and not hiding it very well."

"Some men wear their hearts on their sleeves, others give a woman only the occasional glimpse," she commented dryly.

"Maybe there's some underlying fear? Ever think of that? Clearly *I* can't wear my heart on my sleeve. I'm running this outfit."

"Don't worry. I've long since got the message."

"Have you *really*?" He flicked a diamond-hard glance at her. "Maybe you're not as good at interpreting as you think. Anyway, as a favour to me, don't give Rob the slightest encouragement. He doesn't need it."

"What, not even a smile?" Her blue eyes sparkled with challenge.

"Next thing you know he'll want to stay on longer." Keefe's answer was crisp.

"I don't think so," she disagreed. "There are lots of girls out there."

"Not like *you* there aren't," he clipped off. "Damn this thing!" He began to pull on the bandana around his neck to loosen it. They were all wearing protective bandanas. Hers was sapphire blue; Keefe's a bright red. The colour on him was wonderful, setting off the polished bronze of his skin.

She had never seen a man so impossibly dashing. "Anyway, it's like I said. I'm not going to compound your worries. I'm going home."

"Are you, Sky-Eyes?" He turned his dark head abruptly, pinning her gaze.

She took a quick fluttery breath. He hadn't called her *Sky-Eyes* since she couldn't remember when. "You know perfectly well I have to. You're my *fantasy* lover, Keefe," she said on a bitter-sweet note.

"Now you tell me. You dream of me." He looked straight ahead.

"Nightmares mostly." She laughed, but it came out off-key.

"But very *real*."

"*Very* real," she admitted, thinking of the torture of awakening to find he really wasn't there in the bed beside her.

"Even at their worst you want them," he said.

"One ought to be able to take medication for *want*."

"Maybe *want* is wired as much into the brain as the flesh." He broke off with a groan. "Look at Rachelle! Early morning isn't her scene. Why did she want to come?"

"Hopefully to see me take a tumble," she suggested, laconically.

"My sister is far more likely to be the one taking a tumble." His reply was grim.

"I hope not! Even under provocation I have no heart to wish any harm on Rachelle."

"Only on me."

"Don't be ridiculous, Keefe," she said sharply, rising above the difficulties that had been thrown in their way. "*You're* the person I'd miss most in the world. Not that you don't know it," she added, with a helpless flare of hostility.

He laughed beneath his breath, reaching across to lightly tap her hand. "Some things, Sky-Eyes, we can't change. Much as we fight it."

An hour later, the vast landscape was drenched in blazing sunlight. They cut a swathe through a section of Djinjara's great herd, which was moving in a slow, snake-like formation of well over a mile, undulating towards water. Riders surrounded the herd, keeping them in line with little effort. They exchanged waves. One of the aboriginal stockmen was giving voice to a native song not unlike a chant. Not only the cattle were finding the lilting sound calming, even though it had grown very hot by now. As always, they hoped for an afternoon thunderstorm to bring the blessed rain. Hope was everything on the desert fringe.

Jinjin was a moving mass of waterbirds, spoonbills, shags, white-faced herons with long pointed beaks, huge flocks of ibis. The pelicans wouldn't come into the swamps until they had good rains. Soaring red gums threw their long leafy arms over an amazing green carpet of lush grass with countless little wild-flowers in all shades of purple. Their sweet fragrance was satu-rating the air. Obviously the whole amazing area was flourishing on the moisture drawn from beneath. It was alive with droning bees and dragonflies and multicoloured butterflies that drifted about like spent petals raining down from the trees.

"You'd swear the old guy knew we were after him," Keefe swept off his Akubra to savour a moment of cool relief

"Not here, boss," Jonah called. "Bin here, though. Ya can see all the tracks. Mebbe this mornin'. Can't be far."

"We'll take a ten-minute break," Keefe decided, already starting to dismount. Everyone was tired. So tired. But deter-mined. There was a job to be done.

Skye followed suit. She was fading more quickly than she had thought. The shimmering heat over the spinifex plains was unholy. There was one plus, however. Her mare, with her thoroughbred lines and fine aristocratic head, was as smooth as silk to ride. That gave her extra confidence.

"This is awful!" Rachelle staggered up to them to complain. "I feel like I'm about to pass out." Her smooth olive skin was mottled with heat rash. Skye felt really sorry for her. No use to say, "You shouldn't have come, Rachelle." That would have been tantamount to waving a red flag in front of a bull.

Keefe looked at his sister with concern. "You wanted to come, Rachelle," he reminded her. "It *is* terribly hot. We're in for another dry storm. Why don't you relax for a while, cool down, then call it a day? We're over the worst of it, but there's more to come. The mob can't be far away."

Robert walked towards them, raising a hand. "It doesn't get much better than this," he enthused, his good-looking face aglow with heat and excitement. No brumby chases where he came from. No real rough and tumbles. "What a picturesque place!"

he exclaimed. "It has to be seen to be believed. You couldn't even count the butterflies. But no brumbies, alas!"

"We'll find them," Keefe said with conviction.

"How's it going, Skye?" Robert transferred his gaze to Skye, thinking she looked a vision even after a tough ride. Her beautiful skin was flushed, honey-gold wisps of hair escaped from her thick plait to stray around her face: her eyes were as vivid a blue as the sky.

"Don't worry about *her*," Rachelle broke in fiercely, obviously feeling very sorry for herself. "This is a real drag. I'll probably get stung by one of those damned bees." She swatted the golden-green air. "I could do with a cup of tea."

"Sorry. No tea," Keefe rose to his feet. "Tea later. We have to catch up with the mob. Old Man Mooki is onto us."

"Damn Old Man Mooki !" Rachelle cried out, in a fit of bad temper.

"Rachelle, I'm in no mood for mutiny." Keefe turned on his sister very quietly. "I understand you're tired. You've got right out of the way of things. We'll ride on, and you can head for home. Keep to the line of lagoons."

"I want Skye to come with me." Rachelle's dark glance veered from her brother to the silent, but sympathetic Skye.

"I'll come," Robert offered very gallantly when he was thoroughly enjoying the experience.

"I don't want *you*," Rachelle announced rudely. "I want Skye."

"Only Skye's riding with me," Keefe told his sister, this time in a no-nonsense type of voice. "So is Rob. He's having a ball. You can easily find your way back, Rachelle. I can spare Eddie to go with you. Just take it nice and easy. Drink often from your water bottle."

"Thanks for nothing!" Rachelle cried hotly.

"It's yourself you have to blame." Briefly Keefe touched her shoulder. "Mount up now. The rest of us have to keep moving."

"Wait and see. I'll probably get sunstroke." Rachelle issued the dire warning. She had so hoped to see Skye drooping from exhaustion. No such luck.

"No, you wont," Keefe assured her. "You're carrying the McGovern banner."

CHAPTER FIVE

THEY finally caught up with the mob at a borehole. Roughly thirty wild horses, very tricky to catch. Old Man Mooki was the big black stallion that had run for years with his motley mob and ever-increasing harem, some of them mares he had taken from the station. Many attempts had been made to yard him in the past but Mooki had great legs, hence great speed. These days he wasn't as tough as he had been, but was still a formidable opponent.

"Let them drink their fill." From the shelter of the trees, Keefe issued the order just above his breath. "Slow 'em down. Then we'll try to drive them towards Yalla Creek. The bed is dry and the banks are steep. With any luck at all, the sand will wear them out."

Muscles tense, they awaited their moment.

Sharp old Mooki sensed them before they got anywhere near them. The colts threw up their heads as though at a signal. The mares began to snort and kick up. Next minute they were off, in a thunder of black, bay, piebald and chestnut bodies. They were moving so fast it seemed like they didn't have a hope in hell of catching them, Skye thought, hot on the chase. The mob, with Mooki in the lead, was doubling back towards the trees, unshod hooves pounding up a great billowing cloud of red dust, tangled manes and tails whipping in their own momentum.

They spread out, five of them now with Rachelle and Eddie out of the game. For the plan to succeed they had to head Mooki off. Turn him round. The mob would follow. It took nerve, but they forced themselves on, trying to ignore the heat of the day. Gradually the mares came down to a canter, one of the mares in foal dropping out of the race. The rest of the harem was slowing. Mooki and the colts were dead set to fight for their freedom. Keefe had plotted their course of action in advance. Yalla Creek wasn't all that far off. The sandy bed would prove heavy going for all the horses, including their own. The danger was that the youngsters in the mob would endeavour to get to the opposite side of the creek. The trick was not to give them the opportunity.

Keefe thundered past her, his bush shirt stuck to his back with sweat. He was taking chances, but he was a splendid horseman and his big gelding had endurance and a fabulous turn of speed.

Incredibly, out of nowhere a group of adult emus, standing nearly two metres high, decided to join in the chase. They must have felt threatened in some way because they put on a tremendous burst of speed—they were capable of sixty kilometres an hour—outrunning the tiring horses. It was a fantastic sight and would have been very funny if it hadn't been so dangerous to man and beast.

Heart in her throat, Skye found her second wind. She picked up her own speed, fanning out wide with Rob fanning away to her left. What if an emu decided to veer across their tracks? Years before a mounted stockman had been killed in a freak encounter with an irate emu protecting its nest. The only thing that surprised her was that a mob of kangaroos hadn't joined in. Give either species, just a hint of a chase and it was on!

Ahead Keefe and one of the stockmen had Mooki boxed in. Skye and Rob brought up the rear, with the remaining stockman going to their assistance. The brumby stallion was as good as penned. Only not to be outdone, Mooki took a mighty plunge into the creek, his hooves threshing about in the loose sand, his heaving sides lathered in sweat. A few of the colts hesitated, as though they knew they'd be bogged down in the sand, but the others followed their leader.

Inside ten minutes it was all over. The flightless emus, satisfied there was no threat being posed to them, trotted off sedately on their long grey legs. Keefe took his pick of the worn-out colts. The others, including the old war horse, Mooki, he let go.

"Really should shoot the ugly old thing!" Rob muttered. "He's a real pest."

"No need." Keefe would only shoot a horse when he absolutely had to. "Mooki is on his last legs. Have to hand it to him. He's a game old guy. What we have to do now is yard the colts. Not a bad bunch. We should be able to turn them into good working horses."

It turned out to be a hollow victory.

"I don't like the look of that sky." Keefe stared upwards with a frown on his brow. He had been sensing trouble for a while now. Familiar as they all were with the dry electrical storms, many times he found himself relying on a mix of intuition and experience for further developments. The mushrooming masses of steel-grey and black were almost directly overhead. It would be a miracle if there was rain in them. Still, the odd miracle did happen.

Thankfully they had finished constructing a makeshift holding yard, using stout coolabahs for posts. The colts had gone in quietly enough but now they were starting to mill about as glaring silver-blue flashes of lightning rent the heavens, followed by loud booms of thunder.

"Better take cover," Keefe shouted over the abruptly rising wind. Their own horses were tied up securely. The stockmen set to arranging a tarpaulin as some sort of shelter. "Go on, Skye. Move it," Keefe ordered, over the howl of the wind. This was one time he wished she weren't there.

"You'd better move it too," she shouted back at him. "I don't like the look of this either." There could be a short sharp deluge, or the whole thing would pass yet again. It was those jagged lightning bolts that posed the danger.

"I'm not going to stand here arguing." Keefe seized her, easily gathering her up with one arm and sheltering her with his body. They made a race towards shelter but didn't make it before a lightning bolt, like a gigantic flashing mirror, shot down the sky like a missile and buried itself in the centre of the tallest gum. The strike was so bright it seared the eyes. Momentarily blinded, Skye felt Keefe's strong arm tighten to steel as he pitched her beneath the tarpaulin where she went sprawling on her hands and knees. Slightly winded, when she opened her eyes it was to see him turning back to free the penned colts.

The huge gum tree was still holding but fire was blossoming all over it so it stood like a towering armed statue alive with electric-blue flame.

The screams from the colts were horrifying; near human in terror, severely unsettling the station horses that were out of harm's way. Eddie had sprung to attention, going to Keefe's aid. Sooner or later the tree was going to explode. What then?

Skye started praying for a miracle.

Please bring on the rain.

She couldn't remain in the shelter. Surely they needed every pair of hands. Shakily she rose to her feet, feeling pain around her midriff where Keefe had grabbed her. Swiftly she made the judgment she would be best employed helping Rob tackle the far corner of the yard. Her bandana would have to act as a glove. She ripped it off, wrapping it tightly around her right hand. There wasn't a second to lose.

Keefe caught sight of her out of the corner of his eye. "I told you to keep back, Skye," he roared. "We'll handle it. Do what I tell you."

"I'll be okay!" she defied him, realising she was probably the only person on Djinjara who would dare to.

The truly bizarre thing was the wonderfully intoxicating smell of the burning tree.

"Hurry, Skye, we can do it!" Rob yelled to her, thrilled by her sheer guts. The heat was so intense they risked getting scorched but the focus was on freeing the wild horses.

She couldn't run away and hide. She had to face it. Do her bit.

Keefe's end of the makeshift yard predictably fell first, quickly followed by a general collapse. The terrified horses bolted out of the wrecked enclosure, galloping in a frenzy of fright for the open plain.

"Get to the gully." Keefe threw out an imperative hand, racing back to where the station horses were tethered. He untied the terrified animals, sending them on their way with a hard slap on the rump.

"Do you *ever* do what you're told?" Keefe got a fierce grip on Skye, half lifting her off the ground as they made a run for the gully, where he plunged them both in. It was from there, standing thigh deep in yellow brackish water, that they watched the gum tree come down with a mighty roar, sending up a billion sparks and a high, spiralling tongue of flame. That intoxicating smell of burning eucalyptus wood saturated the air.

Then came the smoke. Not good. That started them off coughing. Keefe buried Skye's head against his chest, his bush shirt sodden with gully water.

"Phew!" he exclaimed hoarsely. "I've never seen anything like that in my life."

Tentatively Skye lifted her head, her sensitive nostrils flaring at a new scent on the air. Sulphur. "Keefe, I think it's going to rain," she said, wonder in her voice.

Keefe threw up his water-slicked dark head, his expression matching hers. "It is!" he said in amazement.

"Gosh, isn't that wonderful?" The moment seemed so ecstatic, words just bubbled up as if from an underground spring. "Want to kiss me?" she challenged, turning up her wet, glowing face.

"Do I!" He reached for her with tremendous urgency. The rain came pelting down… He continued to hold her, kissing her fiercely, never moving his mouth from hers. Mouths and bodies were fused wetly, unmistakably passionately together. They appeared to be oblivious to everyone and everything, even the rounds of clapping and the gleeful whoops!

Time to go home, Rob Sullivan thought, stunned by all he had witnessed. Now this! Keefe was a magnificent guy.

I guess he needs a magnificent woman.

The night before she was due to fly out of Djinjara on the first leg of her way home—Robert was heading back with her—Skye was invited up to the Big House for dinner. The invitation had been issued by Lady Margaret. She understood it had to be obeyed. She felt a violent tug of war on her emotions. She desperately wanted to be with Keefe before she left and she wanted to spend that last evening with her father.

"Go, love, go!" Jack expressed his encouragement. "Lady McGovern thinks the world of you." He paused for a telling moment. "So does Keefe."

"The kiss got around?" Skye faced her father across the table.

"Yeah, well, what did you expect, love? We all know you and Keefe share a bond. I sort of thought of it as…affection?"

He sounded worried, Skye thought. How had he missed her real feelings for Keefe? He was her father after all. Or had he deliberately chosen to hide from what had been right under his nose? Damaged people did. "You have a problem with me kissing Keefe, Dad?" she prompted, fully aware her father was a man who, in his own words, "kept his place". Was he worried that he could possibly lose his job as a result of this new development?

"Problem?" Jack's expression suddenly relaxed. "As I heard it, he grabbed *you*!"

Skye reached for his hand. Now wasn't the right moment to confide in him. "It was just one of those things. You know how it is. The rain coming down at that precise moment was fantastic. Like a gift from Heaven. It put out the fire."

"Still, a *kiss*?" Jack, not to be put off, searched her eyes.

"A kiss, Dad. That's all."

Jack scoffed. "A single kiss can change a life. I should know. So how is this kiss going to affect everyone at the house? I reckon you ought to prepare yourself for some attack from Rachelle. By the way, Scott's girlfriend turned up this afternoon when you were out taking photographs."

She nodded. "I noticed a plane fly over when I was taking shots of Manguri." She referred to Djinjara's revered desert monument. "By Scott's girlfriend, you mean Jemma Templeton?"

Jack nodded. "That's the word. Plain girl, but very sweet and gracious. Too good for Scott, I fear. He won't be faithful."

"I expect not," Skye sighed. "You think they'll make a match of it?"

"I'm more interested in what's going on between you and Keefe." Jack continued to study Skye's face. "It seems to me in a perfect world, you'd be perfect for each other. But in the *real* world there's me, your dad. Plain old Jack McCory, station overseer, a man who had to leave school at fourteen. You can take your place anywhere, you're a beautiful, educated woman, but I'm just good old Jack. Are you anxious about that, love?"

Skye's tender heart melted. "How could I possibly be anxious about you, Dad? I love you. Never mind with the McGoverns. Anyway, Keefe thinks very highly of you. You wouldn't be overseer if you couldn't handle everything that's thrown at you."

"True." Jack felt quite secure in his own capabilities as Djinjara's overseer. "But *socially*, I mean. The McGoverns are Outback royalty. We both know that. Look at it from the family's point of view."

"You're jumping too far ahead, Dad." She strove to slow him down, though she herself was concerned about the McGovern's reactions.

"If Keefe kissed you—in front of everyone—it means he couldn't care less about what anyone thinks," Jack reasoned. "I see it as the equivalent of a commitment. Especially from Keefe. It wouldn't mean much coming from Scott, but Keefe is something else again."

"I can't argue with that," she said quietly. "But I'm sure the family is expecting Keefe to do a whole lot better than me. Best to face it squarely, Dad."

"Damn it all, he *couldn't* do better," Jack stoutly maintained. "But we both know the McGovern clan are first-class snobs. That Rachelle has given you hell over the years."

Skye sighed. "She has in her way, but it's not so much snobbery, Dad. Rachelle has convinced herself I robbed her of her brother's affection. It's not true, but that's the way she feels. She doesn't have a lot of insight into her own behaviour."

"Have you and Keefe come to any sort of agreement?" Jack asked tentatively. "You don't have to tell me if you don't want to. At least, not until there's something to say."

"There's nothing *to* say, Dad." She shook her head. "Keefe and I have always shared a strong bond but we haven't moved on. There are all sorts of difficulties."

"I can see something is weighing heavily on your mind.

Don't worry, I won't ask. I'll wait for you to tell me. You're the best daughter in the world." He covered her hand with his own.

Jack drove her up to the house at seven sharp. She had anticipated being asked to dinner at least once so she had packed a pair of black evening trousers worn with a simple black top with a sapphire-blue satin trim. She clipped on silver earrings and a rather lovely silver cuff. Black high heels and she was ready to present herself for McGovern inspection. She had learned Jemma's parents had arrived with her. The father, Farleigh Templeton, had been piloting his Beech Baron.

Keefe was waiting for her in the hallway. Immediately she felt that manic upsurge in her blood. It was hell to be so passionately in love with him. She should stay away from him entirely.

You can't do that. He's in your blood.

And there it was again. The question of *blood*.

"You look beautiful, very *chic*!" His brilliant gaze flared over her, taking in every last detail.

The pride in his voice made her heart ache. How had she found the strength to deny him when he had wanted her? Yet she had. There was such a cloud hanging over them.

"You know the Templetons are here?" He took her arm, his long fingers a caress.

"Dad told me. Maybe they want to put a bit of pressure on Scott?" she suggested.

"I wonder if that would be wise." Keefe's expression went wry. "Right now I can't think Scott would make a good husband. He has a bit of maturing to do."

"How would you rate yourself as a potential husband?" She gave him a sideways glance.

"What a question!"

"Maybe you can't or won't bring the same singularity of purpose you apply to everything else to settling on the right woman."

"Stop it, Skye," he warned, catching her hand and pressing his thumb into the palm. "God, I wish you weren't going back tomorrow."

"I must." Just his thumb working her palm, yet the movement radiated sexuality. Her entire body was aquiver. "There's bound to be something pressing to claim me. By the way, you'd best tell me now. Has Rob given the family the tip-off about our un-premeditated kiss?"

"To my knowledge Rob hasn't said a word," Keefe said. "And really, Skye-Eyes, that had to be one of the best kisses of all time."

"Agreed." She couldn't help but smile. "But you took a risk. The news has flown around. Dad spoke to me about it. I would say he's concerned."

"About what, exactly?" Keefe asked coolly. "You've learned nothing from him about your mother?"

"My mother was Dad's mystery woman, Keefe."

"Was there *nothing* he asked her?"

"Seems not." She shrugged wryly. "Dad deemed it a miracle when my mother said she would marry him."

"Not much of a courtship," he said bluntly.

Skye came to a halt, her eyes a blue flame. "Dad's love for my mother was *real*."

"I don't doubt it." Keefe spoke with a mixture of frustration and impatience. "I'll pick my moment carefully to speak to Gran. I suppose an interrogation is what it amounts to. Even if we *are* related in some way—it seems we're both enmeshed in that one—it can't be all that close."

"Yet we've always had feelings for one another, haven't we? Strong feelings. A strong bond."

His lean fingers tightened around her arm. "So what does that prove?" He offered it like a challenge.

"It proves there's a strong possibility cracks in our relation-ship might open up."

* * *

They were all assembled in the very English-looking drawing room, the huge area divided by a splendid triple arch and lit by two magnificent matching Waterford crystal chandeliers. Insolent Scott and a smiling Farleigh Templeton stood in front of the white marble fireplace, filled for most of the year with a variety of lush indoor plants and blossoming branches. Over the mantel hung an enormous rectangular, very important-looking Georgian mirror, reflecting the backs of the heads of the two tall men.

There was no shortage of serious antiques in the Big House, Skye thought wryly. Yet they mingled happily with more exotic items from India and the Orient. Lady McGovern herself had until fairly recent times been a great collector of just about everything: paintings—one would have thought they had enough—porcelain; beautiful pieces of furniture; exquisite rugs. And books. Lady McGovern loved books. They were stacked on just about every table. Skye, a book lover herself, had absolutely no argument with that. She only wished she could grab a few. She spotted Margot Fonteyn's biography side by side with Robert Helpmann's on the library table in the entrance hall as they had come in.

Rachelle had cornered Rob, who was looking more than a little rattled. A youthful-looking Meredith Templeton, far better endowed than her daughter in the looks department, was in the midst of an animated conversation with Lady McGovern, with Jemma looking quietly on. They all broke off to stare at Skye as she entered the room with the Master of Djinjara.

The two of them seen together were stunning. Perfect foils for each other, Lady McGovern thought. Keefe so dark of hair and bronzed of complexion; Skye the blue-eyed, golden-honey blonde. Skye, being Skye, was giving no thought to the impact of her own beauty, unaware she was catching all the light. Of course they had all heard versions of that burning kiss. She, for

one, heard *everything* that went on at the vast station. Some
things she wouldn't tell. Things that were secreted in her heart.
Not that she had one hundred per cent proof. Just the awful
nagging anxiety that had never left her. The bond between Skye
and her beloved grandson forged in childhood had reached the
dangerous stage.

Such a shame, a shame, a terrible shame… Both would be
badly wounded. That's if it was the truth. Lady McGovern took
turns at belief and disbelief. Too fearful of going further. Lives
could be destroyed. But knowing her grandson as she did, she
knew he wouldn't rest until he had the truth by the throat. Her
unwillingness to speak of the past—the secrets she had buried—
she accepted now would have to be revealed with all their wider
implications. Not only Keefe and Skye would be devastated.
What about Jack? Sometimes nothing was as it appeared to be.
Sometimes the truth destroyed.

Dinner was over. Skye walked with Keefe through the home
gardens, under palm fronds and low-arching branches freighted
with summer blossom. Above them a glorious starred sky:
Orion, the mighty hunter, Alpha, Centauri, Sirius, watchdog of
the night sky, the sparkling river of diamonds, Lilah Lilya, the
Milky Way, and burning bright over the sandhills the five points
of Jirranjoonga, the Southern Cross. Around them a wonderfully scented desert landscape. They might have been inside a
bush cathedral. Silently, as though locked in their own
thoughts, they reached one of the pavilions that had been built
at various points around the extensive grounds. This one, hex-
agonal in structure, featured white trelliswork that supported
a prolifically flowering king jasmine. After the intense heat of
the day, the desert quickly cooled off, so the air was sublimely
fresh.

Without a word, Keefe put his strong hands to her slender

hips, trapping her against him. "Alone at last!" His striking face bore an expression that held both hunger and pain.

She sighed deeply as an answering emotion engulfed her. Sensually she leaned into him. So thrilling! "Did you see their faces?"

"Okay." He drew back, a faint edge to his voice, knowing his family had heard about the kiss. "I saw their faces. But I thought dinner went well. The Templetons are very pleasant people."

"They are. Even so, it was easy to gauge everyone's surprise. Correction—make that shock."

"Who would care?" he said impatiently. "There couldn't be a woman on earth who makes me feel like you do. Come closer to me, Skye. I can't seem to get you close enough.'

Unable to help herself, she fitted herself against him. They were a perfect physical match. "This is what it comes to in the end, isn't it?" she asked poignantly. "We need to make love."

"Evidently I want it more than you do," he told her with a twisted smile.

"I wouldn't be too sure of that." She turned her head this way and that so he could nuzzle her neck. Impossible to *think* when her whole body was transformed into a column of sensation.

"What bothered me more was the way Scott kept directing looks your way." He lifted his head abruptly to search her face.

So Scott had. Looks that had made her feel she needed to protect herself. But she couldn't tell Keefe that. Thwarted desire only too often turned to hate. "People don't change," she said very quietly.

"He won't bother you." His vibrant voice held a distinct rasp.

"He can scarcely do that as I'm going home."

"So you keep saying." He pressed his mouth to the sensitive spot beneath her ear. Not content, he slipped off her earring and put it in his pocket. Then he returned to teasing and gently nipping the lobe. "I thought Djinjara was your home?" he muttered. "I detest these separations."

She gave a little discordant laugh. "Just think, if we were anywhere else—in the city instead of on Djinjara—I suppose I could be your mistress?" There was just a glimmer of goading in her voice. "Your sister finds it *unthinkable* you could fall in love with me. Your grandmother too looked very watchful. She's fond of me but I definitely don't figure in her plans."

He broke off his ministrations, stepping out of the role of lover. "Much as I love Gran, I make my own plans," he said firmly. "You ought to know that."

"Then what are we *doing*, Keefe?" She sought an answer.

"Could you forget me?" he countered with intensity.

"Sometimes I wish I could," she burst out emotionally. "Sometimes—"

"Sometimes, sometimes...do you how much I ache for you?" Keefe lowered his head, covered her mouth so effectively it cut off her breath.

He kissed her until she was whimpering, desperate to fall into his bed.

"This is torture," he muttered. He was speaking for both of them. His tongue parted her lips again, making urgent contact with the slickness within. It was an intense encounter. No time for tenderness. Only raw passion, made more ravenous by the prospect of being parted. He was holding her so powerfully, her juddering back was arched against the vine covered trellis. It was *insane*—someone might come—but she was letting herself simply melt. His hand, imperceptibly trembling, had pushed down into her low-necked top, his fingers finding her already swollen nipple, working it and her into an erotic frenzy. She could feel his hard arousal. Her own core had long since gone liquid in response.

One of his long legs drove hers apart. They strained ever closer with the primitive desire to be naked. However lightly she was dressed, Skye felt her clothing to be as restrictive as a spacesuit. There was only one end to this kind of love-making. Where they were and who they were was all but obliterated by a consuming passion. Such was the level of intensity she wanted to tear at his clothes, press her mouth against his naked chest. Her hand moved to the buttons of his shirt. She wanted skin, not fabric.

"Someone is coming," he muttered in her ear. Even then he had to say it twice.

"Oh!" She strained to hear. Then the sound of a too-familiar voice, "They must be around here somewhere."

Skye forced herself to move. She was having difficulty trying to regulate her breathing. Only Keefe, in a gesture that wasn't at all hurried, clasped her arm. "Sometimes I love my sister. Other times I loathe her. Let's get out of here before she moves in on us."

A few minutes later Rachelle, hot on the trail, followed by a reluctant and embarrassed Jemma and a silent Scott, found them strolling companionably along the wooden bridge that spanned the lily pool. There was nothing in their demeanour to suggest this wasn't simply a friendly after-dinner stroll yet when Keefe turned to answer a question from Jemma—something to do with the waterlilies—Scott seized the opportunity to move too close to Skye's side.

In the darkness his hand trailed insolently down over her back. He took the insult a step further, pressing his fingers into the sides of her breasts. "I bet you two have had it off," he whispered in her ear, taking advantage of the cover afforded by Rachelle's over-loud voice. "Didn't want *me*, though, did you?" he muttered. "Only Keefe would do. But that's *all* you are to him, sweetheart, a groundsheet."

It was an outpouring of jealousy and venom. On the verge of slapping his face with all her might, Skye brought herself under control. "I pity poor Jemma," she muttered with the utmost contempt, spinning to face him. "You're a pig!"

It was an insult but from the smile on Scott's face he appeared to enjoy it.

Indeed, Scott was thinking there was no reason why he shouldn't give Skye hell. His strong attraction to her had never wavered. It leapt to a consistent high every time he laid eyes on her. It seemed entirely reasonable to him that if a man wasn't allowed to love a woman, he might as well do an about-face and hate her. After all love and hate were but two sides of the same coin. Her beauty alone charged his anger. How in hell was he supposed to marry poor old Jemma? She was as prim as a convent-trained schoolgirl. No excitement there. No extravagant desire. Just a dreary safe match. He wouldn't even consider it only Jemma would bring with her a handsome dowry. What had he to lose really? Jemma would love him no matter what he did. And he fully intended to do as he pleased. She was a fool to trust him. But, then, she was the sort of woman who could blind herself to the foibles of the man she loved.

At this point, Scott's complex feelings towards his brother turned savage. He was shot through with envy. Why should *Keefe* get everything he wanted? Why should Keefe get Skye? There was something in the McCorys' background that needed to be investigated. Some kind of crisis involving Skye's mother. He had always assumed Jack McCory had got her pregnant, thereby forcing a marriage. Why else would she have married him? She had been a lady from all accounts. What the hell was Jack McCory? A stockman on the lowest rung of the ladder. How had Gran allowed it? He had never heard his grandmother mention let alone discuss Catherine McCory in his entire life. Yet Catherine McCory had been buried in the McGovern graveyard.

There had to be a reason. All of a sudden Scott was determined on knowing what.

CHAPTER SIX

LADY MARGARET MCGOVERN was sitting in front of her triple-mirrored dressing table, staring sightlessly at her own reflection. It revealed a deeply troubled eighty-year-old woman whose features still bore the vestiges of great beauty. Lady Margaret was waiting for her beloved grandson Keefe to join her. She dreaded the thought of anyone overhearing their discussion. Rachelle wasn't above eavesdropping. Neither, for that matter, was Scott, but they were downstairs with Jemma and her parents, playing cards. Rachelle adored card games and she was a very good chess player. Lady Margaret knew full well the Templetons and, of course, Jemma herself had their hearts set on a match with Scott. They had made that perfectly plain. Lady Margaret had wanted—had indeed tried—to speak to Jemma. To warn her? But she despaired of Jemma now. That young woman would be deaf to anything in the least negative she had to say about Scott. She was convinced Jemma knew in her heart that married life with Scott would be far from easy, but it was obvious Jemma preferred to be miserable with Scott than happy with anyone else.

So there it was! A marriage that would somehow endure or inevitably crash. Only time would tell.

This conversation with Keefe had to be kept entirely confidential. That was why it was being conducted in the privacy of her bedroom. Not that she planned to initiate anything. She would wait on Keefe's questions, then try to steer a safe course through a sea littered with icebergs. Nothing much in Cathy's background to be worried about. Her personal history was something else again. Stick with the background. The wonder of it was she hadn't been called to account long before this. Such a heavy burden! She would be glad to lay it down. Keeping secrets was a curse.

Keefe knocked on the door then entered on his grand-mother's summons.

He had to smile. It was as much a command as a simple response to his knock. As long as he could remember, his grandmother had been very much in command. Keefe opened the door into the richly furnished bedroom, with its canopied bed, antique furnishings and fine paintings. The sitting room, equally opulent, was to one side, dressing room, bathroom to the other. His grandmother was seated in a splendid gilt armchair, one of a pair she and his grandfather had bought at a Christie's auction many years before. The antiques had all but taken over, he thought. But his grandmother had always indulged her passion for collecting. Perhaps to a fault.

She was still wearing the violet silk dress she had worn at dinner but she had taken off her double string of perfectly matched pearls. They were so big that on someone else—outside Royalty—they would have been mistaken for costume jewellery. Not so his grandmother.

The expression on her face was mask-like as usual, but he knew the mask covered a seething cauldron of emotions. Either way it rent his heart. He loved his grandmother, even if he was aware of her manipulative qualities and secretive nature. She had such *presence*.

"Sit down, dear," she said, indicating the other chair with a graceful wave of her hand.

Keefe laughed. "I think I'll take the sofa, Gran. I'd hate to break one of those gilded legs.'

"Don't be silly, darling," she chided. "Your grandfather used to sit in them. Your grandfather bought them, for that matter. For me, of course."

"A lot of years have gone by since then, I think." Keefe chose to lower his six-foot-plus frame onto the sofa, which was covered in a beautiful, white patterned blue silk. "You look tense, Gran," he began, knowing a moment of anxiety and regret that this conversation had to come about. Since his father's death his grandmother, a permanent fixture in his life, was looking decidedly frail. "I don't want to worry you or cause you upset, but there are some things I need to know."

"You love Skye?" Lady McGovern cut to the heart of it.

He had no intention of denying it. That would be a betrayal of the woman he loved. "I've always loved her. You must know that. I loved her when we were kids. I'm madly in love with Skye, the woman. She's everything I want."

"So what is it you wish to know?"

The question was asked in such a way there couldn't have been a thing in Skye's background that wouldn't bear scrutiny.

Keefe's striking features grew tight with controlled anger. Here it was again. The long-maintained silence; the stonewalling, what had to be a cover-up. "I want to know all about Skye's mother's background," he said in a quiet voice that nevertheless demanded she listen. "I want, Skye wants—and her wants are more important than mine—some kind of resolution on this. The not knowing is impacting heavily on our relationship. You were obviously very attached to Skye's mother. It was on your say-so she was buried in the family cemetery. No one outside the family ever has been accorded that privilege—call it what you like."

"*Privilege* is what *I* call it," Lady McGovern said severely, attempting to hide her trepidation behind matriarchal power. She knew it wouldn't work with Keefe. He was Master of Djinjara now. She was the McGovern dowager.

"Tell me who Catherine McCory really was. The little you've revealed over the years just isn't so. She's never been spoken about within the family. Dad, to my knowledge, rarely mentioned her, yet he was very kind to Skye.'

"Who wouldn't be?" Lady McGovern raised her thinly arched brows.

"She *was* related to you, wasn't she? Come out with it, Gran. We've all taken that on board. Was her maiden name really Newman? So far we have been able to find a record of a Catherine Newman entering the country from the UK for two years before she first came to visit."

"We? You and Skye have been checking?" Lady McGovern's expression turned steely.

"*I* have someone on it, Gran." He cut her short. "I can't allow you to override the fact I love Skye. I want to marry her but I need to be able to think ahead."

"Dear God!" Lady McGovern threw up her hands in horror. "How could you betray *family*, Keefe? I don't believe it!"

"With all due respect, Gran, you might be the one who's been doing that," he retorted bluntly. "It hasn't been easy to go behind your back but you, yourself, are the cause of that. Would you answer the question please? What *is* the mystery? Was Catherine sent out here because of a certain incident, her behaviour perhaps? Could she have been a little wild in her youth? She was dead at twenty-two. She appeared to have had no one. No family. It's as if she didn't belong anywhere. You took charge of her. I want to know why. I believe it's your duty to tell me. Skye certainly has a right to know. Far from investigating, Skye actually fears delving into her mother's background. You must know that. It's an instinctive thing, call it intuition. For the past couple of years Skye has been full of unease. So have I. But why *unease* exactly? Both of us have it in our heads we're somehow related. It has stopped us from going forward. But it couldn't be *close* surely, so what's the problem? Now's your time to tell me. Put certain issues to rest. I can't lose Skye. I can't allow her to move away from me. It's not on. So tell me, what brought Catherine to Australia? What brought her to *you*? Djinjara is the McGovern spiritual and ancestral home, but it's just about as remote as a young girl could get from a home in England. I should warn you to tell the truth. A lot rides on it."

"Warn me?" Lady McGovern stared back at her grandson in shock.

"Yes, warn you, Gran," he confirmed quietly, taking her thin trembling hand. "I fully intend to marry Skye, but not until this matter is cleared up. Can't you see both of us need reassurance, Skye most of all? The mystery if there is one, needs to be solved. I need to set her mind at rest. I can't imagine for the life of me why there has *been* all this mystery surrounding Catherine Newman. I need enlightenment right now."

"Neumann," Lady McGovern corrected, looking away from her grandson's dynamic face. "Katrina Neumann. Katrina was a wild child. She was the daughter of a dear childhood friend of mine, Leonora Werner. We went to school together. I often vacationed at Leonora's beautiful family manor as a girl. We were playing in the garden when we overheard a conversation between Leonora's mother, Iona, and her husband, Axel. Axel was accusing Iona of being unfaithful to him. Leonora wasn't his child. Previously he had doted on her and Leonora on him. Lord knows, Axel Werner had many an affair himself, but there again the double standard. He was quite the playboy, very blond, blue eyed, very handsome, German born. Leonora's mother swore that whoever had told him such a thing was out for some kind of sick revenge. Perhaps one of *his* lovers?"

"That must have been terrible for your friend." Keefe frowned, trying to process all this unexpected information.

"Terrible for us both, but naturally Leonora felt the shock most violently. We ran away as fast as we could. We had to stop when she was became ill. I could only kneel and hold her head while she retched her heart out. That was the start of it all. Leonora's parents separated soon after that, divorced. Leonora wasn't mentioned in her *father's* will, although she was an only child. She never contested it, believing herself to be illegitimate. Who knows, maybe she was? One wouldn't like to count the number of cases where the husband isn't the biological father. I promised Leonora when she was dying that Katrina would have safe haven with me if she was ever in need of it. Iona blamed Leonora, shockingly unfairly, for the break-up of her marriage. Leonora left home at age seventeen, she'd been at boarding school with me most of the time. She and her mother never spoke again."

Keefe shook his head incredulously. "It's a sad story, Gran, but it hardly warrants all this secrecy. Unless Skye's mother came to you pregnant with no place to turn?"

"No, no!" Margaret McGovern vigorously shook her pure white head.

"I'm asking you again, Gran," he said tautly, wanting to keep her on track.

"Katrina wanted to put half the world between herself and the past." Lady McGovern was showing her agitation. "She came on her own to Australia. She knew about me, of course, from her mother. It took great courage what she did. She could have had a splendid life. Personally I believe Leonora *was* Axel's child. Axel was very blond, blue eyed. But then so was Leonora, Iona and Katrina," she sighed. "The look and the colouring passed to Skye. I used to think I saw a resemblance to Axel Werner in my friend. Even in Skye."

"DNA could have solved it but then it wasn't available in those days." Keefe frowned.

"Good enough reason for a lot of women to fear it now it is," Lady McGovern shot back, her tone harsh. She began to flex her arthritic fingers.

"So what you're saying is at some time Katrina aka Catherine met Jack McCory, who is still a fine-looking man, fell in love with him, maybe became pregnant before they got around to getting married. Is that it? Lift your head, please, Gran. I can't see your eyes."

Lady McGovern felt like she was suffocating, a pillow held over her head. Airless, struggling for breath, she answered, "I've always believed Katrina married Jack McCory when she found herself pregnant. What has caused me endless trauma over these long years is that I don't believe Jack is Skye's father."

A deadly silence filled up the opulent room.

Keefe sprang up from the sofa, a man pole-axed. *"Dear God!"* His exclamation of shock resounded like a rifle shot.

"I can't bear to say it again," Lady McGovern told him, very piteously for her.

"Then who, Gran?" Keefe at that moment was laying full blame on his grandmother's shoulders. "Put a name to your fears. But be very, very careful. My father was a great man. He was a married man. Maybe his marriage didn't work out the way he hoped, but he was no adulterer."

Lady McGovern blinked rapidly. "What are you saying, Keefe?" Her tone soared. "What are you thinking? Your father, Broderick, never! Please calm yourself."

"I'm calm enough," he retorted angrily. "I repeat. Who?" Keefe, realising he was shouting, reined himself in.

Lady McGovern drew a long quavering breath. "Jonty," she managed at long last. "My dead son, Jonty. Your Uncle Jonathon.

As a revelation it had never crossed Keefe's mind. He

slumped back onto the sofa, holding his head in his two hands. "Uncle Jonty?" he asked in patent disbelief. Uncle Jonty, who had taken a fatal crash off his motorbike while rounding up a few head of cattle. Uncle Jonty, who had died at roughly the same age as Katrina Neumann.

Lady McGovern looked across at her splendid grandson, seeing his tremendous shock. "I could be wrong," she said, very timidly. "But they fell in love."

Keefe felt the tension in every knotted muscle of his body. "God, Gran! We've been focusing on Catherine and all along you've been worrying yourself sick thinking Uncle Jonathon could have been the father of Katrina's child. Which would make Skye my first cousin."

"Exactly." Lady McGovern drew a jagged breath, wondering if she was about to have a panic attack. "Of course, first cousins have married, but—"

"A damned big *but*!" Keefe cried, making no excuse for swearing in front of his grandmother, something he had never done. Skye would be horrified. She could even call a halt to their relationship, even if he already knew he was prepared to go ahead. *No matter what*. His mind was working furiously. He wasn't exactly certain but he was pretty sure there was no legal or moral impediment to first cousins marrying. If his grandmother's revelation was true, he knew in his heart it would have a devastating impact on Skye. And Jack. No getting away from it! "Stop there, Gran," he said with the voice of command. "Just stop. I need time to take this all in."

Right outside Lady McGovern's door, one ear pressed against the woodwork, a third party stood and listened. Keefe's voice, deep and resonant, carried at any time. When he shouted—he did so rarely, no need to when everyone stood to attention—the sound carried into the carpeted hallway.

So Skye McCory was a close relative after all! That was enough to break up any family. Enough to break up a passionate love affair. This piece of information, which had come as just as much of a shock as it had to Keefe, cried aloud to be used…

Skye spent all morning in court. She was seated just behind Derrick Sellway, a big blond handsome thirty-five-year-old man in an expensive dark suit. Derrick was the barrister representing her client. She had done her job to the best of her ability, assembling all the information necessary for Derrick to plead their client's case and hopefully win her a fairer deal. This was a particularly messy fight over money. Not big money as money went, but rather an unholy war between a brother and sister who had gained far bigger legacies from their late father's estate, and the other sister, much younger than the other two, their client, presenting her case to the court for a fairer deal. The brother and elder sister were prosperous people very much acting together. The younger sister had come through a sad divorce and had been left holding the children, in her case twins. She had had a falling-out with her father over her choice of a husband. But now the husband was gone. Literally fled overseas. Their client's circumstances had been considerably reduced. Skye thought she had done enough background checking on the brother and elder sister. In her view—and she hoped in the view of the court—a whole lot of undue influencing had gone on with the ailing father, obviously in an effort to gain, if not the entire estate, the lion's share.

Derrick was doing a fine job of presenting the facts to the court. He had just the right appearance and a fine, persuasive speaking voice. She had high hopes for her client, who was trying to pick up the pieces of her shattered life. Skye genuinely liked and admired her. Now it came down to what the court thought…

The afternoon was spent at a community legal centre where she did pro bono work from time to time. The numbers of women in distress; the numbers who couldn't afford legal representation! The case she had elected to take on was just another in a long line of domestic abuse cases. She wouldn't have any difficulty obtaining a restraining order against the husband, even though she knew only too well some men didn't know the meaning of the word "restraint". Such men picked their victims. Her client, a pretty, vulnerable woman with very low self-esteem and badly hurting, was just as likely to return to the abusive marriage no matter how much counselling and free representation she received. That was the sad part. Still, one had to try. The bravest fought free if only for the sake of their children. Even then, no one was assured of a good outcome. There was terrible danger in making an enemy of a violent man.

It was well after six when she drove into the underground parking area of her apartment complex. She had cancelled a work-related function. That upset Derrick, the high flyer, who appeared to have settled on her, quite without encouragement, as a suitable wife. Both of them were lawyers. They had much in common, except, on Skye's side, love. Derrick was attractive, clever and dryly amusing, inclined to be pompous but able to take a joke against himself. They had spent a good bit of time together one way or another. The only thing wrong: he wasn't Keefe. There was only one Keefe. Nothing could change that.

Inside her apartment she went about switching on a few lights, taking pleasure in her surroundings. After a lifetime with the McGoverns, having access to the Big House with all its splendid furnishings, she had acquired "taste without the big bucks", as a friend had once said. She had been admiring Skye's latest acquisition—a large abstract canvas titled *Purple Haze*—at the time, a surreal sky, line of hills, boulders tumbling down it into the highly swelling waves of the dark blue sea. Was that a sea-tossed small boat in the middle? She thought so. The sea reflected in just the right spots the purples, pinks and amethysts of the sky. The artist was young, clearly very gifted, but not as yet in a position to ask big money. Even so, it hadn't been cheap, neither would she have expected it to be. The painting looked stunning on the living-room wall. It was mounted above the three-seater sofa and matching armchairs. The colours she loved prevailed in the room, the blues and golden hues, the accents of lime green and amethyst.

It occurred to her she was hungry. She had been constantly on the go, missing lunch with only a welcome cup of tea and a biscuit at the community centre. Swiftly she changed out of her smart grey business suit worn with a blue silk blouse, hanging it up before pulling a loose caftan over her head. On the job she usually wore her long thick mane pulled back from her face in some way. Now she pulled the pins out of her updated knot, setting her hair free. A nice cold glass of Sauvignon Blanc would go down well. Maybe smoked salmon and scrambled eggs, a green salad? She only wanted something light.

Just as she was pouring the wine, she was surprised by the sound of the buzzer on her security video unit. Who could be buzzing her at this time of the evening? Whoever it was, she intended to answer or ignore the call, depending on who showed up on the brightly coloured screen. She paused, put down her wineglass then went to check the video picture.

At first she couldn't make out who it was, he was so tall. In the next second the man's head came into focus as he moved nearer the security door.

It was Keefe! She pushed the talk button, saying breathlessly, "Come up." She pressed the unlock button, glancing around quickly. All was in order. Her blue caftan was a bit see-through, but this was Keefe after all. He knew every inch, every curve, of her body. But what was he doing here? Why hadn't he let her know he was coming into town? It was almost too much excitement to handle. Her heart was beating in double time. Was he here on McGovern business, or had he brought her some kind of news? Thrilled as she was by his totally unexpected visit, she sagged back against the wall. No rationality to it, just an intuitive sense that something could be wrong. She couldn't think further…

When she opened the door to Keefe she felt the same electric jolt she always felt at the sight of him. She stepped right into his outstretched arms. He held her with one arm around the waist, shutting the weighted door after him. He didn't speak. Instead, he lowered his head to kiss her with passionate intensity, gathering up her body and holding it close against his as though her satiny woman's flesh possessed some special magic for him.

"You're here?" She showed her surprise when at last they pulled apart.

"Sorry I didn't let you know." His brilliant eyes saw through to her inner trepidation.

"That's okay." She drew him by one hand into the living room. "It's wonderful to see you. That's if you're *real*." She turned back to soak in the sight of him. He always looked sublimely handsome to her eyes; the beautiful dominant male, his expression brooding, which struck her as also romantic, his aura beyond compelling. He was wearing street clothes, a fitted casual jacket over designer jeans, an open-necked white cotton shirt with fine multi-stripes beneath. This was the first time he had ever been in her apartment, and she saw him take a quick, enveloping look around.

"Your sanctuary from the world?"

"Like it?" she asked.

He inclined his dark head. "You've got great taste in everything." He walked towards *Purple Haze*. "This makes quite a statement," he said. "Is it a boat out there in that spectacular ultramarine sea?"

"*I* think so. I'm glad you do too. Would you like a glass of wine? I've just opened a bottle of Sauvignon Blanc."

"A Scotch would be better if you've got it," he said, shouldering out of his jacket and placing it over the back of a Chinese chair. Next he rolled back the long sleeves of his shirt to the elbow, the gold Rolex on his left wrist gleaming in the light.

"One Scotch coming up. I always keep a bottle on hand. Don't like it myself."

"But the odd colleague or two does?" He turned back to look at her. The overhead lighting in the galley kitchen was turning her hair to spun gold. It glanced off the gauze of her long dress, the contours of her beautiful breasts, clear to his gaze. His need for her; his *desire* was incurable. He wondered if such a powerful connection was rare.

"Actually, it's a female colleague of mine who can really knock it back." She laughed. "Ice?"

"Just a cube or two." Hands thrust into the pockets of his jeans, he walked slowly towards a set of four desert photographs she'd had framed and hung—two up, two down—on the end wall. "You're an artist yourself. These are very good. You shot them on Djinjara."

He knew his land. "My impressions," she said. "I love photography. I love it even better than practising law. There's so much heartache in what I do. So much I can't prevent."

"I can imagine." He paused a breath away from her, inhaling her fragrance. "We're going to have a talk, Sky-Eyes."

"I thought so." Now she gave vent to a troubled sigh. "You've spoken to your grandmother?"

"I said I would."

His expression was enigmatic. "So what did you find out?" She set about pouring a measure of single malt Scotch into a crystal tumbler, aware of her trembling hand. She walked to the refrigerator to release two ice cubes from the dispenser on the door. Playing for time. Her heart was hammering in her breast.

"Come and sit down." He took the tumbler from her. "You look magical. I'm reminded of the way Jack always called your mother his princess. I *love* the dress."

"Caftan." She tried to smile, but butterflies were flitting madly about in her stomach "I usually slip into something light when I'm on my own." She curled herself into one corner of the sofa, watching him take a quick swallow of whisky. "Tell me, whatever it is." Following his lead, she sipped her citrus-scented wine, then set her glass down on the long red-laquered Chinese chest she used as a sofa table.

Keefe told her what he knew. Up to a point. The question of her paternity he held back. He feared her reaction. He could see she was already reeling with shock.

"So my mother's name was really Katrina Neumann? But that's a German name."

"A strong German connection," he confirmed. "Your great-grandfather Axel Werner was German born. Perhaps the Neumanns were involved with Werner in business."

"And Dad was so infatuated, so far gone, he made my mother pregnant?" she asked in disbelief. "It could have been a disaster. I don't believe Dad would have let himself do that. Not before marriage. I mean, it was such a risky relationship. God, I don't believe this!"

Keefe studied her in silence. Because he loved her so deeply he was absorbing her upset, which was proving far greater than his own. The beautiful shining masses of her hair stood out like a halo around a face that was unnaturally pale. "I admit it's quite a story. And it doesn't end there."

"Oh, no," she moaned. "Not another sexual secret?"

"A little darker than we both supposed."

Skye sat straight, the lawyer in her coming to the fore. "Spell it out, Keefe. Keep nothing back. Though I fear you've managed to up to date."

Keefe's tone turned grim. He was starting to doubt she could handle this. "Gran believes—she has no actual proof of it, please hold fast to that, Skye—that your mother was romantically involved with my Uncle Jonty."

Skye's stoic expression changed to one of sheer astonishment. *"What?"* For all her legal training she couldn't fasten on this new development. Was it fact or fiction?

"It never occurred to me, either," he told her, head bent. "I was just a little kid when Uncle Jonty was killed. We've been looking in all the wrong places."

Skye felt like all the oxygen had rushed out of her body "Oh, my God!" she gasped in horror, putting a hand to her heart. "Why didn't we just leave this alone?" Tears stood in her beautiful blue eyes. "I *knew* you were keeping something from me, something that would drive us apart."

"Never! I won't let it," he said forcefully. "We'll meet this head on. Come here to me, Skye." He caught her to him, pushing her head back against his shoulder. "We can work this out. We can get to the bottom of things."

"Can we indeed?" She spoke as if she was relinquishing all hope. "We're first cousins. Isn't that what you and your grandmother believe?"

He tightened his arms powerfully around her, not about to ever let her go. "So what? What point is there in jumping the gun? It could be quite untrue. It's something Gran has fastened onto down the years. She has no real proof. Either way, I'll be damned if I'll let you go. The cousins bit isn't even a real issue. It's the shock. Our souls are linked."

"Of course. We're first cousins," she whispered, feeling too devastated to move.

"Even if you *are* Uncle Jonty's child and something inside me *screams* you aren't, it's legal for first cousins to marry in most countries of the world. The UK, Australia, most of the United States, Europe, the Middle—"

She cut him off, fiercely. "Don't tell me the law, Keefe. I'm a lawyer, remember?"

"Then use it to your advantage," he clipped off, more fiercely than he had intended but he was so afraid of losing her. "Use your expertise to straighten out fact from fiction, Skye. Gran is eighty years old. She's caught up in the taboos of her day. Medical geneticists have known for a long time there's no harm in first cousins marrying, no strong biological reason. Royalty did it all the time. There are far higher risks associated with inherited diseases and disorders within a family. Children can be born with very serious problems from the healthiest of parents. It's well documented."

"You don't have to convince me," she said sharply. "You'd marry me knowing I could be your first cousin?" She shut her eyes tightly as if to block him out. "Is it possible *your* Uncle Jonty's blood is beating in my veins?"

"It's possible, yes," he said flatly. "But highly improbable. I prefer to go on *my* gut feelings. I have never at any time had a feeling of overstepping any boundary."

"Boundary?" Outrage overcame her and she began to thump his chest. She wanted to make him see her pain and the devastation her father would suffer if such a thing were true. It couldn't be allowed to happen. "You *want* me, Keefe McGovern. Are you telling me want makes it all okay? After all, you *always* get what you want."

"Okay so *I* finish up the bad guy!" There was a steely glint in his eyes. "One small crack in the edifice and your lifelong love for me disappears."

"Maybe that part of my life is over," she said wildly. "Magic to mayhem! Your Uncle Jonty my father? God, no!"

"Stop it, Skye. Please stop now!" He trapped her flailing hands, holding them fiercely tight. "I know what a shock this is for you. Spare a thought for me. I've had some bad moments myself, trying to absorb it."

"So *you've* had a hard time. Imagine that! For all I know, you could have been harbouring these suspicions for some time, suspicions that have caused you to back off then come on strong. The see-saw effect," she said bitterly. "I see it now. You and your grandmother have nurtured a terror I could be Jonty's child." Her beautiful face was a mask of pain and outrage.

"I assure you Jonty never entered my mind." He gave a short, hard laugh. "I'm no liar. Not even you get to call me one. So you can apologise right now."

She stared into his daunting face, seeing he, like her, was deeply disturbed. "Okay I'm sorry, but I'm in despair. So you don't think Uncle Jonty. That leaves Dad. No one else, is there?" Frightened, she flashed onto something quite macabre then she began to pull away from him, the colour completely gone from her face. "Who else, Keefe?" She waved her hands about in agitation. "No, that's too, too *crazy*! Could you possibly have believed even for a split second it might have been your *father*?"

With an oath, he swooped. "If I *did* confront such a fear," he confessed harshly, "I swear it hovered in my mind for just that, a split second. My father was a great man. An honourable man. I admit I've had moments of wondering who your biological father might be if not Jack. We all knew so little about your mother and her past. There was no openness as there would have been with anyone else. What was the big mystery? We were left trying to shift around the pieces of a puzzle. Could it have been someone out of your mother's recent past? Someone she had fled? Never for me was it someone with a McGovern face. Only Gran managed to convince herself you're Jonty's child. There's no proof. Gran jumped to conclusions. As a lawyer you know that's no way good enough. There must be proof."

Skye's heart shrivelled. "Your grandmother is a highly intelligent woman. A mother and a grandmother. A woman with a lot of experience of life and human nature. She must have seen my mother and Jonty together. They must have been together often. My mother stayed at the house. She lived with the family on and off. I've *rarely* thought about your Uncle Jonty. I wasn't even born when he died. He played no part in my life, though I knew his was a tragic story. But no more than my mother's. My *dad* has always been there for me. And he *is* my dad." She broke off in acute distress. "God knows what he'd do if he was told otherwise. I think he'd just ride off into the sunset and never be seen again. He worshipped my mother. He adores me. No. Absolutely *no*! Keefe, your *Uncle Jonty* is not my father. Jonty is *dead*."

Gently but very firmly Keefe held her, upset by the tremors that racked her body. Her suffering tore at his heart. "A DNA test would expose the truth."

She broke his strong grasp. Using the sheer force of her anger and outrage, she flew to her feet. "You think for one moment I'm going to go up to Dad and say, 'Listen there's a chance I'm not your daughter, but Jonty McGovern's'?" There was so much emotion in her voice it broke. "I wouldn't be surprised if he dropped down dead. I'd have to get out of your life, Keefe, before I destroyed my father's."

Here it was. His greatest fear spoken aloud. The destruction of their love. "You think I'd let you do that?" He too shot to his feet, towering over her. "Do you really think I would make you so unhappy? I *love* you, Skye. We have to work this out together. No way will I let you leave me. But tell me honestly. Don't you at least want the truth?"

"Do *you*?" she lashed back. "What if your *heir*—our child—is born with some defect?"

His handsome face turned to granite. "Such a child would be accepted, loved and cared for," he said sternly. "Use your educated mind, Skye. You're not of my grandmother's generation. Why do you suppose the most highly civilised countries on earth allow cousin marriages? Anyway, that's not *my* thinking. You're *not* my cousin."

"Then who the hell am I?" she shouted, seriously overwound.

"You're Jack McCory's daughter."

"So why do you always call him Jack instead of referring to him as my dad?' she challenged, blazing hostility in her blue eyes.

Keefe was forced to recognise the paradox. "I've always called him Jack," he answered, knowing it sounded lame. "What else would I call him?" he fired. "Now, that's enough!" He hauled her back into his arms. "I've flown all the way to see you. To speak to you."

"You're a fiercely busy man, after all." She pushed wildly against him, feeling shame that right in the middle of it she was seized by sexual longing. She wanted him so badly she felt mortified.

"Don't turn hostile, Skye," he begged. "Either you love me or you don't. Either you'll be my wife or you won't. Are you listening?" He shook her lightly. She was all eyes with shock.

She broke off, exhausted, like a boxer pitted against far too formidable an opponent. Outclassed. Outweighed. Slowly she raised her hands in a gesture of surrender. "Oh, Keefe, what are we going to do?" This was the man who had taken her virginity. But hadn't she given it up to him as though it had been ordained? She'd had him inside her. Inside her body. Inside her heart. Inside her mind. She couldn't love another man. Not after Keefe. There would only be Keefe. Yet never in her wildest dreams had she seen Jonty McGovern as anything but a McGovern tragedy.

"The best way out of this is to get Jack's DNA," Keefe said, in a calming tone of voice. "No need to ask him. The effects, as you say, could be tragic. We test your DNA against his. He wouldn't have to know. *Ever.* We could gain, Skye, not *lose.* You're convinced Jack is your father. I'm convinced you're not my cousin. Why don't we allow our intuitions to reign?"

She thought that at any minute she might faint. "Don't secrets trash lives?" she said with great sorrow, feeling the full brunt of this last revelation. "Your grandmother felt she had a duty to me. But she couldn't bring herself to acknowledge me. I was Jack McCory the overseer's little daughter. She wasn't going to have illegitimacy darken your door. A blemish on the splendid McGovern record. McGovern money paid for my fine education. I've always been asked up to the house. But *never* acknowledged, for all her beliefs. And to think she's functioned all these years believing me to be her granddaughter."

"Oh, Skye!" he groaned. What his grandmother had done was beyond him.

She gave him the saddest smile. "The McGoverns are such snobs."

"That would be very worrying if it was true," he said shortly. "My grandmother did what she thought to be right."

"If that had have been me, I don't think I'd have been able to function at all. Turning your back on your dead son's child?" Her voice trailed off.

"Only you're *not!*" he said with far more conviction that he actually felt. "Gran is an old lady. She has lived by her lights. We have to leave it at that. No point in heaping blame on her frail shoulders. I'm sure she has suffered in her way. The irony is she got it all wrong. She would never have seen Jack as a suitor for your mother. Jonty, on the other hand, would have been. It's a class thing, as you claim."

"Don't I know it!" She heard the bitterness in her own voice. "So how do we go about this thing?"

"You could leave it to me." Tension was in his body, the slant of his taut cheekbones, the set of his chiselled mouth. "A hair from Jack's head would do it. Easy enough to get."

"Like some horrid soap opera." She held a hand to her pounding head.

"No soap opera, Skye. This is real life. We have to know the truth. Whatever it is, it changes nothing between us. Jack need know *nothing*."

"Because there's *nothing* to know!" She whirled away.

"Don't ruin what we have." He was on her in a heartbeat. 'I love you. I need you. I want you. There *has* to be a resolution. We're living in an uncertain, unresolved present. We must look to the future. I won't let the past rule our lives."

She didn't even try to strain against the cage of his arms. Hunger for him had gained ascendancy, flooding her veins with sexual heat. She took a deep shuddering breath. "Let's face it, your power over me is too complete."

"No more than yours over me!" he countered fiercely, rapidly becoming blind to everything but his need for her. He was ravenously, painfully aroused. "Nothing and no one will take you from me and you *know* it. Let me love you. Don't struggle. Nothing else makes sense."

She leaned heavily into him, feeling deep down in her body the little jolting currents of electricity. "You win, Keefe," she said in a subdued voice. "You always win. Do what you want."

"Do we have an option?" He stared down at her with such naked desire her senses reeled. "It's this *not* knowing that is complicating our lives."

Her blue eyes were ablaze. "I love you, Keefe McGovern," she said emotionally, "but if any harm comes to my father, I swear I'll disappear from your life."

"Don't say that." He put an urgent finger to her lips. "You're in shock."

"Certainly I am." She was possessed by a sense of foreboding. "But I mean what I say. Whatever the outcome, I want your word my father is to know nothing."

"You have it. Need you ask?" He didn't want to be angry with her—she was distressed enough—but he was.

"You don't have to do anything," she said, coming to a decision. "We're talking about *my* father." Her whole demeanour had changed. "I have a case before the court. There should be a ruling mid-week. I could get a colleague to stand in for me if I had to. That way I could fly back with you. Spend the weekend with Dad. Be back in the office late Monday."

"If that's what you want. I'll arrange a charter flight to fly you back. No need then to lose time changing planes."

"Good, then that's decided." She spoke crisply, on the surface in charge of herself. What lay beneath was searing confusion.

"I didn't say it was a good plan." Keefe kept his eyes on her. "It's the *only* plan."

"Well, my heart isn't in it."

"And you think my heart is? Jack is the key to unlock the secrets of the past, Skye, not Gran."

"Yet your Uncle Jonty must have been in love with my mother," she reasoned. "At least seriously attracted to her. Your grandmother would know."

"You think I haven't considered that?" Keefe's tone was terse. "He probably was. But, God, he was just a kid. They were both a pair of kids. Maybe they were just flirting with each other. It was Jack she turned to."

"You mean she knew she had no future with Jonty." She didn't bother to hide the raw pain.

"I don't mean that at all." He shook his head, clearly upset.

Yet she persisted. "My mother was a protégée of your grandmother's. What was she doing meeting up with a station hand?"

Keefe was careful to answer. "Love will find a way. *We* know that."

"That's not really an answer."

"It's the best I can do," he said, his expression taut. "Getting Jack's DNA will provide us with an answer once and for all."

"Dad's birthday is at the end of the month. I'll say my surprise visit is an early birthday call. God, I could weep for the lie!" she said poignantly.

"It's not wrong to do this, Skye." He was losing the battle to bank down the tumult in his blood.

"So back to Djinjara. Home, sweet home! Only I've never felt like I had a real home."

"It takes a woman to make a home. *You're* the woman to make a home for me. For us. For our children. If you're not as strongly committed to your life as a lawyer as you'd once thought, you'll have an opportunity to forge another career as a photographer. I'll give you all the help you need." His hands began to move over her, every caress eloquent with desire. "In the end there's only you and me. It's always been like that. If it turns out you're my cousin, so be it! No one will stand in our way."

She let her head fall forward onto his chest. "You *want* to believe, Keefe," she said quietly. "So do I."

"Look at me."

She raised her head, her long lashes sweeping down on her cheeks. She was sick of it all. Sick of the torment. Her need for him was causing ripples to run the length of her body. Keefe's mouth descended hungrily on hers…

He was the most heart-breakingly ardent and masterful lover…

All else was silenced.

CHAPTER SEVEN

His back wedged against a tree, Scott lit up a cigarette, took a deep drag, all the while watching Jack through a veil of blue-grey smoke. They had spent all day at the toughest, most back-breaking work of all, driving the cattle out of the lignum swamps. Most of them had clean skins, not many bore the Djinjara brand. A couple of rogue bulls got clean away. They could be picked up another time. The weary stockmen were sitting about on fallen logs, talking quietly among themselves and gulping down scalding billy tea. The Chinese cook had big thick slices of freshly baked damper ready for them, smothered in either home-made jam or bush honey. Ugh! Unlike Keefe, he liked to sit apart from the men, welcoming his own company. He lifted his eyes to the blindingly blue sky. A falcon was floating above the yarding area, nearly motionless on an upper current. Bonding with station employees had been left out of his make-up. Come to think of it, he was, by and large, a loner by nature. Either that or he wasn't into friendships. A psychological profile might even categorise him as an outsider.

Outsider or not, he had fantasised about Skye more times than he could remember. Even when he was with Jemma, it was Skye he held captive in his arms. Why were Keefe and Skye spinning their wheels about the possibility of being first cousins? As far as he knew, it was perfectly legal for first cousins to marry. He knew quite a few second cousins within landed families who had married and raised healthy broods of kids. No, it was McCory they were worried about. How McCory would react. He knew their overseer to be physically brave. He pitched into the most difficult and dangerous of jobs. He was an excellent overseer, much admired among the nation's top cattlemen. It was his mental state that might bring McCory to his knees.

Once he knew.

Scott drew the cigarette smoke deep into his lungs. He would wait until sundown, and then follow Jack to his bungalow for a little chat. Jack would be most surprised to have him for a visitor. It had never happened before. Keefe was due to fly in before noon next day. That's if he could drag himself away from his precious Skye. At that moment Scott would have given anything to have what his brother had:

Skye McCory.

Don't do this, a warning voice started up inside his head. *Don't do it. Up until this point you haven't done anything really bad.*

That was the decent half of him talking. The McGovern half. But he knew as he continued to stare across at tall lanky Jack McCory, laughing amiably with the men, that he *was* going to do it. He had a vengeful streak, so raw and bitter it even stung him. His brother could have any woman he wanted. With Skye out of the way, the competition might have a chance. Think of it that way. It seemed incredible to him that his Uncle Jonty had mated with that other troublemaker, Cathy-Katrina, whoever she was. But such was the power of a beautiful woman. They could turn a man into a hero or a villain. He could justify his actions on the grounds of pushing his beloved brother back from the brink. And he *did* love Keefe. It was Skye he hated. Skye who had looked at him with scorn and contempt in her eyes. No woman was allowed to do that. This was the only way he could figure out to split her and his brother up. That overheard conversation between Keefe and their grandmother had been handed to him like a gift. Gifts needed to be opened up…

Rachelle met her in the entrance hall, hostility naked in her dark eyes, her chin upthrust at an arrogant angle. "You're here to see my grandmother."

Skye nodded, studying Rachelle with a hint of pity. The sooner Rachelle made a life for herself the better. She was twenty-six years old. She had never held down a job in her entire adult life. It wasn't that she lacked intelligence, even high intelligence. Rachelle lacked any real purpose in life. Sad but true— money often robbed the inheritors of wealth of drive.

"Why are you looking at me like that?" Rachelle burst out, feeling as though she was under a microscope. If the truth be known, underneath it all she felt admiration for Skye and what she had achieved. Not that she was ever going to show it.

"Is there a correct way to look at you, Rachelle?" Skye asked mildly. "I've always wanted us to be friends but your friendship has never been on offer. Now, I'd like to see Lady Margaret. Keefe has already spoken to her. She's expecting my visit."

"You're the last person I want as a member of my family," Rachelle told her vehemently.

Skye was stopped in her tracks. Could Keefe have possibly taken his sister into his confidence? He could have only been at the homestead thirty minutes at the outside, before going off on station business. He had promised to arrange this visit with his grandmother. "So you must think something is happening?"

Rachelle didn't hesitate. "I'm not such a fool I don't know you and Keefe are joined at the hip. It's even possible you're beginning to get the upper hand. What are you seeing Gran about?"

"I see no reason not to tell you, Rachelle. I want to speak to her about my mother."

"There's been a hell of a lot of mileage in your mother's story. From all accounts she was a lady, even, would you believe, connected in some way to an aristocratic family, yet she married your father. Another shotgun affair, I suppose."

A bolt of molten anger shot through Skye, but she ignored the insult. "That's why I want to see your grandmother. There are a lot of things still unclear. Excuse me, please, Rachelle. You really need to lighten up for your own sake as much as anyone else's."

Keefe took the Land Rover, driving out of the compound, heading for Yellow Creek where some of the men would be yarding clean skins. He had briefed Jack before he had left. First on the agenda was to clear out the lignum swamps. He had every confidence in Jack to carry out his orders to the letter. He had a lot of respect for Jack. As he drove out of the trees that surrounded Yellow Creek and into the sunlit yarding paddock, his eyes skimmed the busy stockmen, looking for his overseer. No sign of him. One of the men, Whitey, a part aboriginal with a fine head of snow-white curls, was standing over by the truck, having a gash in his arm treated. Obviously Whitey had come too close to a rushing bullock's horn. Usually the shouts and calls around the yards were cheerful, but this afternoon everyone seemed a bit subdued.

"Where's Jack, Whitey?" he called, starting to feel an element of unease. He strode to the truck, fallen bark crunching under his feet. He paused to take a look at the man's arm. It was a bad gash but Whitey as usual appeared unconcerned. "Your shots are up to date?"

"Sure, boss. Jack not bin here. Not all mornin'. Jonah checked around. No one has seen 'im. Jonah checked the bungalow, thought mebbe he was sick. Not there neither."

"Where's my brother?" Keefe asked.

"Him and Bill were pushin' some cows and calves for a drink. That'd be Kooreena Waters. Bound to find 'im there."

"It's Jack I really want," said Keefe, swatting near violently at a fly. He was worried. Always a man to rely on his gut feeling, his feelings about Jack McCory and his whereabouts weren't good. It was unheard of for Jack not to be on the job. Someone must have seen him. Had he left a note at the bungalow? Had one of the nomads that moved freely across the vast station sighted him? He couldn't have simply gone away. Whatever forces were at play, confidence that all was well was starting to drain out of him.

With a single steely gesture he brought the men into a circle. "Jack is always on the job, regular as clockwork."

"Are you worried about 'im, boss?" Eddie, the leading hand, asked.

"Yes. By the look of it, so are the rest of you. Jack should be here. I want you all to spread out. We need to find him. We need to think accident. He could be hurt. He could have taken a fall from his horse. Unlikely, but something could have happened. We have to consider an encounter with a snake. Even a blasted camel in heat. Jake, you take the truck. Bill the utility. Head back towards the line of lignum swamps. Jack could be chasing up a few that got away. The rest of you, take the horses. Each man in a different direction. Report to me when you're done. We need to find Jack."

Back at the home compound, Keefe began a systematic search of the bungalow. What was he looking for, a note? Nothing in any obvious place. Skye would have seen it, although she wouldn't have been in the bungalow long. He had arranged a meeting between Skye and his grandmother the minute he'd arrived back at the house. Skye desperately needed proof of her identity. A DNA test was the only way to go. He couldn't free his mind of her saying that if any hurt came to Jack he would lose her for ever. People in shock said such things. That was his only comfort.

Skye had left the front door open. A breeze was sweeping in. Keefe went to close it. Only then did he see the grey envelope that must have flown off the hall table and headed towards the old grandfather clock, where it was stuck between the clock and the wall. For a few moments he stared at it in silence then he walked the few paces to pull the envelope out of its hiding place. It was addressed to him.

Keefe, promise me you won't come looking for me. I'm going out into the desert to think.

Jack.

Think? Blow your brains out? The note and the unsteadiness of the handwriting was a sure sign Jack was a very disturbed man. What had happened and very recently? He trusted his grandmother absolutely not to summon Jack for a talk. Other than his grandmother and himself, no one else knew of the conclusions they had reached. Jack would be back. He had to believe that. On the other hand, he had no intention of following Jack's request. He would have the whole station out looking for him. He would alert the nomadic aborigines. They saw everything in their travels. Even in the *mind's* eye. He would take up the chopper. He just knew he wasn't overreacting.

God, he would have to tell Skye. He checked to see if Jack had taken his rifle.

He had.

Both women stared at Keefe in shocked silence. Lady McGovern was the first to speak. "What *is* it, dear?" He cut a powerful, very daunting figure.

"I don't exactly know." He frowned. "Not yet. We can't find Jack. He could have had an accident."

Skye sprang to her feet, instantly in a panic. "Have you checked everywhere? Spoken to the men?"

"Need you ask?" He took hold of her arm to steady her. "You'll want to join the search, I know. So follow me. Don't worry, Gran." He turned back to the frail old lady. "We'll find him." It was spoken like a foregone conclusion.

But dead or alive?

They came on Rachelle tiptoeing down the stairs. "What the devil are you doing?" Keefe called to her, swiftly closing in with Skye in his wake.

"Something is going on, isn't it?" Rachelle looked from one to the other. Both looked extremely tense. A dead give-away.

Keefe stared at his sister, his black brows knotted. Rachelle as a child had always been a great one for hiding behind doors, curtains, sofas anywhere she could overhear private conversations. Could she possibly have been outside their grandmother's bedroom door the night when they had been having their very private conversation? It didn't seem likely. Rachelle had been deeply involved in the card game when he had left the room.

"My father is missing, Rachelle," Skye burst out raggedly, wanting to push Rachelle out of the way. She didn't trust her at all. "Keefe has sent out a search party. Would you know anything about his disappearance?' She did something awful then. She seized Rachelle's arm in a painful grip.

"Me?" Rachelle pulled away in shock. "What do you take me for? I have no idea what the men are doing! Not interested either. He could have taken a fall from his horse. Happens all the time. Horses are dreadfully unpredictable creatures, especially when they're spooked."

"You *know*, don't you?" Driven by worry, Skye, the taller, went to shake her. "Tell us what you know."

"Are you mad? Let go of me!" Rachelle struggled wildly but Skye held on. "Keefe, make her let go of me."

Keefe took Skye away, holding her firmly by his side. "We need you to answer one simple question, Rachelle. The truth, please. Have you spoken to Jack McCory in the last couple of days?"

"Jack McCory's a friend of mine?" Rachelle asked acidly, raising her brows heavenwards. "How dare you lay hands on me, Skye McCory. I have no idea what the two of you are getting at."

"Well, I'll tell you," Keefe rasped. "For a lot of your life you've made a habit of eavesdropping, Rachelle."

"It's not a crime, is it?" Rachelle flushed violently with embarrassment.

"When the Templetons were here and you were enjoying yourselves playing cards, I went upstairs to talk to Gran. Did you follow me?"

"Follow you?" Rachelle asked cautiously, eyeing first her brother then Skye.

"Answer the question." Skye's voice rose sharply. "Did you overhear what Keefe and your grandmother were saying?"

Rachelle's face visibly paled. "I may have been guilty of eavesdropping in the past. In this family it's the only way you find out anything. But I swear I didn't follow you upstairs. Ask anyone."

"They've all gone home."

"Scott hasn't. Ask him."

A shudder passed through Skye. "Did Scott go upstairs? Did he leave the room?"

Rachelle fought the impulse to cry. It wasn't something she normally did, but the upset was contagious. "I'm sure he didn't. He watched when he didn't play."

"You're certain of that?" Keefe questioned. "I mean, you get engrossed in the game. I've seen you too many times."

"Why don't you tell me what's going on?" Rachelle to her horror felt a tear trickle down her cheek. "Everyone hates me."

"Rubbish! You go out of your way to be unpleasant. You've done your best to upset Skye over the years. But no one hates you, Rachelle. I love you. Be assured of that. I just live in hope you'll get yourself together. So we can take it you didn't speak to Jack."

"Definitely not!" Rachelle's dark eyes flashed. "What could I possibly say to him anyway? What could it be that would make Jack McCory disappear?" Slowly she turned to focus on Skye, lifting her hands in a gesture of supplication. "I swear to you, Skye, I would do nothing to upset your father. I've just lost my own father. I think about him all the time. Whatever has happened, I could play no part in your father's disappearance. I beg you to believe me."

Skye remained staring into Rachelle's brimming eyes. At last she said, "I do believe you, Rachelle. I'm very sorry if we've upset you. We're tremendously worried about Dad."

"You can't find him anywhere?" Relieved, Rachelle dashed her tears away with the back of her hand.

"I'm afraid not."

"So there are places I can search," Rachelle offered.

"Thank you for that." Skye started to turn away, her mind crowded with fears for her father's safety.

"The best thing you can do, Rachelle, is go keep Gran company," Keefe said. "She's as distressed as the rest of us. I'm taking the chopper up. I'm confident we'll find Jack in the desert. But I need to conduct the search before nightfall."

"All the luck in the world!" Rachelle called, feeling chastened.

When they were gone, she lowered her head for a moment, biting her lip and thinking back hard… *Had* Scott been there all the time? She wasn't one hundred per cent sure. What *was* it

Keefe and Gran had been discussing? Whatever it was, it had a bearing on Jack McCory's disappearance. Rachelle began to murmur a little prayer for his safety.

Please, God, please protect Jack McCory.

They had two hours before darkness. The men on the ground had searched steadily without finding any trace of the overseer. He let the search go on even though Jack had written he was heading into the desert. He could have been laying down a false trail.

From the air they looked down on an infinite landscape of savage splendour without sign of human habitation. A man in a moving vehicle would be easily exposed in this trackless wilderness. Without a good supply of water, that man could easily die. Many had lost their lives in the country's vast interior; great deserts covered almost half the continent. Fiery red sand dunes rose up from the plains, peaking and curling like the waves of the inland sea of pre-history. Between the giant swells the troughs were clothed in the ubiquitous spinifex and thick clumps of hardy grasses, stunted trees of mulga and mallee. There was very little protection from a blazing sun out here. On the gibber plains in the distance, the large boulders, rocks, stones and pebbles glittered like some incredible mosaic. Above them the mirage shimmered in silvery glass whirlpools.

It was in its way fantastically beautiful—especially to Skye with her photographer's eye—only she had no mind to admire it. Her father could be dead or dying down there.

Eyes peeled, they scoured the vast empty expanses, with their dried-up red clay pans and ancient watercourses that appeared like white veins amid the red. They had been flying for approximately thirty minutes when Skye, who had her head turned in the opposite direction to Keefe, tapped him urgently on the shoulder.

"Down there. Could that be the station Jeep?"

"If it is, Jack has used dead branches and bleached grasses

to screen it from view." Immediately Keefe brought the chopper down low… They weren't all that far off being earthbound. Both of them had picked up the image of a vehicle now.

Feet from landing, the downdraft of the rotor flattened the tall spears of the spinifex grass and churned up a mini-duststorm. Skye struggled to free herself from her seat. She was so agitated Keefe had to take over. "Try to keep calm, Skye," he told her. "We need to keep calm, okay?"

"I'll try." She was having difficulty just swallowing. Her heart seemed to be occupying her entire mouth How much of a lie was her life? It didn't seem to matter now. All that mattered was finding the man she called her father alive. Nothing could destroy the love they had for each other. She was desperate to tell him. How many bereaved families had missed just such a chance to tell their loved ones how greatly they were loved and needed?

Feet dug into the desert sand, with the red whirlpool slowly abating, Keefe lowered a hand to her shoulder. "I want you to wait here." He spoke with habitual authority. "Promise me you'll do that. Wait until I give the signal. You have to trust me, Skye, to know what's best."

"You think he's killed himself, don't you?" She could hear the panic and grief in her voice.

"I think Jack's got more guts than that," Keefe clipped off. "Maybe he's just plain drunk and sleeping it off. Give me a minute and I'll find out."

It was the longest minute of her life.

I'll do anything, God. I'll give up Keefe, the man I love with all my heart, if I have to. I'll tear out my own heart. Don't do this to me, Dad!

What she was offering was self-sacrifice.

Keefe stepped out of the makeshift shelter, waving his arm in an all-clear. "Right, Skye," he yelled. "You can come now."

Gasping for breath, the heat scorching her neck, she covered the distance as quickly as she had covered any distance in her life, powered by sheer desperation to check on her father's condition. The loose sand and the unforgiving heat coming off it was making the going tough, but she was tougher. As she reached Keefe, she half stumbled and he caught her up, hauling her into his arms. "Stop tearing yourself to pieces, Skye. I can't bear it. Jack's in a bit of a mess, but he's going to be all right."

It was moderate rather than severe dehydration Keefe had diagnosed quite accurately, though that situation could have swiftly changed. It didn't take long for even a physically fit man to succumb to killer dehydration in the desert. Especially a man who had polished off a bottle of whisky.

With her head bent low to clear the overhang of branches, Skye entered the shelter. Her father was sitting on the sand, a man at rock bottom. His head and his torso were soaked from the contents of a canvas water bottle Keefe had poured over him. Unlike her, Keefe had had the presence of mind to take it out of the chopper and bring it with him.

"Dad?" Realising she was shouting with relief and gratitude, Skye reined herself in. "Dad, Dad!" Love shone from her face and her voice. "What an awful fright you gave us. Don't you dare ever do it again. Don't you *dare*. You hear me?"

Jack, conscious but weak and dehydrated, somehow managed a smile. "What are you doing here, love?" His look of desolation was pitiful, yet his blue eyes flickered with sudden light.

"Where else would I be?" Skye felt the tears roll down her cheeks. The sight of her father so reduced, plus the reek of alcohol, was almost more than she could bear. She threw herself down alongside him, swooped on him, gathering him close and raining kisses on his cheek covered with harsh stubble. "We've found you. Now we're going to take you home. It's all right, Dad. Everything is going to be all right."

"I'll go get the other water-bottle," Keefe said, getting up off his haunches to make the return trip to the chopper. He turned away, hiding a face white with fury.

He *knew* now what had happened. He just *knew* who had gone to Jack to fill his ears with black bile. He aimed to take action. Even so, payback time never felt so bad.

CHAPTER EIGHT

BACK on Djinjara it wasn't easy to get Jack to take to his bed. But it was heartening to see that slow, increased water intake, plus a cooling shower, had brought about a positive result.

"That's an order, Jack," Keefe told him firmly, long used to men obeying him. "Stay in bed. I've called in Joe McPherson to check you out, just to be on the safe side. You're BP is a bit low. Probably your body will need days for the cells to plump up again. But you're looking better."

"Do as Keefe tells you, Dad," Skye urged, taking her father's hand to offer comfort.

"Unless I'm *not* your dad," Jack murmured, in a very distressed voice.

Skye's blue eyes flashed up at Keefe, then back to her father "What are you saying?" she quavered.

"You *know*, sweetheart." He stared at the white sheet that covered him, not her.

"I know nothing of the kind." Skye stoutly maintained the lie. It was *white*, wasn't it? Well, she wasn't a saint.

"But you *want* to know?"

Skye's helpless shrug signalled her defeat. Another long look passed between herself and Keefe, who was standing on the opposite side of her father's narrow bed.

"Tell us what you *think* you know, Jack." Keefe drew up a chair, speaking quietly, persuasively to his overseer.

"I know precious little," Jack admitted with a tortured smile. "God knows, I never did ask questions. I adored Cathy, Katrina, whatever her real name. I loved her. I know I'm just an ordinary bloke, but I was sure she loved me. She told me I was the loveliest, kindest man in the world." His voice broke.

"Of course she loved you," Skye maintained hotly, taking her father's hand. "And so you are a lovely kind man. Who told you all this, Dad?" She was convinced it was Rachelle, who had appeared genuinely upset by her father's disappearance, but that alone didn't ensure Rachelle was innocent. She was such a devious person.

"It wasn't Rachelle." Keefe looked across at her, reading her mind. This was no time to push Jack.

Skye was aware he was giving off signals. But she felt compelled to ignore them. She had to get to the bottom of this. "Was it Scott?" Scott, who had long desired her, now hated her. It had to be Scott. That was his nature.

Keefe spoke gently. "Will you confirm that, Jack?"

Jack subsided miserably into the pillows. "Leave it for a little while, will you, Keefe?" he quietly begged. "I feel a bit under the weather at the moment."

"Of course." Keefe pushed back his chair and stood up resolutely. "It doesn't matter anyway, Jack. I know it was my brother." His handsome face was set like granite. "Rest easy, Jack. I'll take care of this. McPherson will be here shortly to take a look at you. When you're feeling better we'll arrange a short holiday for you. Be assured, your job is as safe as ever."

As Keefe strode from the room, Skye hurried after him, reaching out to grasp his arm in an effort to detain him. "What are you going to do, Keefe?"

He turned back, studying her beautiful, agonised face. "Leave it to me, Skye," he said, not about to accept interference, even from her. "We both know it *was* Scott. He meant to hurt you through your father. He didn't give a damn what happened to Jack. Jack will confirm it in his own good time."

"Yes." She sighed with deep regret. "Scott's aim has always been to destroy what we have."

"Except revenge is a double-edged sword. Now the sword is going to fall on him."

Keefe turned away. She felt compelled to run after him. He looked so angry, so menacing and he was a very strong man. Superbly fit. Scott would be no match for him. "He's your brother, Keefe." She gripped his arm, feeling the anger and bitter disillusionment that raged through him. "Tell me what you're going to do. If you love me, you'll tell me."

"*If* I love you?" He caught her up so powerfully she was momentarily off her feet. His brilliant eyes slashed incredulously over her face. "How can you even *say* it?"

She was shaking right through her body. "I'm frightened, that's why. Please tell me, Keefe. I couldn't bear for *you* to get injured. Scott wouldn't play fair. He can't seem to help himself."

"I told you to leave it to me," he repeated harshly. "Believe me, he won't stand a chance. Then I'm going to banish him. Next, I'm going to order Rachelle to find herself a job. Any job, just so long as she gets up off her pampered backside."

Skye strangled a laugh. "Wouldn't that be something?"

"This could have ended very badly, Skye. You know that."

"Dad would never have taken his own life." She had to convince herself of that. "He just wanted time to think."

"Only time was running out." Keefe's retort was grim.

She stared up into his darkly disturbed face. "We're no further than we were before. I can't possibly ask dad for a DNA sample. Not now."

"The plan goes ahead." He bent to press a hard kiss onto her mouth. It burned like a brand. Just as he had intended.

"If you can be patient, you'll find Jack is prepared to give it. He's a good man. Doing what *you* need is part of Jack's goodness. I'd strongly advise you to let him bring up the subject himself. Now, don't try to detain me. I'm going in search of my brother." He released her so quickly she staggered a little. "There's absolutely *nowhere* Scott can hide. Nowhere I can't find him."

Dr Joe McPherson of the Royal Flying Doctor Service flew in an hour later, and carefully checked Jack over. No questions were asked apart from those about Jack's symptoms. Dr McPherson handed Skye a list of things to do to help her father recover quickly. Hospitalisation wasn't called for. Maybe a bit of counselling later. No reference was made as to what the counselling might be for, but obviously Joe McPherson knew. He tended to know everything about the people in his vast practice.

Afterwards Jack slept. When he awoke it was to find Skye by his bedside, quietly reading a book of poetry. "Feeling better, Dad?" She closed the book—she hadn't been taking all that much in—setting it down on the bedside table. "Anything I can get you? A cup of tea?"

"Tea would be lovely," he said. "My throat is so dry."

In a matter of minutes Skye was back, allowing her father to sip the tea in silence before taking the empty cup from him.

"That was good," Jack sighed, allowing her to plump up the pillows. "It's dark.'

"Eight o'clock, Dad."

"Has Keefe come in again?" Urgency was in his hoarsened voice.

"Not as yet." She shook her head. "But he will. You don't have to talk, Dad, if you don't want to. Not *ever*!"

"Only it's my plain duty to talk," he said with a wry grimace. "I don't know *what* I intended to do, darling girl, out there in the desert. I was temporarily off my head. But the desert makes a man feel as small and unimportant in the scheme of things as a grain of sand. My excuse is I was in a terrible state of shock."

"I know that, Dad." Skye covered one rough calloused hand with her own.

"I didn't deserve Cathy," Jack said. "I don't deserve you."

Skye held back tears. "Now you're being way too modest." She smiled.

"Maybe just plain stupid," Jack answered brusquely. "Just a naïve old cowhand. You want to know for sure, don't you?"

Skye held his blue eyes. "I'm sure you're my dad. That's all that matters." She pressed his hand tightly.

"I don't think so." Jack's answer was uncharacteristically grim. "You love Keefe?"

"With all my heart. Minus the part you've got." She tried for another smile. "We want to marry, Dad. Keefe is insistent. But I can't see to a future with a cloud hanging over our heads. First, we get *you* right. I couldn't have borne to lose you, Dad. Remember that when you're feeling low. Behind you, there's *me*. Never forget you have to answer to *me*."

"That's my girl!" For the first time Jack gave a big open smile. "I knew Cathy had a bit of a crush on Jonty," he revealed, gently scratching his chest. "God, he was handsome and so full of life. A McGovern. Only Jonty was more or less spoken for. He was involved with one of the Corbett girls. Louise, as I recall. A pretty girl, a very suitable young lady, but not a patch on your mother, who was a genuine beauty. As you are. I was sure Cathy understood that."

"So it was accepted that Jonty McGovern and Louise Corbett belonged together?"

"That was the word. At any rate, Louise had a nervous break-down after Jonty was killed. He always was a bit of a daredevil, taking unnecessary risks, yet a tragic accident all the same.

Cathy, too, was tremendously upset. Everyone was. Jonty was so young to be taken like that."

Skye gave his cheek an encouraging stroke. "How did you get to know my mother so well?"

"Like I've always told you, sweetheart. For me it was love at first sight. How it happened was like this, something of a miracle for me, I can tell you. Lady McGovern charged me of all people to take Cathy out on trips around the station. I was always considered to be very trustworthy and responsible. Personally I always believed she sent me out with Cathy so Cathy couldn't be with Jonty."

"That could certainly have been true," Skye said, with a lick of bitterness. She still hadn't forgiven Lady McGovern. Perhaps she never would. "So on these trips you got to know one another very well?"

"Darned right!" Jack replied with conviction. "We hit it off from the beginning. I want you to know I behaved like a true gentleman all the time. Dozens of times I wanted to kiss her. The urge got more and more powerful every time we were together. But I never laid a finger on my Cathy except to assist her in some way. Getting in and out of vehicles. Dismounting. That sort of thing. In a short space of time we became really good mates. I was always skilful in the bush, a good bushman. I've always been close to the aboriginal people. They showed me lots. I, in turn, showed Cathy lots. She loved this place. She never wanted to leave. She didn't talk about her past. I accepted her background must have been painful. I never pried. She would tell me when she was good and ready, I reckoned. Only I lost her. Maybe I was *meant* to lose her," he said in one of the saddest voices Skye had ever heard.

"Don't say that, Dad." She let her head rest against his, listening to him draw in a ragged breath.

"There are jealous gods up there, Skye. Believe it. One

shouldn't love anyone too much. Love and loss go hand in hand.
If you lose the person you love, your heart is ripped from your
body."

"I believe that." She spoke from the depths of her deep, passionate and abiding love for Keefe.

"Now, let's see about this DNA test," Jack said briskly, as
though they had been discussing it all along.

"Not necessary, Dad." She looked him directly in the eyes.
She was aware of the DNA profiles for close relationships such
as first cousins. She was also aware that the results were incon-
clusive. It was her father's DNA that was needed.

"We'll do it!" he said firmly. "I'm certain in my heart you're
my child, Skye. I refuse to dishonour your mother and her
memory. Cathy would never have done that to me. At first I was
shocked out of my mind by what Scott told me. He has such a
dark streak. But I've been over and over it out there in the desert.
She wouldn't have done it. That wasn't my girl, my Cathy. If it
was Jonty McGovern's child she carried, she would have told me.
She knew I would have helped her in any way I could. I would
have been shocked but, God, I loved her. I saw myself as her protector."

"I believe you about everything, Dad" Skye tried to fill up
the raw aching spots in her with trust.

"And I believed in Cathy," Jack said. "Lady McGovern got
it all wrong. The thing is, love, and you have to take it into
account, she never for one moment considered me as a likely
suitor for Cathy. God forbid! Cathy was a lady. Say what you
like, the old lady is a snob. Can't help it, you see. To her I simply
didn't count. It *had* to be Jonty. Jonty was the father of Cathy's
child. Let's prove it to her once and for all that she was wrong."

Keefe called at the bungalow an hour later.

"How's Jack now?" Voice pitched low, he walked into the

comfortable living room, his height and physical magnificence making the adequate space seem claustrophobically small.

"Sleeping peacefully," she said, picking up on his deep distress. "You spoke to Scott?"

Keefe nodded, putting out his arm and drawing her to him. "Among other things," he said bluntly. "He's up at the house now. Packing. He'll go to wherever I send him. It was going to be Moolaki. It's now Emerald Waters in the Gulf. He'll be up close and personal with the crocs."

"Oh, Lord! How did he take it?" Skye stared up at his taut face, seeing the underlying distress.

"He was absolutely *delighted*. What else?"

"You're upset."

"Of course I'm upset!" His silver eyes flashed. "Scott is my brother. He can fill me with a black rage—he's such a liar—full of bitterness and resentment. He has always wanted to be me, even though he has no real insight into what that entails. He's a terrible disappointment, but he's still my brother."

"I understand that, Keefe." She did. "I know you're suffering. But I need to know this. Are you blaming me in some way?"

"Good God, what are you talking about?" He stared down at her with a knotted frown.

She broke away, going to the door that shut the living room off from the hallway and closing it. "Remember years ago when Scott came after me?" she questioned, a searching look in her eyes.

He cut her off at once. "I'll never forget it."

Something in his manner set off a perverse spark of anger. It had been an extremely stressful day. Both of them were nearing the end of their tethers yet—or perhaps because of it—she couldn't stop. "You may deny it now, Keefe, but you practically accused me *then* of being the catalyst in the whole episode. I was the innocent victim yet didn't you say at the time that Scott wasn't such a monster. Remember?" she challenged. "What was I again? *Temptation on legs*, according to Scott. You appeared to agree. I've had a lot of trouble with that one," she said.

Keefe stood there, disgusted by the havoc Scott had wreaked on them. He could see the tension and the hurt—the remembered and the present—in every line of her body.

"I hurt you," he acknowledged. "I didn't mean to. But it was so *difficult* then. I was sick with concern about you, disgusted with Scott, but, forgive me, I saw you in the heat of the moment as what he said. Temptation. From a little girl you had turned into the most beautiful, alluring woman right before our eyes. Even level-headed men can become a little crazy around a woman like that."

"Like *me*, you mean?" She hugged herself, her arms wrapped around her body like a shield. "I don't see *you* acting crazy!" Her eyes were huge with delayed shock. "I don't see you acting powerless. You're the all-conquering male. You're Keefe McGovern, the cattle baron. Admired and respected by all. You could have any woman you want."

"I believe I've answered all that," Keefe's expression was that of a man nearing the end of his tether. "Over and over. *You're* the only woman I want. *You're* the only woman I'll ever want. Stop now, Skye. It's been one hell of a day. We'll talk in the morning. Thank God Jack is safe." He turned to move away, but she couldn't let him go without *touching* him, feeding off his strength. Whatever the frustrations, whatever the difficulties, she could never be deprived of the sight and sound of Keefe.

"I'm sorry. Forgive me," she whispered, putting her hand on his shoulder and staring up into the dark intensity in his face.

"Nothing to be sorry for," he muttered, pulling her to him and taking her mouth. "Come riding with me in the morning." His arms wound powerfully, protectively around her. "At dawn, just the two of you. You being here and me at the House is much too

cruel. I need to make love to you, hold you through the night."
His breath rasped in his chest. His body was tuned to such a pitch
he didn't think he could take any more of these frustrations. Time
after time. He wanted to close the door on the lot of them. Erect
a huge barrier between Skye and himself and the demands of the
outside world. Jack just had to be Skye's biological father. Their
whole future appeared to ride on it. Skye was a woman of strong
passions. Strong convictions.

"I need to wake up beside you," she murmured back. She had
thought in her brightest moments that their being together was
pre-destined, now she was constantly reminded of the promise
she had made to a God who had shown her mercy. She had her
father back.

It was probably the most dramatic entrance Rachelle would ever
make in her life. She charged up the short flight of front steps
and onto the porch, crying out Keefe's name. In the next instant
she crashed into the living room, her face ghostly white. "You've
got to come," she gasped, bending over to hold a hand to the
stitch in her side. "Scott is going off his rocker. He's shouting
at Gran. It's going to give her a heart attack if he keeps it up.
He's accusing her of loving you more than all of us put together.
He said you're sending him away to be eaten by the crocs. I hope
they get him," she cried with savage gusto. "He said you hate
him and it's all Skye's fault. That she's our *cousin*. Our *first*
cousin, Uncle Jonty's child. Is that true?" Rachelle's dark eyes
were nearly starting out of her head.

"No, it's not!" Keefe wasn't going to be caught up in speculation. For a start, even he wasn't certain. He went to his sister's
side, enfolding her shaking body in his arms. "Quiet now, Chelle.
Hush. Get your breath back. I'm on my way."

"I'll come with you," Skye said, in no mood to brook an ob-
jection. How could Scott do this to his eighty-year-old-grand-

mother? Lady McGovern's health since the death of her son, Broderick, had markedly declined.

"Me, too." Rachelle sobered, enormously gratified by the comfort she had found in her brother. "Will your dad be okay?" She looked at Skye, who nodded.

"Dad's asleep. It's the sleep of exhaustion."

"We're all glad he's back where he belongs, Skye. I mean, I haven't been much of a friend to you."

"But you can be a tremendous help in the future." Skye had no difficulty offering an olive branch.

Keefe drove the Jeep to the base of the homestead's stone steps. He sprang out of the vehicle with the uncoiled strength and liquid grace of a jungle cat. And, it had to be said, something of their ferocity too. The two young women followed him more slowly, Rachelle for the first time in her life clinging to Skye's hand.

"I can't believe Scott could turn on Gran like this," she wailed. "He's always been volatile. This time he's blown a fuse."

"Where are they, Chelle?" Keefe called from over his shoulder.

"Gran's bedroom. Keefe must have hurt him," she confided to Skye in an aside. "His face is a bit of a mess."

"Keefe wouldn't have hurt him too much." Skye hoped. "He knows his own strength. He wouldn't turn the full force of it on his brother."

"Scott well deserves it," Rachelle said, appalled by her brother's behaviour. "Gran is absolutely off limits. He nearly scared me to death. Gran wasn't showing any of it. She's tough. But she's old now. Scott really does have a vicious streak."

The two of them followed Keefe up the grand staircase at a rush, but he had already disappeared down the corridor. The house was silent. Yet neither young woman found this calming. "If he's caused Gran any harm I'll never forgive him," Rachelle said dazedly. "I'm so glad you're here with me, Skye. I can't possibly keep going the way I am."

They found Lady McGovern with her two grandsons in the bedroom. Rachelle went immediately to her grandmother, kneeling at her feet. "You okay, Gran?" She searched the distinguished old lady's face.

"I'm fine, dear," Lady McGovern said, though she looked far from fine. She looked old and frail. "A bit flustered, that's all. It would take more than Scott's inexcusable abuse to carry me off."

Skye, undergoing a delayed shock reaction, was suddenly hit by a dizzy spasm. She slumped back against an antique chest, nearly toppling the exquisite Chinese vase that sat on it.

"Skye?" Keefe crossed to her, guiding her into one of the armchairs. "Put your head down for a moment." He eased her golden blonde head forward, keeping his hand on her nape.

"I'm okay." She brought her head up after several seconds.

"You bet she's okay." Scott, who had been sitting with his head in his hands, suddenly came back to life. "Like we actually *need* her in the family."

"You're unstoppable, aren't you?" Lady McGovern lamented. "You need professional help.'

Scott flinched, his eyes locking on his grandmother's. "I can't believe you said that, Gran. I would never hurt you. I just wanted you to see things *my* way."

"Don't even try to justify *your* way," Keefe told his brother coldly. "Gran's right. You need counselling. After that, you can take over at Emerald Waters. If you don't want to, fine. You and Rachelle have a very healthy trust fund. You can do as you like. The problem is, Scott, you don't appear to have any real insight into your own behaviour. It's deplorable. With the right help maybe you'll be able to straighten yourself out."

"How can I begin to walk straight?" Scott gave an agonised laugh. "I've had to walk in *your* shadow for twenty-six years." He spoke as though he perceived that to be the sole cause of his troubles. "I had no choice in the matter. I was the second son. I was *unwanted*. Wouldn't surprise me."

Lady McGovern looked sadly at her younger grandson. "You were very much wanted, Scott. Wanted and loved. What's going on here is some lack, some liability, in yourself. You're eaten up with jealousy and resentment. You're a mess, my boy. And that mess has to be cleaned up."

Scott swung his angry accusing glance Skye's way. "What about the mess *she's* made? You said yourself you thought she was Uncle Jonty's kid. There's always been a dark underbelly in this family. Skye sure doesn't look like Jack McCory."

"Jack McCory is a good man." Lady McGovern held up her hand as Keefe went to sharply intervene. "The sad thing is I've gone for far too many years not fully appreciating what sort of man he is. Cathy loved him. She tried to tell me that, but I couldn't *see* it. I thought she was infatuated with Jonty. I was blind to what was right under my nose. Jack McCory has proved himself to be a man of integrity. It was a terrible thing you did, Scott, presenting Jack with what could possibly be ill-founded assumptions. I may not be able to forgive myself for that."

"It's fact!" Scott sneered, a nerve twitching in his cheek. "The thing is, what are we going to do about it?"

"No *we*." Keefe's tone lashed. "None of this is your concern, Scott." He rested his hands on Skye's shoulders. "Skye and I are to be married."

Please, God, yes, yes, Skye silently begged. She couldn't continue without hope.

Scott's chin quivered with rage. "It'll be over in a matter of months. It's a natural reaction not to want to marry your first cousin."

"Oh, shut up, Scott," Rachelle raged. "For once in your life mind your own business. You're just jealous. I always knew you fancied Skye. But I'm ready to back whatever Keefe and Skye choose to do. First cousins can marry. No problem. Annette Kingsley—I went to school with her—married her first cousin, Brett. They have a couple of lovely kids now. You've allowed yourself to be eaten up with jealousy and envy. We've all had to live with it. You'll be better off away from here. So will I. All these years you've been trying to live Keefe's life. Time to get one of your own. I plan to."

"I want you off Djinjara tomorrow, Scott," Keefe said. "When you can return is entirely up to you."

Scott stood up, lurching to the door. "Stick your offer of Emerald Downs," he said. "I've got money. No one wants me here anyway, so I reckon I might travel. Become a playboy or a beach bum. I just can't hack marrying poor old Jemma."

"You'll be doing her a big favour," Keefe said in a deeply ironic voice.

"But Skye now!" Scott's dark eyes glowed hotly. "You mean to have Skye McCory?"

"I've already said so." Keefe didn't spare his brother his contempt.

"I won't be expecting an invitation to the wedding, then?" Scott gave Keefe then Skye an insolent salute.

"Right on!" Keefe followed his brother up, determined on seeing him to his room. "Move it, Scott. You need to pack."

CHAPTER NINE

SKYE stayed inside with her father all morning. Scott was due to fly out at noon. Events had been tough on everyone. The family was upset. So was she. It was terrible to be thought of as "the enemy", which was obviously the way Scott felt about her. She wasn't such a fool she didn't know behind the intense dislike lay a very different emotion, equally unwelcome. Scott was just as much attracted to her as he had ever been. It was part of his condition—sibling rivalry carried to the nth degree—to hunger for what his older brother had. It had started in Scott's boyhood. It had carried through to Scott the man. She knew there were areas of grief and a kind of defeat in Keefe in relation to his brother. Keefe had tried endlessly to help Scott. It hadn't worked because Scott wouldn't allow it to work. That would take away his *raison d'être*. She worried that perhaps part of Keefe was subconsciously shifting some of the blame onto her. She had seen it before, but she wouldn't tolerate it now. Keefe loved his brother for all his aberrations. That was what family was about.

She had given her father an edited version of what had happened the previous night, telling him the family had agreed Scott needed professional help to enable him to overcome his problems.

"He'll carry them to his dying day, poor lad," Jack said, his expression saddened. "Hate to say it but a lot of families have the odd man out. So what about young Jemma? Is she still in the equation?"

Skye shook her head. "For a time Jemma will suffer. She does love him. Why I don't know. I've never heard him offer her an affectionate word. There's no explaining this love business. The choices we make, even if they don't fit our needs."

"No explaining life," Jack said with a wry laugh. He was looking so much better, recovering well. "So what did the old lady say? Never darken my door again?"

"Nothing like that, Dad." Skye refilled their coffee cups. "Scott's family love him. The tragedy is he doesn't recognise it."

Jack nodded. "It's as you say. We all make choices in life. Some choices lead to great happiness, others to suffering. The trouble is we don't know at the time. Now, when do we get this test done? The sooner the better, I guess, though I'm at peace in my mind."

The implications were so strong, so possibly traumatic that Skye had deliberately blocked her mind to any other result than that Jack was her biological father. "I've been thinking about that. In the course of my work I've dealt with DNA testing on behalf of clients. All of them paternity tests, as it happens. One involved a large inheritance, only my client's late father *wasn't* her biological father."

"So she missed out?"

"On half of it. I managed to convince the rest of the family she had a definite entitlement and we would fight for it. The case was settled out of court. My client received roughly one quarter. They were a greedy lot. It wasn't the money, it was the not belonging that broke my client's heart. As far as the tests go, it takes about three or four days from the time a sample is received at the laboratory. Keefe wants you to have some time off. Why don't you come back with me? You love Sydney. We can do lots of things together."

"And it would make things easier for this testing?"

She nodded. "We're both on hand. It's Lady McGovern that has to be convinced. She's lived all these years with pure supposition. It's worn her down. Time to set her free."

"But I'm your dad no matter…right?" There was a humble note in Jack's voice.

"You bet you are!" Skye lightly punched his arm. "That's the way it is. That's the way it's always going to be. You're my dad."

She had arranged to meet Keefe mid-afternoon. Same old meeting place. They were desperate to be alone. There was so much to discuss. And above and beyond that, she craved the physical closeness. How could she bring herself to renounce Keefe? How *could* she? That was her torment, adding a great urgency to her prayers. Was it possible to bargain with God, she thought, then forget all about one's promise when the drama was over? Much as she brooded on it, she couldn't think so. It hadn't been a light promise. It had been a solemn vow. Scott had committed a crime, going to her father with his revenge-filled revelations. Now Scott had flown away, leaving the consequences of his actions behind.

She took her favourite mare, Zemira, from the stables. Zemira had that little bit of a devil in her. They forded the numerous water channels that criss-crossed the station. With some she underestimated the depth of the channel at the centre. The water came up to her knee pads, but she would dry off soon enough. The heat of the day was still intense. In the distance she could see a mob of cattle, a thousand or so, being turned in a huge wave towards water. No life without water. A great bull called Samson led the mob by several yards, his dominance on display. Heifers came respectfully behind. The lowing and bellowing—mothers for their calves—even at a distance, rent the air.

On the plain, the landscape was painted in bold colours, rust red with great splashes of dark gold from the spinifex and multiple shades of green and grey-green from the native grasses. Some of the tall grasses were flushed along the tops with tiny yellow wildflowers, bright as coins in the sun. As always, the mirage was abroad. From a distance it took the form of a silver sea, deep enough to swim in. The early explorers had headed off towards those silver seas only to tread never-ending fiery red sands.

The peace and quiet of the hill country was remarkable. Silence *could* speak. It spoke to her. Silence brought her a much-needed measure of peace. Skye attended first to the mare then she spread out a rug in the sun-dappled shade of the bauhinias. Native passion fruit were growing nearby. The pungent fragrance she inhaled with pleasure, drawing it deep into her lungs. With her pocket knife she split a couple of fruit, putting each half to her mouth and letting the pulp slide sweetly tart and thirst quenching in a cool stream down her throat. Delicious! She settled herself on the rug, looking out on the vast panorama.

What to a city person was a trackless, untamed wilderness of flaring red soil, blazing blue skies and the beautiful, but treacherous mirage held for her all the magic of the Dreamtime. This giant desert landscape was deep under her skin. She thought it would take more than a lifetime to photograph it in all its moods. Inevitably her thoughts turned to the coming of the wildflowers. No city person could imagine what it was like, riding through an ocean of wildflowers that ran on mile after mile after mile, away to the horizon. She wanted to capture that sight on camera. That time would come. All that was needed was a cyclone, even heavy monsoon rains in the tropical north. The great inland river system would fill and overflow, preceding one of the most brilliant spectacles one could witness in a lifetime.

After ten minutes of waiting she climbed to the top of the hill to gain a vantage point. Keefe had told her he would be driving a station vehicle. He had been with the station vet for most of the morning but the vet had been scheduled to take a return helicopter flight at 1:00 p.m. to a neighbouring station. One hand shading her eyes, she stood and waited, twirling a bauhinia flower a shade restlessly between her fingers. A pair of kangaroos, a blue-grey female, considerably smaller, and a bright red male, a good six feet on its haunches, were indulging in a little love play down on the flats. The female was showing her affection by placing her short left arm across the male's broad back, tenderly kissing his muzzle. Sex, it seemed, made the world go round.

If only she had her camera! She was in her element here. The very nature of the landscape, with its great desert monuments, rock piles and stunning ramparts, its flora and extraordinary fauna, lent itself to spectacular shots. Kangaroos were fascinating to watch; large groups of them—as protection against dingo attack—getting around the countryside with their unique hops, standing up staring about while taking a break from grazing. Even the pugnacious males' battle for supremacy was thrilling, though it could become a life-and-death affair; two adult males fighting for the honour of taking off the desired female, leading the mob, mostly both.

Five minutes later she was rewarded by the sight of a Jeep speeding across the flat. The heavy tyres were sucking up the sand, sending up spiralling red willy-willies filled with grass seeds and grit.

The waiting was over! She felt such a tremendous rush of emotion she had difficulty swallowing… What she felt for Keefe was outside her control. Whatever happened—whatever the outcome of the DNA testing—she knew there would be no real future without him. But like many women before her faced with life-transforming trauma over an invisible oath given before

God, she would have to stick with her religious beliefs. No one could ever say real life was easy.

He pulled her close, drawing her into his brilliant gaze. They kissed open-mouthed. Long sustained kisses. She kept nothing back. Neither did he.

This is what love is. The giving without stint.

It wasn't only her mouth and her arms she opened wide to him. She gave of her spirit. If she *had* to—if the worse came to the worst—she could live the rest of her life knowing she had once known a great love.

"There'll be protection in one of the caves," Keefe said urgently. He fixed his gaze on the hills with their innumerable caves and shelters. They desperately needed total privacy.

"The one with all the little stick people making love." She took his outstretched hand, her legs atremble. Aborigines over tens of thousands of years had been using rock facings for their art, drawing and incising carvings on countless rocky outcrops, some never seen by the white man.

The deep roomy cave Skye had chosen was full of hidden art. The drawings executed in a range of ochres. They could be understood immediately—men and women making love, beneath trees, alongside creeks with birds and cloud symbols overhead. The positions were very realistic. Even stick figures could bring a blush to the cheeks. Strikingly the male figures were wearing headdresses of birds' feathers.

This wasn't by any means the richest gallery on Djinjara, but it was one of the most accessible and it had a benign aura. It was no exaggeration for her to say the main gallery had the power to make the short hairs on her nape stand to attention. Tribal people believed a Dreamtime spirit had made its home there. She believed it too. She certainly wouldn't dare to photograph the rock drawings. Not that Keefe would allow her to.

No one needed to bring the anger of the Great Ones down on their heads.

"How did it go with Scott?" She stood at the neck of the cave, watching Keefe check the thick yellow sand over. Little lizards scurried for cover, heading for the rock walls.

"Badly!" he threw over his shoulder.

A warning tremor shot through her. "Don't want to talk about it?"

"What is there to say?" He turned back to her, his silvery eyes contrasting strikingly with the deep bronze of his skin.

"Is he still blaming me?" She hadn't intended saying it but, despite that, it came out. There was just something in Keefe's expression that bothered her and spun resistance. She knew she had mulled far too long over that incident that had happened years ago.

"He's blaming you because he can't have you," Keefe said.

She shrugged as if it didn't matter, when it mattered a great deal. "Scott is the type who only wants what he can't have. He lets things fester in his mind."

"I know."

Waves of remembered resentment rose, making it difficult for her to speak. "So what are you going to do?" she asked. "Let worry over your brother affect our lives? He's not worth it, Keefe."

"I know that too," Keefe retorted grimly. "Falling in love with you was out of his control. I can surely understand. It was out of my control."

That jolted her heart. "Maybe I'm a witch!"

He gave a twisted half-smile. "You have powers. Don't let's talk about Scott any more," he said, his voice strained. "He's gone."

She let her fingernails dig into her palms. *Stop now. Keefe is right.* Instead, with the inbuilt perversity of women, she went at it. A fully fledged accusation. "So you can't have us both. Is that it, Keefe? Is that what's gnawing away at your heart? I can see you're upset. I understand it but I won't allow Scott to come between us. Some part of you thinks I have. That's the truth, isn't it?" She whipped out the challenge. "It will *always* be the truth. Scott won't change. We'll all die hoping."

His eyes burned over her and settled on her beautiful mouth. The most seductive woman's mouth he had ever seen. "Skye, please…let it go," he begged. "I can see all Scott's faults and failings but I love my brother. We're the same blood."

"What if *I* turn out to be the same blood?" She was passing beyond caution. "You're none too sure, are you? You and your grandmother."

That too she hadn't intended to say, but what the hell! She was in desperate need of reassurance. Torn between love and pride.

Keefe moved to her side, taking her firmly by the shoulders. "I've *told* you. I don't give a damn who you are. You're *my* Skye, my sun, moon and stars, my woman. You dazzle me. I love you more than anyone else on earth." He knotted a thick swathe of her hair around his hand, tipping back her head, hunger for her a different kind of torment. What was happening inside her he wasn't quite sure. All he knew was she was frantic about Jack and his well-being, just as he was worrying terribly about that crazy spontaneous vow she had made about giving him up as some sort of bargain with a God he didn't know if he believed in. The terrifying thing was, Skye *did*.

"I'm taking Dad back to Sydney," she told him quickly, the words crowding into her mouth. "You said he could have some time off.'

Keefe beat off frustration. He wanted her so badly he was in physical pain. "Of course he can. The break will do him good."

"We can get the paternity test done there." She was dismayed by the glacial tone of her voice. "Should take less than five working days. Then comes the denouement. He's my dad—the man who raised me, but not my biological father. I couldn't keep the results from him. He would want to see the results with his own eyes."

"Oh, for God's sake, let there be an end to it, Skye," Keefe raged. "This has to be settled once and for all. The *not* knowing is far worse than the knowing. I don't expect any revelations. Jack *is* your father. He *knows* how much you love him. I believe he'll hold up whatever the outcome."

"Then you're a darned sight more certain than I am. But, then, you're always so *sure*. Outcomes have to be what *you* want."

Her upraised hands were fluttering like agitated birds. He caught them. "I'm sure you love me, Skye. Nothing can obliterate that. But you're just superstitious enough to abandon me if you don't hear what *you* want. It's been a bad time for us both. I lost Dad. I'm trying to keep it all together. Then we lose Scott. It's *you* I can't lose. Is that clear? I can't bear to argue any more with you. There are supposed to be two theories for arguing with women anyway. I know from long experience of you that neither of them work. Life is full of obstacles. Together we can overcome them. No matter this business with Jack, what could be worse than for us to be parted?"

"Well, Jack's not *your* father, is he? Your answer seems to be that we just don't talk too much!" She was trying to tamp herself down, but fear and the heat of irrational anger was in her throat. Getting angry was a harsh relief. If only this whole business of paternity was a bad dream. She had no real faith her father could accept a negative outcome with any degree of serenity. An unwanted truth could kill him. Second time around. There was so much confusion in her mind, yet as they stood locked together, like a man and woman in combat, sizzling heat waves were rising all around them. The sparks could only billow into flame.

Keefe locked a steely arm around her, his eyes with a diamond-hard glint. "We don't talk," he muttered fiercely. "Talking is getting us nowhere. We make love."

She flung her long hair over her shoulder. "Go on, then! Shred my heart!"

So it was wordless, the well of desire bottomless.

Then came the gasps, the sharp little cries, the moans that went hand in hand with sexual excitement. He worked her out of her clothes, kissing every part of her creamy flesh as it became exposed. Tears streaked her cheeks. He licked them off. Each time her entered her, it was different. Nothing was quite like the last time. He was the most marvellous, accomplished lover, always astonishing her, showing her more and more things about herself, and her own body. Their love-making was becoming a long journey she hoped would never end. Two people could make their own magic; shut out the world.

The scent of him! The sweet, sweet flavour of his skin. Enormously complex feelings went into her surrender to the all-dominant male. He smelled tantalisingly of wood smoke and burnt eucalyptus leaves. She stared up into his brilliant eyes as his lean body covered hers, bearing down on her with a powerful, exultant rhythm. Her breasts, so satiated with feeling, were crushed beneath him. Her trembling legs were locked tight around him. She didn't know where she ended and he started. There was no distinction. They were two people, but one flesh. It was so piercingly perfect, nothing else mattered…

When it came time to leave Jack decided it was his duty to remain on Djinjara.

"Keefe needs me, sweetheart," he told Skye, an element of bravado in his voice. "Too much is laid on him. It's a killer job. I'm the overseer around here. I value my position. Besides, I'm as fit as a fiddle. You can see that. You go off with your samples and in due course you'll let me know."

Some note in his voice brought tears to her eyes. "Well, if that's what you want, Dad," she said gently. She could read his suffering.

"It is, love." Jack patted her shoulders with hands scarred by years of roping, fencing, mustering and other hard physical work. "I'm going to leave everything to you. I don't think I could bear the hanging around waiting, anyway. Far better for me to get back to work."

"If that's your decision, Dad. But you have nothing to agonise about. You're my dad, pure and simple. Don't fail me, Dad. I need you."

"Whatever the outcome, sweetheart, "Jack said, "I'll reconcile to it."

Except Skye knew he wouldn't.

Keefe had organised a private jet charter company to fly her back to Sydney, clipping hours off her time. Take-off was scheduled for 8:30 a.m. Another blazing blue day. Keefe drove her to the airstrip, which had been upgraded to accommodate small- to medium-size jets. The jet she was flying on could comfortably seat six passengers. There was to be one stop at Myall Downs to pick up a party of three cattlemen, all known to Skye, all Outback identities.

There was no exuberant display of love and affection between them. Rather an inflamed awareness and tension. Neither had the power to alter the outcome of this testing to suit their purpose. She felt perhaps unfairly that Keefe was scornful of the appeal she had made to the Almighty to save her father, and her subsequent vow. He might as well have been an atheist for the incredulous view he took of it. He wasn't bothering over much hiding it from her.

"Promises are often made under terrible stress. What sense is there in trying to hold to them?"

"I'd come with you if I could."

She shook her head. "You can't possibly get away. Look after Dad for me?"

"Jack is stronger than you think, Skye." He bent to kiss her, catching a burst of her special fragrance, wildflowers and sunshine. "Let me know the minute you have the results. *Before* Jack, naturally."

She gave a taut little smile. "We're all on tenterhooks about this, aren't we, no matter what we say?"

Keefe shook his head, crisply businesslike, if only on the outside. "No doubts or bothers from me. I love you. I need you. I refuse to let you go. I'm sure the Almighty has handled a lot of broken promises in His time. We have to put the past behind us, Skye."

Only the past would never die.

She delivered the samples for testing the same day. She had used this particular laboratory several times. It had an excellent reputation, fast, accurate and completely confidential.

"We'll have the results back to you by Friday, Ms McCory," the technician, Sarah, told her in her friendly fashion.

"I'd appreciate it."

She arrived back at the city building that housed her law offices, only to be confronted by a very angry-looking, burly middle-aged man, fast losing his hair.

God, here's trouble.

It never rained but it poured. His face looked familiar. Not a good face. An alcoholic's face. Ah, yes, Gordon Roth. A mean man. There were dangers that went along with representing women in distress. Like violent husbands who terrorised their wives and kids.

"Skye McCory?" He caught up with her, faded eyes glaring. "You're the one that's been representing my wife, Emma. Emma Roth."

Skye stepped back a pace. "What is it you want, Mr Roth? You really shouldn't be talking to me."

"So high and mighty!" he sneered. "Think you've won over my wife, don't you? She wants a divorce. Good for you. Bad for me. You've made bad blood between us, lady. I can tell you that. Emma loves me. We can get back together."

Did such men ever learn? "I doubt very much if your wife is going to give you a fourth or is it a fifth chance, Mr Roth. And you can't tell me anything, so please step aside. Your wife has a restraining order in place against you for domestic violence. You had your chance to be heard at the court hearing. A *judge* decided to grant the restraining order to your wife. That could become permanent if you violate that order. You cannot harass or stalk me. You must understand that. Break the law and you could face imprisonment."

"The law! What's the law?" he shouted, waving his arms and drawing immediate attention to the two of them standing at the entrance to the building. "Stinking, rotten solicitors, the whole legal system is geared against men," he raged. "I'm no threat to Emma. Or the kids."

"Were that only true, Mr Roth. Allegations of abuse have been proven in court," she pointed out in a toneless voice. "Now, I really must go, but with a warning. Don't attempt to harass me. I promise you, you'll be sorry."

He gave her an evil look. "I know where you live."

One of the senior partners of the firm, coming out of the building, sized up the situation in an instant. "On your way, whoever you are!" she called in her most carrying, magisterial voice. "Skye, are you okay? Is this man harassing you?"

"He's on his way, Elizabeth. Aren't you, Mr Roth?"

He swore and made a crude gesture in their direction by way of goodbye.

"Sometimes we really do need protection," Elizabeth Dalkeith said very quietly and seriously, taking Skye's arm. Elizabeth had never fully recovered from seeing a family court judge shot dead right in front of her. "If that man gives you the slightest trouble—even a phone call—you're to let me know immediately."

"I will, Elizabeth. I promise."

Silently Skye prayed Gordon Roth would never show up again.

She had trouble concentrating on the outstanding files on her desk. Friday couldn't come soon enough. She knew it was normal enough to start harbouring doubts, especially when lives hung in the balance. Nevertheless, what she thought of as her disloyalty upset her intensely. She really was giving herself hell over all this. Keefe might believe—or chose to believe—his much-valued overseer could survive a tremendous emotional blow. She was far from sure. Another source of deep shame. She had started calling her dad *Jack* in her mind. Maybe with all this worry she was becoming very slightly unhinged?

Only there *had* been something between her mother and Jonty McGovern. Lady McGovern, a shrewd observer, couldn't have been that far out. What was more telling, Lady McGovern all these years hadn't let go of her belief that her son, Jonty, dead at twenty-two, had fathered Skye. Had no one else noticed an involvement? Keefe's father, Broderick? The rest of them, Keefe, Scott and Rachelle, had been children. She knew Keefe was deeply stressed when he allowed very little to stress him. He had a big job running the McGovern empire. He had also suffered the double loss of his father and brother.

Where had the idea of a conspiracy started? With Lady

McGovern, of course. And yet Jack was convinced Cathy had loved him. Jack in his youth must have been a handsome man. He was still a man women found attractive. There didn't have to be a conspiracy behind it. Through the days and the long restless nights she couldn't stop herself from going over and over different scenarios. Keefe wanted to marry her no matter what the outcome of the DNA testing was. There was no impediment after all, but her heart and soul were sore and shaking.

They had rescued Jack once. Would they be called on to do it again? Jack's whole life would implode with a negative outcome. So would hers, but such was her love for him that it was Jack she agonised about. Whatever the outcome, he, not Jonty McGovern, was her dad.

The results were delivered to her office in a large manila envelope marked *Confidential*. She heard voices in the corridor, a couple of her colleagues, so she rose swiftly and closed her door. She wanted no interruptions. She was far too much on edge to begin to hide it. Bracing herself, she opened the envelope. Her head was spinning dizzily. Too much coffee. Too little food.

She began to read. As she neared the bottom of the document, her nerveless fingers let go of the pages.

Skye bowed her blonde head and wept uncontrollably. Nobody could argue with a paternity test when it had a probability rating of ninety-nine point nine.

Keefe rode down to the yards where Jack and his aboriginal offsider, Chilla, were breaking in the best of the brumbies. Where Jack was tall and whipcord lean, Chilla was a small wiry man, both with a wonderful way around horses. They made a top team. The brumby they were breaking in when he arrived, a ghost grey, the sunlight dancing off his unkempt coat, was one of the mob that they had allowed to escape the day of the lightning strike. It was smallish in size, short legs, but powerful enough through the hind quarters. He waited until Jack had the quivering animal standing calmly on the sand, before gesturing to his overseer for his attention.

Jack ducked between the rails and came towards him, his lean, weathered face shadowed by the wide brim of his battered old Akubra, a flash of brilliant red from the bandana around his throat. "Yes, boss."

"I have some news for you, Jack."

"Oh, Gawd!" Jack's face started to work. But he stood in place, ramrod straight, a man receiving sentence. Normally so laid back, Jack was having the greatest difficulty gaining control of his emotions. Keefe put him out of his misery.

Jack swept off his dusty hat, throwing it so high in the air that several things happened at once. The brumby plunged, causing a lounging Chilla to spring to attention; scores of Technicolor parrots rose shrieking from the trees and a little mob of wallabies nearby bounded frantically to higher ground.

"Goddamn right!" Jack yelled. "I knew it. I knew it. My little Cathy would never have betrayed me."

Keefe put out his hand. Jack shook it. "You can't get anything clearer than that, Jack," Keefe said, enormously relieved to be the bearer of good news. "No argument from anywhere. Your belief in your wife—Skye's mother—has been totally vindicated. I'll have to talk to my grandmother. Set things straight. All these years she has laboured with entirely the wrong scenario firmly entrenched in her head. It's quite tragic." He gave a rueful smile.

"But now we *know*," Jack said, his expression so full of life and elation he looked ten years younger. "It was Jonty, you know, that was keen on Cathy. Not that I blamed him. She was like a ray of sunshine. He was so young. We were all so young. Poor Jonty!"

Keefe sighed. How little anyone knew what lay ahead in the

future. "Let me say again how sorry I am my brother had to upset you."

Jack ducked his chin. "Upset us all. He sure did, boss, but that's over. I really appreciate you coming to tell me. How's my girl?"

"My girl too, Jack." Keefe flashed a smile. "We talked for a long time on the phone." Indeed, their long conversation would always remain in his memory. The joy and the enormous relief in her voice, the outpouring of love. "I'm taking the weekend off to join her," he said, hugging the thought of their passionate reunion to him when in his own way he had been through hell. "Want to come along?"

Jack laughed aloud. He knew the score. "You don't need *me*," he said jovially. "I'll be seeing her soon. Give my beautiful girl—our beautiful girl—my love."

"Will do, Jack," Keefe said with a backward wave. He remounted his horse, riding away while Jack, on a wave of euphoria, turned back to his mate Chilla, calling, "Get the big one in here, Chilla, the roan. He's the pick of the bunch. Between the two of us we can turn him into a darned good working horse."

CHAPTER TEN

HE HAD to wait longer than he expected. It was dark now and the tenants who worked had had ample time to make their way home. Consequently, there was no movement around the entrance. He planned on slipping through the security door, either when someone entered or left the building.

Startling him—he was so engrossed in his plan—a taxi pulled up with a screech directly in front of the swish apartment complex. A young man on the hippy side got out, calling to someone still inside the taxi. "Check with Thommo. See you all around eight!"

While he watched and awaited his chance, the young man loped towards the entrance and Gordon Roth, waiting in the garden shadows, closed in quickly.

The security door opened at the click of a button. The young man became aware of the burly guy standing just behind him, almost breathing down his neck, definitely invading his space. Where in the heck had he come from? "You goin' in, mate?" He kept his tone relaxed. One didn't mess with a guy with a face like that.

"Yes," Gordon Roth leaned forward, crowding the young man further. "I was just about to buzz through to my friend.'

"What friend would that be, then, mate?" Something about

this burly guy was making the hitherto carefree young man uneasy.

"What's it to you?" Gordon Roth shot back, a flicker of rage in his eyes. "Anyway, she's waiting for me. We're going on to the theatre."

The young man's glance darted away. He hadn't missed that flicker. So much rage about these days. Road rage, home rage, work rage. A bad sign of the times. "So okay, then, enjoy yourself," he said, clearing his throat. The woman friend he reasoned must be pretty hard up. The guy looked as though he regularly gave women a belt in the mouth. He let the guy get away to the lift—he had no wish to go along for the ride—so he pulled out his mobile to feign a call. Anyway, the lady friend would have to be okay with the guy before letting him in.

Skye heard the knock on her door with a start. She wasn't expecting Keefe quite so early. But he was here! She had been busy preparing a meal for them both in the kitchen; a scallop salad for starters, and two lovely fresh Tasmanian salmon fillets served with marinated cucumber, avocado and green mango. Feeling extraordinarily elated, she moved with light, dancing steps to her front door.

Keefe! Every last impediment to their marriage had fallen away.

She didn't bother fixing her eye to the peephole. She threw open the door, a radiant welcoming smile in place.

"Oh, my God!' She stood transfixed, staring at her visitor with horror.

Find your breath. Steady up. Keefe is coming.

Gordon Roth loomed over her, one heavy foot in the doorway. "Shocked, are we?"

"Why wouldn't I be?" She knew a flash of outrage so intense she was able to summon a forceful tone: "Get away from my door, Mr Roth. I have a friend coming. He's with the police."

Fat fingers reached out to pinch her cheek. "I don't think so, blondie. Let go of the door. I don't want to hurt you. Not for the next half-hour anyway. I'm here to talk. Let's keep this civilised."

"Civilised isn't breaking into my apartment," she answered sharply. "You could get into a lot of trouble over this."

"Trouble? I'm in enough trouble." Roth scowled, his blue eyes so faded they looked colourless. Pebbles. Dead.

"There's always more," Skye was quick to remind him. "You haven't been inside a jail as yet."

"Maybe I've been lucky!" He managed a laugh.

"And maybe your wife was too terrified of you to press charges. You won't bully me, Mr Roth. We've got nothing to say to each other. I strongly advise you to be on your way."

"You lawyers give a lot of advice." Abruptly he lashed out, pushing her backwards so she slammed into the hall console. "Let's go inside, shall we?" He got a painful grip on her arm, forcing her into the living room.

"Nice, nice!" His gaze swept the room. "How well you live! Now, everything will be fine, so relax. It was you who talked my wife into applying for a divorce. All you have to do now— if you know what's good for you—is convince her I'm worth another chance. I'm not letting my kids go. No way! They love me. Emma's a liar. She always was."

Skye was amazed at the calm disdain in her voice. "You can't talk to me about things like that, M. Roth. You must speak to your own solicitor. Kevin Barclay, isn't it?"

"Sacked 'im!" Roth said, thrusting his chin at her. "He was on my wife's side. Never said so, but even an idiot could tell."

"How did you get in here?" Skye took a pace away. *Keep him talking.* Keefe would soon arrive. Keefe could handle anything and anyone who came at him, even a snorting bull like Roth.

"People are careless." Roth waved the question away. "It was easy. Some young dude let me through."

"He shouldn't have done that. What did you say to him?"

"I said I was meeting up with a lady friend." Roth smirked.

"And you've had lady friends, haven't you, all through your marriage?" Skye stared back accusingly, one hand massaging her bruised spine.

Roth's expression turned grim. "You've been checking up on me, have you?"

Skye nodded. "Brothels, you name it."

"I don't do nothing other guys don't do. Especially guys who have a rabbit for a wife."

"Not even a rat could enjoy life with you," Skye said with contempt. She was getting a taste of what poor Emma had had to endure for years.

"A pity you said that!" The pebble eyes ran over her face and body. She was wearing a long halter-necked dress printed with flowers. He eyed her high, taut breasts, the skin that gave off light. "You're a real looker, aren't you? Never had a woman like you. I'm wondering what it would be like."

Her stomach flipped. What she saw in his eyes was *hate*. Not just for her. Or his hapless wife. For all women. She realised something terrible could happen to her. Gordon Roth was one step away from being crazy.

Behind them the phone in the kitchen rang, startling them both. "That will be my policeman friend."

"Leave it." Roth's warning was rough. "You heard me. Don't move."

She froze.

Another sound came on top of the strident ringing of the phone. A couple of raps on the front door.

Only one person it could be. *Keefe*. Immediately that steadied the wobbles that had invaded her limbs.

Seeing the change in her, Roth grabbed her, holding her body tightly in front of him like a hostage. As indeed she had become. They heard the door open.

"Not a good idea to leave the door unlocked, Sky-Eyes," Keefe called, his tone a mix of chiding and dead serious.

Skye drooped against Roth's restraining arm, overcome by relief. Then came fear, not just for herself but for Keefe. For all she knew, Roth might be carrying a gun.

"Care to step inside for a moment, Mr Policeman?" Roth's gravelly voice clanged metallically.

Keefe made a lightning response. He materialised in the living room like a genie materialised out of a puff of smoke. "Whoa!" He held up his hands, palms out, much as Skye had seen him steady a fractious horse. "What's going on here?"

"A little negotiation." Roth's face flushed a violent red.

"Okay," Keefe answered reasonably, acting on his judgment of the situation. "But first I suggest you let Ms McCory go." He held his furious anger well under control. "You're only making things worse for yourself, whoever you are. What are you doing here anyway?" As he spoke, Keefe advanced slowly but steadily, a tall, powerfully lean figure.

"I've got a weapon!" Roth yelled in an excited voice. "Like to see it?"

"Nice and slow," Keefe answered, sliding his hand inside his own jacket. "I have one too. Unluckily for you I'm a crack shot. I suggest, before this goes any further, you let Ms McCory go."

"Please, don't let any of us get hurt." Skye found her voice. "This is Gordon Roth, Keefe. I represent his wife. She has a restraining order in place against him for domestic violence. She wants a divorce."

"Now, why doesn't that surprise me?" Keefe said, moving to stand directly in front of them. "Let…her…go, Mr Roth." His tone was quiet, but every word carried tremendous weight.

To Skye's immense shock Roth caved in. He released her,

using brute force to pitch her at Keefe, who fielded her deftly, taking a few seconds to steady them both.

Roth had his opportunity. He made for the door. Events were getting too much for him. He didn't have a weapon at all. The other guy did. Not that he would need it from the look of him. Oddly enough he didn't look like a copper, though he had an expression like granite.

Keefe had no difficulty closing in on him. He grabbed the back of Roth's shirt, bunching it and jerking him backwards. "Gotcha!"

Roth grunted in surprise. How had the cop moved so fast?

Keefe spun the big burly man like a steer, forcing him to the floor and planting a hard knee into his back. "Something to tie up his hands, Skye," he ordered, "or I could just knock him out. Funny about you bully boys," he mused, kneeing Roth harder. "You only target defenceless women."

Skye raced back with a length of picture cord she had on hand. "Sorry to be so long."

"No need to apologise. This will do nicely." Skilfully Keefe tied Roth's hands nice and tight. "You might give the police a call. This guy ought to be locked up."

"You can say that again!" Skye held a hand over her fast-beating heart.

Face down on the carpet, Roth was groaning in pain. "Are you gunna let me up?" Incredibly, he felt sorry for himself. He was in agony. The cop was using undue force, weighing down on him like a ton of cement bricks.

"No time soon," Keefe answered nonchalantly, when he badly wanted to smash Roth's face in. "Not hurting you, am I?"

Fiercely Roth got off a string of obscenities.

"Don't worry, when the police arrive, they'll let you up," Keefe consoled him. "That's the good part. The bad part is you'll be facing charges. Even then you can count yourself lucky, you truly worthless cur."

* * *

The police were at the door in under eight minutes. One of the officers handcuffed Roth, who, with a face screwed up as if he'd been mugged, protested violently about police brutality.

"He's not a copper, mate. Don't you know that?" the restraining officer said, keeping a straight face when he badly wanted to laugh.

Roth was led away and their statements taken. The police left with a warning: never open the door to anyone unless you know and trust them. They both seemed surprised they had to tell that to a lawyer. It was a lesson Skye would never forget. She knew more than anyone that there were a lot of angry, very frustrated people out there only too willing to take out their anger on anyone who got in their way.

"I was stupid," Skye admitted. She and Keefe were at last alone. "And once again you've had to come to my rescue."

They sat in silence for a moment, both their minds returning inevitably to the past and the distressing incident with Scott that had done all of them so much harm. Now the frightening encounter with Roth.

"Thank God I was there for you on both occasions," Keefe said on a fervent breath. "Deep as our bond has always been, we've moved ever closer over the years, if that's possible. No one will ever seek to harm you when I'm around."

"You were cast as my protector," she said, revelling in his role. "I thought it was you, of course, with Roth. I didn't even bother to check the peephole."

"That's what he was relying on." They sat together on the sofa, Keefe cradling her to him with one arm. Inside he was stunned by what had happened—what could have happened—to the woman he loved. On the outside he remained calm and supportive. "These guys that beat up their women have one thing in common. They're bullies for sure, but cowards most of all. Why do women continue to live with men who threaten them and their children? I don't get it."

His toying with her hair had gentled her exquisitely. Here was a man who could calm her at a touch, yet arouse her at will. "It would take a woman to be in that position to know. Murder-suicide is a fact of life. Women have to deal with that terrifying thought. Frustrated men turn psychotic. The frequency of it happening is shocking. Sometimes it seems to me I'm in a dangerous job. A few years back Judge Henry Rankin was shot dead outside the family law courts."

Keefe's frown deepened. Even with Roth in custody, the muscles at the back of his neck were still knotted with fury. "I remember you telling me that. One of your bosses was involved, wasn't she?"

Skye nodded. "Mercifully she was only a bystander, a friend of Judge Rankin's. She's never been the same since. Apparently the incident keeps coming back in flashes."

"I should think it would," he said grimly, his fears for her having sky rocketed. "Your boss must be one gutsy lady."

"She is." Abruptly her voice cracked and the held-back tears escaped onto her cheeks.

"Don't, *don't*, my love! I'm here. You're safe." Keefe pulled her across his lap. "I worry about you and what you do. Did you know that?"

"I worry about you too. It's pretty savage, what can happen on a cattle station." Day-to-day injuries, as she well knew. From time to time deaths.

"I can handle it. Which brings us to decision time. Are you completely happy to make a life change?" He waited intently for her answer. His need for her wasn't simply the overwhelming physical hunger he had for her. That was always present. But so many links went into making up their powerful bond. Now it was a question of dealing with their past experiences. They had resolved the most threatening issue, the one that had loomed so largely in tearing them apart, now it was time to discuss their hopes and goals for the future.

"Above anything I want you to be happy," Keefe said. "I want you to feel fulfilled not just as my wife and the mother of my children if we're so blessed, but as an individual in your own right. You hold down a difficult, demanding job in keeping with your high intelligence. Is it conceivable, do you think, my love, you could become bored and restless with too much time on your hands?"

"Bored?" She turned up her head. "On Djinjara?"

"Well, I know you love it." He dropped a glowing kiss on her mouth. "But—"

"No buts," she said, easing back voluptuously into his strong male body. "Have you forgotten my interest in photography?" she teased.

"Not at all. But how serious is it? I know you have exceptional talent."

"Why thank you, kind sir!"

"Okay. You know I'll help you in every way I can. Your happiness is paramount. Everyone marries with the hope of being happy. Not every marriage survives."

She sat straight. "Listen, what are you trying to do, put me off?"

"God, no!" He actually shuddered. "What a thought!"

"You're thinking about your mother and father?"

"How could I not!" he replied, rather bleakly. "My parents' marriage wasn't a great success. You know that."

"But the great thing we have in our favour, Keefe, is that I'm Djinjara born and bred. I love our desert home as much as you do. It's taken overlong, but we've finally sorted out the ghosts of the past. You've told me your grandmother and Rachelle want our marriage to go ahead?" She searched his brilliant eyes.

"I don't intend to be wafted off by flights of angels until I see my first grandchild." Keefe reported his grandmother's words verbatim. "Rachelle almost broke my heart asking very tentatively did I think you might allow her to be a bridesmaid."

"Wh-a-t?" Skye was betrayed into saying sharply, then quickly recovered. "And what did you answer?" She modified her tone. Keefe's family would be her family.

"I'm sure she'll want you, I said. Did I do wrong?" He gave her a down-bent mocking smile.

"No, of course you didn't. But that's only because I love *you* so fiercely." Skye returned to burrowing her head into the curve of his shoulder. "I'll love you until my dying breath."

"Hey, no talk about dying," Keefe protested. He was still feeling shock waves over Roth. With an urgent hand he swept her hair to one side so he could press kisses down the column of her neck. "You can never stop living. With *me*."

"So why don't we get married right away?" She was only half joking. She didn't think she could bear to be parted from him for another second.

"Okay with me!" he answered without hesitation, then paused, his expression thoughtful. "But not, I think, with all the people who will want to come to our wedding. Anyway, *think,* my one and only love. You can't possibly deprive me of the sight of my beautiful bride in all her regalia. I will want all the trimmings."

The depth of feeling in his voice would have made any prospective bride deliriously happy. She was over the moon. The future she had been so desperate about was now set. "And you'll get all the trimmings," she vowed, her mind woman-like already running ahead. "The glorious wedding gown—it will cost a fortune—the long veil, the train, the hand-made wedding shoes, something borrowed, something blue, the most exquisite bridal bouquet. Four bridesmaids. Two flower girls." It was all coming to life as she spoke. Designs, colours. "A magnificent Djinjara setting. Reception in the Great Hall."

"God, I can't wait!" Keefe pulled her ever nearer.

"Neither can I!" Her answer was a peal of joy. "Dad is at peace with the news?"

Keefe pressed a kiss to the blue pulse in her temple. "Just like I said. I invited him to come along but he said the two of us wouldn't need him. He sends his love for now. Finally his Cathy, your mother, has found her rightful place in our lives."

"Lord be praised!" For a moment Skye experienced in amongst the joy a sharp sense of loss. She would have given anything to have a few beautiful memories of her mother. Even a *single* memory. Very sadly that had not been her lot.

"It hasn't been easy for you, has it?" Keefe asked gently, as ever reading her mind.

"I always had *you*." There was a deeply emotional catch in her voice. "The great bond we shared has helped me through life."

"I feel exactly the same." That was Keefe's simple answer.

"Our children will be born out of love," she said.

"Indeed they will!" He joined his mouth to hers. It was more than an intense kiss. It carried a solemn vow.

"And Lady Margaret is happy we're *not* first cousins?" she breathed against his lips, unable to resist the sliver of irony.

"Cousins? God, girl, you're my *twin*, my other half," he cried. "Believe me, Gran is thrilled. A great burden has been lifted off her frail shoulders. She meant it when she said she was going to stick around until she can hold our first child in her arms."

"And the one after that," Skye said, her happiness absolute. Her vision had such clarity. The two of them making their journey hand in hand through life. Partners. Full partners. In every way. It filled her mind with glory. "I suppose it would be too much to hope Scott can get his act together?" She briefly sobered.

"You said it, Sky-Eyes." Keefe's answer was laconic. "Scott's a man in charge of his own future. I guess he has a perfect right to go to the devil if he so chooses. We'll just have to make do with the entire McGovern clan plus most of the Outback."

"Wonderful!" She was floating high again on emotion. "Only you haven't officially asked me to marry you.".

"Watch this!" Before she knew what he was about, he tumbled her off his lap, falling to one knee on the plush rug, taking her hand. He turned it over, spread her palm wide. Then he bent his raven head to press an ever-deepening kiss into her palm. It sent little electric jolts all over her highly receptive body. "How old were you when you first asked me to marry you?" There was devilment in his eyes. "Five, wasn't it?"

She gave a little laugh, her expression both tender and alluring. "I was always a precocious child and you were always my prince. You used to call me 'little buddy'."

"You *were* my little buddy then. Now you're my woman, soon to be my wife. I can love you and take care of you better than any other man on earth."

"You'd better!" she teased, exhilaration in her eyes.

"Oh, I will." He leaned forward to kiss her lips, luscious as strawberries, taking his own good time. Slowly…very slowly… drawing the tip of his tongue over the pillowy contours, tracing the outline…all the while feeding her hunger….

Her arms draped themselves around his neck. "You're the best kisser in the world," she exulted. "The *best*!"

"And we're not finished yet," he said with thrilling ardency. "Skye Catrina McCory, will you do me the great honour of becoming my bride?" He stared into her eyes, thinking them the most beautiful blue he had ever seen. His daughters simply *had* to have eyes like that. "Would you please raise your left hand?"

"Right hand for the Bible." She tried to laugh, but there was a decided shake to it.

"Left hand for engagement rings," he pointed out.

She threw her head back in surprise. "You haven't *got* one surely?"

"Not on my person, no. But give me a moment." He sprang up with characteristic litheness, moving across to where his jacket was folded over an armchair.

"Quickly, quickly!" She gave in to a helpless moan. "The suspense is killing me."

He came back to her, and then with an exaggerated courtly flourish knelt at her feet. "I had hoped things would go more perfectly tonight—"

"Don't you dare speak about Gordon Roth," she cried, love and longing rising high in her breast. "I'm not going to allow a miserable creature like him mar our great moment."

"I should think not! *Voilà!*" He opened up a small box covered in dark blue velvet. "Name me one beautiful blue-eyed woman who doesn't have—or should have—a magnificent sapphire?" he challenged. "You think it's beautiful?" His gaze, earnest and intense, sought her approval.

"Oh, Keefe!" She made a little sound of awe and heady delight. "It's *so* beautiful. I'm going to need all night to tell you."

"Don't worry, I'll keep you awake so you can," he promised, silver eyes glinting. Gently he slid the exquisite sapphire and diamond ring down over her knuckle into its resting place. "With this ring I seal our pact. Together we walk through life hand in hand. Man and wife."

"A big amen to that!" She answered on a prayerful breath. The high sense of occasion was accompanied by overwhelming emotion, blocking her throat with tears. "It's very scary, loving you so much," she confessed.

He answered with raw emotion. "My darling, you scare me, too. That's what comes of loving so intensely." He reached for her hungrily, drawing her down onto the rug beside him. Gently he settled her on her back, loving the way her honey-blonde hair fanned out around her flushed, excited face, pulsing with light. "I want to look at you. I want to love you." For long moments he placed his hands on either side of her head, staring down at her.

"Now can't be soon enough!" The heat of passion was making its blistering path from her head to her toes.

"So what do you think?" His voice was as smooth and rich as molten honey. "Will I make love to you here, or will I carry you down the hallway to bed?"

For answer Skye threw up her slender arms, ecstatically locking them around his neck and drawing his beloved head down to her. She was literally thrumming with love and desire.

"Here is *perfect* for me," she said.

THE HOMETOWN
HERO RETURNS

BY
BETH KERY

Beth Kery holds a doctorate degree in the behavioural sciences and enjoys incorporating what she's learned about human nature into her stories. To date she has published more than a dozen novels and short stories and writes in multiple genres, always with the overarching theme of passionate, emotional romance. To find out about upcoming books, visit Beth at her website at www.BethKery.com or join her for a chat at her reader group, http://groups.yahoo.com/group/BethKery/

Prologue

He'd followed her for three blocks, undecided whether he would call out or just fade back into the shadows of their mutual memories. The weight of the past had frozen his vocal cords, but the sight of her graceful figure drew him like a magnet.

He repeatedly told himself there was no reason for so much trepidation. There was nothing between Mari and him now. The common ground they once shared was shadowed by his shame for his father's actions as well as the bitterness he felt toward Mari for refusing to see or speak to him for half a lifetime.

He nearly did a complete turnabout in the revolving doors of the Palmer House Hotel, telling himself it would be best to just walk away. But at the last second, impulse drove him to speak her name.

"Marianna."

She glanced around.

Mari's eyes—God, he'd forgotten their power. The

sounds in the bustling, luxurious hotel lobby faded as the color washed out of her cheeks. He felt a stab of regret. It'd been the sight of her breathtaking face that'd compelled him to pull up short and call her name.

For a few seconds, they remained motionless. The single word he'd uttered had been the first they'd shared since they'd both lost loved ones in one cruel swipe of fate's hand.

"Marc," Mari mouthed.

"I was at your performance and I followed you," he explained rapidly. When she continued to stare at him, her expression rigid with shock, he realized how strange that sounded. "I just wanted to say…you were wonderful."

She set down her cello case and straightened, seeming to gather herself. Her small smile seemed to give him permission to step closer. "Since when does Marc Kavanaugh listen to anything but rock music?"

"Give me some credit, Mari. A lot can change in fifteen years."

"I'll grant you that," she replied softly.

He couldn't stop himself from devouring the sight that had been ripped away from him so long ago. She wore the black dress that was standard apparel for a symphony member. The garment was simple and elegant, but it couldn't hide the fact that womanhood had added some curves to Mari's slender form.

In all the right places, Marc acknowledged as his gaze lingered for two heartbeats on her full breasts. He glanced down at her hands and noticed she was twisting them together, betraying her nerves. Mari was a cellist—a brilliant one. She had the hands of musician— sensitive and elegant. Even though she'd been young and inexperienced when they'd been together so long ago, she'd had a magical touch on his appreciative skin.

"Look at you. Marianna Itani, all grown up."

"You, too."

Maybe it was his imagination, but her lowered glance seemed almost as hungry as his inspection of her had been.

She returned his smile when she looked into his eyes. "Every inch the newly elected Cook County State's Attorney."

"How did you know about that?"

She shrugged. "I read about it. I wasn't surprised. It was a foregone conclusion you'd excel at whatever you did. You always got what you wanted, once you made up your mind about it." She swallowed and glanced away. "I was sorry to hear about your divorce."

He raised an eyebrow. "I'm sure that didn't make any headlines. How *did* you know about that?"

She looked uncomfortable. "I still have a few contacts in Harbor Town. I keep in touch."

Not with me though, Mari. Fifteen years of silence. Marc banished the flash of frustration, knowing how fruitless the emotion was.

"Right." He nodded, understanding dawning. "I wouldn't be surprised if Walt Edelmann over at the Shop and Save was the first person to know about my divorce outside of Sandra and myself. It's almost supernatural the way that man acquires gossip."

Her radiant smile made a dull ache expand in his chest. "Do you think Walt still works at the Shop and Save?"

"I know he does. I don't go back to Harbor Town often, but, when I do, I always see Walt. He's a standard fixture. He and my mother chat almost every day, which is code for exchanging juicy news."

Her glance ricocheted off him at the mention of his mother. The light from the lobby chandeliers made the dark gold highlights in her brown hair gleam when she lowered her head. "Well…you know how small towns are."

"Yeah, I do," he replied gruffly.

She stirred beneath his stare. The moment wasn't as awkward as it was tense. Charged. He waited, wondering what she would say. He was having trouble finding words himself. He and Mari were almost strangers to each other now. It was odd, the paradox of connection and distance he felt with this woman, as though they each stood on the opposite side of a great chasm of grief, joined only by a thin, ephemeral thread.

Still, that cord was strong enough that it had tugged at him this afternoon when he'd seen the newspaper article about the San Francisco Orchestra playing at Symphony Hall; it had made him ask his administrative assistant to buy him a ticket to the performance. It had fueled his impulsive decision to follow Mari to her hotel.

He nodded in the direction of a crowded lounge. "Can I buy you a drink?"

She hesitated. He was sure she was going to say it wasn't a good idea. He might have agreed with her five minutes ago, before he'd been stunned by the visceral impact of standing so close to her…of seeing her face.

"I have a suite. There's a separate room where we could have a drink and talk. I mean…if you'd like," she added when he didn't immediately respond.

Seeing the slight tremble in her lush lips had mesmerized him.

He blinked, wondering if he was seeing things he wanted to see, not reality. In eyes that reminded him of rare cognac, he saw the glow of desire, a heat that hadn't been entirely stamped out by the weight of tragedy.

"That sounds like a great idea."

She nodded, but neither of them moved. The bond

he'd shared with Mari since they'd been sunburned, carefree teenagers in Harbor Town—a bond formed by love and battered by grief—chose that moment to recall its strength and coil tight.

He stepped forward at the same moment she came toward him and enfolded her in his arms. A convulsion of emotion shook her body.

"Shh." His hand found its way into her smooth, soft hair. He fisted a handful and lifted it to his nose. Her scent filled his head. Desire roared in his blood.

"Mari," he whispered.

He pressed his mouth to her brow, her eyelid and cheek. He felt her go still in his arms when he kissed the corner of her mouth. She turned her head slowly, her lips brushing against his. Their breaths mingled. A powerful need surged up in him, its primal quality shocking him. He possessively covered her mouth.

When he lifted his head a moment later, she was panting softly through well-kissed lips.

"Lead the way, Mari."

"I can think of a thousand reasons we shouldn't do this," she whispered.

"I can only think of you."

She put her hand in his and they headed toward the elevators that led to the rooms.

Chapter One

Five weeks later

Mari understood, for the first time in her life, the full meaning of the word *bittersweet* when she returned to Harbor Town after nearly fifteen years. The feeling strengthened when she left the empty office complex on the north end of town and saw Lake Michigan shimmering through the trees.

"We're not far from Silver Dune Bay here, are we?" she asked Eric Reyes as he paused beside her. She waved goodbye to Marilyn Jordan, the real estate agent who had just shown them the commercial property.

"Fancy a swim, do you? It's hot enough for one, that's for sure." His grin faded. "Mari? Are you okay? You're very pale."

She brushed a tendril of hair off her sweaty brow and steadied herself by leaning against the wall of the building. She swallowed thickly, trying to calm the nausea swelling in her belly.

"I'm fine. I think I caught a bug. The guy who sat next to me on the plane was coughing nonstop for the whole trip."

Eric studied her through narrowed eyes. Mari was suddenly reminded that her friend was a doctor, a very gifted one by all accounts.

"It's nothing, Eric," she assured him. "It comes and goes. I'm sure this heat isn't helping matters any."

She stepped away from the wall, willing her queasiness to ease. She didn't have time for illness. This was a trip she'd needed to make for a long time, and she'd planned to complete her mission in a quick and dirty fashion. Because of her impulsiveness with Marc Kavanaugh five weeks ago, her desire to take care of business and get out of Harbor Town as soon as possible only intensified by the hour.

She forced a smile and walked with Eric toward his sedan.

"Were you one of the daredevils who used to jump off Silver Dune? It's got to be a forty-foot drop to the bay," she reflected as Eric unlocked the passenger door of his car. In her mind's eye, she pictured her summertime best friend Colleen Kavanaugh leaping off the tall dune without a backward glance, her long blond hair streaming out behind her like a golden cape.

Mari had always been a little in awe of the Kavanaughs' fearlessness. All the children had seemed to possess that indefinable, elusive quality that Mari thought of as American royalty—the golden, effortless beauty, the easy confidence and quick smile, the love of a dare, a fierce temper and an even fiercer loyalty to those they loved.

"It's fifty feet, actually," Eric replied once she was

seated in the car. He shut her door and came around to
the driver's side. After he flipped the ignition, he immediately turned the air conditioning on high to cool
the stifling interior. "And yeah, I took the leap plenty
of times in my day."

Took the leap.

Mari had only had the nerve to leap once in her life.
She still could see Marc staring down at her, his mouth
quirked in a sexy, little smile even as the rest of his
features were softened in compassion for her fear.

Stop thinking so much, Mari. Just jump.

She *had* jumped, back when she was eighteen years
old. It'd been the summer her parents had been killed.

Foolishness had caused her to take a similar reckless
leap five weeks ago in Chicago. As a thirty-three-year-
old woman, Mari hardly had the excuse of a girlhood
infatuation any longer, yet something fluttered in her
belly as she clearly recalled Marc pinning her with the
blazing blue eyes as he fused their flesh. She heard his
desire-roughened voice in her ear.

I've waited for this for fifteen years, Mari.

She clenched her eyelids shut and placed her hand on
her stomach, not to soothe her nausea this time, but to
calm the thrill of excitement and wonder the memory
evoked. When she opened her eyes, she saw Eric's curious glance raking over her.

"So are you going to keep me in suspense or what?"
he asked as he pulled onto Route 6.

"What do you mean?" she asked warily, still under
the influence of the carnal memory.

Eric gave her a bewildered glance. "I'm wondering
what you think of the property, Mari."

"Oh!" She laughed in relief. For a second there, she'd
thought those physician's eyes of his had x-rayed straight
into her skull and read her thoughts. "I *do* like the office

space. Very much. It's in a private area, and I love all the sunlight. It's nice that it's so close to the woods and the lake. There's plenty of room for The Family Center to grow as we get new funding and programs. Thank you so much for doing all the preliminary groundwork before I got here, Eric. You and Natalie have done a hundred times more than I'd expected."

"It wasn't that much, especially with all the research and ideas you sent us. Plus, you'd already compiled most of the paperwork for the state."

"Most people will think I'm nuts for doing this—a cello player opening up a facility for victims of substance abuse," she muttered.

Eric's dark brows quirked upward. "Good thing the Reyes aren't *most people* then."

Mari smiled. Of course the Reyes weren't most people. Eric and Natalie had been just as impacted by the effects of substance abuse as Mari and her brother, Ryan, had.

And the Kavanaughs…

It'd been fifteen years since a drunk Derry Kavanaugh, Marc's father, had gotten behind the wheel of his car. Marc's father had caused a three-way crash that night, killing himself, both of Mari's parents and Eric's mother. The accident had left Eric's sister, Natalie, scarred—damage both physical and psychological.

This was the old wound that Mari had felt compelled to return to Harbor Town and try to heal. Not just for herself or Eric or Natalie or Marc, but for anyone who had ever been impacted by the devastating effects of substance abuse.

Eric grabbed her hand as he drove. "Nat and I are right here in Harbor Town, and we're one hundred percent behind you on this. Are you *sure* you don't need any of the money from the lawsuit? Do you really think it was the best idea to transfer all of it over to a trust for The Family Center?"

"Of course I'm sure. You know I've planned to start this project with money from the lawsuit for years now. I never could touch that fund for anything else. It just seemed like—" she paused, trying to find the right words "—that money was meant for something bigger than me. I just haven't had the time to get things moving until now. Besides, I'm selling the house on Sycamore Avenue. That'll give Ryan and me a nice nest egg."

She glanced out the window at the rows of perfectly maintained lakeside cottages. Each and every one looked to be occupied with vacationers. The population of Harbor Town swelled in the summer months.

She smiled wistfully as she watched a little girl with a dark ponytail run around the corner of a house. She'd sported a pink bikini and an inflatable green dragon around her waist.

"I'm not sure I'll ever have the time I need to do what needs to be done," she murmured.

Eric wiggled her hand in his before he let go. "You know what I think you need? I think you need a little fun and relaxation, Harbor Town-style."

"What did you have in mind?"

"The Fourth of July festivities, of course. Don't tell me you've forgotten the downtown parade."

Mari laughed warily. "How could I forget such a spectacle?"

"Let's go have a peek, get an ice cream, goof off. There's plenty of time later to sit down and talk about the plans for The Family Center."

"Eric…" Mari hesitated, hating the idea of being seen in such a public place. Marc had mentioned five weeks ago that he rarely returned to Harbor Town, but she knew that his sister, Colleen, still lived here, as did their mother, Brigit. At the thought of running into either of them—especially Brigit—dread rose.

"Mari," Eric said gently. "You have nothing to be ashamed of. Isn't that one of the reasons you wanted to start up The Family Center, to get past the pain of our history, to make something positive come of it? You can't do that by hiding in your house the whole time you're here."

Her eyes felt moist as she stared blankly out the window. Eric was right. Surely it was part of her own healing to remember not just the bitterness but the sweetness associated with the quaint lakeside community.

"All right," she replied softly. "Let's go to the parade."

Mari stood next to Eric on the curb of Main Street. A boisterous crowd of locals, vacationers and day-trippers surrounded them. A trombone blared off-key, startling her. She glanced up at Eric, and they shared a smile.

A huge sailboat float, surrounded by the smiling, waving men and women of the Arab-American Business Council, followed the marching band. Harbor Town was one of many quaint Michigan towns that lined the lakeshore, drawing vacationers from Detroit and Chicago and everywhere in between. A small population of Arab-Americans had settled in many lakeside communities over the past several decades. Harbor Town was often held up as a banner example of how a minority group could not only blend with a community, but enrich and improve it. Her parents had belonged to a Lebanese faction of eastern orthodox Christianity—the Maronites. Despite the minority status of their religion among Arab-Americans, Kassim and Shada Itani had taken comfort in having others around who shared so many common cultural elements.

"Oh, look! It's Alex Kouri," Mari exclaimed as a distinguished man in his sixties marched past. His eyes widened incredulously as his gaze landed on her, and he waved and mouthed her name.

Mr. Kouri had been one of her father's closest friends. Both of them had been Detroit-based businessmen who had brought their families to Harbor Town for summer vacations. Mr. Kouri and her father would frequently drive back and forth together from Harbor Town to Dearborn, Michigan, on Friday and Sunday evenings, leaving their families to idle away the hot, summer weekdays while they worked at their corporate jobs.

Mari noticed how gray Mr. Kouri's hair had become. That's how her father would have looked, had he lived.

She saw a woman standing at the curb, her rapt attention on Mari and Eric, not on the parade. *Still as nosey as ever,* Mari thought with a flash of irritation, recognizing Esther Fontel, the old neighbor from Sycamore Avenue. The woman had once ratted her out to her parents when she observed Mari sneaking out her bedroom window and down the trusty old elm tree to join Marc on his motorcycle one hot summer night. Mari still recalled how angry her father had been, the hurt and the disappointment on her mother's face.

Until she'd turned fifteen, Mari hadn't fully understood the impact that her parents' ethnicity and religious views would have on her. Her brother had dated and enjoyed any number of summertime, teenage dalliances in Harbor Town. When Mari became a young woman, however, she'd learned firsthand that Ryan and she would not be treated the same when it came to dating. Especially when it came to Marc Kavanaugh.

Marc and Ryan had been close friends since they were both ten years old. Her parents had actually both been very fond of Marc, and he was a regular visitor in the Itani vacation home.

But the summer Mari had turned fifteen, everything had changed—and Marc Kavanaugh had quickly moved to the top of her parents' list of undesirable dating partners for Mari.

Mrs. Fontel looked pointedly across the street, and Mari followed her gaze. She stared, shock vibrating her consciousness. Two tall, good-looking men with healthy, golden tans and dark blond hair stood in the crowd. Her gaze stuck on the one with the short, wavy hair. He had a little girl perched on his shoulders.

He looked just as good in shorts and a T-shirt that skimmed his lean, muscular torso as he had in the gray suit he'd worn in Chicago, Mari thought dazedly.

Her glance flickered to the right of Liam and Marc, and Brigit Kavanaugh's furious glare struck her like a slap to the face from an ice cold hand. Marc's stare was fiercer, though. It seemed to bore right through her across the span of Main Street.

It felt like someone had reached inside her and twisted her intestines. He'd said he only returned to Harbor Town a few times a year, she thought wildly. What were the chances he'd be here for the same handful of days she was?

She shivered despite the heat. It was Independence Day. Tomorrow would be the anniversary of the crash. Perhaps the Kavanaughs had gathered to visit Derry Kavanaugh's grave. Why hadn't she considered that possibility?

She jerked her gaze back to the parade, making no sense of the flashing, moving, colorful scene before her eyes, still highly aware of him watching her. He'd always been able to melt her with those blue eyes. She could only imagine the effect they had on the people he'd cross-examined in the courtroom.

Mari had certainly felt the power of his stare during that night in Chicago.

He must be furious at her for not showing up at their agreed-upon lunch, for not returning his calls…especially after what had occurred between them in that hotel room.

"Well, if it isn't Mari Itani," Liam Kavanaugh drawled under his breath.

Marc followed Liam's gaze, too surprised by his brother's statement to comment at first. He immediately found Mari in the crowd. She wore her long hair up and a casual, yellow dress that tied beneath her full breasts in a bow. The garment set off Mari's flawless, glowing skin to perfection. Not to mention what that innocent-seeming ribbon did to highlight the fullness of her curves.

"Mari Itani?" Marc's sister Colleen asked incredulously from behind him. "Where?"

"Stop pointing, Liam," Brigit Kavanaugh scolded when Liam tried to show his sister where Mari stood.

"Did you know she was back, Mom?" Marc asked sharply.

"I knew it. She's just here to get the house in order before it goes on the market. Can't believe she and Ryan have waited this long to sell it, but obviously they haven't been hurting for money," Brigit replied bitterly.

"Mommy, can we follow the parade down the street? I want to see Brendan again. He looked so funny," Marc's niece, Jenny, begged from her perch on his shoulders. Marc's nephew, Brendan, had marched in the parade as part of the Harbor Town Swim and Dive Club.

Colleen laughed and reached up for her six-year-old daughter. Marc bent his knees to make the transfer easier.

"Aren't you coming, Uncle Marc?" Jenny asked, tugging on his hand once her feet were firmly on the ground.

"I'll stay here and keep Grandma company. Tell us if Brendan trips or anything," Marc replied.

Jenny grinned broadly at the prospect and yanked her mother down the sidewalk.

Liam chuckled. "How come sisters always want to see their brothers humiliated?"

"Probably because brothers make it their mission to ignore their sisters," Marc muttered, his gaze again fixed on the vision in yellow across the street.

"It looks like Mari grew up real nice," Liam murmured as he rubbed his goatee speculatively. Liam wore sunglasses, but Marc sensed the appreciative gleam in his brother's eyes as he studied Mari. When he saw Marc's glare, Liam just raised his eyebrows in a playful expression that said loud and clear, *so sue me for noticing the obvious.*

He felt like he was still recovering from a sucker punch to the gut.

At first, he'd had the wild thought that her presence in Harbor Town was somehow related to what had happened in that hotel room in Chicago. When he saw how Mari made a point of avoiding his gaze, though, he wondered.

"Is Ryan with her?" Marc asked slowly, not liking the idea of Mari's insolent brother residing down the street from his mom, even if it was just for a few nights. Ryan Itani's behavior during the lawsuit hearings stood out as one of the worst in a collection of bad memories from that time of his life.

"No. Ryan's still in the Air Force, doing a tour of duty

in Afghanistan. I just heard Mari was here to sell the
house, and I saw the car in the driveway, so I guess it's
true. It's none of my business. I'm just relieved they're finally selling. That house has been a blight on Sycamore
Avenue for fifteen years now. Mari and Ryan wouldn't
even rent it out to vacationers."

"You'd have just complained if they'd rented it out to
vacationers, Ma. Besides, Joe Brown keeps the place in
good shape."

Liam paused when Brigit shot him an annoyed
glance. Marc smirked at his brother. *You walked right
into that trap, sucker.* Liam should have known better
than to say something *reasonable* when it came to the
topic of the Itanis. Hadn't they learned years ago that
when it came to matters of grief and loss, logic went the
way of friendship, compassion…love?

Straight to hell, in other words.

"Who's the guy with Mari?" Liam asked once their
view was no longer obscured.

Marc froze. He'd been so focused on Mari he hadn't
noticed the tall, good-looking man standing next to
her.

Brigit sniffed at Liam's question.

"That's Eric Reyes. He's a doctor now. I'm sure Mari
and him have plenty to talk about. Gloat over, more
likely. I think I'll go and catch up with Colleen. There's
nothing left to see here," Brigit said before she departed
in a huff.

So *that* was Eric Reyes. The seething, skinny kid
he recalled from the court battle for his father's estate
had grown into a formidable-looking man. Had his
mother said *doctor?* Reyes must have used the money
he'd received in the lawsuit to send himself to medical
school.

Fury burned in his chest. Not about the lawsuit. He

was a state's attorney, after all, a victim's advocate first and foremost. Marc had long ago come to terms with the fact that in catastrophes like the one his father had caused, the victims' damages weren't likely to be covered merely by insurance. A good portion of his father's personal assets had been ordered liquidated and disbursed to the Itani and Reyes families.

He'd never been able to make his mother see things as he did. Feeling as if she and her children were being punished for Derry's crime, Brigit had been bewildered and hurt by the other families' legal actions. Brigit had needed to sell the family home in Chicago and relocate to the summer house in Harbor Town. She'd been forced to pay a good portion of a lifetime's savings, including her children's college funds, in order to legally amend for her husband's actions.

The crash had meant crushing loss and grief. The lawsuits had built walls of betrayal and fury between the families involved.

Mari had never actively taken part in the proceedings. Her aunt and older brother had kept her protected in Chicago following her parents' deaths. She'd been young at the time—only eighteen. As he studied Mari's averted profile, Marc wondered for the hundred thousandth time what she thought of the whole affair, what she'd thought of him all these years. The topic had never come up during that intense, impulsive night in Chicago.

They'd been too involved in other things.

He grimaced at the thought. He couldn't help but feel the stark symbolism of having shared something so intimate with Mari only to now be standing on opposite sides of a Harbor Town street.

Reyes put his arm around Mari's shoulder and stroked skin that Marc knew from experience was as soft and smooth as a new flower petal.

It made sense, Mari together with Reyes. Blood was thicker than water, but shared, spilled blood was perhaps even more binding. Isn't that what they said about soldiers who watched each other's backs in wartime? They'd do favors for each other that they might refuse to do for a family member.

I can't compete with that, he thought darkly.

He wasn't sure he wanted to. Not after Mari had made a point of abandoning him following their soul-searing reunion.

"Are you going to talk to her?" Liam prodded.

He twisted his mouth into a frown. "Something tells me she doesn't want to have anything to do with me."

Liam's eyebrows shot up. He opened his mouth to say something, but when Marc turned a grim face to him, he closed it again.

By the time Marc entered Jake's Place accompanied by Colleen and Liam at ten that night, Colleen had commented on his bad mood. Marc had gone from preoccupied to morose as the day had progressed. He'd convinced himself that Mari was right to avoid him. Their impulsive tryst in Chicago had been a mistake, some kind of residual, emotional backfire from their charged history together as kids.

He'd just gotten a divorce eighteen months ago. Hadn't he made a firm pact with himself that he wasn't going to consider any serious relationships for quite some time, anyway?

No sooner had they stepped into Jake's loud, crowded, front room when Marc saw her. She sat in a booth across from Eric Reyes, laughing at something he'd just said. Even though Marc had decided just seconds ago that Mari and he were best separated by two thirds of a continent, his feet seemed to disagree with his brain.

This had nothing to do with logic.

He plunged through the crowd, ignoring Colleen's shouted question. His entire awareness had narrowed down to a single, precise focus.

Mari's eyes widened in surprise when he strode up to the booth.

"Let's dance, Mari."

Chapter Two

Mari stared mutely up at Marc. The man's full impact struck her just as powerfully as it had when he'd unexpectedly tracked her down in Chicago.

God, he'd turned into a beautiful man.

His once-light hair had darkened to a burnished gold. He wore it short now, but the conservative style couldn't suppress the natural wave. Whiskers shadowed his jaw. He looked just as good in a suit and tie as he did in the casual white button-down shirt and jeans he wore at present, but Mari knew which outfit Marc preferred. The wildness of the Kavanaugh spirit could never be disguised by the packaging of refined clothing.

He was still as lean as he'd been at twenty-one, but he'd gained some muscle in his chest and shoulders. She dragged her eyes off the tempting sight of his strong thighs and narrow hips encased in faded, extremely well-fitting denims and met his stare.

He looked good enough to eat—*and* furious. His

eyes glittered like blue flames in his tanned face. Just before he walked up to the booth, she'd been telling Eric she was feeling exhausted after their busy day. Yet one look at Marc, and her blood was pumping madly in her veins, washing away every hint of fatigue.

"Uh, sure," she replied. She couldn't think of a good reason to refuse a dance without sounding rude or highlighting the significance of the encounter. If she agreed, surely people would just assume it was a casual dance between two old sweethearts.

Neither she nor Marc spoke as he led her to the edge of the crowded dance floor. The cover band was playing an '80s classic with a good beat. Marc put his arm around her waist, and they began to move as naturally as if their last dance had been yesterday.

Mari kept her gaze averted from his face, but she was hyperaware of every point of contact of their bodies, how well they fit one another…how perfectly they moved together.

She'd thought something similar five weeks ago when they'd finally made love.

Heat flooded her cheeks at the memory. So much emotional baggage separated them. Why was it, then, that being in his arms felt so right—so natural?

She recalled watching him dress as morning sunlight had peeked around the heavy draperies in the Palmer House hotel room. Marc needed to get back to his condo to shower and then rush to a meeting, but they'd already agreed to have lunch.

And dinner.

From the bed, Mari was admiring the shape of his long legs as he stepped into his pants when he caught her staring. He paused and they shared a smile that brought to mind the night spent in each other's arms, the nearly unbearable pleasure of touching each other, of complete communion after so long and after so much.

Marc's cell phone rang, breaking their stare. He ignored it, but after a pause, it started ringing again.

"Maybe you should answer," she murmured with a smile. "Sounds important."

Gleaming with heat, his eyes remained fixed on her, while he reached for the phone.

"Hey, Mom," he said.

It'd been like a bucket of ice water had been tossed in her face.

Everything had come back—all the anguish, all the grief, all the memories of why they'd been ripped apart so long ago.

Ryan had once told her Brigit Kavanaugh had confronted him after a day in court. "Don't you understand that I lost my husband in that accident? I'm mourning just like you are. Why are you trying to punish me further by taking everything away from my children? Have you no pity?" Brigit had tearfully asked Ryan.

The memory of her brother's encounter always made Mari recoil in pain. She hadn't been around during the court proceedings, but distance hadn't been able to diminish her knowledge of all the hurt between the Kavanaughs and the Itanis.

That's why, after Marc had left the hotel room, she'd packed her bags and caught the first flight she could back to San Francisco. Some things just weren't meant to be.

Even if they did feel so right.

Their thighs, hips and bellies slid together provocatively as they danced. Every once in a while, the tips of her breasts would brush his ribs. Her nipples felt achy, overly sensitive. It excited her, their furtive, subtle, rhythmic caresses. A strange brew of emotions simmered inside her—nervousness, uncertainty, longing...

Arousal.

She stared over Marc's shoulder, not really seeing anything. She was hyperfocused on the sensation of his hard, shifting body and too mesmerized by his masculine scent. She experienced a nearly overpowering desire to lay her head on his shoulder.

"I don't suppose it would do me any good to ask you why you blew me off in Chicago, would it?" His gruff, quiet voice caused a prickling sensation on her neck.

She flushed and avoided his laserlike stare. "I would think the answer was obvious."

"Nothing is *obvious* when it comes to you and me, Mari. Nothing has ever been easy, either. It was my mother's phone call that did it, wasn't it? That's what made you run? I knew I shouldn't have answered it," he said bitterly. "I only did because I'd been trying for weeks to coordinate communication between my mother and my sister, Deidre, in Germany, and they were supposed to have talked the night before. I had a feeling it might not have gone well for my mother. Their relationship had been strained for years...."

She met his stare when he faded off. For a moment, she was trapped in his gaze.

"We don't have to dissect the reasons, Marc. Suffice it to say that Chicago was a mistake."

"I don't agree," he stated flatly.

"We'll just have to agree to disagree, then." She noticed the tilt to his jaw—the Kavanaugh pride and stubbornness in full evidence. She sighed and groped for a way to change the volatile topic. "I'd forgotten what a good dancer you are," she murmured.

"I'd forgotten how hard it was to hold you in my arms

and not be able to make love to you later. It's a memory I'd rather put to rest for good, Mari."

Her breath froze on an inhale. His blue eyes blazed hot enough to melt her.

So much for safe topics.

She blinked as if awakening from a trance and took a step away from him. "Don't, Marc."

"Don't what? Make it harder than it already is? Too late," he said softly. His mouth quirked at his double entendre.

Mari was so busy staring at his sexy grin that she didn't resist when he pulled her back into his arms. He didn't miss a beat when the band started playing a slow ballad. The man really could move on the dance floor. As if he needed that extra edge. He was already more attractive to her than he had a right to be.

He gathered her close, so close that Mari became highly conscious of the how thin the barrier of their clothing was, of how little separated them from touching skin to skin.

"Just relax. Didn't anyone ever tell you there's a time for arguing and a time for...dancing?"

The annoyed glance she threw him was more defense than genuine irritation. The truth was, her reaction to Marc worried her. It'd be convenient to say that being around him only evoked all those old feelings, but the reality was, her physical reaction to Marc as a woman was even stronger than it'd been as a girl.

Exponentially so.

Mari held herself rigid as they swayed to the music, but her resistance could only last so long. Her flesh seemed to mold and melt against his of its own accord as if her body recognized its perfect template, even if her brain refused to acknowledge it. A warm sensation settled in her lower belly.

When Marc opened his hand on her lower back and applied a delicious pressure, Mari gave up the fight and rested her cheek between his shoulder and chest. She sighed, inhaling his scent. He smelled delicious—spicy and clean. Her eyes fluttered closed when she felt him lightly nuzzle her hair with his chin. His warm lips brushed against the side of her neck. She shivered. Every patch of skin that his mouth touched seemed to sing with awareness.

When the final note played, her head fell back. She found herself staring into Marc's eyes, which had gone from blazing to smoky. Her breasts were crushed against his chest. The contours of his arousal were abundantly clear to her given how close they pressed.

It was as if a spell had fallen over her. It must have, for her to be having such intimate thoughts—such intimate feelings—in the midst of a crowded, noisy bar.

A crowded, noisy bar in Harbor Town, of all places.

She pulled back from Marc's embrace and touched her fingertips to her cheeks, mortified to feel how hot they were.

"Excuse me," she murmured before she twisted out of his arms.

The water from the ladies' room sink barely cooled her burning cheeks. Her heat had sprung from an inner source that wasn't so easily extinguished. Her eyes closed, she folded a wet paper towel and pressed it to her face, trying to regain her equilibrium.

He could knock her off balance so easily—still and always.

The thought of walking out there and facing Eric and the other patrons mortified her. Marc and she had been practically glued together on the dance floor. At the recollection of Marc nuzzling and kissing her neck—and of her not only allowing it, but loving it—shock washed over her.

She needed to get out of the bar. She needed to get out of Harbor Town altogether, as quickly as possible.

She'd apologize to Eric tomorrow for her abrupt abandonment.

Someone—a woman—called out to her as she fled the noisy establishment. Mari glanced over at the bar and glimpsed Liam and Colleen Kavanaugh watching her. She read excitement and a hint of concern in Colleen's aquamarine eyes. Part of her was glad to see Colleen's willingness to speak with her after all these years, but she was too discombobulated at the moment to renew old friendships. Panic pressed on her chest.

How could she have ever thought it was a good idea to return to Harbor Town? How could she have misled herself into believing Dr. Rothschild when her former therapist had said she had unfinished business in the little town and a bone-deep desire to heal?

She burst out the front door of Jake's Place, gulped the warm, fresh air she'd been oxygen-deprived. It didn't occur to her until she reached the parking lot just what—or who—it was she was escaping. A pair of hands settled on her shoulders and spun her around.

"Marc," she said in a strangled voice. She hadn't realized until that moment she'd been dreading his touch and anticipating it, as well.

"Don't run from me, Mari. Don't run from this."

She swayed closer, to him, inhaling his scent. Nobody smelled like Marc. She wanted to believe that this was something they could solve. Her body wanted to believe him…wanted to trust in Marc, longed to be swept away by a dream.

A girl's dream.

She met his blazing eyes.

"Marc, we can't. Not again," she whispered. She started to move out of their embrace, her fear returning, but he stopped her.

"What is it, Mari? What's your problem with me?" he asked quietly. She saw wariness shadow his face, felt it rising in his tense muscles. "Is it that you think I'm a killer by association? I'm not my father, damn it. I barely finish a beer if I drink at all. I'd throw myself off the top of the Sears Tower before I got behind the wheel of a car drunk. *I* didn't kill your parents."

She blinked in shock at the sudden appearance of his anger. They'd tacitly agreed to stay away from the minefield of this topic in Chicago.

"I never said you did."

"I lost my father in that crash, as well," he said.

Her throat tightened. "I know that. *Surely* you know that."

"I don't know what I'm supposed to think except that you believe I'm guilty by association. I don't know, because you've never really told me, have you? You walked away five weeks ago. You left when we were together and refused to speak to me for fifteen years. One night, we were on the verge of becoming lovers, and the next, we were separated by the news of the crash. Within days, you were gone and thousands of miles separated us, as well."

"Marc, we were kids. I'd lost almost my entire world," she moaned.

"You came back to Harbor Town. You must have had a reason."

"I did have a reason," Mari said. Her gaze deflected off his face. What would he think about The Family Center? Her fantasies about opening it never included having to tell Marc about her plans. What if he thought the project was odd...or worse, self-righteous on Mari's part? He'd probably never understand how much she'd thought of him while making her plans…of the young man she'd loved and lost so many years ago.

She closed her eyes, trying to banish her chaotic thoughts. All she wanted at that moment was to escape this volatile situation with Marc.

"I didn't come back to Harbor Town for you. And I don't want to talk about the past with you, either, Marc."

"Who do you want to talk about it with? Reyes? Is it okay to talk about things with him? Because you're both victims, while I'm the son of the monster who robbed you of your parents?"

"Marc, *don't*. Please."

It pained her more than she could bear to see the raw hurt on his handsome face. A need arose in her to soothe his sadness, to somehow ease his anguish. The knowledge that she was powerless to do so caused the swelling, tight sensation to mount in her chest. She was stunned at how easily that old wound had opened when she saw his expression of disillusionment.

His expression suddenly shifted. He caressed her upper arms in a soothing motion. "Jesus. You're shaking. I'm sorry—"

"What's going on, Mari?"

Mari's eyes widened at the sound of the hard voice behind them. She looked over Marc's right shoulder and saw Eric standing there, looking furious. Marc twisted his chin around.

"Oh, look," Marc muttered with subdued sarcasm. "If it isn't the other victim, here to save Mari from the beast. What are you going to do, Reyes? Start a brawl with me in the parking lot?"

"Marc—" Mari called out warningly, sensing the volatility inherent to the moment.

"No, Kavanaugh. That'd be your M.O., if I recall correctly," Eric replied.

She grabbed hold of Marc's shoulders and tried to get him to face her when he turned toward Eric. "Marc—"

"I'm betting he never bothered to tell you about that. Did he, Mari?" Eric asked. "I know Ryan wanted to keep that story from you—how Kavanaugh clobbered your brother in the parking lot of the courthouse after the judge made his final decision about the lawsuit?" His upper lip curled in contempt, Eric glanced at Marc.

Marc closed his eyes in what appeared to be frustration and mounting anger. After a second, he met her stare. She read regret on his features.

"I thought Ryan would have told you," he said, for her ears only. "I thought maybe that was part of the reason you avoided me all these years."

Something about her expression must have told him the truth—that Ryan never *had* told his little sister about their fight.

"I was twenty-two years old at the time, Mari. It was a long time ago."

Marc and Ryan used to be inseparable, the best of friends. A powerful sadness swept over her.

"Is there a problem?" someone called out sharply.

Eric turned and saw the youngest male Kavanaugh stalking toward them. Mari had heard from Marc that Liam had become a decorated police detective. She could easily believe it was true. He looked like he was about to make a drug bust in a Chicago alley as he stormed toward them.

"Walk away, Reyes," Liam barked, blue eyes blazing. "Why don't you hurry back to that slick house on Buena Vista Drive that my mom's money paid for?"

Eric's mouth dropped open in shock. "You son of a—"

"I wouldn't finish that if I were you," Liam muttered, jaw rigid.

Mari was distantly aware of Jake's front door opening and closing again, but her attention was on the sparks flying between Liam and Eric. Eric's hands were still balled into furious fists.

"What's the matter, Reyes? Worried about bruising those delicate surgeon's hands?" Liam taunted softly. His cocky grin dared Eric to hit him.

Mari groaned when she saw the flash of fury in Eric's dark eyes as he started toward Liam.

"Eric, don't—" Mari called out, but Marc was already moving to intercept them.

"Cut it out, you two," Marc barked. He reached to restrain Eric, his muscles flexing hard beneath his shirt.

But someone else got to Eric first. A hand tapped him on the shoulder. Eric turned, his back to Mari. He remained firmly planted on his feet, but jerked when someone landed a punch on his jaw.

"Leave my brothers alone, Reyes."

Mari gaped when she recognized Colleen Kavanaugh.

"Get her inside right now," Marc growled at Liam, his eyes blazing.

Liam looked like he was chewing nails as he regarded Eric. For a second, Mari worried he'd refuse to obey Marc's taut command, but then he grabbed his sister's arm and murmured to her.

Colleen stumbled on the gravel, her sandaled feet moving reluctantly as Liam led her back to the bar. She twisted around and pinned Eric with a baleful stare. He didn't move, just stood there as if frozen, gazing after the retreating Kavanaughs. Mari heard him curse softly beneath his breath as he stared at Colleen's beautiful, tear-dampened face.

Soon only she, Eric and Marc remained in the parking lot. She couldn't fully identify the expression on Marc's face as his gaze flickered over her, then Eric, then her again. It was as if every imaginable emotion frothed inside him at once in that charged moment. His mouth looked set and hard when he turned and walked toward Jake's Place.

Mari exhaled shakily.

Eric and she regarded each other silently in the dim parking lot lights as the band finished a raucous tune. The final chords faded off in the hot, still summer night. She sensed that Eric knew, as she did, that they'd just narrowly escaped a volatile explosion of emotion.

Nausea rose in her like a striking snake, taking her by surprise. She gagged and bent over, coughing.

"Mari?" Eric's voice sounded shocked and concerned. He touched her back. "Are you okay?"

She swallowed with effort and straightened shakily. "I...I don't know. I just felt sick there for a minute."

"Come on. Let's get you home. This is the last thing you needed to deal with on top of not feeling well."

But as Eric led her to his car, she turned to watch Marc disappear inside Jake's and willfully tamped down the desire to go after him.

Chapter Three

The second Marc joined his mother on the front porch his gaze immediately traveled down Sycamore Avenue to the sandstone, Arts and Crafts-style house down the block. A dark blue sedan sat in the driveway. Mari's car had been notably absent when he'd returned this afternoon from their annual visit to Harbor Town Cemetery.

I didn't come back to Harbor Town for you, he vividly recalled her saying last night. He leaned against the porch railing and crossed his arms below his ribs. What *had* she come back for, then?

He inhaled deeply of the fresh air. It always seemed to take several days into his summer vacation to get the city soot out of his lungs. The sky had turned a pale blue, tinged with lavender, but above the beach at the end of Sycamore Avenue, crimson, pink and gold splashed across the horizon. It would be sunset soon—Harbor

Town's most famous tourist attraction. How many of those sunsets had he watched with Mari in his arms?

He jerked his mind into the present.

"When did you say you were headed back to Chicago?" Brigit Kavanaugh asked. She'd placed her sneakered foot on the pavement, stopping the porch swing's movement.

Marc knew she'd noticed him staring at Mari's house. Not that it was odd for him to look at the Itani vacation home on his rare visits to Harbor Town. His eyes had been trained long ago to stray toward that house. Even his ex-wife, Sandra, used to take note of it, usually with a flippant, sarcastic remark, on the few occasions she'd accompanied him to Harbor Town.

"I was thinking about staying on a couple days past Brendan's party," Marc said, referring to his nephew's tenth birthday celebration.

"Really? Do you think work can spare you that long?"

He shrugged. "The county can undoubtedly do without me."

"Marc," Brigit scoffed with a smile. "You're a state's attorney, for goodness' sake. You have over a thousand employees working under you."

"Most of whom are gone for the holiday. I've never taken off more than day here and there since entering office. I have the vacation time. I might as well use some of it. It's not like I haven't been working from here, anyway."

All of the Kavanaugh children had taken jobs that would somehow prove they were hard-working, sacrificing, *worthy* members of society, Marc mused. His sister Deidre was an Army nurse on her fourth tour of duty. Liam was a twice-decorated detective on the organized crime squad of the Chicago Police Department, and

Colleen was a psychiatric social worker who worked with high-risk teenagers with emotional and substance abuse problems.

Survivors' guilt.

Their father's final actions had left its mark on all of them.

His mother usually wanted her sons to stay on as long as possible for these annual Independence Day visits. She seemed to want Marc long gone at the present time, though. He tried to ignore the flare of irritation he felt at that fact. Brigit loved him. She remembered how much he'd been hurt by Mari's refusal to see him after the crash. Maybe she just didn't want to see him get hurt again.

The porch swing resumed the rhythmic squeaking noise that blended so hypnotically with the sounds of the locusts and the Lake Michigan waves breaking on the nearby beach.

"You'd do best by staying away from her," Brigit said, finally saying the words he knew she'd been thinking since the parades yesterday.

"Maybe you're right. But that doesn't seem to be stifling the urge to do the exact opposite."

Brigit exhaled at his quiet admission. "After all they did to us—"

"Mari never did anything to us. As for what Ryan and his aunt did, it's not that different than what most people would have done in the same situation."

"She ignored you! She took that money—blood money! After all this time, you've forgotten the effect it had on me—on *us*."

"I haven't forgotten," he said, stung. "Maybe it's never occurred to you that Mari and I might have memories, too, Ma, memories outside of Dad and the crash and the deaths—and the *grudge*."

Her face pale and tense, she brought the swing to a halt and stared at him. He hated seeing her pain, but damn it, what he'd said was true. He exhaled heavily, trying to rid himself of his anger. He wasn't mad at his mother, necessarily, but at this whole situation.

He almost heard Brigit building her arguments in her mind. Marc had become a lawyer like his father, but it was his mother who'd taught him the skills for making an airtight case.

"You want Mari because she's the only thing you've wanted and couldn't have."

Marc started. "That's a hell of a thing to say. Do you really believe that?"

"I do," Brigit said quietly. "You're my oldest son, Marc. I carried you in my body, and I watched you grow from an infant to a man. Do you really think I've never noticed that once you set your mind on something, you make it happen, no matter what kind of storm you cause in the process?"

Marc scowled. He couldn't believe he was hearing this from his own mother's mouth. "You make me sound like a spoiled brat. I've worked like hell to get anything I've ever had. And I've failed at plenty of things. What about Sandra?" he demanded.

"I said anything you ever *wanted*. If you'd wanted Sandra more, the two of you would still be married."

Marc gave his mother a hard stare, warning her not to tread on that private territory. He'd heard her out after he and Sandra had decided to split, but that decision was his and his ex-wife's business, not Brigit's. His mother changed gears, just like that.

"Mari never married, I hear," Brigit said levelly.

"No," Marc conceded, not sure where his mother was going with her comment.

"Her brother is the only family since her aunt died a

few years ago. I don't think Ryan would take too kindly to having Mari get involved with you again."

"You really care about what Ryan Itani thinks?"

"No. But if you care about Mari, *you* should. Would you really consider alienating her from her only relative?"

Marc rolled his eyes and stood. "You're assuming Mari would even be interested. I haven't seen any indication of that so far," he muttered bitterly. His mother's comment hit home, even if he tried not to let her see it. He knew he should leave Mari alone. He knew he shouldn't stir up the frothing cauldron of their shared history.

Problem was, he already *had*. He'd touched Mari again. He'd held her naked against him while her shudders of pleasure and release had vibrated into his body and mixed with his own.

It was too late, Marc realized with a grim sense of amazement. Something had happened in those ecstatic moments that couldn't now be ignored.

He noticed movement out of the corner of his eye. He swung around like a hound catching the scent and he saw Mari walking toward her car, her long brown hair bobbing in a ponytail. As she was opening the car door, she paused and looked furtively down the street. Their gazes locked for a few electric seconds before she ducked into the car.

The screen door squeaked open. Combing his longish blonde hair with his fingers in a distracted fashion, Liam sauntered onto the front porch. He looked a little taken aback when Marc charged him.

"Give me the keys to your bike," Marc ordered tersely.

Liam's bewilderment dissipated when he glanced over Marc's shoulder and saw Mari's car backing rapidly out of the driveway. He dug into his short's pocket and handed Marc the keys to his motorcycle.

"Fill it up with gas while you're out, will you? Unless whatever you're doing gets too interesting, that is," Liam said with a mischievous sparkle in his eyes. Marc grabbed the keys and jogged down the porch steps, ignoring his mother's burning glance of disapproval.

Mari had risen early the morning following the Jake's Place fiasco, determined to refocus on her mission. She breakfasted with Eric and Natalie Reyes to discuss more plans for The Family Center. Afterward, she and Eric went to the real estate office to sign a lease, and then to an office furniture and supply store to arrange for items to be delivered to the Silver Dune Bay facility.

She spent the rest of the day making the old house presentable to prospective buyers. Without really knowing why she did it, she paused in her manic scrubbing at 5:17 p.m., walked to the front door and cautiously peeked out a window. A silver sedan passed with three people in it, Marc at the wheel.

She'd somehow known he was near, even though she'd been doing her damnedest to deny his presence in her mind all day. She returned to her cleaning and tried to turn her thoughts in another direction, but failed.

Later that evening, she stood at the front door and gazed onto the tree-lined street. How the hell had she ended up here at this point in her life? Mari wondered. Seeing the crimson sky at the end of the street caused hundreds of other remembered sunsets to blaze to the forefront of her mind. She was hyperaware of the handsome, white house built in the Colonial Revival style up the street.

After the end of a doomed, four-year relationship with James Henry, an investment banker from San Francisco,

Mari had experienced a desire for a fresh start. That inner push had set her plans into motion. She'd wanted to be free of her past once and for all and that meant returning to Harbor Town.

Too bad her grand scheme for a clean slate and healing had turned into a maelstrom of mixed emotions.

By late evening, her stomach had started to growl. She took a shower, pulled her hair into a ponytail and dressed in shorts and a T-shirt. Her heart was skipping rapidly when she exited the house and headed for her car. Something compelled her to look up the street at the Kavanaugh house.

Sure enough, Marc was leaning against the porch railing, his head turned, watching her. For a few seconds, it felt as if she couldn't breathe.

She got in her car and drove to a little diner on the edge of town called The Tap and Grill. After the friendly counter lady had brought her an enormous turkey sandwich to go, she drove aimlessly through the town's quiet, tree-lined streets, finally ending up on scenic Vista Point Drive, overlooking the beach.

A motorcycle roared, breaking the sleepy silence, as she parked at the side of the street. She opened the car door and leaned over to the passenger seat to grab her sandwich. A shadow fell across the steering wheel.

She turned around to see Marc standing between her car and the open door.

"I hope whatever's in that bag is enough for two."

Mari glanced out the back window, noticing the gleaming black and chrome motorcycle parked down the street. She'd peeked out of her windows enough lately to know the vehicle belonged to Liam. Apparently Marc had forsaken a bike years ago for the handsome, conservative sedan she'd seen him driving. Memories of Marc and her brother, Ryan, tearing down the street on their motorcycles, looking like young summertime gods with their deep tans, sunglasses and wind-tousled hair, washed over her.

"Did you follow me?" she asked him warily.

He shrugged, his stare never leaving her face. "I figured you wouldn't answer the door if I knocked at your house. When you finally broke cover, I thought I better take my chance or risk not seeing you for another fifteen years."

She gave him a hard look. He quirked one eyebrow.

"We need to talk, Mari. Please."

Against her will, her gaze lowered to his shadowed jaw and tanned throat. She shivered when she recalled how the stubble had felt brushing against her neck that night in Chicago, grazing ever so lightly against the sensitive skin covering her ribs. The sight of his insouciant male good looks only increased her caution.

Or her reaction to them did.

"So if I let you come with me to Sunset Beach, that's all you'll try to do? Talk?"

He sighed. "I'm not planning on coming on to you on the beach," he replied drily.

She rolled her eyes at him as she aggressively swung her legs out of the car, daring him not to move back and give her the space she required.

His only reaction to her wary acquiescence was a slight grin. They said nothing as they made their way down the private sidewalk that ran between two mansion-sized homes. When they hit the white sand beach, Mari led them over to the manmade breakwater that consisted of stacked lengths of cut, unfinished logs.

She plopped down on the breakwater. Marc sat down next to her. She studied him through the corner of her eye. He wore a pair of cargo shorts and a dark blue shirt that failed to hide the breadth of shoulders or hint at the sleek muscles Mari knew lay just beneath the soft fabric. He managed to make the casual beach-wear look sexy as hell. She could just see him as a tall, lanky, cocky fourteen-year-old sporting a new pair of sunglasses, standing on Sycamore Beach and clutching his skimboard, the sunlight turning his hair into a havoc of incandescent gold waves.

She handed him half of her sandwich wrapped in a napkin.

"I was only kidding about sharing. Eat your supper," he murmured, giving her a sideways smile.

"You know how they make sandwiches at The Tap. It's huge." She insistently pushed the sandwich toward him. Maybe he noticed the irritation in her expression, because his eyebrows rose, and he accepted the food, probably to avoid an argument.

The fiery, orange-red sun looked like it was slowly quenching itself in the shimmering, dark blue water. They ate without speaking. For the first time, it struck her how odd it was that the beach was empty.

"Isn't Sunset Beach public anymore?" she slowly asked Marc as she held up the paper bag so he could deposit his rumpled napkin inside it.

He shook his head. "Mom told me the home owners hereabouts bought it from the town a few years back. It's private now."

Mari stopped chewing and glanced warily at the af-fluent residences nearby.

"Don't worry. They aren't going to call the cops on us. Unless we make an ugly scene or something," Marc said when he saw her uneasiness over trespassing.

She took a swig of the bottled water she'd ordered with the sandwich. She offered the bottle to Marc, and he drank, too. Mari glanced away from the strangely erotic sight of him placing his mouth where hers had just been.

"I don't plan on making a scene," she said briskly, shoving the wrapper and the remainder of her sandwich into the bag. "And you're awfully quiet for someone who insisted we had to talk."

"I just didn't want to ruin the peaceful moment."

She raised her eyebrows. "Implying that whatever you have to say is the opposite of peaceful?"

"If it involves you reacting to it by refusing to see me again… Yeah, there might be some serious waves."

Mari kicked off her flip-flops and stuck her feet in the cool, fine sand. Despite her attempts to calm herself, her voice still cracked when she spoke.

"Marc… You saw what happened last night as well as I did. All that animosity, all that hurt. It'd be irresponsible of us to…you know—"

"I think *I* know, but do *you?*"

"What do you mean?" she asked slowly.

"I wasn't planning this little reunion, Mari. But now that it's happened, I'm not willing to just walk away from it, either. And I'm not talking about sneaking down to your house and having some hot, vacation sex with an old fling." His gaze flickered down over her neck and breasts and he added gruffly, "Although I think we both know that scenario has its appeal. The point is, you mean more than that to me. It was a hell of a thing to see you Chicago and realize that was still true, after all these years. I'm a practical guy. It's kind of hard to run from the truth when it's staring you right in the face."

Mari swallowed thickly in the silence that followed.

"It would never work out," she said after a moment, her voice so quiet it almost couldn't be heard above the sound of the waves breaking gently on the beach.

"I don't think you're so sure about that. I think you want to *act* like you're sure—" her heart surged against her breastbone when he reached up and caressed her jaw with large, gentle fingers "—so it'll be easier to push me away."

Her spine straightened and he let his hand drop to the wood embankment. "I'm not being selfish. I'm trying to be wise," she explained. "I don't want you to be hurt. I don't want my brother to worry. I don't want your mother to be angry. I don't want—"

"What about you? What about what *you* want, Mari?"

She looked out at the dark waters, worrying her lower lip with her front teeth. She was highly aware of him leaning toward her.

"Because here's the thing," Marc muttered near her left ear, causing her neck to prickle in awareness. "I think you were worried about all those things when you left Harbor Town fifteen years ago, when you cut off all ties with me. I think you were thinking about what was *wise* instead of what was *right*."

She glanced at him furtively, but when she saw the expression on his face, her gaze stuck.

"I think you were considering what you thought your parents would have wanted you to do in that situation, Mari."

Anger flared in her breast at his mention of her parents. "I don't have to listen to this."

She started to stand, intent on getting away from him at that moment. He halted her with a firm hand on her shoulder but it was the earnestness in his deep voice that truly restrained her.

"I'm not saying it was wrong. I understand. Your folks were suddenly gone—something you'd never dreamed of as a possibility, even in your worst nightmares—so you did what you thought they would have wanted if they were alive. The rebellious daughter who lied to them and snuck out to see the guy her parents forbade her to see vanished fifteen years ago."

"So what if she did?" Mari challenged. "You're *making* my point, not talking me out of it. I *had* been behaving like a selfish, lying, thankless brat. Sometimes it takes a crisis before you realize how foolish—how hurtful—you've been acting."

"And I'll bet after they died, there were times you would have done anything to take back your rebellion against them," he said quietly. "But there was nothing heartless in what you did, Mari. You were acting like a typical teenager. You never purposely hurt your parents."

"Only because their deaths got in the way of them ever fully realizing what I was doing," she cried out.

"So that's it? You're going to carry around the guilt of a teenage girl inside of you forever? Be a martyr to your parents' cause?" he asked harshly.

This time he didn't succeed in stopping her when she stood. Marc caught up to her several feet away from the surging waves. He placed his hands on her shoulders and turned her around until she faced him.

"I'm not blaming you for feeling guilty, Mari. God knows I haven't been immune to the emotion. I'm not blaming you for staying away for all those years, either. But here's the thing…"

She realized that tears were streaming down her face, even though she hadn't been aware of feeling sadness, only anger and shame and hurt. She stared up into Marc's shadowed face and knew she was experiencing something else in that moment, no matter how tenuous that emotion was.

Hope.

She didn't move, despite her charging heart, when Marc leaned down until their faces were only inches apart. "...you're not an eighteen-year-old girl anymore. You're a woman. Tell me that if you met me for the first time in Chicago that you wouldn't be intrigued by the chemistry between us."

"That's wishful thinking, and you know it," she said in a choked voice. "We *aren't* strangers. We can't escape the past."

"I'm not suggesting we can. But we can deal with it. Or at least we can try."

A shudder went through her at his words. He placed his hand on her back and softly rubbed her, soothing her even though he probably didn't understand her sudden anguish.

We can deal with it.

Was it true? It stunned her to realize that a big part of her doubted they could successfully face their demons.

The realization hurt. Wasn't that why she'd returned to Harbor Town? Because she'd convinced herself there was a chance people could heal, even in the most difficult of circumstances? Did she believe it for other people but not herself?

A moan escaped her throat, and Marc enfolded her in his arms. Hot tears scalded her cheeks, as if they'd been held inside her body for too long and finally boiled over. She pressed her face against his chest. Years of pent-up emotion poured out of her while the waves anointed her bare feet with cold, clean water and Marc held her, helping to ease her anguish.

God, the things she wanted to say to her parents— how sorry she was for not appreciating them more, how much she'd regretted over the years that she hadn't been the daughter they wanted, how much she'd needed their calm, steady presence as a child...how much she loved them.

She'd had similar thoughts thousands of times, but tonight, here on the beach with Marc Kavanaugh's arms surrounding her, Mari knew she'd never fully felt the impact of those regrets.

After several more emotional minutes, Mari slowly became aware of Marc's warm mouth pressing her head as he occasionally murmured to her in a quieting fashion. When he kissed her ear, she shivered in his arms. Her crying slowly ceased as she became more aware of him.

"All I'm asking is that you at least *try*." His rough whisper so near her ear caused her to still in sudden sensual awareness.

"I'm not sure I know how, Marc. It seems like too much, thinking about some of this stuff." She sniffed and turned her face into his shirt. "It's so…"

"What?" he asked quietly.

He cupped the back of her head. She leaned back and looked up at him.

"Big. Intimidating."

"I'm bigger."

She went entirely still when she saw his slow, potent smile cast in moonlight.

"Don't be so cocky," she admonished, even though she couldn't help but smile at his immodesty.

He chuckled and pressed her head back to his chest. "I only meant that I'm stubborn, and more than willing to try." Neither of them spoke for a pregnant moment. "As far as strength goes, I think you're underestimating yourself, Mari. All I'm asking is that you give us a chance. All I'm asking is that you don't run."

He must have sensed her uncertainty, because he spoke coaxingly near her ear.

"Just agree to see me, spend time with me, for the next week or so."

"That's all?" she asked doubtfully.

He drew her against his hard length, making sure she wasn't left in doubt of his desire for her.

"I want you. I always have. I've never made a secret of it…not that I could." She glanced up at him to see his small smile. "But I'll go at your pace. As long as I know you're not running, I'll be happy. Well…at least pacified."

She sighed. She wished she could know it if was right, wished she could be certain.

"Take a risk, Mari."

Her gaze leaped to meet his. Was he a mind reader?

"All right," she whispered. "But I can't guarantee anything. And I want to take things slowly…test out the waters." *See what kind of effect our being seen together has on your family and friends like Eric and Natalie Reyes,* she added privately. She grimaced at her thought, realizing Marc was right to suggest she considered everyone else's feelings before her own.

He pulled her closer. He didn't say anything, but she found herself wondering if he thought the same thing she did. They'd learned fifteen years ago that life was tenuous. People who thought happiness was guaranteed, that security was a certainty, were living in a dream.

But did that mean the dream wasn't worth seeking?

Mari didn't know the answer to that. So she did the best she could. She put her arms around Marc's waist and tried to exist on the knife's edge between doubt and desire. Despite her uncertainties, she became focused on the sensation of Marc's body against hers. She closed her eyes. For a few delicious moments, she was only aware of the soothing sound of the gentle surf and Marc's spicy male scent.

She opened her heavy eyelids when he murmured her name. Much to her amazement, she found herself nuzzling his neck just above his collar, exploring the textures of his skin against her lips. He felt so good. Tasted so good, she added to herself when the tip of her tongue sampled him. He said her name again, more insistently this time. She leaned back and saw the gleam in his eyes as he stared down at her upturned face.

She waited with sharp anticipation while he slowly lowered his head and pressed his lips to hers. It wasn't a chaste kiss, but it was gentle…a promise of passion rather than the thing itself, a sweetness to be savored on her searching lips. She craned up for more of his taste and cried out softly when he lifted his head, depriving her.

"We'd better go," he said, his voice ragged.

"What? Oh…okay," Mari murmured, feeling bereft in the absence of Marc's tender kiss. Hadn't she been the one to tell him not to try anything on the beach, and yet here she was, tempting him into kissing her with all the power she knew he had?

So much for taking things slowly, Mari thought irritably as they went to retrieve the sandwich bag and headed down the lamp-lit sidewalk to the road.

She felt dazed and unsettled about what had just happened out there on that moonlit beach. Had she really just told Marc Kavanaugh she'd see him?

"Uh, I'll see you.… I'd better be…" She fumbled uncertainly after she'd unlocked her car door, highly aware of Marc standing just behind her on the quiet street.

"Yeah. You'll see me."

He sounded so restrained. Wasn't he going to kiss her again? At least touch her?

"Okay, then," she mumbled. "Good night."

He said nothing, increasing her confusion. She slammed her car door and turned the key. Harbor Town seemed as if it'd been cast under a drowsy enchantment, Mari thought as she drove home on the darkened streets. If the kids were out playing on the peaceful summer night, they must be playing hide-and-seek, because she saw no one on her short ride home.

Until she pulled into the driveway and stepped out of her car, that is.

She heard the roar of the motorcycle. Marc pulled up behind her, cut the engine and dismounted the sleek bike. She sensed tension in his shadowed form as he stalked toward her.

"I said I wouldn't accost you on the beach, but I didn't say a word about your front yard."

He took her into his arms and covered her mouth with his.

This kiss was everything his former one was not: hot, consuming. He spanned her upper back with his hands in a blatant gesture of ownership, her breasts pressing tightly against his ribs.

Mari moaned as he explored her mouth thoroughly, and she submitted to his bold claim. She wrapped her arms around his waist and held on while lust surged in her blood, enlivening her flesh. It never occurred to her to question the sudden inferno of her desire. Logic and the result of Marc's kisses were mutually exclusive events.

She panted softly when he lifted his head only to lower it again and press his mouth to her neck. She couldn't think straight with him nibbling and kissing, his teeth occasionally gently scraping her skin, causing her nipples to tighten in excitement. His hands moved over her, coaxing her to enter a sensual fog. She leaned her head back, granting him more access. Her eyelids parted into slits, and she found herself staring at the dim streetlight.

A quick, flashing picture arose in her imagination—Brigit Kavanaugh standing on her front porch, staring down Sycamore Street as her son publicly ravished Mari Itani in her driveway.

"Marc," she whispered hoarsely. "People will see."

For a moment, she thought he hadn't heard her as he continued to ravenously explore her neck with his mouth, but then he abruptly stopped. He grabbed her hand and pulled her toward a lush maple tree. Mari jogged after him. The tree's thick canopy of leaves provided a cover the streetlight couldn't penetrate.

He positioned her with her back against the tree trunk and immediately swooped down to kiss her again. Their private, adult game of hide-and-seek on this hot, Harbor Town night only increased her ardor, She didn't respond passively but caught his tongue and created suction, loving his raspy groan of arousal in response.

Heat flooded her lower belly and sex. She sighed in sublime satisfaction at his hard pressure against her tingling flesh. She knew firsthand just how much Marc Kavanaugh wanted her in that moment, and it was delicious, heady knowledge.

His stroking hand encircled her neck and then found a breast. He fondled the sensitive flesh with a knowing touch, making her kiss even more hungry…more desperate. A moment later, he lifted his head. The night surrounded them like enfolding velvet as Marc lifted her T-shirt up over her breasts.

Mari moaned when she felt pleasure pinch at her nipple and simultaneously between her thighs. Marc's long fingers moved, scooping the flesh over the top of her bra, pushing down the cup. His fingertips whispered across the now-naked, puckering nipple, and Mari bit her lower lip to keep from crying out.

"Such beautiful breasts," he whispered before he molded her flesh into his warm palm and continued to pluck the crest.

Mari whimpered as her desire swelled into full bloom. And when his warm mouth enfolded her nipple, she couldn't prevent herself from crying out. His tongue was the gentlest tease one moment and a demanding lash the next. She shifted her hips restlessly. Marc must have instinctively understood how she ached, because he palmed the juncture between her thighs.

Mari's eyes sprang wide as pleasure jolted through her flesh. This was crazy. They were in her front yard, for goodness' sake. Things had moved from an impassioned kiss to heavy petting so quickly that she'd lost all good sense.

And she'd said she wanted to take things slow. How could Marc take her body from room temperature to boiling so fast?

When Marc deftly began to unfasten her shorts, she protested, but very weakly. "Marc, we really shouldn't."

She gasped at the sensation of his long fingers slipping beneath the silk of her panties. When she felt him find the evidence of her arousal, he groaned harshly. Mari leaned her head against the tree trunk, gasping and whimpering while Marc stoked her body into a raging fire. When she cried out anxiously, he muttered next to her lips.

"Let go, Mari. I'm here. I've got you."

Marc.

Always tempting her senses, teasing her into feeling her courage. She found herself responding as she always had to his challenges. He put his left arm around her, holding her against his body when she shattered.

The lulling sound of the locusts penetrated her consciousness. She blinked her eyes open slowly as convulsions of pleasure still shimmered through her flesh.

"See, Mari? Your body trusts me. You just have to let your mind trust me, as well." He kissed her, quick, fierce…hungry.

"Let's go inside," he said.

Mari heard his gruff voice through a thick haze of combined arousal and satiation. She opened her mouth, an agreement on her tongue, when someone called out from the sidewalk.

"Marc?"

Mari's breath froze on an inhale.

"Liam?"

Marc's response made her jump. She frantically pushed away from him and started righting her mussed clothing.

"Uh, sorry to bother you," Liam called. "I saw the bike."

She put her hands on Marc's shoulders and shoved. "Go on. Talk to him," she whispered. Even in the midst of her mortification and disbelief at her wantonness, Mari missed his hard heat.

"I got a call from my captain," she heard Liam say. "I need to get back to Chicago tonight, but I should make it back for Brendan's birthday party. Mom said you were staying. Can I take your car? You can keep the bike and we'll switch when I get back."

Mari felt like a fool standing in the dark shadows of the tree when Liam surely knew she was there. She smoothed her hair, but there was nothing she could do about the heat and color in her cheeks—the telltale signs of her impulsivity when it came to Marc. She held her chin up as she joined the two men at the edge of the yard.

"Well, as I live and breathe, if it isn't Mari Itani," Liam said, deadpan.

She met Liam's amused glance and broke into a grin. She couldn't help it. Liam had always made her laugh.

He held out his arms invitingly. "Give me a hug, girl. We never got around to saying hello last night."

She went willingly, gasping when Liam squeezed her so tight her breath whooshed out of her lungs. Marc tapped his brother's elbow after several seconds.

"Haven't you got some emergency in Chicago?" Marc prompted.

"Oh, right," Liam agreed. He grinned devilishly as he released Mari. "I guess I should let you two get back to whatever emergency you were attending to behind that tree."

Mari glanced at Marc furtively. "Don't hurry away on my part, Liam. I was just about to go inside."

"Mari," Marc growled a quiet warning, which she ignored.

"Good night, both of you. Liam…it was wonderful to see you," Mari said before she hurried toward the house.

"Nice timing," she heard Marc say with dark sarcasm.

She flew up the front porch steps to the sound of Liam's low, male laughter.

Chapter Four

The beachgoers would love the new day, Mari decided. She peered through the screen door the next morning. Bright sunshine had turned Sycamore Avenue into a picture of small-town Americana, complete with white-washed fences and robins twittering in the lush, mature oaks and maples.

She glanced toward the top of the street, her gaze lingering on the Kavanaugh house. It stunned her, how nervous she was about seeing Marc again. How excited.

He was just a man, after all.

But she was lying to herself, and she knew it. She'd never reacted to anyone as she had to Marc. She'd done her share of dating over the years and almost married James. Several of those men, most notably James, had accused her of being obsessed with her career—aloof and distant.

Some quirk of nature had made her anything but aloof with Marc.

She turned her attention back to the house, determined to tackle the dusting before the day got away from her. Surely she had more practical things to consider at the moment besides reigniting an old flame.

She retrieved some rags and lemon-scented polishing oil and buried herself in some honest, physical labor.

A wave of nausea forced her down the ladder several hours later. She supposed she should eat something. She pushed a few tendrils that had come unbound off her perspiration-damp face. Applying some elbow grease to what seemed like miles of mahogany built-ins, wainscoting and trim really worked up a sweat. She was in the kitchen eating some crackers to calm her stomach when she heard footsteps on the front porch.

She froze. It was him; she just knew it. With a mixture of trepidation and anticipation, she went to the screen door.

It was Marc, all right. He waited at the door, his arms crossed beneath his chest, his knees slightly bent. He leaned back on his heels in a relaxed, thoroughly male pose. Their gazes immediately met through the screen door. She saw his eyes flicker briefly down before he met her stare again. At that brief visual caress, her nipples prickled in awareness against the fabric of her bra and form-fitting T-shirt.

"Is that her?" someone asked in a hushed voice.

Marc's jaw tilted sideways even though he continued to meet Mari's gaze. "That's her." Marc's voice lowered in a mock conspiratorial whisper to the young boy who stood next to him.

Marc wasn't alone on her front porch. She hadn't initially noticed, thanks to Marc's powerful presence. No sooner had she seen the tall boy when another child—this one sporting a long, white-blond ponytail—peeked around Marc's thigh.

"Hello," the little girl said.

"Hi," Mari replied, charmed by the child's huge, blue eyes and sober expression.

She opened the screen door. Her gaze flickered up to Marc, who was warmly watching her. Leave it to him to bring the two children—his niece and nephew?—to lighten the tension of their meeting.

Marc touched the top of the little girl's head. "You can come out of hiding, Jenny. Mari won't bite. I don't think so, anyway."

She rolled her eyes at Marc before she smiled and beckoned her visitors into the house.

"You two wouldn't be Colleen's kids, would you?" Mari asked over her shoulder as she led them down the hallway to the kitchen. She'd heard that, unlike the other Kavanaughs, Colleen had married and had children.

"Yes, Colleen Sinclair is our mom," the boy said. His adult tone made Mari's smile widen.

"Marianna Itani, meet my niece and nephew, Jenny and Brendan," Marc said as they entered the sunny kitchen.

"You said her name was Mari, not Marianna," Jenny said to her uncle under her breath, as if she was politely trying to correct his error.

"Mari is short for Marianna like Jenny is for Jennifer," Marc explained.

"Oh," Jenny uttered while she studied Mari with interest. "You look like a princess."

"Jenny," Brendan groaned, clearly embarrassed by his little sister's forthrightness.

Mari smiled at the girl. "Thank you. You look very much like your mother did when she was close to your age. And it's a pleasure to meet both of you. Would you like something to drink? Some lemonade?" she added when both children nodded.

Mari poured lemonade and searched through her meager groceries for a snack that might tempt the children. She found a small bag of gourmet, chocolate chip cookies and placed several on a plate. Marc watched her while the kids looked around the large kitchen with interest.

"Brendan told me this house was haunted," Jenny said as Mari handed her a glass of lemonade and set the cookies on the oak table.

"I did not," Brendan said, blushing. He was blond, like his sister, although his hair was a shade or two darker. He obviously had already spent a lot of time at one of Harbor Town's white sand beaches, given his even, glowing tan. Despite Brendan's dark eyes, Mari couldn't help but be reminded of Marc at a similar age.

"You *did*. Every time we play outside after dark at Grandma's, you say it," Jenny replied before she took a sip of her lemonade and daintily picked up a cookie.

Mari glanced at Marc, and they shared a secret smile. As a child, Colleen had been both a lady and a hell-raiser. It seemed her daughter shared a similar bent.

"Do you mind if we look around?" Brendan asked Mari.

"Feel free, although there isn't much to see," Mari said. "Least of all any ghosts, I'm afraid."

Brendan looked slightly disappointed at this.

"Leave your lemonade on the counter," Marc directed before the children scurried out of the kitchen.

Mari glanced at Marc, laughter in her eyes. "They're beautiful."

"Yeah," Marc agreed. "They're great kids. It's Brendan's birthday the day after tomorrow. He'll be ten, but I swear, sometimes it feels like he's about to turn thirteen."

"Wants to be fully independent already, huh?"

She heard one of the children speak in the distance. It struck her suddenly that she was alone here in the kitchen with Marc.

"Yeah. Colleen has her hands full with Brendan." Marc's low murmur made Mari think he might have become just as aware of her in that moment as she had him. "He keeps needling to let him go to the beach with his friends—no supervision."

"We used to go on our own at Brendan's age," Mari mused.

"Yeah, but we grew up in a different world. Our parents were lucky to see us for meals, and they wouldn't have seen us then, either, if we weren't starving. We lived on the beach during the summer."

They shared a smile at their memories. She recalled the golden afternoons, taking a break from her adventures with the Kavanaugh children and to return to Sycamore Avenue for dinner, her mother humming while she cooked, her father on the back terrace reading the newspaper from cover to cover or ineffectively trying to make his creeping hydrangeas bloom. Mari and Ryan would bolt their meals and dash outside again to play freeze tag or Red Rover with the Kavanaughs until one of their parents' voices rang out in the night, ending their summertime bliss until the next morning when it would resume again with the fresh promise of a new day.

"Looks like you've been working hard," Marc said, nodding at the wood cleaner and mounds of dust cloths on the counter.

"I'm trying to get the house in shape to be sold."

"Seems sad, thinking about someone else living here. I have a lot of memories about this old house."

"Yeah," she whispered, studying his strong profile as he glanced around the room.

A half hour later, the children sat cross-legged on the front porch while they played *Operation*. The batteries in the toy had long since petered out, but Brendan and Jenny didn't seem to mind. Each just watched with a tight focus as the other removed the little plastic bones from the tiny holes in the patient and called foul when they believed the surgical instrument had touched the edges of the wound.

Much to Mari's amazement, Brendan had discovered a closet in the basement filled with old board games, mementos and photos and even a few of Mari's and Ryan's yearbooks. She hadn't been the one to clear out the Dearborn family home years ago; Ryan had seen to that. Most of the furniture had been sold at an auction after their parents' deaths, although she and Ryan had kept some pieces from both homes. Ryan must have brought some of their belongings from Dearborn to Harbor Town years back. It made her a little melancholy to think of her brother carefully storing away those remnants of their childhood.

"Who did Colleen marry?" Mari asked Marc, who sat next to her on the porch swing.

"Darin Sinclair."

Noticing his hushed tone, Mari glanced over at him.

"Colleen met him while they were both at Michigan State. Darin was an Army ranger. He was killed in Afghanistan almost two years ago."

Mari's gaze zoomed over to Brendan and Jenny, their blond heads bent over the board game, speaking to each other in low tones. Suddenly Colleen's children's adult manners made perfect sense. They'd lost their father so young....

Maybe Marc noticed her shocked expression, because he grabbed one of her hands in both of his. He rubbed her wrist with a warm, slightly calloused palm. She shivered.

"I'm sorry I mentioned it," he said. "I understand Ryan is stationed in Afghanistan. He's in the Air Force, isn't he?"

Mari blinked. "Yes. Ryan's a Captain...a pilot. He's stationed in Kabul. He'll be coming home to San Francisco in two weeks. I'm counting the days." She put her other hand on top of his, accepting the comfort he offered her without conscious thought. Tears smarting in her eye, she glanced up at him. "I wasn't thinking about Ryan just now, though. I was thinking... It seems so *unfair,* after everything Colleen went through as a kid, to have to endure more as an adult."

His expression turned grim. The next thing she knew, his arm was around her, and her head was on his shoulder. The porch swing squeaked as they swayed. Mari watched Brendan and Jenny play while Marc stroked her upper arm, and she breathed in his scent.

"Do you know what I think, Mari?" he asked after a moment. "I think you've had enough of cleaning house and being sad. I think you and I need to go to the beach."

She lifted her head and looked at him. He wore a small smile, and his expression carried just the hint of a playful dare.

"I shouldn't," she whispered. "I have so much to do."

"Like what?"

Mari hesitated. It would have been a good moment to broach the topic of The Family Center. His mood was so light, though, so warm. She found herself wanting to avoid the weighty subject.

Or perhaps she was just a coward, and was avoiding having him misunderstand her intentions...judge her.

She waved lamely toward the house. "I have cleaning to do."

"There are better things to do on a gorgeous day like today than dust, Mari."

She gave a bark of laughter. Confronted with Marc's wry challenge, she couldn't seem to help it. It was so strange to feel this swelling surge of life, like sap rising in an old tree. She'd grown so used to being careful to maintain her control, of walling off the impulsive side of her nature that she only knew existed because of the man who sat next to her.

"I don't have a swimsuit," she said, her gaze locked on his well-shaped mouth.

"Colleen and Deidre left a dozen suits over the years. I saw them behind the towels in the linen closet. Come on," he said. "There are still some good times to be had in Harbor Town. The only thing that's required is that you let them happen."

She had a hundred other things to do besides idle away the day on the beach with Marc. Still, part of her clung to the promise in his blue eyes.

"The real estate agent is going to be here any minute," she stalled.

"Perfect. I have some work to finish up before we go. The meeting with the agent isn't going to take all day, is it?"

"No, but…" She paused when he gave her a pointed glance.

"You always get your way, don't you," she said softly.

Her heart squeezed in her chest at the sight of his potent grin.

"That remains to be seen, but I'm the optimistic type. How about if I pick you up at two?"

* * *

Later that afternoon, Marc waited on Mari's front porch while she changed into the swimsuit he'd brought. He'd kept his expression impassive when she'd given him a *you've got to be kidding me* look when he'd handed her the bikini.

"There's more air than material to this thing," she'd accused as she'd held up the skimpy bathing suit.

"What?" he'd asked innocently. "You used to wear bikinis all the time."

"I'm not a teenager anymore. Honestly," she'd scolded.

He'd glanced over her. "You've got even more of a reason to wear a bikini now than you did when you were seventeen, Mari."

The roll of her eyes had told him she thought he was full of it, but Marc had only been telling the absolute truth. The vision of Mari naked in the Palmer House Hotel's room would undoubtedly be burned into his memory until the day he died. Her beauty had matured into the type that could make a man a little nuts, if he let it.

He glanced up when the screen door opened and Mari walked out onto the porch. Her brown hair was up on her head, but a few wisps of it fell around her flushed cheeks. She wore a red tank top and jean shorts that showed off her long, shapely legs. He let his gaze trail over the sight of bare shoulders that reminded him of smooth honey. His body responded to the sight of her like a cord jerked tight.

Still. After all these years.

"All set?" he asked gruffly as he stood.

She nodded and glanced away. He'd started to get used to Mari's hesitancy around him—her nervousness. When he saw the color in her cheeks deepen, he wondered if it'd truly been anxiety she'd been experiencing, though.

He'd already picked up a lunch for them from The Tap and Grill. After he'd stowed it and the canvas bag she carried in the storage receptacles on Liam's bike, he noticed Mari's expression.

"What?" he asked.

"I'd forgotten we would be—" she waved vaguely at the motorcycle "—you know...using Liam's bike."

He knew what she was thinking, and he thought it was best not to comment. She, too, recalled driving around Harbor Country years ago, the cycle vibrating with power beneath them, Mari pressed so tightly against his hips and back that not even a granule of the white, sugary sand from one of the beaches could have made its way between them.

He just grinned and handed her a helmet. Her wariness faded when she took in his expression. He was relieved to see her lips curve in amusement. He'd expected her to insist on taking her rental car instead of the bike. She was in the process of fastening the helmet when she paused. Marc glanced up the street where she was staring. He saw his mother standing at the top of the steps of her house. She was watching them.

"Let's go," he said quietly, noticing how Mari's smile had faded at the sight of Brigit. "That sun is broiling me. I need a swim."

He straddled the leather seat. The engine roared to life. He waited while Mari climbed on. When he felt the pressure of her thighs surrounding his and her arms around his waist, he took off down the driveway, the feeling of Mari's supple body pressing against him, making him forget his mother's condemning glare.

"Where are we going?" he heard Mari shout behind

him after they'd ridden down Route 6 for ten minutes or so.

"Tranquil Lagoon. Have you ever been?" he asked over his shoulder.

"No, it doesn't sound familiar."

"Colleen introduced me to it a couple of years back. Most of the locals don't even know it exists."

After following a serpentine road that branched from the rural highway to a drive that consisted of crumbling concrete and burrowing weeds, Marc stopped the motorcycle at the top of a bluff and shut off the engine.

"We'll have to walk the rest of the way," he said.

He grabbed the two bags and headed down a grassy trail that sloped at a steep angle. Mari slid in her tennis shoes, fell into him and apologized. He turned and took her hand while she righted herself.

His body buzzed with a sexual tension that was getting increasingly difficult to ignore. He'd told Mari he'd go slowly with her, and he'd do his best to stand by his word. He was a man, not a saint, though. And Mari tempted him like he couldn't recall ever being tempted.

He kept her hand in his once she'd steadied herself. They picked their way down the steep, overgrown path. Several large locust, elm and oak trees blocked the view of the lagoon when they reached the bottom of the surrounding dunes. When they broke away from the cover of the trees, he heard Mari gasp in pleasure.

"Oh, it's lovely," she murmured as she stared out onto the horseshoe-shaped body of water. Massive dunes surrounded the inlet on three sides. Its choppy waters a brilliant blue that reflected the cloudless summer sky, Lake Michigan sparkled outside the narrow mouth of the lagoon. The lagoon absorbed both the hue of the sky and the surrounding foliage, making it a deep teal. The placid waters made a perfect mirror for the lush green trees.

Marc led Mari over to a spit of sand at the edge of the water. No one else was in sight. He set down their bags in the shadow of a large white boulder and whipped off his shirt. Mari did a double take at his rapid disrobing.

"What? I'm burning up," he said. Not just from the hot sun, either, he thought wryly as he considered the last quarter of an hour spent with Mari pressed against him, the hum of the motorcycle only increasing his sensual awareness of the woman behind him. He kicked off his shoes and waved at her clothing. "Come on. Don't tell me you don't want to take a dip."

"I do." She seemed a little dazed.

The way she was staring at his chest made him forsake courtesy. He headed toward the lagoon. He needed a slap of cold water against his skin. It wasn't going to do him any good to stand there and watch Mari strip down to that little bikini he'd brought her, as much as he wanted to do just that.

He resurfaced from a short swim a minute later and turned toward the shore. He saw Mari standing waist deep in the water and swam toward her. She was smiling at him when he surfaced five feet away.

"Feels good, huh?" he asked.

He was captivated by her eyes as she nodded. She had the most beautiful eyes he'd ever seen—a rare color, like brown infused with amber.

"It feels wonderful. The water is a little warmer than the lake itself this time of year," she said and moved her hands as though caressing the surface of the lagoon.

Marc's gaze traveled up the path of an elegant arm and lingered on a smooth shoulder. The need to touch her swelled in him, but he refrained.

With effort.

"I see the suit fits all right," he said as he glanced at her breasts, barely restrained behind two scraps of gold cloth.

"Get that grin off your face, Kavanaugh," Mari said, rolling her eyes.

"Am I grinning?" Marc laughed, ruining his innocent look.

"You know you are."

He continued to chuckle as she plunged into the water, covering herself from his gaze. She surfaced several feet away from him, standing in water that covered her from the chest down. She wiped the water out of her face and gave him a censorious look.

"It's one of Deidre's swimsuits," she said reprovingly. "You know how small she is. One of Colleen's would fit me much better. Not that I'm telling you anything you don't know," she said, giving him a disgusted look.

"Do you think I notice stuff like that? They're my sisters, for Christ's sake."

"You never noticed that Deidre is petite and delicate?"

He snorted. "I don't know what you remember about Deidre, but my sister is anything but delicate. She's been known to run into the line of fire and hoist a wounded soldier over her shoulder before carrying him to safety."

"She did that?" Mari asked, her eyes going wide.

Marc nodded, not particularly fond of this latest example of his sister's reckless bravery. "She won the Army Medal of Honor for it. Thank God, she's been transferred to Germany, far from active battle."

"You must worry about her a lot," Mari said as she took a step closer.

"Like you do about Ryan," he murmured.

A hush fell over them. A robin twittered in the distance.

"I'm sorry about the way you found out about Ryan and me fighting after the trial all those years ago," he said.

She glanced up at him, her sad, sober gaze tearing at him a little.

"You weren't there, Mari. To say emotions were running high during the court proceedings is a huge understatement."

"You and Ryan used to be so close," she whispered. "Sometimes…" She stared at the narrow opening to the blue lake and made a hissing sound of frustration.

"What?"

She shook her head. "I just wish the crash had never happened."

"You're still angry about it."

Her gaze shot to meet his. "I didn't say that!"

"It wouldn't surprise me if you were. Who wouldn't be angry about having their parents unexpectedly stolen from them one stormy summer night?"

He saw her throat convulse as she swallowed. He realized he was holding his breath when she took another step toward him in the cool water.

"My parents weren't the only thing I lost," she whispered.

Desire sliced through him as he looked down at her face. He held himself on a tight leash, but he didn't want Mari to know that. Not at that moment, he didn't.

"If you're referring to me, I'm standing right here," he replied.

She started, blinked and looked away. "I *was* referring to you. But I was referring to more than that. I was thinking of my childhood. My security. My belief that everything would always be the same.… That even when things got bad, I'd wake up the next day, and everything would be fresh and new. I lost all of that, that summer," she said softly.

"We all did."

"I know," she said quickly. "I know it. I meant to tell you that the other night in the parking lot, but things got out of hand so fast. I never blamed you, Marc. Never. How could I?"

He shrugged. "Other people managed to. It's human nature. When the perpetrator of the crime dies along with the victims, people look to the family. Blame has to be cast somewhere."

"But that's ridiculous!"

"I'm not saying it isn't. But people need to do something with their anger, with their helplessness." He shrugged. "I see it all the time in my work. Victims need to find a target for their angst. My mother has lived with that refrain for fifteen years. In the beginning, she got nasty phone calls, hate mail, pranks were pulled. People in town ostracized her. Some of them still do. It hasn't been an easy road for her. People say she should have been harder on my dad about his drinking. Maybe one of us kids should have stopped him somehow. Maybe *I* should have. I was old enough. That was what my opponent for the State's Attorney position thought…and made a point of mentioning about a dozen times during the campaign," he added wryly under his breath.

"You're kidding."

He shrugged and glanced away. In all honesty, he'd repeatedly wondered if he might have done something to prevent the crash.

"You were twenty-one years old," she whispered. "Please tell me you don't actually believe any of those allegations."

"No. I don't," he said after a moment. "My dad

was responsible for his actions. Does that mean those criticisms didn't eat at me at times? Of course not. It's natural to wonder how you could have done things differently."

"How could you have known what your father was going to do on that night? You had your own life. You hardly were thinking about *Derry* any more than I was thinking of *my* parents at the time."

She'd spoken in a pressured rush. Marc recognized the moment she realized what she'd just said. Color rushed into her cheeks.

Of course neither of them had thought of their parents that night. They'd been in bed together, their love on the brink of consummation.

Marc shoved aside the emotion-packed memory with effort.

"Deidre holds my mother responsible for a lot of what happened with the crash. She thinks my mother was in denial about my father's drinking problem. That's why she doesn't return to Harbor Town in the summer like the rest of us. Actually, Deidre refuses to come to Harbor Town, period."

Marc sighed when he saw Mari's horrified expression. He'd brought her here for a casual outing, a chance for them to reconnect over something besides their volatile past.

"Let's not worry about it, okay? Not now," he murmured.

He gave in to his need and placed his hands on her damp shoulders. She went still beneath his touch. He slipped a finger beneath the cloth of the swimsuit where it tied around her neck.

"I just thought the color would look good on you, that's all." He noticed her confused expression. "That was the reason I picked this suit. The main reason, anyway," he said as he watched himself idly stroke her. He met her stare. "Gold—like your eyes and your skin."

"Marc."

Her breath fell across his lowering mouth. He kissed her softly, and she responded to his coaxing caresses, feeding his desire with a distilled sweetness he associated exclusively with Mari. His muscles tensed when he felt her fingertips touch his chest, her movements striking him as curious but uncertain, featherlight and quick, like ten drops of water scurrying over his skin. It hurt a little to feel his body respond so wholeheartedly to her taste and feel and to have to restrain himself, holding back what seemed so natural and right. When they'd been young, it'd been a serious trial.

As an adult man, it was nothing less than torture.

Her eyes seemed to smolder beneath her heavy eyelids when he finally lifted his head to study her. The need to press her soft, lithe body against his length in the calm water nearly choked him, it felt so powerful. He placed his thumb, a placeholder for his mouth, on her lower lip and rubbed, a reminder to Mari that while he'd do his best, there was only so much a man could do to control human nature.

"I'll race you to the mouth of the lagoon."

"What?" she asked, looking dazed and beautiful.

"I'm trying to control myself, Mari, but it's hard."

Her eyes widened at his abrupt, gruff statement. She blinked, as though coming out of a trance.

"All right, let's swim then," she said breathlessly.

Thankful for the rush of coolness across his overheated body, he submerged himself in the water.

Chapter Five

They swam, and they ate the sandwiches Marc had brought and they swam again. They talked almost non-stop, as though they were trying to make up for fifteen years of separation in one afternoon. Mari hesitantly asked him about his divorce, but she soon discovered there was no reason for discomfort on that front. Marc spoke without rancor about his ex-wife. He explained how they'd grown apart and how they'd wanted different things.

"I suppose that can happen to any couple," Mari murmured, thinking of herself and James as she idly dried herself with a towel. "People grow. They change. There's no guarantee they'll change in the same way."

"Maybe," Marc replied levelly. "But if you care enough about the person to begin with, there's more of a cushion to weather the changes."

He sprawled on the blanket to soak up the sun's rays. He went on to tell Mari that Sandra had disapproved wholeheartedly of him running for Cook County State's Attorney, and how his choice had been the nail in the coffin of their marriage.

"She insisted I only wanted experience at the State's Attorney's Office as a springboard for a cushy job at a law firm. When I said I planned to run for the job, she couldn't believe it."

Mari didn't reply for several seconds as she studied his strong profile. "I've heard that you head up the second largest criminal justice system in the entire country. It's an extraordinary feat, Marc. I...I was really proud of you when I heard you'd won the election."

He lifted his head off the blanket. "You were?"

She rolled her eyes, both flattered and discombobulated by the fact that he seemed genuinely pleased by her compliment. "Of *course*. Do you—" she glanced away from his piercing eyes "—regret it?"

"Becoming a state's attorney?"

"No. You and Sandra splitting."

He exhaled and lay back, staring up at the blue sky and fluffy clouds. "No. It was the right thing to do. If anything, I regret entering into the marriage so impulsively. I was too young. Maybe I was grasping for something to hold on to."

He glanced over and noticed her small smile.

"What?" he asked.

Mari shook her head and looked away from the enticing vision of him lying there wearing nothing but board shorts and water droplets.

"I was just thinking you must be one of the most eligible bachelors in the state."

He rolled his eyes. "If anyone thinks that, they're either crazy or have never experienced the fallout of divorce. I hardly consider myself to be in the marriage market. Avoiding it like the plague, more like. What about you? Do you have any regrets, Mari?"

"With my career? No. I've never once regretted my work. You must remember how much I loved playing, even when I was a girl. My choice of career was an easy one. I've felt nothing but blessed since the day someone actually paid me to do what I love."

"You're fortunate."

"I am. Maybe too much so."

His brows went up.

She laughed self-consciously. "I've had a boyfriend or two tell me that I'm *too* serious about my career."

"Ah. We have that in common, then. Fortunate in our choice of career, unlucky at love. It's funny, though.... I'd always pictured Mari Itani to be the type to master both her career and romance like a pro." His mouth quirked with humor, but his eyes were warm as they studied her. "Figured you'd be married with at least five kids by now and be busy training them for the family orchestra."

Mari whipped her towel at him in playful reprimand. Hearing Marc tease her had caused embarrassment and pleasure to surge through her in equal measure. There was little doubt she'd once expected to settle down and start a family with him.

Funny, how the dreams of a girl still had the power to move her.

Soon, the sun's warm rays lulled Mari as she lay on the blanket they'd spread on the beach. Admiring the gleam and flex of his strong back muscles, she watched through heavy eyelids as Marc again wandered into the lagoon to cool off and swim.

When she awoke, her right cheek was pressed against her extended arm. She glanced around sleepily, not moving her head, wondering why she felt so content when she wasn't immediately certain where she was. She saw the blue-green water of the lagoon wink in the periphery of her vision and recalled the day in a flash. Everything was quiet.

Where was Marc?

She abruptly turned onto her back and bumped into the answer to her question. He was right there—his arm bent at the elbow, his head in his hand, his long body curved around her. Only an inch or two separated them. She laughed in startled amazement when she saw his blue eyes studying her.

"What are you doing?" she asked.

"What does it look like I'm doing?" he countered in a low, husky voice that only added to her sense of delicious lassitude.

"It looks like you were watching me sleep." His gaze flickered over her neck and breasts, and made her skin tingle.

He smiled. She stared up at him, mesmerized by the longing in his blue eyes. "I was thinking about all the nights I missed watching you while you slept," he replied in a hushed tone.

A strained silence ensued.

"Did you think about me? When you left for San Francisco?" he asked.

"How can you ask me that?" Her eyes burned when she blinked. "It was hell, that first year after the crash. My aunt was worried sick about me, I lost so much weight and I couldn't sleep through the night. I'd wake up in a panic."

"Were you having nightmares?"

She shook her head. "I'd dream I was back in Michigan and that everything was perfect. I'd dream my parents were still alive. I'd dream of being with you again."

She reached up and caressed his jaw. "Waking up was the nightmare."

His nostrils flared slightly at her words. His eyes looked fierce. He leaned down and pressed his mouth to hers.

She sighed in surrender. It was just the two of them. They weren't hurting anyone by acknowledging their unique bond. The past receded. Surely there was nothing stronger than this moment, than this feeling?

He lifted his head too soon for Mari.

"Marc?" she whispered, disappointed at his withdrawal.

His mouth slanted in irritation. He glanced up at the thick foliage behind them.

"What—?" she asked, startled when he abruptly sat up. Mari heard voices behind them. She sat up, as well, twisting to look behind her.

Three teenagers—two girls and a boy—reached the bottom of the path and walked onto the white sand. They hesitated when they saw they weren't alone, but then the boy said something Mari couldn't catch, and they headed down the spit of sand, granting Mari and Marc space, if not privacy.

Marc glanced back at her, the heat in his eyes still very much present, and gave her a wry smile. She laughed softly. They were a little old to get caught fooling around on the beach. She tried to ignore the sharp stab of regret she experienced and reached for her tank top.

They dressed and packed up their belongings, speaking sparingly to each other as they trudged back up the steep path. She noticed how far the sun had dipped in the western sky as Marc got on the motorcycle.

"How long did I sleep?" she asked as she climbed up behind him.

"Over an hour."

"Really?" she asked, flustered. It was out of character for her to nap for so long, if at all. Had Marc watched her that whole time? "I'm sorry. I've been a little tired ever since the trip," she murmured as he shifted the cycle to an upright position.

"Don't be. I didn't mind." The bike roared to life.

Mari had thought the spell that had settled on them in the lagoon had been broken by the arrival of the teenagers, but she'd been wrong. She held on tight to Marc's waist and pressed her chest to his back, her cheek to his shoulder and watched the trees and picturesque farms pass by as he drove on country roads for miles. When Marc turned the bike down a long, narrow drive, she noticed a handmade sign featuring a peach and a fluffy pie: McKinley Farm and Orchard—Pick Your Own Fruits and Vegetables and Savor the Harvest at the Cherry Pie Café.

She dismounted from the motorcycle and removed her helmet. Marc had turned off the engine in a gravel turnabout featuring signs in the shape of pointing fingers. Cherry Orchards. Strawberry, Blueberry, Blackberry Picking. Peach, Plum and Apple Orchards. Lake Michigan, the Cherry Museum, Country Store, Restrooms and the Cherry Pie Café.

"Have you been here before?" she asked, grinning.

"Never," Marc replied. "But who can resist a place called the Cherry Pie Café?"

Mari pulled her tote bag out of the storage bin. "I'd like to change before we look around," she told Marc.

Marc also retrieved some folded clothes from the bin. He grabbed her hand and led her down a quaint path featuring bright flowers and a tiny bridge over a burbling stream.

Wearing a sundress, she came out of the bathroom

a few minutes later. She saw Marc standing at the entrance to the Cherry Museum. He'd changed into a pair of cargo shorts and a white, collarless shirt that made his bronzed skin glow in comparison. When he turned and looked at her as she approached, he broke into a wide grin, his teeth flashing in his sun-darkened face.

"What were the chances of *that?*" he drawled, staring at her sundress, patterned with red cherries.

She joined him in laughter until he reached out and grabbed her hand, leading her out into the gorgeous summer evening.

They picked up a little wooden basket from a receptacle and wandered into the cherry orchard. Again, they talked little, speaking with their eyes and small smiles, both of them comfortable in the silence as they filled the basket. Only the sound of a bee or two buzzing contentedly in the trees and the gulls calling in the distance reached Mari's ears. She idly wondered if the farm was deserted, because they saw no one. It was as if an enchantment had fallen over the place.

She quickly learned they weren't alone on the farm, however, when, their basket nearly overflowing with cherries, they exited the orchard. She glanced up at a clicking sound and saw a white-haired man wearing khaki shorts and white socks, taking their picture.

He was smiling when he lowered the camera a moment later.

"Hope you don't mind," he called. "I saw you while I was in the next grove over. You make quite a picture in that dress, ma'am. The photo would look great in my brochure." The man's kind eyes glanced over at Marc, and he nodded cordially. "With your permission, of course."

They approached the sunburned man and exchanged greetings and handshakes. As she suspected, he was the owner of the farm, a man by the name of Nathan McKinley. He told them that he and his wife had bought the farm last year and moved there from New York, looking for an escape from the city grind. It seemed right, somehow, she thought as she watched Nathan and Marc talk pleasantries, that the only person they'd conversed with during these golden hours was someone new to the area, a stranger to their past.

"You two should check out the café," Nathan said. "We have lake-view seating and the best cook in Harbor Country."

Marc glanced at her, his eyebrows cocked in a query. Mari nodded eagerly. She was in no mood to return to town at the moment. In fact, she wished this stolen day with Marc would never end.

They sat at one of the small tables in the cafe. Looking as large and picturesque as the Mediterranean Sea, Lake Michigan sparkled to their right. The only other occupant of the café was a brown dog whose tail wagged in friendly welcome when they sat, although he appeared to be too drowsy to move from his reclining position in the cool shade. The view was spectacular as the sun started to sink toward the lake, but Mari hardly noticed it. Her attention was all for the man who sat across from her.

The best cook in Harbor Country ended up being Nathan's smiling wife, Clarisse. Nathan's boasting about her cooking hadn't been without merit. Mari was surprised and pleased by the delicate, flavorful sauce on her Cornish hen, which was accompanied by mouthwatering mashed potatoes, garden-fresh steamed spinach and homemade cherry tarts. After Clarisse had cleared their empty plates, and Mari had requested a bag of the tarts and some homemade cherry salsa to take home, they lingered at their table, enjoying the view.

"I'm not surprised Nathan wanted to get a picture of you," Marc said after a while.

Noticing his warm gaze, she paused in sipping the remainder of her tea. "I know. How funny that I picked this dress to bring."

Marc reached across the table and covered her hand with his.

"I don't mean the dress," he said. "You're glowing, Mari."

"Am I?" she laughed, made a little self-conscious by his heady stare. "I got some sun today. We both did."

Marc shook his head, a small, quizzical smile on his lips. "It's not the tan."

Clarisse's arrival broke the delicate bubble of the intimate moment. Mari and Marc thanked Nathan and Clarisse profusely and promised to tell everyone who would listen about their wonderful farm and café.

A wistful sadness came over Mari as she climbed onto the motorcycle and Marc drove down the lane back to the main route. Night settled slowly on their return to Harbor Town.

She didn't know for sure what to expect when Marc pulled into her driveway. She released him reluctantly, having grown used to the convenient excuse of holding him so close while they were on the bike. He kept his feet planted on the concrete of the drive while she dismounted. Mari smoothed her dress and tried to read his expression, but his face was cast in shadow.

"I'm leaving the cherry tarts," she said as she removed her tote bag from the storage unit. "Give them to Brendan tomorrow at his party for me, will you?"

Marc turned the ignition on the motor and silence fell, interrupted only by the waves hitting the shore rhythmically on Sycamore Beach.

"Why don't you give them to him yourself? Come to his party with me."

Mari froze in the action of hoisting her bag to her shoulder. "What? No, Marc. Of course not."

"Why not?"

Her chest tightened when she heard the stiffness of his tone.

"It's a family party," she murmured. When he didn't reply, she continued. "Surely…surely your mother is going to be there?"

"She'll be there. What's that got to do with me asking you, as well?"

"Oh come on, Marc. It's got everything to do with it. I don't want my presence to ruin a family celebration."

"There's no reason your presence should ever ruin anything," he stated bluntly.

"But there *is*," Mari shot back. "There is, and you know it. It would be rude of me to show up and make your mother feel so uncomfortable at a family function. Excuse me for saying so, but it's disrespectful of you to suggest it."

He leaned toward her enough that she caught sight of the tightness of his lean jaw. "How do you figure that?" he demanded. His voice had been quiet enough, but she sensed his anger. The old, familiar feeling of helplessness rose in her.

"It's disrespectful and selfish to deliberately do something that would make Brigit unhappy."

"So I'm selfish for wanting to be with you."

"Yes. No," Mari sputtered. "I mean, it's selfish in this particular instance."

"What about this afternoon?" Marc replied briskly, reminding Mari all too well of his skills as a prosecutor. "My mother would have preferred I didn't spend it with you. Was I selfish then? My mother thought I should have worked things out with Sandra. I suppose I was selfish every time I went against her wishes, though. Right?"

"No, Of course not," Mari seethed. "That's not what I meant. This situation is different."

"I know it." His loud bark made her jump. "But that doesn't make it wrong for me to want to be with you."

She opened her mouth to make a blistering comment—how dare he try and make her seem like she was being petty for bringing this up?—when someone called her name. She blinked and peered through shadows thrown by the bushes lining the yard.

"Eric?" she called, thinking she recognized her friend's voice.

"Yeah," Eric replied. After a few seconds of silence, he stepped into the light of the streetlamp. He glanced warily from Mari's stiff expression to Marc's angry one.

"It was such a nice night, I thought I'd walk over and see how things went with the realtor today. Is everything okay?"

"Yes, of course," Mari replied quickly.

Eric's gaze flickered over to Marc. "Do you have some time to talk? I had some good news today. I've wanted to tell you about it all day, but I couldn't reach you on your cell."

"I…well, sure," she said, flustered by the turn of events.

She jumped when the motorcycle's engine suddenly roared in her ears.

"'Night," Marc said.

"Marc…*wait*," she called as he began to turn the cycle around in the drive. She saw the tilt of his chin and suddenly knew for a fact that the golden day had come to an abrupt end.

Eric and she stood immobile, watching as Marc tore down the street in the opposite direction of the Kavanaugh house.

"Sorry. I didn't mean to interrupt," Eric said uncertainly. "It's just that I think I found the perfect manager for The Family Center today."

"Really? That's great."

"You don't seem as excited as I thought you'd be." He glanced down Sycamore Avenue. "Mari…are you *seeing* Marc Kavanaugh?"

Her spine stiffened at Eric's incredulous tone. She felt beleaguered and on edge, having her idyllic day with Marc end this way.

"Why do you ask it like *that?*" she bristled.

"It…it just seems a bit surprising."

"Does it really? It doesn't seem strange to me at all!" she said a little shrilly. Her emotions seemed to be reaching some sort of crescendo in her body. A strange, indefinable feeling had risen in her as she'd watched Marc ride away. She felt exhausted and yet prickly with adrenaline. She was vaguely queasy. In the back of her mind, she had the niggling thought that she was now hotly defending to Eric something she'd just been denying with Marc, and that upset her even more.

"Well… Cut me some slack, Mari, but yeah," Eric said slowly. "It does seem a little unusual, at the very least."

"Marc and I were involved years ago, before the crash. Maybe you didn't know that. Listen, Eric. I'm thrilled that you think you've found someone for the manager position. But I'm not feeling very well. You'll have to excuse me at the moment. I'm sorry."

"Mari, wait. Are you okay?"

She felt intensely guilty about treating a friend in such a fashion, but Mari couldn't seem to stop herself.

Eric's question went unanswered. She hurried up the front steps and into the darkened house. Without pausing to set her bag down, she rushed into the downstairs powder room and—much to her shock—threw up.

A moment later, she flushed the toilet and brushed her teeth. Leaning against the bathroom sink, she stared at herself in the mirror. A cold sweat had broken out all over her skin, and her face had gone pale beneath her tan. She started when she saw Eric's face appear behind her in the mirror.

"Mari?" he asked tensely.

"It's okay," she said shakily, noting his worried expression. She turned on the tap and filled her palm with cool water, then pressed it against her cheek. "I...I guess that bug is still bothering me."

"Seems like an awfully strange bug to me. I'm going to make an appointment for you with an internist I know at Harbor Town Memorial."

"No, Eric, that's not necessary."

"It *is,* Mari," Eric countered.

A trickle of unease went through her when she noticed how sober his expression was.

Chapter Six

Mari felt so good the next morning that she had herself convinced her illness last night had been the result of strong, conflicted emotion. Eric was kind enough to have arranged a lunch for her and Allison Trainor, the nurse he thought well-suited for the manager position of The Family Center. It had turned so hot and humid outside that they opted to eat indoors in the air-conditioning versus the sun-soaked terrace of the Captain and Crew Restaurant downtown.

"Your qualifications are exceptional," Mari mused as she perused Allison's resume for the tenth time.

Allison possessed both social work and nursing degrees and had significant managerial experience in hospitals and substance abuse rehab programs. Even better, Allison was not only warm and kind, but confident and down-to-earth.

Mari looked up as the waitress cleared the remains

of their lunch. "Eric says he knows of your work. So, as far as I'm concerned, the job is yours if you want it."

Allison looked pleased. "I accept. When Dr. Reyes told me about your plans for The Family Center, I was hooked. I like the idea of a treatment facility for people struggling with substance abuse combined with a place where family members can get education, understanding and support. What you plan puts a positive spin on a topic most people would rather ignore."

"I really want the emphasis to be on education for the community—clubs, workplaces, schools. Substance abuse is a community problem as well as an individual one. The stigma attached to it keeps us from seeing that."

"Agreed." Allison leaned back and gave a sigh of relief. "I wish all job interviews could be this easy."

Mari laughed. "Having people you trust make recommendations makes a big difference. Speaking of which, I don't suppose you have any recommendations for a clinician—someone to run educational, support groups and do individual therapy? He or she would also need to be comfortable giving public presentations."

"I do know someone. I don't know if she'll take the job, but she'd be perfect. Her name is Colleen Sinclair and she lives here in town."

"Colleen?"

"You know her?"

"Yes. We were friends…once," Mari said thoughtfully. "I wonder if she'd consider it."

"I can speak to her about it, if you like," Allison offered.

Mari remembered Colleen calling out to her at Jake's Place the other night. What had occurred next out in the parking lot had thrown a damper on any hope she'd had that she and Colleen might possibly resume their friendship.

Still… Mari thought the opportunity seemed too good to pass up without at least exploring the possibility. She wanted the best people working at The Family Center, and Colleen not only had the right credentials, she had the personal experience of dealing with the ramifications of substance abuse. Colleen was a survivor.

"I'd like to talk to her about it myself, actually. I happen to know she's busy with her son's birthday party today, but I'll try and contact her tomorrow."

Allison had needed to hurry to get back to her current job at the hospital, so Mari was alone when she exited the bustling restaurant. The bright sun blinded her as she stepped from the dim interior.

A petite woman plowed into her. Both fumbled to stop a plastic container from falling on the sidewalk.

"It's all right. I've got—" The older woman stopped talking when she glanced up at Mari.

"Brigit." Mari blinked. She hadn't stood this close to her in years. Marc's mother had aged extremely well. Mari's tongue felt numb with shock. "I'm sorry. The sun blinded me there for a moment."

Mari nodded nervously at the container. "That must be Brendan's birthday cake. He and his sister came to visit me yesterday. They're such lovely children—"

Abruptly, Brigit stepped around her and marched away without another word, her spine ramrod straight.

Ice poured into Mari's veins. She stood there on sunny, muggy Main Street, her skin tingling and her limbs starting to tremble. The unexpected encounter with Brigit Kavanaugh had a profound effect. She'd dreaded running into her, and now she had…in the literal sense.

In Mari's younger years, Brigit had always been so

warm toward her, so welcoming. Neither of Brigit's daughters had been interested in her hobby of wildflower collection, but Mari had come to share Brigit's passion. They had gone on several jaunts together in the local meadows, searching for elusive flowers they'd earmarked in Brigit's *Wildflower Field Guide*.

Now, Brigit refused to speak with her and apparently loathed her, Mari thought as she recalled the cold, furious expression on Brigit's face. Having someone look at you with something akin to concentrated hatred wasn't an experience Mari was used to having.

Especially when that someone had once been a friend.

She sat down on one of the chairs outside Kate's Ice Cream Parlor for a moment until she regained her composure to walk back home. All the while, one thought kept circling in her mind.

Marc wanted me to attend that family party.

She stood and crossed Sutter Park. Children shouted gaily from the playground.

She should focus on what she needed to accomplish in Harbor Town. She should finish her mission and get out of here. It all made perfect sense.

Or at least she'd thought it did, until she climbed the steps to her house and made her habitual glance up Sycamore Avenue to the Kavanaugh house. The vision of Marc staring down at her as she awoke rose in her mind's eye.

I was thinking about all the nights I missed watching you while you slept.

Longing tore through her, so sharp it stole her breath.

Marc and Liam were the only two people remaining that evening after Colleen and Brigit took a horde of

Brendan's friends and Jenny to Kate's Ice Cream Parlor on Main Street. They sat at the kitchen table, covered with half a dozen pizza boxes, plastic cups, a half-eaten birthday cake, soda bottles and an array of toys and party favors. They'd volunteered to clean up, but neither brother seemed too anxious to get started.

"I've been wanting to talk to you about something," Marc said. "You've lost weight. You look like crap."

Liam scowled and scraped his fingers through his mussed, shoulder-length hair. "I've been too busy to work out lately. Or get a haircut. Not all of us have the leisurely schedule of a gentleman lawyer."

"I'm a government employee, not a fat cat. But that's not my point. You're working undercover again, aren't you?"

Liam's mouth turned hard. "Can't keep much from you, can I, counselor?"

Connecting the dots and not particularly liking the resulting picture, Marc just studied his brother for a moment.

"It's that corrupt cop investigation, isn't it?" Marc asked.

Liam raised his brows and slouched insouciantly in his chair, and Marc had his answer.

As the county's top prosecutor, Marc lived and breathed the same air as Chicago cops. He knew when something was up; he sensed when cops were jumpy.

"That inner ring of dirty cops is dangerous, Liam."

Blue eyes flashed. "You think I don't know that?"

"Just be careful. You'd put Mom in a grave if something happened to you. She's worried enough about Deidre."

"You have some nerve, accusing Deidre and me of being martyrs. Who do you think we learned it from, Mr. Defender of Victim's Rights?" Liam accused.

Marc didn't fall for the bait, just continued to hold Liam's stare until his brother sighed and glanced away.

"You sound like Mom. I told her I'd think about quitting the force when I'm done with this assignment, but not before. So the only thing I can do is tell you I'll be as careful as I always am. I don't have a death wish."

You sure as hell act like you do sometimes.

Marc bit his tongue to keep from saying the words out loud. He'd said enough for now. It wouldn't help things to start a fight with Liam.

Liam grimaced when he lifted his elbow off the table and saw that a miniature plastic hockey puck was stuck to his skin. "I guess we better start cleaning up," he mumbled.

"Right," Marc agreed unenthusiastically.

"They say we're in for a hell of a storm later on tonight," Liam said as he stood. He picked up the empty bag of cherry tarts Mari had donated for the party. "Hey…weird about you and Mari being back in town at the same time, huh?" Liam asked with affected casualness.

"Yeah," Marc replied shortly. He carried a stack of pizza boxes to the garbage.

"Marc."

He turned, something in Liam's tone making him cautious.

"I…I never told anyone. About the night of the accident. About Mari being at the house with you."

Marc narrowed his eyelids as memories of that fateful summer night assaulted him.

Liam's panicked shouts from downstairs had interrupted an intensely private moment between Mari and Marc fifteen years ago. In fact, they'd been about to make love for the first time as a storm brewed on the horizon. The news of the wreck had put a stop to that.

The crash had jolted Mari and him onto complete different life paths.

He was more than a little shocked at hearing Liam speak aloud about a topic that had been forbidden between them through some unspoken fraternal oath. Maybe it was Mari's presence in town, or maybe it was the threat of a storm in the thick air—the still, oppressive atmosphere not unlike that of the night of the crash—that had made Liam break the silence.

"It must have been rough, being with Mari that night," Liam said, his voice gruff, cautious.

Marc didn't reply, just resumed clearing the table.

Liam always had possessed a talent for bald understatement.

Mari kept herself busy that day by meeting the furniture deliverymen at The Family Center and arranging what items she could on her own. She'd dropped in on Natalie Reyes's accounting practice and spoken to Natalie about the status of the center's operating license and some other financial matters. They'd ended up chatting for hours. Natalie was one her favorite people—so quiet and reserved, yet so warm and giving once she accepted you into her private world. Mari knew Natalie rarely went out in public, self-conscious about the scarring on one side of her face. Mari had hoped her involvement in The Family Center would bring her out of her self-imposed confinement somewhat, but, so far, her friend remained shrouded.

Afterward, she returned to Sycamore Avenue where she spent the better part of the evening practicing her cello.

When she played, she entered a familiar, focused trance where she lost all sense of place and time. But, suddenly becoming aware of how hot it was, she paused to wipe sweat off her brow, change into a button-up, thin sundress, and open up a window in the bedroom, not that it helped to alleviate the stifling atmosphere. She resumed practice.

Isn't the air conditioner working? she wondered a little while later. She set her cello and bow aside and went downstairs to the thermostat.

"Do *not* tell me," she whispered in disbelief when the air conditioner didn't respond. In the distance, she heard thunder rumble ominously. She hadn't noticed a storm was approaching. With her air conditioner apparently on the fritz, she welcomed the prospect of relief from the oppressive heat and humidity.

She glanced at a clock. It was just past midnight. A feeling of sadness went through her. Now that the day was over, she realized that part of her had hoped Marc would seek her out following their bitter parting last night.

She walked out on the front porch. A warm wind swirled, causing the porch swing to jerk and sway. Some leaves skittered down the dark, deserted street, the sound striking her as hushed and furtive. She perched on the swing. Lightning flashed over Sycamore Avenue.

The weather reminded her of the night her parents had been killed. Funny how the realization didn't bring back the horror of rushing to the hospital and hearing her mother and father had been dead upon arrival. Instead, another memory flashed vividly into her mind: the hot, wondrous expression on Marc Kavanaugh's face when he'd looked down at her in his bed. She'd been naked and overwhelmed by desire.

Mari clenched her burning eyelids tight. Grief had wormed its way into that memory over the years, transforming it from a girl's gilded dream into a woman's tarnished regrets.

Tonight, the wonder of that moment had returned. She was so caught up in the poignant memory that she thought she'd imagined it when she heard Marc's voice.

"Mari."

She opened her eyes and spotted his shadowed form standing at the bottom of the stairs to the porch. The longing she'd experienced earlier that day swelled in her chest, making breathing difficult. For some reason, the fine hair on her arms and the back of her neck rose.

"Couldn't sleep, huh?" she asked quietly.

"Who could, on a night like this?"

Neither of them spoke as he came up the steps and sat several inches away from her on the swing.

"Hell of a storm brewing," he murmured as lightning lit up the street clear as day for a brief moment.

"Yeah," Mari replied shakily, wondering if he, too, thought of the similarity between this storm and that one so long ago. Thunder rumbled in the distance. "I'm glad about it. The air conditioner just went out. Hopefully the storm will break this humidity." She swallowed when he didn't reply. Was this what they'd stooped to? Talking about the weather? "How was Brendan's party?"

"He had a great time. He said to thank you for the tarts, by the way. He'd only share them with his best friend, Brian, much to Jenny's dismay."

She heard the smile in his voice and laughed. "I should have gotten a bag for her."

"I think she'll manage to survive on a week's worth of cake and ice cream," Marc said. "Are you interested in Eric Reyes?"

Mari started. She'd been lulled by his low, light tone. The switch in topic took her by surprise.

"Interested?"

"Yeah. Are you seeing him?"

"No…he's just a friend. A good friend."

She could only make out his shadow, but she saw him slowly nod his head.

"Ryan introduced me to him, years back. We've kept in contact, mostly by email over the years," Mari explained.

"Ryan must have met him during the lawsuit hearings."

"Yeah." A gust of wind caused the porch swing to shudder, despite Marc's firmly planted feet. She inhaled for courage. "I saw your mother downtown today."

"You did?"

"She didn't mention it?"

"No, she didn't. How did it go?"

"Not well," Mari replied with a mirthless chuckle. "When she realized it was me who'd bumped into her, she gave me the cold shoulder. Walked away without a word."

Marc cursed under his breath. "I'm sorry."

"It's not your fault," she said.

He didn't speak for a moment. Mari almost felt him examining her in the darkness.

"Is this your way of saying I told you so?" he finally asked with grim amusement.

She sighed and wiped the perspiration off her brow. "Maybe," she conceded. She fervently hoped to avoid another confrontation with him on the subject, but she wasn't going to apologize for what she'd said last night, either.

"Do you want me to take a look at the air conditioning?"

"Do you think you could actually fix it?" she asked, sitting up straighter.

"I'm not guaranteeing anything, but I can have a look. Let's start with the furnace, since it's inside, and it's about to start pouring. It might be the blower or a belt."

A thought struck Mari as she flipped on the hall light and led Marc to the closed doorway on the right.

"What's wrong?" he asked from behind her.

She glanced down at her skimpy dress and folded her arms over her breasts. In the darkness, she'd forgotten to think about how thin the fabric was. She turned her head warily. Her heart bumped against her breastbone at the vision of Marc in full light. He was wearing his customary beachwear—long cargo shorts that showed off his muscular, tanned calves and a blue T-shirt that picked up the color of his eyes. His dark blond hair had been sexily mussed by the whipping wind.

"Nothing is wrong." She waved at the shut door down the hallway. "The furnace is in the basement."

Her gaze shot away when she saw something flicker in Marc's eyes.

"Yeah. I remember that, strangely." His mouth quirked. "Lead the way."

Mari closed her eyelids briefly when she turned. She'd been so eager to have her AC fixed, she hadn't been thinking…

She flipped on the light over the basement stairs and took the squeaky steps at a brisk pace. She was proud that she didn't blush when she nodded at the furnace situated in a cubbyhole of the unfinished basement. Marc didn't say anything, just went over to it and opened the door that accessed the machinery. Mari stood back, admiring the flex and play of his muscles beneath the blue cotton.

Her heart seemed to skip a beat when he suddenly paused in his poking and walked into the narrow space between the furnace and wall. He opened up the breaker box and flipped a switch. When he returned, he saw humor dancing in his eyes.

"I used to kiss you back in that cubbyhole until my lips were chapped for days."

For a second, Mari's mouth just hung open. She was sure she must have imagined him saying it. She'd been a little embarrassed up in the hallway when she realized two things: one, she was wearing a thin, translucent dress with barely anything on beneath it, and two, she was about to take Marc to their first make-out hideaway. She'd thought he was tacitly agreeing to not make mention of the subject when he saw her discomfort. But here he'd just bluntly pointed out the elephant in the room.

Laughter burst from her throat. Her eyes sprung wide at the strength of her response, and she covered her mouth. She couldn't help it. It must be hysteria. When she saw Marc's grin widen, though, she wondered. How could the sound of Marc Kavanaugh's deep chuckle be anything but right?

"Remember that time when my mom came downstairs to put in a load of laundry while we were back there?" she asked between jags of laughter.

"Yeah," Marc replied as he opened the box he held. "We froze up for about two seconds and then got right back to the thick of things. I don't even remember when your mother went back upstairs again."

"Neither do I."

When she registered his altered expression and fading grin, the unexpected, swelling wave of amusement waned. Heat rose beneath her skin. Marc's gaze lowered to her breasts, which she'd exposed as she tried to cover her erupting laughter. He went still, masculine appreciation gleaming in his eyes.

Mari was a little surprised she couldn't hear the electricity popping in the air between them.

She cleared her throat and looped her arms beneath her breasts. When he met her gaze, she shook her head and rolled her eyes, attempting to package the poignant moment in the convenient mental container of silly childhood nostalgia.

But the moment *hadn't* evoked anything silly inside her. Far from it.

"You just threw a breaker. I reset it. The AC should work now," he said as he shut the door to the furnace.

"That's it?" Mari asked in amazement.

"I don't know. We'll have to go upstairs and see if the AC turns on or not."

She nodded, but neither of them moved. Instead they remained motionless, facing each other.

It felt like she was keeping a volcano of emotion from erupting from her chest. Her inhalation sounded ragged and raw in her own ears. It was really too damn much. Too much history. Too much *feeling*.

"Come here," Marc said, his voice quiet, but firm.

She flew across the room and into his open arms. A convulsion of emotion shuddered through her body and she gasped.

"Why do you fight it so much, Mari?" he asked gruffly as he stroked her back, trying to soothe her.

"I know it'll never work out." Tears shot out of her eyes with the same pressured intensity as her words. "But I can't seem to stop wanting you. Especially…"

His hand, spread on her lower back above her buttocks, paused. "What?"

"Especially tonight," she said, her face pressed against his chest. "You probably didn't notice, but the storm…the night…it's like—"

"The night of the crash," Marc whispered hoarsely.

Her heart seemed to swell at his words. So, he *had*

noticed the similarity of tonight to the one where their lives had been cleaved apart.

He put his fingers beneath her chin. He lifted her head until she looked up at him. She saw her own raw need reflected in his eyes.

He leaned down and caught a tear with firm, grazing lips. His eyes were open, watching…gauging her reaction as he rained kisses on her cheek and jaw, drying her tears, wetting his mouth with her sorrow. When he brushed his lips near the corner of her mouth, she turned to meet him.

She felt him stiffen as though an electric shock had gone through him when their lips touched. She sensed the steel edge of male desire that had leaped into his muscles. He softly sandwiched her lower lip between both of his own, parting her mouth, molding their lips together in a delicious kiss. Mari's eyes fluttered closed as a sensual languor weighted her limbs and heat expanded at her core.

She hungrily slicked the tip of her tongue along the seam of his mouth. A wild satisfaction tore through her when he groaned, deep and rough, and pulled her closer, pressing her tight to his body, taking her mouth in a possessive kiss.

Why was she doing this? She'd told him she wanted to be cautious. Yet here, in this moment, she felt nothing but glorious triumph that she'd inspired such a wholehearted, total response from Marc.

All his former tentativeness evaporated as he boldly explored her. Their flavors mingled, acting like an intoxicant on her brain. One hand clenched mindlessly at his T-shirt, while the other reached and knotted in the thick hair at the base of his skull. Her back arched as he leaned down over her and completely claimed her.

Both of his hands coasted up her back, simultaneously mapping her shape and stroking her.

He paused, both of his large hands spread across her ribs as though he held her heart in his hands. She moaned in rising need. He answered her call and caressed a breast. She moved back slightly, granting him more access. He sealed their wild kiss and lifted his head, watching her with blazing eyes, his nostrils slightly flared. He pressed an aching nipple to the center of his palm and closed his hand over her, gently kneading.

She felt his body tighten and harden in response to that intimate caress. It only fueled her mounting need. When he transferred his fingertips to the erect crest and gently charted the topography of her nipple through the thin fabric, desire ripped through her. She found herself jerking up his T-shirt, desperate for the sensation of his bare skin.

He made a rough sound in his throat. The next thing she knew he was lifting her in his arms. Lightning flashed in the dark, old house, and thunder answered in a ferocious roar. Neither of them spoke as he carried her up first one flight of stairs and then another. Words couldn't contain the fullness of that taut, burning anticipation, a powerful tension that demanded release.

Mari waved at the second door on the left—her old bedroom—her gaze never leaving Marc's.

Buffeted by the wind, the sheer curtains billowed inward when they entered the room. Marc laid her on the bed. When he straightened, Mari's hands flew to the buttons on her dress. He moved quickly, grabbing her wrists and halting her.

"No. I'm going to do it." His low, rough voice made goose bumps rise on her arms and her nipples tighten. "Just give me a second."

He began to undress. The light leaked in from the

downstairs hallway and allowed her to admire the sight of him as he went about his business with rapid efficiency. She was glad; she wanted him to hurry.

She didn't want logic to wriggle into her awareness. Not at this moment.

She knew Marc had shared her desire for haste when he began to strip out of his shoes and cargo shorts like he though his life depended on being naked. Her breath stuck in her lungs at the site of him standing and whipping his T-shirt off with a flex of lean, dense muscle. She eyed the shadow of light brown hair on his chest, following its trail to where it disappeared in his white boxer briefs.

"You're so beautiful."

He glanced up at her shaky whisper.

"No. You're the beautiful one," he said.

The dim light allowed her to see the feral glint in his eyes as his gaze traveled over the length of her. His haste seemed to mount, given the rapid manner in which he finished stripping. Mari glanced down when he stood before her. It hurt a little to look at him; he was so beautiful—proud and elementally male. The room flashed with brilliant white light, and thunder seemed to rattle the very air they breathed.

He sat on the bed next to her. Spellbound, Mari watched him. She couldn't draw breath as he unfastened her dress to the waist. He carefully peeled back the sides of the fabric, exposing her breasts. She convulsed with raw emotion when he just stared at her, his face intent, as though he wanted to take the image to his grave.

"*Hurry,* Marc," she whispered hoarsely.

His gaze leaped to hers, as if he'd caught her meaning. Who better to understand her desperation at that moment? Their joining had been interrupted fifteen years ago by news of mind-numbing loss.

But that was another night. Not this one.

His fingers moved fleetly at her plea. He drew the dress down over her legs then skimmed one hand down her buttock and thigh before reaching for her panties.

"I could never get over how soft you were," he muttered as he rid her of her underwear. She saw how rigid his face was as bent over her. "I always knew you were mine from the first time I touched you."

"Marc," she murmured desperately. Her desire almost hurt it was so strong. The night in Chicago had been wild, but this was a fiercer need that tore at her.

She cried out in protest when he didn't immediately press his weight against her but instead leaned over the side of the bed. He rustled for something in his shorts. She realized he was searching for a condom and experienced a brief moment of combined relief and guilt.

She hadn't even considered protection in the midst of her mindless need.

She watched, mesmerized as he sheathed himself. When he was done, she held up her arms, beckoning him.

He lowered himself. She sighed in relief at his weight pressing against her. His dense muscles were a sensual blessing pressed to her soft breasts, his arousal brushing against her belly and the juncture of her thighs.

She ran her hands over smooth skin encasing dense muscle and bone and opened herself to him. His mouth covered hers possessively as he entered her, her ecstatic cry muffled by thunder.

Rain began to pound on the roof and earth. The elm tree outside her bedroom window thrashed against the side of the house. But that storm was nothing compared to the one happening in Mari's body as Marc slowly staked his claim.

When he was fully sheathed in her, he dropped his

forehead on the pillow next to her cheek, his rib cage heaving. A great tenderness penetrated her arousal. He was the strongest man she knew—male virility personified—but in that moment, he was as helpless with his desire as she was. She caressed his shoulder and ran her fingers in into his hair.

"It's okay, Marc. It's okay."

He rose over her, his facial muscles tight and straining. "I don't know if I can control it," he warned in a choked voice.

"Then don't try."

He started to move.

She understood him perfectly. She existed at the eye of this storm with him. She clenched her teeth tight as her nerve endings began to fire madly with signals of sensual friction, making her want to purr and scream at once. He slaked himself—demanding and forceful—but she met him for every deep, driving thrust, an equal partner in this greedy consumption, both of them seemingly rushing toward the finish line to assure themselves the moment wouldn't be ripped away from them as it had in the past.

The headboard began to clack rhythmically against the wall. Their bodies became glazed with sweat as they both raced for that treasure, grasping blindly for it, requiring it like they required that next gasp for air. Marc reached it first. She held him at her core, knowing she'd forever remember him throbbing deep within her and the poignancy of his rough groan as ecstasy ripped through him. Still in the midst of his climax, he reached between their bodies, finding her most sensitive flesh… demanding she join him in that sweet conflagration.

Her back arched as she followed Marc's silent demand and she shook in a storm of release.

Chapter Seven

Marc propped himself up on his forearms, his neck bent as he fought to catch his breath.

He lowered his head to Mari's and pressed his mouth to her neck, absorbing her movements as she gasped for air. After a moment, he lifted his head. Her breasts heaved as she panted. Her large, liquid eyes were open, watching him.

He glanced down over her face, neck and elegant, sloping shoulders. Had he really just made love to this exquisite woman with all the finesse of a steam engine going at full throttle? He couldn't regret it. His need for total possession had been as easily controlled as the storm that raged outside the window. His gaze lingered on the pale globes of her breasts rising and falling. The delicate nipples were still stiff from desire.

He lowered and kissed the tip, lingering to feel her texture against his sensitive lips. He felt himself lurch in the tight embrace of Mari's body and realized he was segueing rapidly from satiation to arousal again.

"I know you wanted to go slowly, but it wasn't something I could control," he whispered roughly near her breast.

He lifted his head. Lightning illuminated the room, allowing him to see the shadow of uncertainty falling across her delicate features.

He sighed. "I'd better…"

He shifted his hips, letting his actions finish his sentence. Leaving Mari's warm, tight embrace made him grimace. He wasn't ready to withdraw.

Not even close.

"I'll be right back," he told her before he walked into the hallway.

His memory served him in his search for the bathroom. He was once allowed to come upstairs in the Itani summer house when they were little. He and Ryan had been friends, and they had occasionally condescended to hang out with their little sisters, Colleen and Mari.

Until the summer after Mari's freshman year of high school.

Kassim and Shada Itani had apparently noticed the way Marc stared at their blooming, beautiful daughter, and the rules in the Itani household had changed drastically.

Marc had never really thought much about the Itani's ethnicity and religion before that summer. But when Mari had become a young woman, Marc was forced for the first time to realize the vast differences in their backgrounds and culture. He could still recall how stunned he was when he learned how rigidly Mari's dating would be monitored by her parents. They were nowhere near as strict with Ryan.

It quickly became clear to Marc that under *no* circumstances would Mari be allowed to date an Irish-American boy from a liberal, Catholic family. He may have been acceptable as Ryan's friend, but, when it came to Mari, he was a pariah in Kassim and Shada Itani's eyes. Their grins of delight upon seeing him subtly changed over a single summer, replaced by tense, slightly suspicious expressions.

Of course, he and Mari had seen each other, anyway. Not much could stand in the way of two determined teenagers with hormones raging through their blood. Whenever and however they could manage to be together, they did it.

He washed his hands. Thinking about all the tenuousness of being with Mari when they were kids made him anxious to return to her. Would it always be that way? Not if he had his say about it.

He impatiently swiped his wet hands on a hand towel and hurried into the stuffy hallway. Before he joined Mari in the bedroom, he hurried downstairs and flipped the gauge on the thermostat. The AC hummed to life.

"Success," he proclaimed as he entered the room.

"Cocky," she murmured.

She snorted when he plopped down next to her, making the mattress squeak in protest, and immediately began to ravish her neck. He liked the sound of her laughter so much he tickled her with his whiskers.

"Is that a complaint?" he growled between tickles and nibbling her neck. He couldn't get enough of her taste on his tongue.

"Oh no…heaven forbid I'd complain about *that*."

Marc raised his head, grinning. He glanced down, realizing for the first time that Mari had drawn the sheet over her nakedness. He raised his eyebrows, his mirth fading. She stopped laughing, as well, when he tugged the sheet to her thighs. He sobered at the vision of her beauty.

"Please don't hide yourself from me anymore."

He opened his palm along the side of her ribs and stroked her from breast to thigh, awed by how she flowed beneath his hand like warm silk. He met her eyes. Her expression had become as somber as his.

"All right," she acquiesced quietly. "For tonight."

He leaned down and kissed her abdomen. Her taut muscles leaped beneath his lips. Relishing the delicate shivers he evoked from her flesh, he lowered his mouth, exploring the sensitive skin of her lower belly. He wasn't above pressing his advantage.

"Not just for tonight, Mari," he corrected. He skimmed his lips against the satin skin of her inner thigh, and she opened for him with a sigh. "Not ever," he murmured before he lowered his head.

Mari awoke the next morning to the sound of her cell phone ringing in her purse. She opened her eyes. The sunlight streaming through the window was so intense, she had to squint.

She squeaked in panic and raised her head.

"What's wrong?" Marc asked groggily.

For two seconds, Mari just stared incredulously at him. The vision of him—naked, sleep-rumpled and sexy as hell—seemed to score her consciousness. She lay in the circle of his arms. Her head had been resting on his chest. Everything came back to her in a rush: the storm that had raged outside of the house and inside of the bedroom, as well, the sensual hours of making love throughout the night, the complete focus on one another as they tried to get their fill…

Never fully succeeding.

Mari glanced over at Marc's mouth and the succulent flesh of dense pectoral and shoulder muscles.

"It looks like it's late, and I have an appointment at the hospital at nine-thirty, not to mention a ton of other things I need to do today," Mari said.

The drowsy look in Marc's blue eyes evaporated.

"What's wrong? Why do you have a doctor's appointment," he demanded.

"It's nothing," she murmured. She touched his upper arm as a signal to warn him that she was getting out of bed, but instead, she lingered, caressing his bulging biceps with appreciative fingertips. "I've been struggling with a little bug ever since the plane trip from San Fran to Detroit," she said, sighing when she felt Marc's fingers at the back of her scalp.

"You don't seem sick to me."

His low rumble caused her to open her heavy eyelids, which had uncooperatively drifted closed under the influence of Marc's massage.

"I agree. I'm fine. I'm just doing it to humor Eric," she whispered.

His hand ceased moving.

"Reyes?"

Mari blinked. "Yes," she said hesitantly, taking in Marc's stiff features. "He saw me get sick the other night and made a big deal about making an appointment for me. He's a doctor, you know."

"Yeah. I know."

Her mouth fell open but nothing came out. She knew that both Eric and Natalie had used the money from the lawsuit to get educations and improve their prospects. Their mother had come from Puerto Rico years back with little more than the clothing on her back. She'd worked for eighteen hours a day as a maid in various locales to support her two children. Miriam Reyes had drilled the importance of education in her children's heads.

Mari admired Natalie and Eric for what they'd done after their mother had been killed in the crash. How many people won lawsuits only to throw away the money on foolish schemes or unneeded luxuries? Not the Reyes. Instead, they had carefully planned futures for themselves, keeping in mind what their mother would have wanted for her children. No one could replace a loved one with money, but being careful about what was done with that money made a difference.

It did to Mari, anyway.

She swallowed as she glanced at Marc. "So…you found out that the Reyeses used the lawsuit money to get educations. Eric became a surgeon and Nat is an accountant," she said quietly.

"I didn't know—not until the other day," he replied.

"Oh. I…I wonder…"

"What?" Marc asked.

"If…if you ever wonder what I did with my share of the lawsuit money?" She studied the pillowcase. The ensuing silence seemed to ring in her ears.

"Yeah. I've wondered," he finally said.

"I want to tell you about it," she whispered. "It's the main reason I came back to Harbor Town."

He looked puzzled, but his long, stroking fingers resumed their sensual massage.

"When do you want to tell me about it?" he asked.

"How about tonight at dinner? I'll make you something here at the house," she suggested. Mari couldn't help but become preoccupied by his narrowed gaze on her mouth.

"How about if we make love right now, and you tell

me after that?" he suggested. He grasped her shoulders and gently pulled her up several inches. Mari moaned softly at the sensation of their naked skin sliding sensually together. The hand at the back of her head pushed her down to his mouth.

"Oh...that'd be...I..." Mari mumbled incoherently between Marc's kisses. "Marc...I can't...doctor's... appointment."

He leaned back. His smile was part angel and part devil. Mari couldn't fathom how he managed to pull it off.

"Nothing else but your health could make me stop," he said silkily.

Mari snorted doubtfully. He turned on his side, rested his hand and watched her while she grabbed a robe out of the closet. She glanced up and caught him staring at her breasts as she covered them. He sighed and lay on his back, his gaze on the ceiling.

"It's going to be a long wait until suppertime," he said dolefully.

She chuckled and started out of the room to take a shower.

"Mari?" he murmured, all traces of mock sadness gone from his voice.

"Yes?" she asked, turning.

"You'll call me if anything is wrong, as far as the doctor?"

"Nothing is going to be wrong," she said, smiling. She saw his raised brows and nodded her head. "Yes, I'll be sure to call in the rare event I have a dire illness."

"Just call me. Period," he said.

She nodded, hesitant to yank her eyes off the glorious vision of him propped up on the pillows and naked save for a thin sheet draped low on his hips. She shook her head as if to ward off his spell and exited the room.

It was hard to think like a rational human being with Marc around.

Once she reached the hospital, Mari noticed she'd missed a call from her brother. She put off returning his call, none too eager to speak with him when memories of Marc still crowded her consciousness. Instead, she called the number Allison had given her yesterday for Colleen, Marc's sister. She still clung onto the strand of hope that Colleen would at least meet with her to discuss The Family Center and a possible job.

Colleen didn't answer, but Mari left a message with her number saying she'd love to meet while she was in town if she had a chance. If she didn't call back, at least Mari would have her answer.

Eric had made her appointment at Harbor Town Memorial with a friendly, middle-aged, female physician named Estelle Hardy. She kept up such a pleasant, steady stream of conversation while she examined Mari that it hardly felt like a typical doctor's visit. She sent her to the lab and asked her to sit down in the waiting room until the results could be obtained. While she was waiting, Mari saw with a leap of excitement that Colleen had returned her call. Colleen had left a warm message, saying that she very much wanted to meet and could stop by Mari's house after work that afternoon, if it was convenient.

Mari immediately redialed Colleen's number. She got her voice mail at the same time that Dr. Hardy's nurse beckoned to her. Mari left another message saying she'd be happy to have Colleen over at the house at five, as the nurse led her to a consulting room.

She was just ending the call when Dr. Hardy walked in, carrying a chart.

"Well, I think we've figured out the reason for your malaise and bouts of nausea," Dr. Hardy said after they'd both sat down.

"Really? What?" Mari asked, still happily preoccupied with the prospect of Colleen Kavanaugh agreeing to see her again.

"You're pregnant, Mari."

Chapter Eight

Through the roar in her ears, Mari distantly became aware of a familiar voice. She blinked open her eyes with effort. Eric Reyes sounded nervous.

"Mari? Mari…open your eyes, please."

She saw him standing in the consulting room. He looked very doctorlike in an unbuttoned lab coat and with a stethoscope around his neck. He also looked very, very worried, Mari realized. She abruptly sat up on the exam table.

"What's wrong, Eric?" she demanded.

A bewildered, alarmed expression came over his handsome features. He reached out, stilling her from sitting up farther.

"What's wrong with *me?*" he asked dubiously.

She just stared at him, amazed. Disoriented.

"You passed out. Estelle Hardy called me down here. She knows we're friends. Mari, what the hell is wrong?

Estelle refused to tell me—patient confidentiality and all."

For a few seconds, she just stared at him, her mouth hanging open, the news Dr. Hardy had given her minutes ago striking her consciousness like a hammering blow.

"I'm pregnant," she blurted before she could stop herself. She wasn't telling him as much as repeating the shocking news to herself.

"You…you are?" She blinked and looked up into Eric's face. "It's…that's…wow," Eric finished feebly. He inhaled slowly, collecting himself. "I was beginning to wonder, given your symptoms."

"You were?" Mari asked. "Why didn't you say something?"

He shrugged helplessly. "I thought it seemed a little farfetched after you'd told me about breaking up with James five months ago," he said, referring to Mari's old boyfriend.

"James?" Mari repeated dully as if she'd never heard the name in her life.

"Yeah. *James Henry.* The guy you saw for four years?" Eric's grip tightened on her arm. "Mari, I think you need to lie down again. You're white as a sheet."

"No, no, I'm fine," she mumbled. She realized that she was just blankly staring at Eric's face again. It occurred to her he must be wondering who the father was—

Bewildering flashes of images, memories and feelings flooded her awareness, making it difficult for her to concentrate. She saw Marc standing there just inside the revolving doors of the Palmer House Hotel in Chicago, the sight of him striking her as thrilling and sad at once—thrilling, because he'd grown into such a beautiful man, just as she'd known he would; sad, because all evidence of the boy she'd once known was gone forever.

She recalled Marc's fierce, focused lovemaking last night, heard his husky voice.

Not just for tonight, Mari.

Another thought kept buzzing around her consciousness like a persistent fly.

This child was the grandchild of her parents—and of the man who had killed them.

She winced when another thought struck her as she slowly, carefully started to get off the examining table.

Not to mention that the only living grandparent would want nothing to do with my baby.

Mari operated on autopilot for the rest of the day. She straightened up the house for a showing at noon, then stopped by Natalie Reyes' office to pick up the employment contract for Allison Trainor. While she was there, she made an abbreviated copy of the contract so that she could show it to Colleen this afternoon, in case she was interested in the position.

She recalled while driving down Vista Pointe Drive that she'd told Marc she'd make dinner for him that night.

A wave of panic rose in her. She pulled the car over to the side of the road, put the vehicle in park and instinctively placed her hand on her belly in a protective gesture.

"I'm going to have a baby," she said out loud, needing to hear it, needing to let it seep into her consciousness. It didn't help much. Everything that had happened since the thunderstorm last night to the present moment had a surreal cast to it.

After she'd recovered from her faint this morning,

she'd actually sat down and had a discussion with the doctor. Dr. Hardy had made a recommendation for an obstetrician at Harbor Town Memorial, and her nurse had scheduled an appointment for Mari the following week. The information and advice Dr. Hardy had offered hadn't seemed to help pound the strange new reality into her brain, though.

It must be shock, Mari thought as she proceeded down the street again.

On the way home from the grocery store, she noticed she'd missed another call from her brother. She didn't call back. She didn't know if she could bear talking to Ryan when she carried such a volatile secret.

An hour's practice on her cello temporarily quieted the nagging, persistent question—*what am I going to do?*

In the shower, she examined her abdomen carefully, but there was no sign on the surface, anyway, of the miracle occurring in her body. A wondrous excitement rose up in her, and for a few seconds, she had a wild urge to run down the street and charge into the Kavanaugh house to share the news with Marc.

Reality sobered her quick enough, however. She finished showering, blow-dried her hair and dressed in a tangerine-colored linen skirt and matching tunic. She added a leather belt and slid into her favorite brown sandals.

She made some advanced preparations for a dinner she was both dreading and anticipating. Should she call Marc and cancel? It was going to be bad enough acting like she hadn't received earth-shattering news this morning in front of Colleen Kavanaugh, but how could she look at Marc and not blurt out the truth?

Her feelings continued to run the gamut from dread to excitement, numbness to exhilaration. It was crazy.

Mari supposed all the things she'd heard about pregnant women and their out-of-control emotions must be true. She was living proof.

At a quarter to five that afternoon, Mari heard a knock. She put the pitcher of herbal iced tea she'd just prepared into the refrigerator and hurried to the front door. Colleen stood on the porch wearing a pink sundress that showed off her golden tan. She smiled when Mari opened the screen door.

"I would have never thought you could get prettier than when you were eighteen, but I see you've gone and done the impossible."

"I could say the same for you." Mari laughed suddenly and shook her head, overwhelmed with happiness at seeing her old friend again. She waved Colleen inside. "Come in! I'm so pleased you—"

She paused when she saw Colleen glance worriedly toward the Kavanaugh house. "I was about to tell you, I ran over to ask if we could meet at my mother's? I was in the process of dropping Jenny off so Mom could watch her, but Mom's friend Mrs. Aichman called and asked if Mom could take her for her doctor's appointment. I would have just brought Jenny along, but she fell asleep at Mom's. She came down with a cold—it's kept her up for the past two nights—and I hate to wake her. She really needs the sleep. So that's why I'm here early."

Colleen faded in her pressured explanation. Her eyes sharpened on Mari's face.

"I can guess what you're thinking, Mari," Colleen said quietly. "No one else is home. Marc and Liam took Brendan to the beach this afternoon, and I doubt they'll be back for a while. And like I said, my mom just left to run Mrs. Aichman to the hospital."

Mari smiled, trying to hide her nervousness at the idea of stepping into the Kavanaugh house when she was quite sure she wouldn't be welcomed there by the owner.

"I completely understand about Jenny. Why don't we just reschedule our appointment?"

"Appointment?" Colleen said, blue-green eyes going wide. "You make it sound so official. I thought it was just a reacquaintance chat between two old friends."

Two old friends.

"If you're sure it'll be all right—"

"It'll be fine," Colleen assured. "Come on. Let's go catch up on the last fifteen years of our lives."

That's precisely what they attempted to do while sitting on the Kavanaugh's front porch sipping iced lemonade. Mari was having such a nice time chatting with Colleen that she realized an hour had passed, and she'd hardly worried about the news she'd received that morning. She also hadn't spoken to Colleen about The Family Center. She rectified that as soon as she made the realization.

Colleen listened, a sober expression settling slowly on her face as she listened to Mari try and put into words her plans for the money she'd received from the lawsuit so many years ago.

"You never touched any of that money?" Colleen asked in a hushed tone after Mari had talked nonstop for several minutes.

Mari shook her head. "You'll never know…" she began, pausing when her throat tightened uncooperatively. "You'll never know how many times I wondered what that money had been meant for before the lawsuit. Had it been saved for your college funds? Marc's law school? For Deidre's and your weddings, perhaps? Nest eggs for Kavanaugh grandchildren?" She met Colleen's stare and smiled despite the tear that had fallen down her cheek. "It was torture to consider it. I had loved all of you, in a way. I considered just giving my portion back—"

"No," Colleen quietly interrupted. "That wouldn't have been right. It would have offset the balance of things."

Mari's mouth fell open, stunned that Colleen had captured so succinctly the essence of her feelings.

Colleen stared at the glass of lemonade in her hand with a fierce focus.

"I accept the job offer," she said.

"You...you do?" Mari asked, surprised at her decisiveness.

Colleen nodded. "I'll look over the contract, of course. I'm not sure how much notice will be required at my current job, but yes—I want to do it." She glanced over at Mari and smiled. "It seems right somehow, you starting The Family Center and me working there. Like coming full circle."

Mari inhaled and laughed shakily.

"What?" Colleen asked.

"I'd forgotten how formidable you can be at times."

Colleen made a face. "Doesn't go with the blond hair, huh?"

They both laughed.

"There's one other thing you should know, Colleen, before you make your final decision."

"What?"

"Eric Reyes will be working at the Center, as well."

Colleen's amusement faded. "In a full-time capacity?" she asked.

"No, no," Mari assured. "He'll only be volunteering an afternoon or morning every week, but, given what happened in the parking lot the other night, I thought I should mention it."

"I see." She seemed to consider. "Well, I can get past it if he can. We don't have to be best friends to work together for a few hours a week."

Mari sighed with relief.

She caught movement out of the corner of her eye and saw Marc's car coming up Sycamore Avenue. Colleen's glance followed Mari's.

"I'm sorry, Mari," Colleen said.

She gave Colleen a smile of reassurance. Of course, Colleen didn't know what had been happening between her older brother and Mari, but she must have sensed the tension.

"It's okay," Mari assured her. "I was making dinner for Marc tonight, anyway."

"You were?" Colleen asked. She seemed pleased.

A moment later, Brendan bounded up the porch steps wearing swim trunks, flip-flops and a towel around his neck.

"Uncle Liam dared Uncle Marc to do a back somersault off the dunes, and he *did* it!" Brendan told his mom in a rush of excitement. He noticed Mari sitting next to his mother and said a polite hello before he launched into a description of his uncle's dive.

"Marc," Colleen scolded as her brothers came up the steps. "You're going to hurt yourself. You're too old to be doing stuff like that."

"That's what Liam thought," Marc replied. His cocky grin at his brother froze when he saw Mari sitting there.

She realized he hadn't noticed her because of the porch railings. Mari tried to look calm, but suspected she failed awfully. He was wearing a pair of board shorts, a white T-shirt and a pair of sunglasses. For just a few seconds, the man and the boy of her memories blended seamlessly.

"Hey, Mari," Liam greeted her pleasantly, as if it was the most natural thing in the world for them to find her there. "You should have come with us. Marc could have pulled off a double if you'd been watching."

He flinched and laughed when Marc flicked his towel at his calf.

"What?" Liam asked his brother, eyes wide with innocence. "That's the way it always worked, wasn't it? Mari Itani comes around, and Marc suddenly has to double anything he's doing...dive twice as high, swim twice as fast, flirt twice as much..."

"Tackle his brother twice as hard," Marc muttered under his breath as he came the rest of the way up the stairs.

"Man," Brendan muttered in awe as he looked at Mari. "You *should* come with us next time, Mari."

Colleen snorted, but Marc seemed to have forgotten Liam's teasing as he leaned against the rail, his arms loosely crossed, his stare on Mari.

"What are you doing here?"

"Catching up," Mari replied, nodding toward Colleen.

Marc nodded slowly, his laserlike gaze never wavering from her. "You never called me today."

"Oh..." She furtively glanced over at Colleen and Liam, suddenly feeling like she and Marc were in a spotlight on a stage. "I...I forgot."

His eyebrows arched. "Not about dinner, too, I hope."

"No," she replied, trying to be nonchalant. It was difficult with not only Liam and Colleen, but Brendan watching their exchange with apparent interest. Mari wondered if Brendan thought his uncle was going to do a double somersault from the porch to the front yard. "I went shopping earlier and have some salmon marinating in the fridge."

Liam clapped his hands together loudly. "Great. I love salmon."

"Shut up, Liam," Colleen said without heat.

Mari was staring at Marc and laughing when a vehicle pulled into the drive. She recognized Brigit behind the wheel and hopped up from her sitting position like she was on springs. She'd been enjoying herself so much she'd forgotten the time.

"I should be going," she said as she hurried toward the stairs.

Both Colleen and Marc called out to her. Ignoring them, she rushed down the steps. She realized she'd stood up too abruptly. It seemed as if she was walking underwater as she made her way down the sidewalk. Her sense of unreality only deepened when she heard a man's voice coming from down the street.

She knew that voice.

She peered at her house. Wearing jeans and a dark red T-shirt, her brother Ryan stood next to a blue car. He stared back. Even at this distance, she sensed his surprise…his shock. Her feet slowed. Her vision blurred.

Oh no…*not* again…not *now,* she thought in dazed irritation, recognizing the symptoms from this morning in Dr. Hardy's office.

Suddenly, a pair of arms encircled her from the back. Somehow, despite her disorientation, she knew it was Marc. She didn't resist when he took most of her weight and leaned her body back against the length of him.

"It's okay, Mari. I've got you. Take a some nice, easy breaths," Marc's voice rumbled near her ear.

She did what he said and soon the green canopy of the giant sycamore tree overhead resolved into separate, rustling leaves.

"I'm okay," she murmured. She tried to straighten and resume her flight from the Kavanaugh house. Marc allowed her to take her weight back on her feet, but he refused to move the circle of his arms from around her waist. In her new, upright position, she could see directly in front of her.

What she saw made her wish she'd passed out.

Brigit Kavanaugh stood to her right, her face pale and stony as she stared at them. To the left, her brother Ryan stalked down the sidewalk toward the scene. Despite her disorientation, she was so happy to see him. He was safe. Ryan was home. She gave a soft moan when she saw Eric Reyes jog up behind Ryan. She realized it was Eric's car her brother had stood next to a moment ago.

"Ryan? What are you doing here?" she asked through numb lips. She still wasn't entirely convinced she wasn't hallucinating.

Her brother's mouth was clamped tight in a straight line.

"I got sent home early," Ryan said stiffly. "I'll explain later. Let's get you home."

Out of the corner of her vision, she saw Brigit walk past them. Most of her attention was on her brother's fixed, furious expression as he looked over Mari's shoulder. She felt Marc's arms stiffen around her waist when Ryan reached toward her.

"Come on, Mari," Ryan said, never removing his gaze from the man who held her.

"Let go of her this instant, Marc. I don't want them here," Mari heard Brigit say behind them.

"You heard her," Ryan said in such a soft, deadly tone that Mari doubted anyone else heard him.

Still, Marc showed no signs of relaxing his hold. If anything, it seemed as if his arms hardened into steel bands.

"Mari?" she heard Marc ask from behind her.

"It's okay." She twisted until she caught a glimpse of his face. He looked every bit as tense and angry as Ryan. Every bit as dangerous, too.

"I said, *let* go," Ryan seethed.

Fear swept through her when she saw the blazing look of anger in Marc's eyes.

"I'm all right. Let go, Marc. *Please,*" she implored before he said something volatile and this whole keg of gunpowder exploded in their faces.

Marc's gaze flickered to her face. His arms slowly loosened around her.

Mari turned toward him and whispered without meeting Marc's eyes. "Maybe…maybe we ought to cancel for tonight."

Ryan grasped her hand and led her down the Kavanaugh's front walk, Eric joining them at the boundary of the Kavanaugh yard. She glanced back furtively as they reached the sidewalk. Looking young and bewildered, Brendan stood on the front steps. Brigit, Colleen and Liam Kavanaugh formed a semi-circle around Marc. Brigit appeared angry, Colleen and Liam tense.

Mari turned away. She didn't want to interpret the expression on Marc's face as he watched her walk away with Ryan and Eric on either side of her.

Chapter Nine

Mari glanced up after dinner that evening when her brother walked onto the shadow-draped terrace at the back of their house.

When they'd first arrived, Ryan had suggested that Mari go upstairs and rest following her episode of dizziness. Mari had insisted she wasn't an invalid, and that she wasn't going to go lay down when her brother was just returning home from a yearlong tour of duty in Afghanistan. She scolded him for not giving her warning about his early release, but Ryan said he'd wanted to surprise her. Apparently he and Eric—who were correspondents—had been conspiring over the matter. Ryan had wanted to return to Harbor Town to help Mari with The Family Center project. Her happiness at seeing Ryan home and healthy did a lot to ease her disappointment about what had happened at the Kavanaughs, but a sense of unease still lingered as her brother sat down across from her.

"It's strange to be back here, isn't it?" he murmured.

"Yeah, so many memories," she replied in a hushed tone.

A silence ensued. Ryan was six foot three inches tall, a hard-as-nails Air Force pilot, charming and courageous in equal measure. Nevertheless, Mari sensed how he hesitated to bring up the explosive topic of finding her in Marc Kavanaugh's arms. Mari had to admit, she was feeling uncertain around her brother, as well.

She suddenly regretted nothing more than blurting out that she was pregnant to Eric Reyes this morning. Had Eric told Ryan that volatile news on their drive to Harbor Town from the airport? If so, what conclusions was Ryan making? Mari could only imagine, as the news still didn't seem quite real to her, either.

Ryan nodded toward the overgrown trellis. "Dad's hydrangea finally took," he said.

Mari smiled in the darkness. "He fussed over that plant daily, remember? It looks like all it wanted was to be left alone," she said.

"Mari, what were you doing down at the Kavanaughs' house today?"

She blinked. Apparently memories of their father had dislodged the crucial question from Ryan's throat.

"I...I'd been visiting with Colleen. I've invited her to be the clinician and educator for The Family Center. She has excellent qualifications. She said yes." Enough light was leaking through the windows so that she could clearly see how tense Ryan's face had become. Mari slowly let out the air in her lungs. "I see you don't agree with my decision."

"I don't, but since when does that matter? I've always made it clear what I thought of you using all the lawsuit money for this. That money was meant for your future, Mari. Not for some philanthropic project."

"And yet you came," Mari challenged softly. She refused to start up their old disagreement now. What was the point? "You said you wanted to help."

"I do want to help. You. If it's important to you, then it's important to me."

"Thank you, Ryan."

"But I think it's a huge mistake to involve the Kavanaughs."

Mari sighed tiredly and her brother stirred.

"Forget about that damn Family Center and the Kavanaughs for the moment. Let's talk about you," Ryan said.

She glanced up warily. "Me? What about me?"

"Eric told me on the drive from Chicago that you haven't been feeling well. He said I should ask you about it."

"He…he didn't say anything else?"

"No. He didn't. But the moment I arrive in Harbor Town, the first thing I see is you running away from the Kavanaughs and nearly fainting in their front yard. What the hell is going on, Mari? Are you sick?"

"I'm fine. Really. I just… One second, Brigit Kavanaugh was pulling into the driveway and the next—"

Ryan leaned forward intently. "Has Mrs. Kavanaugh been giving you a hard time since you returned? She always did have a strong personality—"

"Ryan, let me finish," Mari interrupted sharply. Her brother clamped his mouth shut, but he still seemed agitated. Mari closed her eyes. This was the last thing she wanted. Ryan was her only living family. She hated the idea of arguing with him when she hadn't seen him for over a year. She was so thankful he was home and safe.

"What I was trying to say," Mari resumed in a quieter

voice, "is that I didn't plan on being, or want to be, at the Kavanaugh house when Brigit returned. I'd gotten up too abruptly from a sitting position, and then I looked down the street and saw you. The combination of all the things—the whole situation in general—made me a little dizzy, that's all."

"What about what Eric said?"

"Eric is worrying too much, Ryan," Mari said wearily. "This has been a whirlwind trip. I've had a lot to do."

"It's been too much for you. I'll take over the sale of the house. I can do anything you need done at the center, as well. Grass mowed, pictures hung, desks moved—I'm your guy."

Mari reached across the table and grabbed her brother's hand. "Thank you," she said earnestly. "You don't know how much that means to me, Ryan."

"Like I said. If it's important to you, I want to be here to help." Ryan's brow crinkled as he stared at her. "You look exhausted. Why don't you go to bed?"

"It's your first night back," Mari protested.

"I'm not going anywhere. At least not for a while. Not until the Air Force has decided I've had enough rest and relaxation and decides to ship me off again."

Dread settled in her belly like lead. "You've just completed your third tour. Surely they won't send you for a fourth?"

His dark eyes narrowed on her face. He seemed to regret his words. "Probably not, it just depends. One thing is for certain. I'm back for a long stretch, if not for good." He squeezed her hand. "Go on to bed. Come tomorrow, you can start ordering me around to do your grunt work."

Mari rolled her eyes and stood. Maybe Ryan was

right. She really did need some privacy to sort out her thoughts. She loved Ryan like crazy. How—and when— was she going to tell him that she was pregnant with Marc Kavanaugh's baby?

How and when was she going to tell *Marc,* for that matter?

She slowly went up the stairs to her bedroom feeling like the weight of the world was on her shoulders. She washed and brushed her teeth mechanically and remembered to take one of the prenatal vitamins Dr. Hardy had given her. When she got to her bedroom, she changed into a short, gold satin gown. The image of the Kavanaughs' tense faces as they stood in the front yard earlier suddenly rose in her mind's eye and caused a swooping sensation in her belly.

Maybe the wisest thing would be to say nothing to Marc at all. Was it really fair to subject a child to all the historical baggage and hurt that existed between their families?

The thought made her feel like two squeezing hands had wrapped around her throat.

She glanced at her bed. She envisioned their impassioned lovemaking last night. How fair was it to not tell Marc about his own child? She couldn't do that to him. She loved him too much.

Mari sat down heavily on the mattress and stared blankly into her open closet. It'd been the first time she'd admitted it to herself. Of course, she'd known she'd loved Marc once, but she'd been a girl…an infatuated, wide-eyed teenager. To acknowledge that the powerful force that throbbed in her breast at that moment was nothing less than the deep, passionate love of a grown woman shocked her to the core.

She was so stunned by her private admission that she was surprised to realize she had the capacity to be shocked even further. The branches on the old elm rustled in the stillness of the night, and Marc's face appeared outside her window.

"What in the world do you think you're doing?" Mari whispered when she'd opened the window.

She stepped back as Marc clambered across the sill. Marc tried to suppress his laughter when he met her stare. She'd looked poleaxed when she'd seen his face in the window.

"I couldn't think of how else to see you."

Mari made a repressive motion with her hand and walked over to a fan that sat on top of the dresser.

"For God's sake, why didn't you just knock on the front door?" Mari scolded him.

His amusement faded. He nodded significantly at the fan she'd turned on so that Ryan couldn't hear them speaking. "You really have to ask me that after what happened today?"

She placed her hands over her eyelids and sat on the edge of the bed. Guilt rushed through him when he realized how fragile she looked. His gaze lowered.

Fragile and beautiful. The little gown she wore left her smooth arms and legs bare and gifted him with the sight of her breasts pressed against very flimsy fabric. He yanked his eyes off the tempting sight of Mari sitting on a bed wearing next to nothing and tried to focus on what was important. She'd almost passed out cold on his mother's sidewalk today, and here he was gawking at her like a horny teenager.

He sat next to her on the bed. "I had to see if you were okay. I was worried."

"I'm fine," she said, sounding exasperated.

"You almost fainted today. What did you find out at the doctor's? Are you sick?"

He saw her throat convulse. "Dr. Hardy said I was perfectly healthy."

"Then why did you almost pass out?"

"Is it really that surprising?" she exclaimed, pulling her fingers away from her eyes and meeting his stare. "Your mother doesn't want me in her house any more than Ryan wants me to be there. This is a stupid, tangled-up mess and I can't believe I was so dumb as to put myself smack dab in the middle of it. I was an idiot to come back to this town!"

"You're not an idiot. You're compassionate and you're brave. I can't tell you how proud I am of you."

She just looked at him, her mouth gaping open in amazement. He resisted an urge to send his tongue through the tempting target of her lush, parted lips. He cleared his throat and forced himself to meet her incredulous stare. "Colleen told me about the center you plan to open for victims and survivors of substance abuse."

"She...she did?" Mari asked him slowly. "I wanted to be the one to tell you. I'm sorry."

He nodded. "Why didn't you tell me?"

"I was planning on doing just that, tonight at dinner," she whispered. "But then—"

"Ryan came home."

Mari nodded. When he saw how dull her usually brilliant eyes looked, he pulled her into his arms. She held herself stiff at first, but as he stroked her back, he felt her muscles begin to mold against his body. He didn't think she was crying, but he sensed she needed comforting, nonetheless. He felt a measure of satisfaction when her arms surrounded his waist.

It must have been a hell of a day for her.

Neither of them spoke for a minute or two, but he had never been more aware of another human being in his life. He held her against him, all the while thinking of her saving that lawsuit money got for all those years and slowly coming up with the plan for The Family Center.

He nuzzled her temple, inhaling the fresh, citrus scent of her hair, urging her to lean back and look at him. She complied. He stared down at her lovely face, glad to see some of her typical vitality had returned to her eyes.

"All these years, I thought maybe you'd forgotten Harbor Town."

"How could I ever forget this place?" she whispered. "It was the place where I'd been the happiest I've ever been in my life…and the saddest. It was the place where I'd lost the most."

He kissed her softly. Her lips felt warm and responsive beneath his.

"And you came back to try and make some sense out of it all," he said next to her mouth a moment later. "To give some purpose to a random, meaningless act that should never have happened." He shook his head slightly, still half in awe. "You're incredible, Mari."

"I'm not incredible. I'm beginning to think it was all a mistake."

"No. It wasn't a mistake," Marc said steadfastly. "I want to help you with it, if I can."

"You do?" she looked up at him, her golden-brown eyes huge in her face.

"Does that surprise you?"

"No. Yes. A little." She bit at her lower lip. "Ryan wants to help, too."

"Does he?" Marc asked, not paying as much attention as he should because he was still enthralled by the vision of Mari's white teeth scraping across her damp, plump lower lip. He blinked when he realized she was staring at him, her brow arched in a query. "Oh," he said as understanding dawned. "So you're foreseeing conflict between the Itanis and the Kavanaughs if we try to work together on this project."

"It did cross my mind."

"It could potentially be a land mine," Marc conceded after a moment.

"It seems like I've done nothing but navigate around a land mine since returning to Harbor Town," Mari admitted bitterly.

"Which brings me to the reason I climbed your tree tonight."

She gave him a wry glance. "I thought you did that because you're an idiot."

He smiled good-naturedly and flicked his eyebrows. "In addition to that. See, it struck me sometime today—maybe it was as your brother came to save you from the evil Kavanaughs—that you and I really need to get out of this town. Just for a few days," he added when she looked at him like he was crazy.

"Marc, I have a million things to do in order to get things started with the Center before I leave the week after next. The last thing I should be considering is leaving town."

"You just said that Ryan was going to help, and Colleen is on board now. Once Liam hears about the news, he'll likely volunteer some of his time. And I'm assuming Eric Reyes is involved in the project?"

Mari nodded doubtfully. "And his sister, Natalie. You remember her?"

Marc closed his eyes briefly and glanced away. He'd remember the young girl who'd been injured and scarred by the crash until the day he died.

"Of course I remember," he mumbled. "You're making my whole point, Mari."

"What do you mean?" she asked, obviously bewildered.

"You said you'd give this a chance," he murmured as he flicked his finger between them. "But *I* don't stand a chance with you while we're here in Harbor Town. There are too many obstacles. Too many memories. It's not a fair playing field."

"So what do you suggest?" she asked, looking wary.

"That you come to Chicago with me this weekend. Just for two nights," he added quickly when he saw her mouth open to argue. "There's nothing that can't be taken care of at The Family Center for a couple days without you."

"I can't, Marc!" she exclaimed. "Ryan just got home!"

"We won't be leaving for a few days, and you'll be back by Sunday," he reminded her. "Ryan is home for a while, isn't he?"

Mari nodded reluctantly.

When he sensed her wavering, he pulled out all his ammunition. He pressed his forehead against hers and kissed the end of her perfect nose. "Don't you think you owe it to yourself to get away from all the distractions for a period of time and just focus on us? Wouldn't you regret knowing that you'd never found out...*for sure?*"

She leaned back slightly, and he saw a world of doubt and longing in her eyes.

"I let you go once, because I thought I didn't have a choice," he whispered hoarsely. "I'm not willing to do that again. If you spend this time with me in Chicago, and you decide to walk away, I'll accept it. But I'm not willing to let you go this time until I know for sure you're certain, *absolutely* certain, that it's what you want. How else can you know that until you spend some time away with me, away from all the history of this town and the people? It's almost impossible to figure out here with everything and everyone around us."

He put his hand on the back of her head and tilted it forward, so that their foreheads once again met and their breaths mingled. Her long hair fell like a drape around them, increasing the sense of solemn intimacy.

"It's only fair, Mari."

"You always could talk me into anything," she whispered.

He smiled slowly.

"Don't be so cocky, Kavanaugh. I'm not so sure I'm happy about that fact," she added. "I can't seem to think straight around you."

"Come to Chicago with me," he entreated in a hoarse whisper.

She bit nervously at her lip. He waited on tenterhooks.

"Okay."

He seized her mouth with his own. He'd waited for that acquiescence. Now that he had it, he didn't bother to hide his hunger for her. She moaned softly when his tongue probed the sweet cavern of her mouth.

She sealed their torrid kiss a moment later, panting.

"Marc...if I go with you, you have to give me some space. I meant it when I said I can't think straight around you. I want to make a well-thought-out decision about whether or not we can have a future. I can't do that if you're always...doing that."

"Doing what?" he asked silkily as he plucked at her lips.

She joined him, despite her protestations, seeking out his mouth, sliding her tongue teasingly against his lower lip until he groaned and kissed her deeply once again. She tasted wonderful, like peppermint and woman and sex. He spread his hands over her satiny-smooth shoulders and pressed her down to the mattress. He came down over her, kissing her all the while, coaxing her until his body throbbed with a dull, insistent ache. Her breasts were a delicious, soft firmness against his ribs.

"*This,*" Mari hissed a moment later against his mouth.

It took his lust-drunk brain a few seconds to understand what she meant. When he recalled their former conversation, he sighed and sat up, trying to ignore the tempting vision she made lying on the bed with her hair spread out around her and her breasts heaving beneath the thin, gold fabric.

She stood and tried to smooth her hair, which Marc had mussed with his fingertips. He watched her, scowling, as she went over to her closet and withdrew a robe. His frown only deepened when she covered herself. She was all serious business by the time she belted the garment with a defiant tug.

"I won't agree to go with you on this trip if you continue to do that, Marc."

"What? Do the most natural thing on earth?" he asked, trying to hide his irritation and failing.

"I'm serious," she said so loudly that he started. He narrowed his eyes on her. She looked desperate. "We both know we're sexually compatible. That's the easy part," she said, the stain on her cheeks deepening. "You brought up this proposition. If you truly want to discover if we have a future together, then we need to do more than…roll around in bed together."

His annoyance evaporated when he saw how nervously her hands moved over her belly. He sensed her fragility in that moment. "All right. If that's what you want, you've got it. I promise to follow your lead in regard to the…rolling around in bed."

She flashed him an irritated glance, but when she saw his smile, she broke into a grin, as well.

"Do you really want to do this?" he asked her.

"Yes. I'll go—if you promise not to push me." She glanced up at him through thick lashes, her gaze flickering down over his chest and abdomen and sighed. "You're very hard to resist."

He leaned back, his arms bracing him on the mattress.

Patience was what was called for with Mari, but he'd never had to tamp down his lust more than this. Maybe he was as aware as she seemed to be that when they made love, no barriers could exist between them. He supposed Mari was saying that some of those obstacles existed for a reason—they were a defense against hurt, against bad judgment.

She had to let down those barriers at her own pace, not his. He wasn't planning on hurting Mari, of course. Look at what'd happened today at his mom's house, though. Marc hadn't wanted that. Pain seemed to be inherent to any scenario that involved Mari and him together.

He was willing to deal with that potential pain, but Mari had to decide on her own if she was willing to endure the bad that might come with the good.

"I guess there are worse things than you finding me irresistible," he murmured ruefully.

She ducked her head, hiding her smile. "Much. But for now…" She nodded significantly toward the window. "Don't break your neck on the way down, Tarzan."

Marc grimaced as he stood and headed toward the window. He was still hard with arousal. "A broken bone might get my mind off some other aches," he said under his breath.

"What?"

"Nothing," he said as he threw one leg out the window and paused, straddling the low sill, his head still inside Mari's room. She watched him with a small smile, her arms crossed beneath her breasts.

"You're sure you want me to go?"

"Quite sure."

"Do you want me to help you out with anything tomorrow?"

She considered for a moment, her mouth pursed. "You could babysit Jenny and Brendan for Colleen. That way we could go over her contract, and I could show her around the facility after she gets off work."

Her eyebrows arched when he frowned. She obviously guessed that he'd have preferred to help out with something a little more hands-on in Mari's company.

"Okay, I'll take Jenny and Brendan to the beach," he conceded. His gaze sharpened on her. "But come Friday morning, we're leaving Harbor Town and everything in it behind for a few days, agreed?"

"Agreed," Mari said.

Marc hesitated when he saw her expression. "Come here," he said after a moment.

She approached the window slowly. When he palmed her jaw he saw tears swell in her eyes.

"What's wrong?" he whispered. "Why do you look so serious?"

"I just don't want to screw up things any further than they already are."

He placed a hand on her hip and leaned forward, pressing a kiss just below her ribs.

"I know you've felt lonely for a long time now," he told her. "But you're not going to be standing alone this time. I promise."

He placed another kiss on her upper abdomen and felt a shudder go through her. He kept his face pressed just below the fullness of her breasts for a few seconds. She smelled so good he needed to concentrate all of his will in order to leave. After a moment, he lifted his head and looked up at her face. She watched him with liquid, fathomless eyes.

"Okay?" he whispered.

She nodded. He leaned forward and kissed her once more—this time on the naked skin above her left breast—and ducked out of the window.

Chapter Ten

Mari arrived at the facility the following afternoon and exclaimed in pleasure when she saw all the bushes and flowers that had been planted. As she alighted from the car, Mari caught a glimpse of her brother carrying a shovel and walking toward the back of the building. Eric Reyes, on the other hand, was crouching and maneuvering a lilac bush into the newly dug earth. He stood as she approached and waved.

"It looks fantastic," Mari enthused. "I can't believe how much you and Ryan have done."

"It's coming along," Eric agreed as he removed a pair of gloves. They were practically the only things he was wearing, besides a pair of shorts, socks and tennis shoes. The sun had deepened his muscular torso to a dark bronze. Mari glanced around when she heard the sound of another car pulling into the lot. Eric's expression stiffened when he saw Colleen step out of the car and start toward them. Mari knew the second Colleen recognized Eric because she halted momentarily and kicked up a few pieces of gravel before she resumed walking.

Mari cleared her throat, acutely aware of the tension in the air as Colleen joined them.

"You two are going to be working together in the future. I'm hoping you'll end up respecting each other as much as I respect both of you," Mari said after she'd greeted Colleen.

She glanced at Colleen, whose chin was slightly raised as she regarded Eric. His expression was also rigid.

Suddenly he smiled, his white teeth flashing in his tanned face. "It's not going to be me starting any fights," he said significantly. "Welcome to The Family Center, Colleen. From what Mari tells me, we're lucky to get you."

Colleen looked a little taken aback, as if she was deciding which parts of Eric's greeting were sarcastic and which parts genuine. "Thank you," she murmured.

Mari sighed and led Colleen into the building to show her around, hoping fervently she hadn't made a mistake by involving both of them. But the fact was, she trusted Colleen and Eric implicitly. It was their working *together* that created some cause for concern.

After they'd toured the facility and Colleen had chosen an office, they sat down together to go over the employment contract.

"Mari… I'll have to tell my mom about the job soon," Colleen said when they were wrapping things up an hour later. "From some of the things you've said so far, I've gotten the impression you were trying to keep the Center under wraps for the time being. Is it okay with you that Mom knows?"

Mari paused in the action of putting a stack of papers

into her briefcase. "Of course you should tell her," she said firmly, although it was trepidation that filled her, not confidence. "She'll have to find out sometime, right? It's inevitable."

"I thought…perhaps *you'd* like to tell her," Colleen said cautiously.

"*Me?* I don't think that's a very good idea. You saw yesterday how your mom feels about me." She sighed when she saw Colleen's worried expression. "Look, I'd like to think that the news about The Family Center will be welcome to Brigit, but I have a feeling she might view it as an insult."

"An insult?" Colleen asked.

Mari nodded. "I hope she doesn't, of course. But that's been haunting me, that your mother might see me starting this project as a sort of sanctimonious slap to the face. It's her town, after all. She might consider it intrusive, as if I'm purposefully throwing the crash into the spotlight again…re-opening old wounds."

"But you're trying to *heal* old wounds. This project is about the future, not the past," Colleen exclaimed.

"I'm so glad you see it that way. But you must see what I mean. Not everyone will agree."

"Like your brother?"

Mari sighed. "Yeah. Like Ryan. He also believes the past should remain safely buried and contained."

Colleen inhaled deeply. "Well, we'll just have to take it one day at a time. People have their opinions, it's human nature. Just because everyone in Harbor Town isn't on board initially doesn't mean we can't change their mind. They'll come around once they see the positive things that come out of The Family Center. The proof is in the pudding, right?"

Mari chuckled, feeling a little less weary. "Bless you, Colleen."

A few minutes later, Colleen checked her watch and gasped. "Look at the time. I'd better get back to make the kids something, or Uncle Marc will have already fed them pizza and Cheetos or something."

"He's not that bad, is he?" Mari asked, grinning.

"No, in all fairness, he's not. Marc would probably throw in an apple and make them drink milk, along with their Cheetos. Liam, on the other hand, thinks pizza ought to be served for breakfast, lunch and dinner, and Brendan totally agrees." Colleen paused in the process of getting her keys out of her purse and glanced at Mari speculatively. "Marc told me you were going with him to Chicago this weekend."

"He did?" Mari asked weakly.

Colleen's aquamarine eyes sparkled. "Yeah. And I think it's a brilliant idea."

"Really?"

"Do you know how rare it is to be given a second chance with someone?" Colleen asked, suddenly sober.

"Colleen, I've meant to say… I'm so sorry about your husband. I wanted to tell you yesterday, but I just never got around—"

Mari was reminded of Colleen's courage when she smiled and stood. "There's no need to apologize, Mari. Darin and I had some wonderful years together. I cherish every moment I had with him. You and Marc should do the same."

"It's hard," Mari admitted. "The future can be so uncertain."

"All the more reason to grab your chance at happiness while you can. I'll talk to you soon," Colleen said before she left the room.

After Colleen was gone, Mari lingered, thinking

about what she'd said. If she looked at it from Colleen's point of view, everything seemed so certain, so clear.

But it wasn't all that cut-and-dried, was it?

Marc had recently been through a divorce. He'd said that a serious relationship or marriage was the farthest thing from his mind. The pregnancy had come from a wild, impulsive moment. What if he wasn't pleased by the news? It was one thing for him to say he wanted to be with her, even when he'd formerly planned to be cautious in the dating arena, but suddenly being strapped with a relationship and a baby was another thing altogether.

Mari locked up the offices, but her thoughtful mood made her stroll toward the woods and the dunes instead of immediately getting in her car. She walked the length of Silver Dune and paused, staring out at the vast, blue lake. The wind whipped her hair around her face. She pictured standing next to Marc on that ledge fifteen years ago.

Stop thinking so much, Mari. Just jump.

Mari wished it was all that simple.

She kept herself busy that night and the following day. Distracting herself with plans and projects for the Center helped her from ruminating on her worries about Marc, the baby, Brigit, Ryan and a dozen other things.

By the time twilight fell on Thursday evening, Mari knew she was going to have to confront Ryan about her plans to go away with Marc the next day. She broke the news while they were cleaning up in the kitchen after dinner.

"A weekend in Chicago?" he asked slowly. "That sounds serious."

"It is, I think," Mari admitted.

"How serious?" Ryan asked, his dark brows drawn together in concern and growing anger.

"Ryan, you're going to have to trust me on this."

"I *do* trust you. I don't trust Kavanaugh. Can't you see the end result isn't going to be good?" he demanded. "There's too much garbage in your pasts, Mari. You deserve something better than that."

"I want to do this. I *need* to do this."

Ryan straightened abruptly from where he'd been leaning on the counter. "His father murdered Mom and Dad. How can you even consider a future with Marc Kavanaugh?"

"It wasn't murder," Mari countered, just as heatedly. "It was an accident!"

"It was reckless *homicide*," Ryan boomed.

For a few seconds, Mari just stood there as her brother's retort echoed in her ears.

"How long?" she asked eventually. When Ryan just pinned her with a furious stare, Mari persisted in a low, trembling voice. "How long are you going to hold on to your anger, Ryan? Mom and Dad are gone. Your anger isn't going to bring them back."

"At least I'm respecting their memory," Ryan said stiffly before he tossed the dish towel on the counter, "which is a damn sight more than you're doing by climbing into bed with Marc Kavanaugh."

Mari didn't get much rest that night. She'd only been asleep for a few hours when she was awakened by the sound of her bedroom window scraping open. A scream building in her throat, she sat up in bed.

"Shhh, it's me."

"Marc Kavanaugh," she scolded in a low, vibrating voice, "I'm going to chop down that elm tree. You scared the daylights out of me. What do you think you're doing?"

"It's Friday morning," he said in a hushed tone. In the

darkness, she saw the shadow of his tall body squeezing agilely through the window.

"It's not even dawn yet," she hissed.

"It's going to be soon. We have to hurry. Come on, get up."

Mari barely suppressed a squawk when he came over to the bed and pulled the sheet off her.

"Have you packed already?"

"Yes, but—"

"Great. I'll take your stuff out to the car while you shower."

Mari blinked when he turned on the bedside lamp. Her mouth was open to protest. But when she saw him— wearing a pair of jeans and a light gray collarless shirt, his hair adorably mussed on his forehead from his tree climbing—he looked so excited and so damn appealing, her irritation faded into mist.

She got out of bed, scowling. She didn't want him to know how attractive she found him at that moment. He already had more power over her than she preferred. "Okay, but this better be worth it. I just got to sleep a couple of hours ago."

"I'll make it up to you. I promise," he said. Pointedly urging her toward the shower, he nodded at the door.

She thought for sure Marc was going to spirit her away to Chicago the second they were both in his car. He surprised her by heading first to The Tap and Grill and returning with a coffee for each of them before turning toward Main Street Harbor.

"Where are we going?" she whispered when Marc told her to leave her purse in the car. Dawn hadn't broken yet. The quiet night and her unexpected awakening had created a hushed, tense feeling of expectation inside her.

"Colleen's boat," he said as they hurried down a long dock, Mari's hand in his. "It used to be Darin's."

"What...? We're going to cross Lake Michigan to get to Chicago?"

Marc's derisive snort was her only answer. Once they reached a moored speedboat, Mari didn't argue when Marc told her to sit down and relax. It would be another hot summer day once the sun rose, but the pre-dawn air was mild and pleasant. A light breeze tickled her cheek as she listened to Marc untie the craft and start the boat.

Within a matter of a few minutes, they'd passed the buoys designating the harbor, and Marc released the throttle. Her curiosity would have to wait. He'd never hear her questions over the roar of the engine. Mari watched the lights of Harbor Town slowly slide to the right of her vision as the boat cut through the water.

Mari studied Marc's silhouette in the darkness when the boat slowed. He was sitting on the back of the seat instead of in it. She realized he was searching for some landmark on the shore.

He abruptly cut the motor, and only the sound of gentle waves slapping against the side of the boat entered her ears.

"This is it," Marc said.

"This is *what?*"

"Come here."

She stood and grasped his outstretched hand. He guided her to the seat in front of him. From that position, Marc was directly behind her, his legs bent on either side of her. He placed one hand on her shoulder and the other along her cheek. He applied a slight pressure until Mari turned her head toward shore.

"Right about there," Marc murmured from above her. The sun had started to rise. Mari could make out the huge shadow of a dune in the distance. She glanced to the right, gauging the distance to Harbor Town.

"It's Silver Dune," she whispered.

"Yeah," Marc replied.

A warm wind whisked past them. Mari shivered, not from the breeze, but from the feeling of Marc's left hand moving along her neck. She went still when he caressed her jaw with his fingertips. When she realized how concentrated her awareness was on the sensation of him close behind her, his legs surrounding her, his stroking hand, Mari rolled her eyes in the darkness. You'd think she was a sixteen-year-old on her first date.

"So what are we doing?" she whispered.

"Watching the sun rise over Silver Dune."

"Why?"

He pressed back on her shoulder, and her head fell in the juncture of his spread legs. Her eyes sprung wide. The location where she her head rested wasn't really decent, but Marc sounded casual enough when he spoke.

"Why not?"

Mari tried to attend to the sunrise, but it was difficult to do, surrounded by Marc's scent and heat. The waves gently rocked them, and Marc stroked her neck and shoulder in the most distracting manner. Slowly, the sky behind the black dune began to turn silver and then to muted gold tinted with rose. Neither of them spoke as they watched the crimson orb of the sun top the horizon and then creep through the woods beyond the sand dune. The trees seemed ablaze. Mari saw a structure in the far distance through the trees and gasped.

"What?" Marc asked gruffly from behind her. His voice sounded close, like he'd leaned close.

Mari twisted her head to try and see him. He groaned, and she realized why. When she hastily tried to lift her head from between his thighs, he rested his hands on her shoulders and kept her in place.

"I can see The Family Center," Mari said quietly.

"I know. I can, too."

The sun topped the tall trees at the top of the dunes and sent its warming rays onto a pale blue, shimmering lake.

"Everyone comes to Harbor Town for the sunsets," Mari murmured after a moment. "But the sunrises are just as beautiful."

"I wanted you to see one."

Mari glanced over at the small town perched on the shore. It looked perfect and fresh, cast in the golden light of dawn. She set down her coffee cup and turned in the seat. When Marc saw what she was doing, he steadied her while she rose to her knees in front of him. His small grin faded the instant before she pressed her mouth to his.

When she leaned back a moment later, and Marc stared down at her, she saw the sunrise reflecting in his blue eyes like glowing embers.

"I know what you wanted me to see," she whispered.

"Do you?"

She nodded and pressed her lips fleetingly to his once again. "You wanted me to see things in a whole new light." She inspected him somberly. "I'm trying, Marc."

He opened his hand along her neck and stroked the line of her jaw with his thumb. "That's all I ask," he said. He nodded toward the shore. When Mari turned, he put his arms around her shoulders and pulled her back against him. "Don't you think that'd be a perfect spot for a memorial?"

"A memorial?" Mari murmured, her cheek pressed against his chest.

"Yeah. A memorial for the survivors of substance abuse. A fountain, maybe, set there at the edge of the trees on the promontory of the dune?"

"It would be. It'd be like a sanctuary, a place to think or pray…"

A place to heal, Mari added in her mind.

"I want to sponsor it," he murmured.

She twisted around and gazed up at him. "You don't have to—"

"I know that," he interrupted. "You don't *have* to do what you're doing, either. Not that this compares to what you're doing, not in the slightest. But it's something I'd like to do, if you'd let me."

"Of course. It's a beautiful idea." She put her arms around his waist and he embraced her in return.

For a few minutes, they bobbed on the blue lake and held each other fast, drinking in the rays of the new day. After a while, he leaned back slightly and put his hand beneath her chin. He tilted her face up and kissed her, chastely at first, but then, as their tastes mingled, with all the focused, fierce passion she associated exclusively with Marc.

"We'd better get going," he said next to her lips a while later.

Looking into his gleaming eyes, she nodded. She took her own seat as Marc started up the boat again.

They returned to the same town she'd known and remembered, but thanks to Marc, Harbor Town looked a little different now in her eyes.

Due to her sleeplessness last night, Mari found herself drifting off when they were only fifteen minutes away from Chicago. When she awoke, they were driving down

Lake Shore Drive with the city to the left and the deep blue lake shimmering to the right of them. She was still blinking into wakefulness when Marc turned off onto Randolph Street. He'd only driven west a half block before he pulled into the parking garage of a high-rise.

"You ready?" Marc asked her a few seconds later, after he'd parked.

Mari nodded, suddenly feeling a little giddy with the excitement of their weekend getaway. He grabbed their bags and led her to an elevator. They stopped in the luxurious, residential lobby so that Marc could collect his mail.

Mari observed with fascination the way Marc transformed from a sun-tanned, easygoing vacationer to a confident, big-city state's attorney right before her eyes. It wasn't a huge change, granted, and he didn't behave any differently in the slightest. The nod of respect a few residents granted him as he picked up a package from his doorman and the wistful, backward glance one attractive, middle-aged woman cast his way allowed Mari to see this different shade to Marc's complex character.

He introduced her to his doorman, Oscar. Oscar treated Marc with equal parts friendliness and deference and seemed to know all sorts of intimate details about Marc's life.

"I've known Mari since I was eleven years old," Marc admitted to Oscar as Mari and the doorman shook hands.

"Oh, the dirt you must have on him," Oscar said with a wink.

Mari opened her mouth, but Marc hastily grabbed her hand and led her away. The sound of Oscar's laughter echoed behind them.

Marc's condo was large and featured a breathtaking lake view. It was decorated in a sparse, austere fashion that she usually associated with a busy man living alone. In Marc's case, though, it didn't strike her as cold, but as utilitarian and elegant in its simplicity. The only contrast to the strong lines and gray-and-beige decor was a wildflower arrangement that sat on the teak dining room table. Mari walked over to it. The huge display looked brilliant with Lake Michigan as its backdrop.

She smiled as she touched a delicate bloom. "The purple iris and yellow daisy," she murmured in amazement. "They're my favorite flowers. I always loved how the yellow was cheerful and the purple was so pensive. Like sun and shade," she murmured, a smile on her lips.

She glanced down and saw a small card leaning against the vase with the words written on it in black ink, *Welcome Mari.*

"How did you know they were my favorites?" she whispered to Marc, who stood watching her from the head of the table.

"I once saw flowers like that pressed on the inside of one of my mother's flower books," he said. "On the wax covering them, she'd written, Mari's favorites, sun and shade."

"Your mother saved them," she said huskily after a moment, touching a soft bloom.

"Yes."

Once the burn of tears had eased, she glanced at him. "Thank you, Marc."

He shrugged. "My assistant, Adrian, deserves the credit for finding them. I don't know how that woman is able to pull off half the things she does."

She smiled. She knew he was trying to play down the surge of emotion she'd experienced, and she loved him for that.

"Come on. I'll show you your room," he said.

He grabbed her suitcase and showed her into what was obviously a guest bedroom, given the lack of personal items on the dresser and bedside tables. Despite its relative bareness, it was still a well-appointed room featuring a lake view and brilliant sunshine flooding through floor-to-ceiling windows. She caught Marc's eye as he turned from setting her suitcase on a low bench. He raised his brows when he saw her amazed, amused expression.

"You didn't actually expect that I was going to put you in my bedroom, did you?" he asked.

"Honestly? I did," Mari said with a laugh as she began to unzip her suitcase.

"Does that mean you wouldn't have minded?"

Mari blinked at the sound of his low voice. He sounded much closer than he had been just a second ago. She glanced over her shoulder and saw him watching her, the hint of a grin on his mouth.

"I would have minded," she told him with a stern look that was ruined by a smile. She turned back to unzipping her suitcase. "In fact, I appreciate you not pressing me about sharing a bedroom. This room is lovely, thank you."

"I'll just let you unpack then," he murmured.

Mari didn't look up until she sensed his tall figure exiting the doorway. If he only knew how much she wanted to surrender completely to the sensual promise in his hot, blue eyes.

Chapter Eleven

He was sitting on the L-shaped couch in the living room, sorting through a small mountain of mail, when she joined him. Briefs and memos nearly bursting out of the supple leather, a case sat next to him on the cushions. He glanced up at her when she sat in the corner of the couch.

"You must have a million things to catch up on with work after being away for a week," she observed.

He carelessly tossed a thick, white envelope onto the wood and glass coffee table.

"To hell with work." He stood and transferred to the cushion next to Mari. He grabbed her hand. "I'm still on vacation."

She laughed. "You needn't feel like you have to entertain me. You woke me up so early this morning, it's not even lunchtime, yet. Work for a while, if you need to. I can only imagine how demanding your job is."

He squeezed her hand. "If you think I'm going to work when I've finally gotten you all to myself, you're nuts."

She started to protest and noticed the way his eyes were fixed on her mouth. She inhaled and caught the hint of his spicy cologne. Heat slowly expanded in her lower belly, a sensation she seemed to always experience in Marc's presence. She covered the hand that held hers and began to idly stroke his index finger, liking how large and different he felt in comparison to her.

"What are we going to do then?" she asked idly.

When he didn't immediately respond, her gaze flew to meet his. He'd been studying her averted cheek and exposed neck like he'd been considering taking a bite out of her. She tried to ignore the thrill that went through her at the thought.

"How about if we take a walk, have lunch somewhere and come back for a swim. There's a nice pool on the roof deck," he muttered.

Mari couldn't help but notice he seemed much more interested in her lips than the plan he proposed. "Okay."

"Mari?"

"Yes?" she asked breathlessly.

"If you keep doing that to my finger, we're not going anywhere."

Mari froze. She looked at their hands resting on the cushion. He'd covered her left hand, but she'd curled the fingers of her right hand around his index finger and had been stroking him slowly. It had taken Marc's heavy-lidded stare and spoken warning to make her realize how suggestive the caress must have seemed.

She released him and stood abruptly.

"I'll just go change then, for our walk." She didn't wait for him to respond before she hurried out of the room.

Mari hadn't been to Chicago for any extended stays since she was a child. She'd come for performances with the orchestra on several occasions, of course, but was usually too tired from traveling, practices and the performance to see much of anything but the interior of Orchestra Hall and her hotel room. She'd forgotten what a lovely city it was sitting next to the topaz jewel of Lake Michigan. Its towering, glittering high-rises and big-city sophistication blended seamlessly with the Midwestern friendliness of its residents.

They walked north along the lakefront among bikers, skaters, joggers and beach-goers. Such a vast sampling of humanity rolled by Mari's view that she challenged herself to be objective in her assessment of the man who walked next to her in comparison. That jogger, for instance, had Marc's height and lean, muscular build, but he didn't move with the confident, easy grace of a born athlete like Marc did. A dark-haired man with an intense, handsome face held his girlfriend's hand as they walked in the other direction, but he didn't look down at his companion with a hot gaze that could make a woman feel like she was the only female on the planet.

"What?" Marc asked when he caught her trying to covertly study him.

"Nothing," Mari said. She tried to hide her smile.

He started laughing at her mysteriousness, and she joined him.

She was being a fool, and she knew it. Wasn't that what they said love did to you?

They walked all the way to Lincoln Park on the lakefront and ate lunch at a little bistro in the park. Afterward, they wandered around the Lincoln Park Zoo without any serious intent and paused at whatever caught their eye. Marc bought her a lemonade, and Mari happily sipped it while she watched from a below-water-level window as a playful polar bear swam back and forth.

"They say humans project all sorts of things onto animals, but I would swear that bear is flirting with you," Marc mused.

Showing off his sidestroke in front of the viewing window, the frisky polar bear plunged in the other direction in the water. It did appear as if he was staring directly at Mari.

Mari glanced at Marc, and merriment swelled inside her. "Jealous?" she murmured.

He just muttered under his breath, grabbed her hand and led her away from the adorable, amorous bear.

On the way back to Marc's, they window-shopped in boutiques on Rush and Oak Street. When Mari saw a swim-and-dive shop, she asked Marc if they could go inside.

"Didn't you bring along the gold swimming suit?" Marc asked when he saw her holding up a sleek mail-lot.

"Yes," Mari murmured distractedly. "But I'd feel like an idiot wearing that thing in public."

She glanced up when he made a disgusted sound. "You're not going to buy a *one-piece,* are you?" he asked, sounding like she was considering the ultimate sellout.

She just gave him a condemning glance and kept browsing. She lost track of what he was doing, but he reappeared by her side a few minutes later.

"Here. How about this one. It's not quite so skimpy, but it's sexy as hell, like something a James Bond woman would wear," he growled near her ear.

Mari glanced over and saw him dangling a white bikini on his index finger. An innocent smile crossed his face.

"It'll look great with your tan," he coaxed.

"All right. You have good taste," Mari conceded after a moment. The suit really was cute and had a good deal more coverage than Deidre's bikini. She reached for it, but Marc yanked it away.

"I'll get it for you. What?" he asked when she protested. "It's the only time a woman has ever told me I had good taste in clothing. I want to be able to brag about it every time I see you in it."

A few minutes later they exited the air-conditioned boutique and stepped into the sweltering heat of the midday sun.

"Let's catch a cab home," Marc suggested, already stepping to the curb in search of a taxi. They were back inside his pleasantly cool condominium within fifteen minutes.

"Do you want anything to drink before we go up to the pool?" Marc offered as he headed directly to the kitchen.

"No, thanks. I'm going to change."

Marc had more than good taste when it came to swimsuits. He knew her coloring and figure to a T. The suit not only fit her perfectly, but it played up all her assets without seeming indecent. The halter-style bra had sufficient padding in it to make her feel covered but still managed to shape her breasts in a flattering manner, creating a sexy, but tasteful, décolletage. The bottoms were very abbreviated boy shorts that hugged her hips and rode low on her belly. Mari turned back and forth in front of the mirror in the guest bath, inspecting her stomach critically. Was it, indeed, swelling a fraction of an inch farther than its usual limit? She didn't *think* so, but maybe…

"Mari? You almost ready?" Marc called down the hallway.

Mari started, her hand perched just below the slight convexity of her belly. It all hit her in a rush again; that was *Marc Kavanaugh* calling for her to join him.

She was cradling the tiny beginnings of their baby in her palm.

"I'll be right out," she shouted.

She scurried into her sundress and studied her face in the bathroom mirror. When Dr. Hardy had consulted with her, she'd mentioned that many women chose to wait to tell family members, friends and acquaintances about their pregnancies until after the eighth week. Miscarriages could occur, and if everyone already knew about the pregnancy, it made it all that much more difficult to have to break the news at every turn.

Most couples were cautious, even when they might be married and have loving, supportive families. She was willing to bet that the majority of the couples Dr. Hardy talked about were married and didn't live thousands of miles apart. Most of those couples didn't have the emotional baggage and charged history she and Marc shared.

Surely she wouldn't be doing too much harm by keeping quiet about the pregnancy for the time being. *Surely* she'd be doing Marc a huge favor by sparing him this news for a short while? He'd feel obligated to make major, life-altering changes, and what if those changes weren't even warranted, in the end?

Mari honestly couldn't decide if she was being selfish by harboring that thought, or if she was being caring toward Marc by shielding him for the moment. She could see the argument both ways.

Nothing had seemed certain to her since she'd seen Marc in the lobby of the Palmer House. It seemed as if the ground beneath her feet had become prone to frequent earthquakes, and her typical confident stance had turned wary with every new step.

She entered the living room and saw Marc standing near the door wearing board shorts and a turquoise T-shirt. His briefcase was on his shoulder, and he had several towels tucked beneath his arm. As usual, his gaze struck her like a sensual caress.

Marc's desire was the one thing she could count on with the certainty of the rising sun. But was that enough to cushion them for what would undoubtedly be the rough ride of the future?

Marc was glad to see they were the only residents on the pool deck besides an older woman who was doing laps. Hopefully the lady wouldn't linger once she'd completed her exercise, and he'd have Mari all to himself. He set his briefcase on a table shaded by an umbrella and joined Mari by a couple of recliners in the full sun.

"It's beautiful up here," she murmured, walking over to the view that featured Lake Michigan to the east and the skyscraper-packed shoreline to the north and south. She turned and smiled at him as he removed his T-shirt. "I can't believe we're nearly the only ones up here."

Marc shrugged and sprawled on the deck chair. "It's like anything else. People tend to ignore luxuries after a while," he murmured distractedly, most of his attention focused on Mari's fingers as she unbuttoned her sundress. "I've only been up here a couple times this summer myself. *Holy...* I'm a genius."

He raised his sunglasses. Mari paused in the action of tossing her sundress on a chair. Marc was too busy checking her out in her new bikini to really take in the amused expression on her face. Maybe the new suit did have more coverage, but it did amazing things to Mari's figure.

"I'm never going to hear the end of it, am I?" she said under her breath as she came down next to him on a recliner.

"Never," he agreed. "A man has to take credit where credit is due, and I definitely deserve huge accolades for finding that suit." He unglued his eyes from the swells of her breasts in the V of the top and lazily trailed his gaze down her belly and curving hips. Her smooth, golden skin looked downright edible next to the white fabric.

"Marc."

He blinked and glanced up from her lap to her face. She was staring incredulously at him.

"What?"

"We're not alone," she whispered.

"All I was doing was looking," he said, flipping his sunglasses back into place.

"Somehow it didn't seem that innocent," he heard Mari say under her breath.

He chuckled and stood. "Want to get in?" he asked.

"I'll wait. I think it's you who needs to cool off," she said wryly as she dug around in a canvas bag and retrieved a magazine.

He laughed, tossed off his glasses and dove into the deep end of the pool. The water was refreshing, but nowhere near as cold as he needed it to be. After he'd swum some laps, he raised his head. A quick survey of the pool told him Mari and he were alone.

He swam to the side and poked his head up over the ledge. Mari was watching him over the top of a magazine with a smirk on her face. He crooked a finger at her in a come-here gesture. She shook her head, her gaze returning to the page. He continued to beckon her silently, however. She finally stood and sauntered toward him. Instead of sitting on the ledge and easing down into the water next to him, giving him the opportunity to touch her honey-colored, smooth skin, she dove straight over his head into the water. He grinned as he watched her swim underwater toward the shallow end of the pool. He plunged after her. When she reached the end of the pool, he was there a split second before her. He leaned his back against the wall, his feet on the bottom of the pool and his legs bent, like he was sitting on an invisible chair. He grasped Mari's shoulders.

"What are you... How did you get there so fast?" she sputtered as her head came out of the water.

"I was inspired," he told her as he pulled her over a few inches so that she was above him. As her buoyant body drifted down to touch bottom, she encountered him instead. She scooped up some water and splashed him in the face.

"Hey," he murmured, not at all bothered. He wiped the water out of his face while Mari pushed her long, wet hair away from her eyes. There was laughter in her whiskey-colored eyes when they met his.

"I'll race you to the other end," she challenged breathlessly.

"Uh-uh," he said quietly as he arranged her so that she straddled his belly in the water, his weight bracing her. Grasping her upper arms, he brought her closer with his hands until her heaving breasts tickled his chest. It felt good—really good—to have Mari's naked skin sliding ever-so-subtly against his in the cool water. "I like it too much right here."

"Do you?" she murmured, her mouth hovering just inches from his, her breath striking his lips in warm, fragrant puffs of air. He placed his hands on her hips, loving the way the curve of them fit into his palms.

"I think you know the answer to that." He slid his hands along her water-lubricated skin. He felt her go still as he traced the beguiling swells of her hips and the indentation of her waist and then her heaving ribcage. "Do you recall how you told me not to come on so strong during this visit, Mari?"

"Yes," she replied, her eyes glued to his mouth. She gasped softly when he shifted his hands so that his forefingers were just below the fullness of her breasts and his palms cradled her ribcage. He felt her heart beating into his palms, rapid and strong.

"If you kissed me right now," he murmured. "I wouldn't be breaking any rules."

"Well, I'd hate to be the one to turn you to truancy."

He held his breath as she slowly leaned forward. She very carefully kissed the drops of moisture off his lips one by one, and then rose to do the same for his nose. He closed his eyelids when she transferred her attention there, her quick, elusive caresses creating a riot of sensation in his body. By the time she'd dried his whole face with her sweet, seeking lips, he was starting to hurt with desire.

Her mouth settled on his. He could just as easily have single-handedly stopped the rotation of the earth than prevented himself from transferring his hands to her upper arms and sliding her closer to him. He gave himself twenty seconds to drown in the taste of her, twenty seconds to show her how much he wanted her, twenty seconds to glory in the fact that her hunger seemed every bit a match for his.

She whimpered softly when he sealed their kiss and moved away from her.

"I think I'll do a lap or three dozen," he muttered before he plunged into the water. He tried to banish Mari's dazed expression and flushed cheeks from his mind's eye as he set a hard, brisk pace for himself, but it didn't really work.

Not in the slightest.

Slightly winded from his swim, he finally rose from the pool. Mari glanced up from her magazine. He gave her a reassuring smile when he saw her uncertain look. The last thing he'd meant to do was make her feel guilty. He was the one who'd asked for it, and, given the same circumstances, he'd gladly suffer his momentary discomfort again just to feel her supple body gliding next to his and her lips caressing every inch of his face.

"Do you mind if I look over a couple things in the shade?" he asked, pointing toward his briefcase beneath the umbrella.

"No, of course not," she assured.

He dried off and settled himself for the next forty minutes, going through his phone messages and making a priority list for things that needed to get done in the next few days. He was proud of himself for staying on task with the alluring distraction of Mari reclining just feet away in a sexy bikini.

Everything was going great until she pulled some suntan lotion out of her bag and started smoothing the emollient onto her long legs. Like a bee drawn to honey, he rose slowly from his seat at the shaded table and walked toward her.

"You need any help with that?" he asked as he plopped down into the recliner next to her.

"I think I can manage."

He didn't reply as he watched her work the lotion into her thighs. She glanced over at him as she poured some more into her palm.

"I thought you were working," she said with a touch of asperity.

He studied every detail of her hands smoothing over her belly.

"I was. I'm not anymore. You have beautiful arms," he said distractedly.

Mari snorted. "Thanks. I don't think I've ever received that particular compliment before."

He smiled and just continued to watch her. He might have looked relaxed to a casual observer, but in fact, his body was tensed like an animal's ready to spring. Why wouldn't anyone tell her she had gorgeous arms? They were like sensual poetry, the way they gleamed in the summer sun, the way she moved them. Why hadn't he told her before?

He sat up when she reached her shoulders.

"Here," he said, reaching for the bottle. "You're going to get it on your new suit."

She glanced at him doubtfully but released the lotion, nevertheless.

"Lean back," he encouraged as he transferred positions so that he was sitting beside her on her recliner. "It's best to be in the exact spot where you're going to lay when you put the stuff on, or else you take the risk of missing the exposed parts."

"You sound like quite the expert on suntan lotion application," Mari said sarcastically as she reclined in the chair.

Marc poured some of the warm liquid in his palm. "Well, I don't want to brag or anything…"

Mari rolled her eyes, but he sensed her focused attention as he carefully began to rub the emollient onto her shoulder, careful not to stain the fabric of her suit.

"You really take this seriously. You'd think you were doing surgery," Mari murmured as she watched him work the lotion into her skin along the line of the suit.

"I'm a perfectionist," he said in a deadpan tone.

She laughed. The smile remained on her mouth while he did her other shoulder. It faded when he squeezed more lotion in one hand and started matter-of-factly working it into the exposed skin in the V of her halter top. From the periphery of his vision, he saw her mouth open to protest, but he just continued rubbing the lotion over the top of a breast with two fingers, sliding and circling over firm, curving flesh. He leaned down farther, taking his time and true to his word, completing the task with meticulous attention to detail.

It was with great disappointment that he finished covering the last, tiny patch of satiny-smooth skin between her breasts at the very bottom of the V. He straightened and screwed the cap on the bottle.

"There. Not a drop on your new suit," he said as he handed the lotion back to her.

He paused when he finally glanced up into Mari's face. Her cheeks had turned pink. Her lips were parted as she panted shallowly.

He'd been so absorbed in the erotic task of putting lotion on the upper and inner swells of Mari's breasts he hadn't really noticed the effect he was having on her. He opened his mouth to apologize, but wouldn't that be a bit disingenuous? Was he *really* sorry?

"I think I'll go take another swim."

She didn't reply as she watched him stand. He hoped she wasn't angry at him, but Christ… How much temptation could a man take?

You're making a lot of selfish excuses, he remonstrated with himself as he sliced through the water. Mari meant a lot more to him than sex. A hell of a lot more. She'd made a point of saying she wanted to see if there was a chance for them beyond their obvious sexual chemistry. She'd said she didn't want to be pushed. And look at how he was behaving. He couldn't help but recall that both Mari and his mother had made a point of saying he always got what he wanted. Was this the kind of thing they were referring to? He wanted Mari—a hell of a lot—and he couldn't seem to stop himself from touching her, no matter what the circumstances.

The thought sobered him.

He did a racer's flip and soared in the opposite direction.

Problem was, his sexual attraction for Mari was all tied up with a ton of other feelings. It was as easy to turn off his physical desire for her as it was to disengage from his emotional attachment.

But he was going to have to try, if this was going to work. He was going to have to try *harder*. He'd never forgive himself if he got to the end of this weekend and had to live with himself for blowing things with the only woman in the world who mattered.

Mari was feeling exceptionally sleepy by the time they packed up their things and headed back down the elevator to Marc's condominium. Maybe it was the heat, or maybe it was because she'd slept only a few hours last night.

Or maybe it was the fact that she was pregnant.

Whatever the case, Marc took one look at her once they'd walked into his cool, quiet living room and suggested she go take a nap. She was so pleasantly groggy that she didn't argue, but wandered back to the guest bedroom, shut the door and fell asleep almost instantly on the bed.

She awoke later, turned over and saw muted evening light seeping around the blinds.

Thank goodness. She hadn't slept for too long. It would have made her sad to think she'd wasted this rare opportunity with Marc by sleeping away a good chunk of time.

She sprung out of bed, completely refreshed.

Pregnancy seemed to have the effect of making her feel either as wrung out as a limp dishrag or energized, as if she could take on the world…maybe even Marc Kavanaugh.

While she showered, she recalled in vivid detail laying there on that deck chair and watching the intent focus on Marc's face while he slowly, carefully drew little gliding circles over the tops of her breasts. Heat rushed through her body and she turned down the hot water a tad. Mari wasn't sure if it was just Marc's effortless sexuality or the fact that her own body was extra sensitive—perhaps because of the pregnancy—but she'd never known she possessed quite so many erogenous zones.

After her shower, she took time and care with her appearance, wanting to look her best. She styled her hair and applied her make-up sparingly—she didn't need much, thanks to her good color from spending the afternoon in the sun. She dressed in a sleeveless, coral chiffon dress she favored because it worked for everything from a casual evening at home to dinner or cocktails out. The chiffon fabric twisted just beneath the V-neck and followed the same tan line as the suit she'd worn today. Her eyebrows went up when she inspected herself in the dress. Maybe her stomach wasn't starting to protrude, but her breasts definitely looked fuller than usual beneath the soft fabric.

She finished off the outfit with gold hoop earrings, a wrist cuff, sandals and then completed her preparation with a spritz of her favorite perfume. Her heart sank a little in disappointment when she entered the large living/dining room area and didn't see Marc anywhere. Had he thought she was going to sleep through the night, and left to run some errands? No—it looked as if he'd set the dining room table for two. In the distance, she heard a shower running in the master bath.

She smiled as she perused his bookcases in the living room. She was glad they were staying in for the evening.

One could always learn so much about a person from their books. Marc's shelves were filled with everything from autobiographies and biographies to historical books and popular thrillers. She pulled out one of three unlabeled black books and murmured happily when she realized it was a photo album of Marc's younger years.

She sat in the corner of the couch and began leafing through the album. Derry Kavanaugh's face leaped out at her from one photo. It was a rare family shot of the whole Kavanaugh family on one of the Harbor Town white beaches. One single moment of happiness had been captured for eternity, Mari thought as she brushed a finger across Marc's adolescent face. Derry's hair was a mixture of gold and gray, and his handsome, smiling face made him look as if he didn't know the meaning of sorrow. The photo had caught Brigit Kavanaugh staring at her husband, love softening her features.

She felt a bond with Brigit in that moment. They were both grown women who had fallen in love with charismatic Kavanaugh men. They had both lost those men in different ways.

If Brigit had a second chance with Derry Kavanaugh, would she take it? She took another look at a Brigit's loving expression as she stared at her husband and had her answer.

Her heart felt a little heavy or full—Mari couldn't decide which—when she turned the page. For a few seconds, she just stared. After a moment, she carefully picked up the wax-paper envelope with the two flowers that had been dried and preserved—the daisy and the iris. She saw the words Marc had quoted back to her written in Brigit's slanted, clear hand—*Mari's favorites. Sun and shade.* The envelope had been placed beneath a photo of her and Marc standing in the Kavanaugh backyard, Marc's arm around her, both of them grinning broadly, sunburned and flushed with first love. She must have been about sixteen, Marc nineteen.

"I took it when I found it at Mom's."

Mari glanced up at the sound of Marc's gruff voice. Through the film of tears over her eyes, she saw that his hair was still damp and that he wore a pair of jeans and a casual blue cotton button-down shirt. She must have had a slightly bewildered expression on her face because he seemed to find it necessary to clarify.

"The flowers, I mean. I figured…you know."

"What?" Mari asked when he didn't finish.

"I figured they belonged here with me."

For several seconds, neither of them spoke.

"I didn't really have anything of yours after you left," Marc explained. "Except for photos." He inhaled and glanced out the windows to the lake in the distance. "Truth be told, I sort of stole it from Mom. I didn't want to have to deal with her questions if I asked for permission for them."

"When did you take them?" Mari asked in a hushed voice.

Marc met her gaze again. "One weekend…after the Palmer House."

Mari swallowed and carefully replaced the dried flowers in the book. She stood and slid the photo album back into its place on the shelf. When she turned, she saw him examining her appearance.

"You look gorgeous. You dressed up. I ordered in some food for us, but we can go out if you like."

"No," she said quickly. "I'm glad you planned to stay in."

His grin caused something to hitch in her chest. "I'll take you for dinner tomorrow night. Some place nice. Tonight, I ordered in from a favorite restaurant—French Vietnamese cuisine. They already delivered. It's warming in the oven."

"Great."

"I have some wine chilled," he said, pointing toward the kitchen. "I'll just…"

Mari stepped forward, halting his exit by placing her hand on his arm. He looked down at her, surprised by her abrupt movement. Standing this close, she could smell the scent of his soap and spicy cologne and could see the flecks of green in the midst of the sky-blue of his iris.

"Thank you," she said.

"For what? Stealing some dried flowers?"

"No. For not forgetting me…for not giving up."

She went up on her tiptoes and kissed him fleetingly on the mouth. When she lowered and looked up at him, she saw that he looked stunned.

"How about that food? I'm hungrier than I thought I would be." She tilted her head toward the kitchen in a silent prompt.

He blinked, seeming to come out of his daze. "Right," he said. "Dinner."

Mari smiled as she followed him. He was usually so confident. It did something to her to see him off balance, even if it had lasted for all of two seconds.

Marc had ordered multiple items, so they opened all the cartons and spooned small portions from each onto their plates. The food was some of the best she'd ever eaten, and Mari didn't think it was just because of the company. There was steamed Chilean sea bass with cellophane noodles and oyster mushrooms; jumbo shrimp, asparagus and scallions; diced filet mignon and yams in a light sate sauce and a lovely salad made with lotus root, cucumber, tomatoes and a tamarind dressing.

Just as Mari picked up her fork to begin, Marc hopped up from his seat. "Hold on… I forgot."

He came back into the dining room carrying a candlestick and brand new taper. Grinning, he lit the candle and sat down across from Mari.

"So proud of yourself, aren't you?" she teased as she forked a succulent shrimp.

"Well, you've got to admit, when you get a caveman to serve you fine cuisine by candlelight, it's a small miracle, right?"

Mari gave a small moan as she chewed the shrimp. "You did *very* well, Caveman."

A while later she leaned back in her chair and sighed as she stared out at the dark blue lake and muted lavender sky. The flickering candle was starting to cast shadows on the ceiling. It would be dark soon. She lazily forked her last bite of salad and chewed it slowly, appreciating the subtle blend of flavors on her tongue.

"I think I've died and gone to heaven," she murmured.

"I'm glad you liked it." He nodded at her full wine glass. "Wine not to your liking?"

"Oh… No, it's fine," she said hastily. "The food was so delicious I didn't have a thought for it, that's all."

"You can take it into the living room, if you like," he suggested. "I got dessert, but maybe we should wait a bit?"

"Definitely," Mari agreed.

He stood and began to clear their dishes. When Mari started to help him, he shooed her off, insisting she take her wine and relax in the living room. Mari obligingly took her full glass of wine, but felt a little awkward since she had no intention of drinking it. She kicked off the sandals she was wearing, perched in the corner of the L-shaped couch and drew up her feet. When Marc joined her a few minutes later, he carried a mug and handed it to her.

"Figured you'd probably prefer tea. It's herbal," he said as he handed it to her.

"Thank you," she murmured, scooting her feet back a few inches to make room for him to sit.

"I was just thinking while I was cleaning up in the kitchen—I'm not used to being around you as an adult. I shouldn't have assumed you drink alcohol." He continued when she stared at him in blankly, "I've never seen you drink since I met up with you at the Palmer House. It wouldn't surprise me if you abstained."

"I have a glass of wine once in a while," she said as understanding dawned. He'd assumed she hadn't drank her glass of wine for reasons related to their past. In truth, she hadn't drank it because of her pregnancy. "What I said was true. It just didn't appeal tonight."

Marc nodded, but his expression was somber. "I mentioned it the other night, but I'll say it again. I'm not much of a drinker, either. I just thought some wine with the food—"

"Marc," she interrupted. "I didn't think twice about you having a glass of wine. You didn't even finish it. Do you really think I'm worried that you're some kind of alcoholic because your father had a drinking problem?"

He shrugged and glanced away. "It's not as if I haven't heard something similar before. My brother and sisters have, at one time or another. All of us were stained by my dad's actions."

Mari opened her mouth to demand the details—who

had dared to insinuate something so ridiculous? How could they possibly justify their allegations, when the Kavanaugh children were practically paragons of virtue, dedication and hard work?—but she closed her mouth when she noticed Marc's rigid profile.

"It's so unfair. I'm sorry," she murmured.

His gaze returned to her face. "It meant a lot, to discover you weren't one of those people judging me for someone else's actions," he said quietly.

She shook her head, her throat suddenly tight with emotion. She cradled his jaw with her hand and moved her fingers, absorbing the sensation of his warm skin, both overwhelmed by his vibrant presence and hungry to experience more of him.

"What's wrong?" he asked her as he studied her through narrowed eyelids.

"Life is so uncertain. I wish…I wish I could always have you like this."

"Like this?" His mouth quirked, and Mari brushed her thumb against his lips. He went still at her touch.

"Just us," she whispered as she moved her finger, studying his texture like her thumb was her only source of sensation. "No one else."

"It is just us. And the future," he said.

"There's the past."

His hand came up and cradled her shoulder. "There's the present, Mari."

The present.

Staring into Marc's eyes, she felt the present moment stretching out to eternity. He didn't move or speak when she leaned over and placed her mug of tea on the coffee table, but she sensed the tension that had leaped into his muscles. She lifted her knee and straddled his thighs, her head lowered. The need she felt couldn't be denied any longer.

She unfastened the first three buttons of his shirt and pressed her face into the opening.

She did what she'd been holding back from doing for weeks now...for years.

She drowned herself in him.

Chapter Twelve

The skin on his chest felt thick and warm pressed against her seeking lips. He didn't have an abundant amount of hair there, but what she encountered delighted her as she rubbed her cheek and lips against it, experiencing the springy, soft sensation. His scent filled her, intoxicated her. She moved her hands, cradling his waist and then sliding up the taper to his ribs, caressing him with gentle, molding palms and eager fingers.

It took her a few seconds to realize he was holding his breath. That changed when she gently pulled aside the fabric of his shirt and kissed a dark copper-colored nipple.

He gasped her name raggedly and tangled his fingers in her loose hair.

He was so hard, so male. Her lips and fingertips couldn't seem to get enough of him. She rubbed her mouth across his nipple, testing the texture with her tongue, thrilling to the sensation of the flesh beading beneath her caress. Her hands moved fleetly, unbuttoning the remainder of his shirt. His abdomen and ribs rose and fell as she explored his naked torso and tasted his skin.

He said something in a low, rough tone when she moved her mouth, raining light, quick kisses on his chest. She couldn't hear him, but interpreted the words to mean desire. He hissed her name when she greedily sampled another small, flat nipple and felt it grow stiff below her tongue and lips.

He cursed and grasped her shoulders, lifting her. He pulled her down to him and seized her mouth, and their separate fires leaped into a single inferno.

He joined her in her quest to explore, to touch…to thrill. His hands molded her back muscles and encircled her waist. She loved how big he was, how much of her he could hold in his grasp. He shifted her slightly on top of him, bringing her closer against him, matching the core of her heat to his.

They groaned into each other's mouths, burning separately…burning as one.

Mari felt liberated. Before, she'd allowed herself to touch Marc's fires, to be consumed by them, even. This was the first time she'd let her own flames run free. Before, there had always been the nagging restraint, the hovering caution.

Not now, though. Not in this eternal moment.

He shifted his hands to her hips, his fingers delving into the soft flesh of her buttocks. They continued to devour each other as he rocked her against him, both of them so hungry, so starved for one another. He moved one hand to the back of her head and held her while he ravished her mouth. His lips lowered, feeling hot and voracious on the skin of her neck. She tilted back her chin and arched her back, offering herself to him, lost in a sea of sensation. His hands moved rapidly as he pressed kisses against her neck and shoulders, sweeping aside the fabric of her dress and the straps of her bra. He peeled cloth off her breasts. Mari cried out in abrupt loss when suddenly his mouth was gone, then gasped as his mouth closed over a nipple. She furrowed her fingers through his short hair and held him to her as she whimpered in sublime pleasure. An unbearable ache swelled inside her, a pain she knew would only be silenced by their joining. He continued to tease her flesh with his mouth and tongue until Mari grew desperate. She reached between them, wild to remove the barrier of their clothing. His head rose when he realized what she was doing. His breath came in short, jagged pants against her damp breasts as they fumbled, united in a fury of need.

Her head fell back and she gasped at the sensation of him entering her.

"Look at me."

She complied with his command. It felt as if she'd explode from the strength of her combined emotion and arousal when she met his fierce gaze. She rested in his lap, quivering. She felt so full…so inundated with him.

They began to move at the same moment as if by some unspoken agreement. He closed his eyes. A muscle twitched in his cheek. She understood the sweet agony. She experienced it with him.

"You've been holding yourself back from me," he whispered hoarsely, his eyes open now, pinning her as she moved over him.

She didn't reply. Her body spoke for her. It was true, but she wasn't holding back from him now.

And she made sure he knew it.

She leaned down and scraped her parted lips against his, caressing rather than kissing. She tasted his sweat.

Their breaths mingled and the inferno inside her grew. His hold on her hips and buttocks tightened and they both became more demanding, both of the other and themselves.

She wanted to hold onto these seconds forever...never wanted it to end.

If it didn't end this moment, she would die.

She held on tight to his shoulders and cried out in pleasure as she succumbed. She heard his low, rough growl as he held her down to him, felt his muscles grow rock hard beneath her clutching fingers. Her name was a fierce prayer on his tongue.

The seconds unfolded into minutes as time resumed its normal cadence. Mari pressed her lips against Marc's pulse as she tried to catch her breath. She felt his leaping heart slow to a steady throb.

Something had happened.

She had the amazingly clear thought through her hazy satiation: She *had* to tell Marc about the baby, and not just because she was obligated. In that moment she wanted to tell him, *longed* to complete the link between herself, this vibrant man she held and their growing child with every living cell in her being.

She whimpered in protest when he lifted her, separating them. He groped for his jeans, roughly pulling them up around his hips.

"No. I don't want it to end," she murmured.

"It's not going to end."

She blinked when she heard the hard edge to his voice. Then he was gathering her to him and standing.

The master bedroom was dim and shadowed. The duvet felt cool against her heated skin when he laid her on his bed. He came down over her.

"It's only the beginning," he said in a gruff whisper and his mouth settled on hers.

* * *

Mari quickly learned he was right. They made love again and then held each other.

She considered how she would tell him about the baby. Now, perhaps, when they held each other and their desire for one another still lingered around them like a comforting cocoon? Her heart felt so full at the moment, though. She didn't want to tell him in a rushing torrent of emotion and end up crying on his chest, feeling like a fool.

Perhaps tomorrow while they were out at dinner would be a safer choice, she thought nervously.

"What are you concentrating on so hard?" Marc interrupted her thoughts.

She glanced up at his face, surprised. "Was I?"

He gave her the slow grin that always caused a funny sensation in her belly and brushed a tendril of hair off her brow. "You looked like you were plotting how to break some terrible news. I have a feeling I know what it is."

She sat up slightly, alarmed. "You do?"

He nodded, suddenly sober.

"I made the criminal offense of not giving you your dessert."

Mari rolled her eyes. He laughed and clambered out of bed, telling her to sit still. When he returned, Mari smiled at the vision of him, naked and magnificent and carrying a tray which he set on the bedside table.

"Dessert is served," he told her, coming down next to her on the bed. He flipped the bedside lamp to a dim setting. He turned and dipped a spoon into a small carton and then a dish.

"What's this?" she murmured when he held the spoon to her mouth.

"Fresh pineapple and homemade coconut ice cream."

Mari opened her lips and sweet, rich flavor burst on her tongue.

"Oh...you're going to spoil me," she groaned.

His teeth flashed white against his tan skin when he grinned. He removed the spoon from her mouth, but pressed the cold, smooth metal against her lower lip, massaging the flesh in a small circle.

"That's the plan," he murmured, his tone a gentle, sensual threat.

He gathered more ice cream and fruit and pressed it once again to her mouth. She laughed.

"You don't have to feed me, Marc."

"We should try and get some of it into your stomach."

"So you can get the rest of it in yours?" she joked as the confection melted on her tongue.

"I'll end up eating plenty, don't worry."

He turned from gathering more ice cream on the spoon. Instead of pressing it to her mouth, however, he placed a dollop on the tip of her breast. Mari barely had time to gasp at the unexpected chill when his mouth was there, hot and agitating. Her eyes went wide at the erotic sensation of bitter cold on her nipple transforming so quickly to delicious heat. She grabbed onto his head and sighed. Did he somehow sense how sensitive her breasts were? How much pleasure he gave her with his fingers and mouth? He seemed so focused on them... as if he somehow knew.

Or perhaps it had nothing to do with her body burgeoning with new life. Maybe her flesh would always react this way to Marc's touch?

The idea was a little disorienting.

He drew on her nipple and her thoughts splintered in a thousand directions. Her eyelids flickered closed as she gave into yet another wave of delicious pleasure.

* * *

Drowning.

He felt like he was drowning in her. Marc had told her last night he drank sparingly, if at all, and that had been the truth, but he could easily become addicted to Mari…to the vision of her smile, the way her muscles quivered in anticipation when he kissed the side of her ribs or her belly, the sweet sounds that came from her throat when he was deep, deep inside her.

After a night and most of the following day, Marc started to feel like a heel for keeping her captive in bed for all that time. Not that Mari seemed to mind, but still. It was another gorgeous sunny day, surely they should try and get out and enjoy it some? They were too enraptured with each other to notice much of anything else.

Nevertheless, they showered and ate a late lunch at the café around the corner. Afterward, they went back up to the pool where they were glad to see they were the only ones present. They took a quick swim and returned to their recliners, the hot sun on his skin feeling more like a sensual caress than usual because Mari was lying next to him.

"Marc."

He blinked when she said his name. He hadn't realized he'd been staring at the sight of her belly and hips sparkling with droplets of water.

"Hmm?" he asked.

She shook her head and laughed. "You're a lecher, you know that?"

"If I am, it's with good reason," he muttered as he reached into Mari's bag. "I've waited a hell of a long time." He regretted his words when he saw her expression go solemn. He held up the infamous bottle of suntan lotion from the day before. "Time to oil up."

Her serious look disappeared as she collapsed into giggles. When he started to smooth the lotion onto her soft, warm skin, though, all the tension he'd felt yesterday returned. His smile faded and Mari's laughter quieted.

He managed to cover her upper arm and right shoulder with lotion before their stares met and held. They both stood by silent mutual agreement and grabbed their things. He took her hand and led her back to his condo.

The fact that they'd held themselves on such tight leashes the previous day added to their sense of haste. Perhaps it was half a lifetime spent apart that heightened their sense of need.

Maybe it was the dark worry that these were stolen days with Mari that added to Marc's desperate hunger for her.

"We have to go back to Harbor Town tomorrow," Mari whispered wistfully next to his chest a while later. They lay entangled on his bed, their hearts still thumping rapidly from their latest explosive joining.

He ran his fingers through her long hair and marveled once again at its softness. "That's a long time away still. I'm taking you out to dinner tonight. We have more than twenty-four hours together," he murmured. "That's plenty of time."

"Plenty of time for what?" she asked, pressing her lips to his chest.

"Plenty of time for me to convince you to spend the rest of your life with me."

He'd said it lightly enough, but she must have caught the thread of seriousness in his tone, because she lifted her head. Her eyes looked dark, soft and velvety in the shadowed room.

"How can you be so certain that's what you want?" she whispered.

"You know me. I'm a decisive guy," he said, smiling in order to lighten the moment. He didn't like the anxiety in Mari's eyes.

"But…but you and Sandra divorced only a year and a half ago, and what about—"

"Are you implying it's a complete impossibility?" he asked as he stroked the nape of her neck.

"Well…no."

He met her stare. "There's still time, then." He pressed gently with his fingertips and she put her head back on his chest. "I think there might be time for a little nap, too. You wear me out, Mari."

He smiled when he felt the vibrations of her small chuckle.

She lay awake and watched Marc sleeping, detailing every line of his face. It was true she had an ocean of doubt about their being together, but she had faith in Marc.

She tried to imagine his expression tonight at dinner when she told him about the baby. She drowsily pictured his look of incredulity slowly morphing to one of amazement and excitement.

And love?

Her eyelids opened heavily a while later. The sound of a cell phone ringing insistently had finally penetrated her deep sleep. She lifted her head.

"Marc. That's yours. They've called back several times now, I think. It must be important."

His eyes popped open. He scowled as he rolled over to the far side of the bed and reached for the phone on the bedside table. He glanced at the caller identification before he answered.

"Yeah?" he asked in a deep, sleep-roughened voice.

A long silence ensued. Mari glanced over at him. His profile was rigid with concentration as he listened to the caller. A sense of unease stole over her lassitude.

"How long has it been since she admitted her to the hospital?"

Mari gathered the loose sheet around her and sat up in the bed, her heart starting to hammer rapidly in her chest.

"Uh-huh. Okay. Yeah. We can be in Harbor Town in a few hours. Traffic should be nothing right now...I know, I understand...I still want to come... Yeah, okay. See you soon."

He hit the End button.

"What is it?" Mari asked.

"It's my mom." He met her eyes before he set the cell phone on the table. "She had a heart attack."

"Oh, my God—" Mari whispered.

"It's not bad," he said hastily, hearing her shock. "She's going to be fine. That was Liam calling. It was relatively mild. The cardiologist told Liam and Colleen she's had high blood pressure and high cholesterol for a while now, but according to the doctor, it hasn't improved with treatment. The cardiologist implied my mom hadn't been taking her medications."

"Did you and Liam and Colleen know—"

"No. She never told us. I thought she was completely healthy," Marc interrupted grimly.

"She *looks* so healthy. She's so slender and active. It's the last thing I would have expected."

"Yeah. Me, too," he said in a flat tone.

Mari's chest ached for him. She knew what he was experiencing.

"Anyway...Liam says they'll likely release her tomorrow, but I still want to go."

"Of course," Mari said. She started to rise from bed when Marc put his hand on her forearm, halting her. She looked over at him.

"This doesn't change anything. Do you understand?"

He seemed to regret the harshness of his tone. He closed his eyes and exhaled. "I only meant… I'm sorry, Mari."

"Don't apologize," she said fervently. "I understand completely. Of *course* you have to go. It's family."

He opened his eyes. "Yeah. But I'm sorry nonetheless."

She nodded and hurried out of bed. The vivid dreams about telling Marc about the baby slowly faded to the background.

Chapter Thirteen

They arrived back in Harbor Town that evening at about six. Mari insisted upon accompanying Marc to the hospital.

"I mean… I won't go into your mother's room or anything—that would upset her—but I'd like to be there for you. If you'd like it, anyway."

Marc had given her a half smile and grabbed her hand. "'Course I want you there."

Once they'd located the unit where Brigit was staying, Mari told Marc she was going to find them something to drink while he went and saw his mother. Her throat was dry after the long drive. She left him to confer with the nurse and wandered through the corridors of the hospital in search of a vending machine.

When she returned to the unit carrying two orange juices, she found Marc talking to Colleen in the waiting area. They were the only two occupants in the room, their backs turned to her. Mari went still when she heard the distress in Colleen's tone as she spoke in a quiet, shaking voice to her brother.

"It's my fault," Colleen said.

"What? How could it be your fault? Don't be ridiculous."

"All right, maybe it wasn't entirely my doing, but what I said to her certainly didn't help matters," Colleen said in a hard voice. She swept her long hair over one shoulder in an anxious gesture and leaned back in the chair. "It was after I spoke to her that she got all quiet. Then her complexion went sort of gray and she clutched at herself like this." Colleen demonstrated by grabbing at the area between her left chest and shoulder. "She said she was having a cramp. It scared the hell out of me."

Marc put an arm around his sister for reassurance.

"Yeah, it must have been scary. But it wasn't because of anything you did or said. The doctor said this has been building for a while. Mom hasn't been attending to her treatment."

"What I said didn't help any."

"I doubt that. What were you talking about?" Marc asked, seeming disbelieving and curious all at once.

Feeling guilty for eavesdropping upon the conversation, Mari had stepped forward to identify herself when Colleen spoke in a low, flat tone.

"I told her about my new job. I told her about Mari starting up The Family Center. At first, I thought her silence just signaled her disapproval, but then I noticed her complexion, how odd she looked—"

Marc suddenly looked over his shoulder, his blue eyes pinning her. Had she made a sound? Mari thought perhaps she had.

A sound of distress.

"Mari," Colleen said breathlessly as she stood.

"Mari?" Marc asked, his voice louder than Colleen's had been.

Mari blinked. How long had she been standing there while her heart hammered in her ears? Marc was coming toward her, his brows drawn together. She stupidly offered him a bottle of juice.

"It's not very cold," she said. "I think the vending machine was broken."

He looked at her like she'd been speaking in Swahili. He put his hand on her upper arm. She started. She hated the way his jaw hardened at her instinctive recoil from his touch, but there was nothing Mari could do.

That old feeling of helplessness had risen in her again.

"I think I should go," she said quietly to Marc.

"Because of what you just heard?" Marc demanded, blue eyes flashing.

"Mari, please don't," Colleen said hastily. "I was feeling sorry for myself. I'm sure what I said to Mom had nothing to do with—"

"You don't believe that," Mari interrupted levelly. She turned back to Marc and handed him the other bottle of juice. He seemed so stunned by unfolding events that he accepted it automatically.

"I'll take you home," he said.

"No. I can walk." She didn't know what had come over her, but she felt strangely calm despite her rapid heartbeat. She met Marc's stare, trying her best to seem reassuring even though she felt powerless at that moment. "Everything will be okay, Marc. I'll get my things from you later. You should see your mother right now."

Marc looked like he was about to protest when Colleen spoke, sounding a little weary.

"I'll take Mari home. It'll take me five minutes. You should go on in, Marc. Mom's waiting for you."

Mari didn't glance back when Colleen touched her elbow. They walked away.

When she arrived home, Ryan came down the hallway, bare-chested and holding a butter knife. He wore a pair of cargo shorts and a surprised expression.

"I thought you weren't coming back until tomorrow."

"We came back a little early," Mari said. She parked her rolling suitcase at the bottom of the stairs and placed her fingertips on her eyelids. When she opened them, she was staring at a steely bicep.

"Cool tattoo," she said dully, examining the artist's rendering of the logo of the Air Force wings morphing into an eagle taking flight. "When did you get that?"

"Two…three years— Who cares?" he asked, interrupting himself impatiently. "Are you okay, Mari?"

"Yeah. I'm just really, really tired. I need to go to bed." She started up the stairs, but turned back. Ryan was staring at her with something close to alarm. "I'm okay, Ryan. Marc's mom just had a heart attack. It took us by surprise, that's all."

His mouth dropped open.

"Like I said, I'm just tired. Can you do me a favor?"

"Of course. Anything."

"I don't want any visitors. No one."

Ryan nodded, looking somber.

Mari sighed and trudged up the stairs. She was too fatigued to think…to feel. She felt as if weariness had soaked into her very bones.

This was the ending to their magical weekend. Somehow, it didn't surprise her.

Her bedroom faced west, so it was bright with sunshine. She began to draw the curtains. When she reached the window next to the elm tree, she made sure it was locked before she shut out the remainder of the golden evening light. She thought of how she'd planned to spend that evening in Marc's arms after telling him about her pregnancy.

But the past had a way of sneaking up on you when you least expected it.

The next day Mari stayed to herself. She kept her cell phone turned off. Ryan treated her as if she was recovering from an illness. He seemed like he wanted to question her, but was too sensitive of her mood to interrogate her, for which Mari was thankful. She needed to think.

She was playing her cello at around one o'clock when she paused, hearing tense, male voices downstairs. She held her breath and tried to make out the words.

It was Marc and Ryan. It sounded like they both stood at the front door. Their voices were muffled, but their volume increased with almost every word.

"She doesn't want to see you," Ryan suddenly shouted, plenty clear enough for her to hear.

"Who the hell are you? Her jailer?" Marc responded, just as aggressively.

"I'm doing what she *asked* me to do, Kavanaugh. She *said* she didn't want to see you."

Mari hastily set down her bow and started to rise—she wouldn't be surprised, given the animosity between Marc and Ryan, if a fight broke out—but then the screen door banged loudly and silence ensued.

She set aside her cello and raced over to the window. She opened the sash and searched the leafy branches, dreading seeing Marc's face…and longing for it. The robins remained the only occupants of the elm tree.

A moment later, she sat on the edge of her bed. She realized distantly her cheeks were wet with tears. The memory of studying Marc's face while he slept yesterday afternoon came back to her in graphic detail.

Such a beautiful man.

What parts of Marc would be in their baby? Would their child have his eyes? His sense of humor? His fierce courage?

Thinking about discovering those wonderful characteristics in their child without Marc there to share those moments caused grief and sadness to slice through her like a knife.

She wrapped her arms around her belly as if she was staunching a wound. Tears gushed down her cheeks. She lay on her side on the bed and suffered in solitude.

She awoke the next morning regretting the way she'd been avoiding Marc. He deserved better than to be turned away at her front door like an annoying salesman. She resolved to call him later. She wanted to ask him about Brigit. Marc must be worried sick about his mother. It certainly sounded as if her heart attack hadn't been a major one, but why hadn't she been following her doctor's orders?

She had an appointment at the obstetrician's office that afternoon, and she needed to complete a few more things for The Family Center. Eric, Natalie and she had planned for an opening at the end of August. She regretted nothing more than how Brigit Kavanaugh had responded to the news of the project, but Mari would move forward, nevertheless. Hesitation now twined with her determination to open The Family Center, but the idea of stopping now when their intentions were so good seemed very wrong, indeed.

Her appointment at the obstetrician's went quickly, much to Mari's surprise. The obstetrician, Anita Carol, was a friendly, African-American woman, a few years older than Mari. Mari told her about the bouts of dizziness and nausea, and Dr. Carol recommended frequent, small meals to keep her blood sugar steady and prevent nausea.

She did a quick exam and told Mari make an appointment for an ultrasound. Mari wasn't planning on being in Harbor Town that much longer but she didn't bring that up to the doctor.

"The baby's father can come to the ultrasound, as well," Dr. Carol said brightly on the way out the door. "We should be able to determine the sex by that time, if you two are interested in knowing."

Mari remained seated on the chair in the exam room after the doctor left. She rubbed her belly through her jeans, feeling hollow inside…empty…*lonely* at Anita Carol's parting words.

She irritably wiped at her eyes when they stung. How could she possibly cry more when she'd shed bucketfuls of tears yesterday?

She came to a standstill outside of Dr. Carol's office when she saw Brigit Kavanaugh. Brigit also halted abruptly in the hallway.

"Brigit. Are you…are you well?" Mari asked once her lungs unstuck and she could breathe again. She anxiously searched Brigit's face. She would never have guessed Brigit had been in the hospital the day before yesterday for a heart attack. Dressed in jeans and a fashionably belted turquoise tunic, she looked quite healthy.

For a few tense seconds, Mari wondered if their chance meeting was going to a repeat of the one on Main Street. She exhaled in relief when Brigit spoke, albeit stiffly.

"I'm fine. They released me yesterday morning. The doctor says there was no significant damage to my heart.

I'm just here to fill some prescriptions at the hospital pharmacy."

"Thank God," Mari whispered.

"You were here for an appointment?" Brigit asked, glancing behind Mari.

"Yes," Mari mumbled. Too late, she turned and noticed where Brigit stared. The nameplate on the door read Anita Carol, M.D., Obstetrician. Brigit's glance flickered down over Mari's abdomen. For an awkward moment, neither of them spoke.

"I heard from Colleen about the project you're starting for the survivors of substance abuse."

Mari tried to swallow but her mouth felt too dry. "I... yes. Can we sit down, Brigit?"

Brigit drew herself up tall. "I assure you I'm fine. I feel very healthy. I'm not going to have another heart attack," Brigit said crisply.

Mari smiled. "Actually, I was asking if we could sit down for me."

The straight line of Brigit's frown quivered. "Of course," she said quickly. "Just over here." She led Mari to a bench in the quiet hospital hallway. "Take a deep breath," Brigit said briskly once they sat. "You've gone pale as a ghost."

Mari followed her advice, trying desperately to calm her rioting thoughts. After several seconds of silence, Brigit spoke.

"I don't suppose you could have started this Family Center in San Francisco?"

Mari blinked at the sound of Brigit's wry tone.

"I didn't plan for it in Harbor Town to upset you. I meant for The Family Center to be a positive thing...a healing thing, not a source of upset."

Brigit looked incredulous. Mari sighed heavily, feeling defeated.

"I'm sorry. I can see you feel otherwise," she said quietly. "I can only pray you'll eventually believe me when I say I never meant to cause you any serious harm or pain."

Brigit didn't respond. Perhaps she felt it was unnecessary, given the circumstances.

"I understand you were with Marc in Chicago over the weekend."

Mari levelly met Brigit's stare. "Yes."

"He's determined to have you, no matter what I say. He's always been that way, as you probably recall." The older woman sighed and looked at the opposite wall. She seemed lost in her thoughts. "Once he set his mind to something, Marc always got his way. Even when Derry died, even after all the money for his law school tuition was taken away, Marc just plowed ahead. He went to the University of Michigan instead of Yale where he'd been accepted and planned to go. The tuition was much less expensive, although far from cheap. He worked two jobs and had to take out loans, but he got his degree with honors. Did he tell you that?"

"No," Mari whispered through leaden lips.

"He wouldn't have said anything, I suppose. Not to you." She turned and looked at Mari. "You were the one thing he wanted and couldn't have. It doesn't surprise me, the way he's pursuing you. It's in his character, I suppose."

"You don't admire his determination in this instance," Mari said.

"Determination? I'd call it stubbornness and pride, wouldn't you?" Brigit shifted her purse onto her shoulder and stood. She hesitated. "Take care, Mari. You don't seem entirely yourself."

Mari remained seated as Brigit walked away.

* * *

Her heart felt like a stone in her chest when she heard the knock at the front door later that evening. She paused in the action of cutting some bananas for a fruit salad. His stance wary, Ryan's eyes flashed as he glanced at her.

"It's okay. If it's Marc, I want to talk to him," Mari told her brother with a reassuring smile. She felt her brother's stare on her as she walked out of the kitchen.

She opened the screen door. "Hi," she said tremulously. Marc stood there on the porch looking beautiful to her, his dark blond hair wind-ruffled, his jaw darkened with whiskers, his blue eyes gleaming in his shadowed face.

"Hi."

A ripple of sensation coursed down her neck and spine at the sound of his low, hoarse voice.

He waved toward his car in the sunlit driveway. "Will you come for a ride?"

Mari nodded. She stepped out onto the porch, feeling like a prisoner walking to the gallows.

Neither of them spoke after they'd gotten into the car. Marc drove to The Family Center. He glanced over to her and gave a small smile when she gasped in pleasure. A painted blue, brown and ivory sign had been placed next to the entrance.

"I hope you don't mind," Marc said as he parked the car and nodded toward the freshly painted sign. "Liam had to get back to work, but when he heard about the Center, he wanted to do something. He commissioned Joe Brown to make it before he left Harbor Town. Joe left him a message saying he installed it Saturday."

Mari was too amazed to speak. They got out of the car and went to examine the sign. Joe had included a small landscape in the corner of the sign, a dune and a sunset. Mari recognized the vista off Silver Dune. Beneath the name of the organization and contact information, a two-word quote had been added.

"Choose hope," she whispered. After several seconds, she glanced up at Marc. He watched her, his eyes like two steady beacons beckoning her to shore. Her throat ached when she swallowed. "I need to make sure I get Liam's number from you. This was so wonderful of him."

Marc nodded and grabbed her hand. They took a rough path through evergreen, oak and maple until the tree line broke and they walked out onto the dune. Lake Michigan looked periwinkle blue beneath the fiery orange, sinking sun. When they reached the end of the dune, Mari turned toward him. She nodded toward the water in the vicinity of where they'd sat in the boat and watched the sun rising several days ago.

"We're back on the shore now," she said quietly. "Watching the sunset again."

His hand came up to cradle her jaw. He whisked his thumb across her cheek. "Sunrise. Sunset. They're all good, as long as you're here."

Mari distantly wondered if her throat would ever stop aching. Lately it seemed to be constantly swelling with emotion. "It's been a difficult trip...coming back to Harbor Town," she murmured.

"Mari, about what Colleen said in the hospital...I know it upset you. But Colleen was worried—"

"I know," Mari said rapidly. She turned toward the lake, missing Marc's caress when her motion caused his hand to fall away. "Of course she was upset. I would have been, too, given the circumstances. It's completely natural."

Out of the corner of her vision, she saw Marc stiffen.

"So why have you been avoiding me for the past few days?"

"I needed to think," Mari said, her gaze on the dancing waves of the silver-blue lake.

He didn't speak for several seconds. When she glanced over at him, she saw his mouth had drawn into a straight line. She'd never seen Marc look so grim. Somehow he'd guessed what she was about to say.

"Don't do this, Mari."

"One of us has to," she said in a hushed voice. "I was right. It would never work, you and me."

"It *does* work," he said, putting his hand on her upper arm. "It always has!"

"For us," Mari replied, just as heatedly. "It works for *us*, Marc. But we're not the only two people on the planet. There are other people…other lives we have to take into account."

"I don't accept that. We're not hurting anyone by being together. What happened with my mother was scary for everyone, but that had nothing to do with you starting The Family Center or us being together. It had *everything* to do with the fact that she's been ignoring her physical health. I've had a long conversation with her about it. She's agreed to take her medication now and follow the doctor's treatment advice."

"I spoke with Brigit, as well."

He paused for two heartbeats. "You did? About what?" he asked warily.

"She seems to be of the opinion that you want me this much because I was the one thing you never could have."

"And you believed her?" Marc asked, anger entering his tone.

"No…at least not totally."

"What's that supposed to mean? *Not totally?*"

She paused for a moment, gathering herself. She waved toward the edge of the dune in the distance.

"Do you remember us standing there on the end of this dune together? It would have been fifteen summers ago. Just weeks before the crash, if I'm not mistaken."

He didn't respond to her quiet question, but she sensed the tension coiling in his muscles.

"I was terrified," she said softly. "Literally. I still have a fear of heights, you know. But I jumped. Do you know why?"

She turned to look at him, but he still didn't speak. She hated seeing the rigid, hard lines of his face cast in the crimson rays of the dying sun. His eyes were usually so alive when he looked at her, but at that moment, they looked cold with dread.

"Because, once upon a time, I would have followed Marc Kavanaugh anywhere. *Anywhere*," she added fervently. She shook her head sadly. "But things changed. And I'm not a child anymore. I have others to consider."

"I see. We're back to this, then. I'm the selfish one, for suggesting we should be together."

Mari closed her eyes and felt tears skitter down her cheek. The wind increased and tossed the trees behind them. The waves hitting the sand beach in the distance sounded lonely. She pushed her blowing hair off her damp face.

"I don't think that anymore. You're not selfish. You're strong. Stronger than I am. You said you would accept my decision after we returned from Chicago." She swallowed convulsively. "Please understand. I'm not strong enough to follow you this time around."

She turned away from the lake and paused. "Ryan and I booked flights back home. We leave tomorrow. I can finish what remains to be done for The Family

Center from there. I'll go inside now and tie up a few loose ends. Ryan can pick me up here later." She lowered her head, praying for strength to continue. "There's... there's something I'll need to speak with you about, but...perhaps it'd be best if it waited until I was in San Francisco."

She glanced up at him. This was by far the hardest thing she'd ever done. Her entire body hurt as if every cell protested at the idea of leaving him. She touched her stomach in an instinctive protective gesture. *This* life was the one that had decided her, in the end. She needed to protect her child from the pain and heartache of their past. Wasn't fate screaming loud and clear that they weren't meant to be together? How many more people would be hurt if they tried?

"Good-bye," she said quietly.

He said nothing, but she felt his gaze on her as she walked back through the trees alone.

Chapter Fourteen

Six weeks later, Ryan and Mari paused by the front door of her condominium. She knew what her brother was going to say before he said it.

"You're not yourself, Mari. I'm worried about you."

"I'm *fine*. You were at the doctor's appointment with me two days ago. You heard it yourself. I couldn't be healthier and neither could the baby."

Ryan looked doubtful. She knew he'd been referring to her spirits, not her physical well-being. Before he could say anything else, she kissed him farewell on the jaw.

"I'll talk to you soon?"

Ryan opened his mouth and then closed it again. "Yeah. Okay. Call me if you need me," he said with a pointed glance before he walked out the door.

Ever since she'd broken the news to Ryan about her pregnancy two weeks ago, he was constantly dropping by and checking her pantry to see if she had enough food, or lecturing her about little things, like when he noticed she'd used a small ladder to change a lightbulb.

She sighed and picked up the bag of items he'd dropped off and carried them to her dining room. Ryan meant well. He was as hyperaware as she was that her baby's father wasn't around to look out for her. When she'd told him who the father was, it had not been a comfortable moment.

Since then, neither of them had mentioned Marc's name out loud.

She still hadn't called Marc to break the news. It just seemed too overwhelming. Insurmountable, in fact. She couldn't seem to build up the energy required to tell Marc they were going to have a baby, if not a future, together.

She set the bag of items on her dining room table with a thud, purposefully trying to scatter her thoughts of Marc. She kept waiting for the pain to fade, but after being in San Francisco for six weeks now, it still hurt to think of him…to recall his face as they stood together on Silver Dune.

She'd kept herself busy with her symphony work and making plans for the baby's nursery. She'd turned over much of the day-to-day preparations for The Family Center to Allison Trainor, Eric Reyes and Colleen. Constantly conversing with the Harbor Town residents—especially Colleen—had made her too depressed. She'd needed to cut back on her interactions for basic survival's sake.

Of course limiting her communications with Eric or Colleen hadn't stopped her from waking up in the middle of the night in a state of panic, feeling as if she'd left something crucial behind. The dreams varied, but the experience of waking in a cold sweat, anxiety clawing at her throat was the same. That, and the inevitable tears that followed.

The experience was very similar to what had occurred when she'd been uprooted and moved to San Francisco fifteen years ago.

It was so hard to keep reminding herself she was doing the right thing when it felt so wrong.

Mari opened the green garbage bag on the table and withdrew a smaller, sealed bag filled with photos. She took out a black-and-white one and smiled at the handsome couple posing for their wedding picture.

"That's your grandma and grandpa," Mari whispered, her hand on her belly.

She definitely possessed a small baby bump now, something that was only identifiable to Mari and a few people who were in the know. She'd taken to talking to the baby, much to her own amusement.

"They would have spoiled you rotten, especially my dad," she told the baby.

She reached into the plastic bag and pulled out a black yearbook. All of the items had come from the Harbor Town basement. The house had sold three weeks ago. Ryan had brought back the remaining family items when he returned to San Francisco. He'd just recently divided them up, however, and brought Mari's share to her condominium tonight. Or at least that's the reason he'd given for dropping by on a Friday night at eight o'clock. Mari knew it really was just an excuse for checking up on her.

Who knew her big, bad, fighter pilot brother could be such a mother hen?

Mari checked the year on the book and saw that it was her own yearbook from her senior year. She'd been seventeen years old, filled with hope and head over heels in love with Marc. It'd been torture for her to be separated from him during the fall, winter and spring, although he would drive up to Dearborn occasionally. His visits had always been short, though, given her parents' disapproval of their relationship.

She opened up the yearbook, smiling wistfully when she recognized youthful, long-forgotten faces.

It was cruel, the way time fell through your grasping fingers.

She paused when she saw a light pink envelope inserted between some pages. She opened up the envelope and realized it was her graduation card from her parents. Below the printed inscription, she saw both her parents' handwriting.

From her mother: *We will always be proud of our beautiful daughter. Always. Congratulations, Marianna!*

She blinked a few unwanted tears out of her eyes so that she could see her father's note.

Mari, Your entire future stretches ahead of you. My advice to you as you set about your journey is to never give up hope. Hope is putting faith to work when doubting would be easier. Know that you will always have our love, Dad.

For a full minute, she just stood there, staring at the message. It was as if she'd just looked up and seen Kassim Itani standing there…saw his thin face and small smile and the knowing twinkle in his dark eyes. The years had collapsed.

Her father had reached out and touched her across the vast barrier of time.

Still holding the card, she walked over to the window and stared out at the glittering high-rises, not really seeing them, but instead seeing her father's face…

And Marc's.

Hope is putting faith to work when doubting would be easier.

That's what she'd done. She'd doubted when she should have hung on. She'd done the wise thing, the rational thing, but everyone knew hope wasn't logical.

"Choose hope."

It took her a moment to realize she wasn't speaking to the baby. She was whispering to herself.

"Your mother is here, Marc."

He did a double take at his administrative assistant's unexpected announcement.

"Where?"

Adrian pointed at the office assigned to him at the courthouse at 26th and California. He had a briefing to attend with some of his top attorneys who were prosecuting a police officer accused of murdering his wife. It was a high profile case and he needed to do a million things before the briefing. All of those things faded in his mind at the news his mother was in his office. Brigit rarely came to the city, let alone to the criminal courthouse.

"Thanks, Adrian," Marc muttered before he plunged into his office. His mother stood from her chair and turned to him. Marc thought she looked healthy enough, but—"

"Is everything all right, Mom?"

"Everything's fine."

Marc gave her a quizzical glance as he deposited his heavy briefcase on his desk. "Why are you here, then?" he asked, bending to give her a kiss.

"I just wanted to speak to you."

"About what?" Marc asked as he settled in his chair.

Brigit also sat. "I was worried. You seemed so distant when we spoke on the phone yesterday."

"I'm fine."

"You're missing Mari."

He blinked, shocked his mother had just said a name that was typically *verboten* to her. It was all the more disorienting to hear Mari's name because he himself hadn't spoken it since she'd left Harbor Town six weeks ago. He said it in his mind frequently enough. Too often, in fact.

"What makes you say that?" he asked, once he'd recovered from the shock of his mother willfully bringing up the topic of Mari Itani.

"Because I know you. It's killing you that she left."

Marc didn't reply, just flipped the pen he'd been twiddling in his fingers onto the desk. He was getting angry.

"What's your point, Mom? You came all the way to Chicago to say I've been missing Mari? So what if I have been?"

Brigit pursed her lips together before she spoke. "I thought perhaps I might be able to ease your misery some."

His laugh was harsh. "I doubt it."

Brigit inhaled deeply and then plunged ahead. "Perhaps. Perhaps not. I wanted to tell you that a week or two after Mari returned to Harbor Town—two days after my heart attack, in fact—I saw Mari at Harbor Town Memorial. She'd had an appointment there."

Marc's brown wrinkled in consternation. "Yeah. She hadn't been feeling well."

"Those dizzy spells. And nausea, perhaps?" Brigit asked.

"What are you getting at?"

"She was coming out of an obstetrician's office, Marc. She told me herself she'd had an appointment there."

He just stared at his mother's face. In the distance a car alarm started blaring loudly.

"I've had my share of children. I know I haven't seen Mari for years, but there's a certain air a woman gets. There are signs. Mari is pregnant, Marc."

He continued to gape at his mother. His heartbeat started to throb uncomfortably loud in his ears.

Brigit cleared her throat. "And I don't think I need to tell you that if she was pregnant, it wasn't with your child."

"What?" he muttered. He felt like he was trying to absorb his mom's words and meaning through a thick layer of insulation.

"Even if you two had…intimate relations once Mari had come back to Harbor Town, she wouldn't have thought she was pregnant after a week. If she is pregnant—or even if she just *thought* so—it couldn't be with your child. Mari must have been involved with someone else, Marc. That's why I came to Chicago. I thought it might ease the sting of her leaving some…to know she must have been involved with another man."

Marc sat forward slowly in his chair. "That's why you came here? To tell me that…you thought it would make me feel *better?*" When his mother didn't respond, Marc dazedly shook his head. "That's one hell of a mean-spirited thing to do, Mom."

Brigit's face collapsed. "I'm doing it for you, Marc."

"No," he stated harshly. "You're doing it for yourself. You're doing it because you want the threat of Mari to disappear for good." He stood abruptly, causing Brigit to start. He reached for his briefcase. "The incredible thing about it is, you did the opposite."

Brigit stood, looking flustered. "What do you mean? Where are you going?"

"I'm going after Mari."

He didn't look back at his mother as he stormed out of the office.

He called to book a flight while he was in the cab. He didn't even bother to go back to his condo to pack anything. This was too important. He was halfway to the airport and apologizing to an assistant district attorney for not being able to attend the upcoming briefing when another call came through on his cell.

He did a double take when he saw the caller identification.

It was Mari.

Why the hell was she calling him now when she'd refused all of his calls since she'd left?

He so forcefully plunged through the revolving doors of the Palmer House Hotel that they kept spinning a full revolution once he was inside. Mari looked over her shoulder at the sound, her eyes huge in her face. For a second he just stood there, dazed.

Mari's eyes. God, would he ever get over their impact?

She turned around. Everything seemed to slow down around him. Sounds became muffled and distant. It was just like when he'd followed her from her concert and walked through these very doors. She'd turned and he'd been compelled to call out when he'd seen her exquisite face.

This time was the same…and it was a thousand times different.

His gaze skimmed over her. She looked incomparably beautiful to him, wearing a dark blue skirt and a soft, cream-colored knit top that clung to her breasts. His eyes rested on the curve of her belly. He met her stare.

"Three months," she said quietly.

"Why didn't you tell me?" he whispered.

Her smile practically undid him. She stepped closer.

"I wanted to tell you about the baby. More than

anything. But I had myself convinced I was doing the right thing by staying away. It took a voice from the past to make me see I wasn't being wise. I was just giving into my fear…my doubts about the future. Our future. I made that realization last night, Marc, and I got on the first plane here this morning. I hope you can forgive me—"

Her words were cut off when he reached for her and lifted her in his arms. He buried his face in the soft fabric of her sweater and inhaled her scent.

"You're sure? You're not going to leave again?" he asked in a garbled voice.

She was pressing small, frantic kisses against his neck and jaw. He felt the wetness of her tears on his skin. "No. Never again."

"You'll stay with me?"

She put her hands on each side of his head and looked into his eyes. "I promise. If that's what you want. I wasn't sure…those things you said about not wanting another relationship—"

"Did you actually think that applies when it comes to *you?*" he asked incredulously. He kissed her with the single intent of silencing her doubts on that front.

"Our future was ripped away from us so long ago," Mari murmured when he lifted his head a moment later. "We've been given a second chance. It's a blessing, and I'm so sorry I couldn't see that before."

"As long as you see it now," he whispered, his mouth hovering next to her lips. He kissed her softly, and when he caught her taste, hungrily. He growled low in his throat before he lifted his head. "God, I love you so much. I can't believe we're going to have a baby."

She smiled. "I love you, too."

He kissed away the tears on her cheek. "The future starts now, Mari."

She took his hand and placed it on the curve of her belly. He went still at the sensation.

"Actually it started twelve or so weeks ago." Her golden brown eyes were filled with joy and amusement as she glanced up at the high-ceilinged lobby. "Right in this very place."

He smiled slowly. Laughter burst out of her throat when he spun her around, her long hair flying in the air. He set her back down on her feet and leaned over her. He spoke to her through nibbling kisses on her lips.

"What do you say we go back up to your room and celebrate our future to its fullest?"

She leaned up and pressed her mouth to his. He held her tight. Marc had the vague, distant impression that they were attracting a few stares from passersby, but he couldn't have cared less. The realization had struck him that he held his whole world in his arms.

His future...*their* future had never shone so bright.

Epilogue

The following spring

Mari thought her heart would burst with joy. The child in her arms had never seemed so beautiful to her as she did at that moment, nor had the man who sat beside her looked so wonderful. She squeezed Marc's hand. He turned to her and smiled.

Perhaps it was the sublime spring day or maybe it was the special event they attended. The priest solemnly continued with his blessing of the lovely memorial fountain Marc had had commissioned to be built at the edge of the woods on Silver Dune.

She glanced down the row of seated visitors and caught sight of Eric Reyes. She smiled when he gave her a quick thumb's up. She was sorry to see that Natalie hadn't been tempted out of her solitude to attend the lovely outdoor ceremony.

Rylee Jean Kavanaugh chose that moment to make a

loud, burbling sound in her sleep. Marc and she glanced down in surprise and concern, but Rylee resumed her peaceful nap, her tiny, rose-colored lips making a rhythmic, pursing movement as she slept.

"She's going to wake up hungry as a horse," Marc whispered.

Mari noticed his devilish grin and the way his gleaming blue eyes flickered quickly over her breasts.

"She's got an appetite like you," Mari whispered back, giving him a mock look of censorship.

Something caught her eye at the back of the seating area. Her smile faded. Marc turned to look where she stared.

"I can't believe she came," she whispered.

They watched Colleen Kavanaugh lead her mother to a seat in the back row. Almost every seat they'd set up in the clearing had been taken. The Family Center had gotten off to an excellent start. Clients attended the ceremony, as did family members, employees and people from the town.

Father Mike continued. "We would like to end this ceremony by having each of you bless this fountain. Those who have survived the pains of substance abuse and those who are trying to find the hope within themselves in order to survive please come to the front, grab a small portion of salt and toss it into the fountain. The salt represents toil and tears, but also stands for hope. Hope is invisible, something we must find within ourselves using the vision not of our eyes but of faith. Your blessings and wishes today may disappear like the salt in the water, but this fountain will be replenished and strengthened by your hope for the future. Please come forward and cast your wishes into this fountain."

People began to stand and join in a line. Mari glanced back halfway through the ceremony and saw Brigit

Kavanaugh sitting next to her daughter. She looked stiff and uncomfortable, as if she'd gate-crashed a party where she wasn't welcome.

Things had improved between Brigit and Mari since she had moved to Chicago, obtained a position with the Chicago Symphony Orchestra and married Marc. Rylee had been born four-and-a-half weeks ago, and a grand-daughter had certainly made Brigit warmer, at times re-minding Mari of the woman she used to know. However, Brigit still became tight-mouthed when any mention of The Family Center was made. That was why Mari was shocked Colleen had persuaded her mother to come.

Mari glanced uncertainly at Marc as they came back from dropping their salt into the fountain. He gave her a small smile of encouragement, and her love for him swelled. He'd been so supportive of everything she'd done with The Family Center. She knew he felt bad that his mother kept up a silent opposition to the project.

Father Mike said a few closing words and a prayer, and everyone started to depart. There was a reception following the ceremony in The Family Center. Mari should get inside there to help.

Instead, she stood. "I'll be right back," she whispered to Marc.

Brigit and Colleen were standing in preparation to leave when Mari approached. She still held a sleeping Rylee in one arm, but she extended her other hand.

"Brigit," she said softly.

Brigit seemed confused, but she hesitantly took Mari's hand.

She led her mother-in-law to the podium that stood in the front. Everyone was milling about or departing, their attention elsewhere, but she sensed Marc's gaze on her like a reassuring touch. She nodded at the gold bowl containing the salt.

"Take some, Brigit."

Brigit stiffened at her words.

"This ceremony is for the survivors of substance abuse," Mari spoke quietly. "That's what you are, Brigit. That's what this place is about. It's about making a future despite the pain of the past."

She saw Brigit's throat convulse. For a second, Mari worried she was going to turn and walk away, but then Brigit reached with a trembling hand. Mari gave her a smile and led her to the edge of the lovely, new, stone-and-metal fountain.

Brigit held out her arm. The grains fell through her parted fingers like solidified tears. The hand that had released the salt found Mari's. Mari felt Brigit's flesh shaking next to her own. She tightly clasped Brigit's hand before they turned away.

Mari and Marc stood in each other's arms later. They stared out at the lake and the sinking sun. Almost everyone had left the reception at The Family Center. Marc had asked her to take a walk with him, and Colleen had happily agreed to watch her niece for a few minutes.

"Every time I think I couldn't love you more you prove me wrong," Marc said quietly from above her.

"I feel the same way about you."

He grinned and lowered his head, nuzzling her nose. "I'm thankful you decided to take the leap, Mari."

"It's only half as scary with you next to me."

"And twice as exciting."

"Cocky," she chastised softly. She went up on her toes and kissed her husband in the golden light of the setting sun.

* * * * *

MILLS & BOON®
By Request

RELIVE THE ROMANCE WITH THE BEST OF THE BEST

A sneak peek at next month's titles...

In stores from 16th November 2017:

- **His Best Acquisition** – Dani Collins, Rachael Thomas *and* Tara Pammi

- **Her Ex, Her Future?** – Lucy King, Louisa Heaton *and* Louisa George

In stores from 30th November 2017:

- **The Montoros Dynasty** – Janice Maynard, Katherine Garbera *and* Andrea Laurence

- **Baby's on the Way!** – Ellie Darkins, Rebecca Winters *and* Lisa Childs

---

MILLS & BOON®

Why shop at millsandboon.co.uk?

Each year, thousands of romance readers find their perfect read at millsandboon.co.uk. That's because we're passionate about bringing you the very best romantic fiction. Here are some of the advantages of shopping at www.millsandboon.co.uk:

* **Get new books first**—you'll be able to buy your favourite books one month before they hit the shops

* **Get exclusive discounts**—you'll also be able to buy our specially created monthly collections, with up to 50% off the RRP

* **Find your favourite authors**—latest news, interviews and new releases for all your favourite authors and series on our website, plus ideas for what to try next

* **Join in**—once you've bought your favourite books, don't forget to register with us to rate, review and join in the discussions

Visit **www.millsandboon.co.uk** for all this and more today!